THE ROAD
TO
ROO INN

Thanks: My eternal gratitude is owed to the following people in no particular order... Yan Spencer @Holy Cow Tattoos for his excellent artwork, Ulla Schrelle for her editing skills, thus ensuring that this book doesn't read like it was written by a small child (a big child is fine!), Krusher Joule for getting me into this whole writing nonsense in the first place, Lemmy for everything, all at the Burgundy Room (Hollywood) and the Doubledown Saloon (Las Vegas) for furnishing me with alcohol, and last but by no means least, my wife Masuimi for her love and support, for putting up with my crap, and for making life an adventure.

I would also like to give a shout out to the following people for their encouragement, inspiration, music, and beer (sometimes all four at once). Cutter (shots!), Digga, Josh Sindell, Tim Shay, Richard Copcutt, Steffan Chirazi, Alex Kane, Jeremy Brown, Big Chris, Chris Cornell (Rest In Peace), Pinch and The Damned, all at Metal Hammer and Vive Le Rock, Laura and Pinup Girl, Kawasaki Motorcycles, Monster Magnet, Motörhead, Clutch, The Dwarves, The Prodigy, Pink Floyd, Orange Goblin, Poison Idea, Slipknot... There are too many bands to mention, we'll be here all day! Lots of love to Sarah and Adam.

Respect to MCs worldwide.

ISBN: 0692898093
ISBN 13: 9780692898093
Library of Congress Control Number: 2017908568
The Road To Roo Inn, Las Vegas, NV

THE ROAD TO ROO INN

MORAT

For Lemmy
1945-2015

CHAPTER ONE

It wasn't going to be easy getting an orc through customs, that much was obvious. It was also becoming increasingly obvious that Zig Zag McClintock *was* an orc, and some of the passengers aboard flight 625 to Sydney, Australia, were starting to get a little twitchy. Thankfully, the cabin lights were still dimmed a soothing blue, the blinds closed to allow people to sleep, but even in this semi-darkness it was clear that something wasn't quite right about the man snoring very loudly to himself in seat 23a. It was the teeth, mostly. It probably didn't help that the young man sitting in 23b, one Vincent Christ, kept disappearing every time they hit turbulence.

"Ladies and gentlemen, this is your captain speaking," said the captain smoothly. "As you can see, I've turned on the fasten seat belts sign just while we get through this bumpy patch..."

Vincent clung to his seat for dear life, apparently under the mistaken impression that it would somehow cushion his fall if the plane were to suddenly plummet into the ocean below. He tried not to think about how far that fall would be, or about the fact that he'd have time to think about that, too, on the way down. Bumpy patch bollocks! Eight hours they'd been bouncing around on this nightmare flight that seemed to be deliberately aiming for bad weather, and thanks to Zig Zag taking *all* the sleeping pills Vincent had endured every stomach-churning minute of it.

Vincent hated flying. Of course, never having flown before today – or was it yesterday? – he'd had no idea that he hated flying, but he *really* fucking

1

hated flying. The boredom had been bad enough, eleven endless hours from Berlin to Tokyo, with his arse going to sleep and his brain wide awake, but this was hell! The plane shuddered and pitched, the cabin staff long abandoning the idea of serving any refreshments, liquid or otherwise. And Keanu Reeves was just about to ruin The Matrix again on a screen the size of a postage stamp. Yes, this was definitely hell!

And then there was the ring.

Since Vincent was eleven years old he'd been the owner, if not the rightful owner, of an invisibility ring that made him vanish whenever he was in danger. In the right hands it was incredibly powerful, and the bounty on it ran into the millions, but unfortunately Vincent's were not the right hands. They weren't even the right fingers! Technically, it was only supposed to work when he was actually *in* danger, but somehow it also worked when he *thought* he was in danger, and so, instead of keeping him safe from harm, it often had a habit of making his life vastly more difficult, by making him invisible on his motorcycle, for instance. Or, like now, making him disappear in public on a very full flight from Tokyo to Sydney.

Vincent poked at the screen to make Keanu Reeves go away, switching the display over to show the flight path. He tried to do some breathing exercises to calm himself down. Not long to go now, an hour and a half, and if the cabin staff had to stay seated for the remainder of the flight then he should be fine as soon as they landed. Mercifully, many of the seats around him were taken by fellow members of the outlaw motorcycle club, Aberrant MC, for whom Vincent was prospecting, and they all knew about the ring, but, still, his disappearing act might cause a few problems with the general public if he couldn't keep his fear under control.

Not that Aberrant MC were a particularly inconspicuous bunch to start with, and already they had caused a minor scene going through airport security. For obvious reasons, Andy One-Leg had raised a few eyebrows when he took his leg off and put it through the X-ray machine, hopping on the spot while he waited to go through the metal detector. Then Vincent kept setting the metal detector off, virtually down to his underpants before they took him away for a pat down. His invisibility ring was the only metal on his person, and wouldn't come off his finger, but for some reason it took a good twenty minutes to ascertain, quite wrongly, that it couldn't be employed as a weapon of mass destruction. Next came Stone, extremely reluctant to take his sunglasses off, as if the airport strip lighting were brighter than the midday sun, cringing at every step.

"Sir, you must take those off," said the uniform, a spotty German with no sense of humour.

"Migraine," pleaded Stone, shielding his eyes. "Blinding headache. I've taken some painkillers so it should pass."

"Sir, you must still take them off."

So Stone took his sunglasses off to reveal what were clearly the eyes of a complete drug fiend and he, too, was promptly taken away for a search that was rather more intimate than necessary. Smiler and Joker both got through okay, though not unnoticed, with Billy Toothless causing people in line to recoil at the stench when he took his boots off. And then came Zig Zag...

Technically Zig Zag was a dworc, half dwarfish, half orc, and an extremely rare breed considering how much dwarfs and orcs hate each other. Indeed, he was not the result of love, but of rape during an orc raid, his mother unceremoniously dumping him in the woods as soon as he was born. But standing at five feet five inches in his socks, he looked more like a small orc than a particularly vicious dwarf, so orc it was. He could pass for an orc child, but never as a dwarf, though it was fair to say that he hadn't been blessed with the most attractive features of either race – leather-skinned, pointy-eared, and with a surplus of nasty teeth. It seemed the only thing he'd picked up from his dwarf genes was a thickness in girth, a height disadvantage, and the uncanny ability to tell gold by its smell. His looks had not been further enhanced when, many years ago, his face had been split in two with an axe and then bound up with dockyard rope.

"Sir, you cannot bring this liquid in your carry-on."

"No liquidsh? What do you mean no liquidsh? I need thish!" protested Zig Zag.

"Three ounces is the maximum allowed in carry-on bags," said the German. "This must go in your checked luggage or you must throw it away."

"But I need thish with me," insisted Zig Zag. "It'sh exshpenshive shtuff, I don't want it getting losht. It'sh shpecial shampoo," he added.

"Shampoo?" said the German, not at all convinced that anyone would want to get this suspicious-looking green goo anywhere near their skin, let alone use it to combat dandruff.

"Yesh," said Zig Zag. "It makesh the hairsh grow schtronger."

The uniform looked down at Zig Zag. Given his height disadvantage it was possible to see the top of his head, and the uniform could see no signs at all that this miracle shampoo was even remotely miraculous. Zig Zag was completely bald.

"It does not appear to work," said the German, perhaps betraying a sense of humour after all.

"Yeah, well, I haven't schtarted yet," muttered Zig Zag.

"Still, it must go in your checked luggage."

"Bollocksh."

The green goo was in fact a powerful magical liniment, and before heading to the airport Zig Zag had vigorously applied a significant amount of it to himself in order to appear even vaguely human. But still, there was only so much it could do. In human form he was not an attractive man, appearing as if he might once have been involved in some horrible industrial accident, or perhaps suffer from the world's worst cleft palate. His teeth were too big for his mouth causing a shower-fitted speech impediment, his thin grey goatee beard almost permanently moist. It might even be possible to feel sorry for him if he didn't look like such a complete bastard, but that's exactly what he looked like, a spiteful little thug with an attitude problem. The recently tattooed face, some sort of Mike Tyson tribal thing, probably wasn't helping much with PR.

And so Zig Zag had been forced to put the liniment into his checked luggage, which had then, most inconveniently, been checked all the way to Sydney for his convenience. Unable to reapply the liniment en route as he'd planned, he had instead taken a large quantity of sleeping pills in the hopes of slowing down the reversal process. Which perhaps it had, but there could be no doubt that it was wearing off fast. At this rate it would have worn off completely by the time they landed, and he would look nothing like the picture on his counterfeit passport. Australian immigration policies on orcs were vague at best, considering they'd never knowingly encountered one before, but it was a safe bet that they wouldn't be pleased.

The passports were also worrying Vincent. Given that he had no criminal record it wasn't strictly necessary for him to have a forged passport at all, but, for reasons that had become abundantly clear in his relatively short time prospecting for Aberrant MC, it was best if as few people as possible knew the club's travel arrangements. At least three of the club's thirteen full patch members were wanted fugitives, and the same number again weren't even human!

Aside from the threat of arrest there was also the very real danger that they'd get thrown into quarantine.

Admittedly, the passports had worked just fine so far, and customs in Tokyo seemed more interested in showing them pictures of drugs and porn to make sure they weren't bringing in any of their own. But still, with all the high-tech security at airports, there was always the worry of getting caught out.

Beside them, in the aisle seat, Stone let out a long and sorrowful moan. Tortured by his migraine he cradled his head in his hands, eyes blindfolded. It had been getting progressively worse, growing from a few urgent stabs every now and again, when they left Berlin, to a constant agony by the time they boarded the next plane in Tokyo. Now, as they approached Sydney, it was unbearable, like his skull was too small for his brain, worse than the worst of hangovers. How was it possible for eyeballs to produce so much pain?

And yet Stone knew only too well where the pain was coming from, and that all he could do was endure it. Follow it. Somewhere, in the vast open space that was Australia, his old friend Derain was sending a distress signal, a psychic SOS so powerful that it completely overwhelmed him. There was no knowing what it meant, only that Derain was in great danger, likely enduring some torture of his own. All Stone could do was get there as fast as possible.

And then, suddenly, the pain stopped.

Stone sat upright and removed his blindfold. He opened his eyes and looked about him, wildly.

"Oh dear," he said. "That's not good. That's not good at all!"

CHAPTER TWO

"Oh dear," said Dum Dum. "That's not good. That's not good at all!"

The image on the TV screen – mounted above the bar at the Rainbow Bar And Grill on Sunset Boulevard – panned back to the scene of the crime, and to a hailstorm of flashing red and blue lights atop an army of police cars. Behind the lights, and very much on fire, was an LAPD squad car that had been painted a rather unpleasant shade of pink, while the bottom left corner of the screen continued to show an artist's impression, rendered in pencil, of two fugitives considered "armed and extremely dangerous". Despite the fact that the TV was muted there could be little doubt who they were. Aberrant MC's sergeant-at-arms, Numb Tongue, and his girlfriend Snow, the club's first ever female prospect.

"Can you turn it up a bit, please?"

"Sure, honey." The cute blonde behind the bar grabbed the remote and aimed it at the screen. It was early evening and the place was relatively empty, just a few poodle-haired tourists trying to decide which enormous pizza they wanted. Guns N' Roses' *Welcome To The Jungle* was playing in the background, barely audible, little more than Muzak.

"...eyewitnesses say that the two bikers, one male, one female, and apparently members of an unknown outlaw motorcycle gang, rounded the corner here at Firestone Boulevard and Graham Avenue, and allegedly discovered four LAPD officers beating a young black man. They stopped their motorcycles and approached the officers, and the officers drew their weapons. When the bikers continued to approach them, one of the officers tazed the male biker and a fight broke out."

The image then switched to a large black lady who, despite full make-up, appeared to be still wearing her nightgown and bedroom slippers. Evidently she was rather amused by the situation.

"It was like something out of the moo-vies," she beamed, as her nightgown struggled to retain her modesty. "Those po-lice, they was beatin' on that man somethin' awful, then Bonnie and Clyde shows up, and aw hell broke loose. The po-lice tazed the man and he be like, "Don't do that!" in uh English accent, aw Hugh Grant only real deep, and tha's when he broke the officer's arm."

The screen panned back to the studio, the images of chaos and the artist's impressions now at the bottom left corner, while updates ran along the bottom centre. Police, it was reiterated, were actively seeking two white bikers, one male, one female, wanted in connection with the assault of four LAPD officers. The male, two hundred and ten pounds and said to be well over seven feet tall, had a shaved head and goatee beard, and was heavily scarred about the face. The female – five foot six, black hair, one hundred and twenty pounds – by all accounts looked like she'd just stepped out of a Victoria's Secret ad. Both appeared to have extensive knowledge of mixed martial arts, and both were, the newsreader kept repeating, considered armed and extremely dangerous. Police had yet to issue a statement about the alleged beating of a young, homeless, black man by the four officers.

"According to eyewitness reports," said the orange newscaster, "the officers were disarmed and then forced to paint their own vehicles..."

By this point the barmaid was watching, too, and she slid Dum Dum a beer across the bar. "On the house, honey," she smiled. "They friends of yours?"

"Family," said Dum Dum.

Family was right. Aberrant MC were the only family Dum Dum had now. His mother had died in a mental asylum when he was a teenager, and he couldn't remember even meeting his recently deceased father. There was a vague blur, a shape with no face, but nothing more. Which was weird considering that his father was a bridge troll; you'd think he'd remember more than a blur, even if they'd only met when Dum Dum was a child. It did, however, account for Dum Dum's size, all six foot eight, three hundred and fifty pounds of him, still shorter than Numb Tongue, but rather more difficult to see around. Having spent most of his life in and out of prison, he'd spent four years prospecting for the club before getting his full patch a little over six months ago, at the age of forty-two. No shit, family was right. He was in this for life. Which in his case, he had learned, could be three or four hundred years.

Up on the screen they cut to the chief of police as he approached a podium that was cluttered with microphones and surrounded by press. His stance radiated authority, but he began with an appeal for calm and an assurance that the allegations of police brutality would be thoroughly investigated. As would allegations that footage of the entire incident had been posted to – and hastily removed from – YouTube. The officers in question appeared not to have been wearing body cameras, but there were dozens of videos of the cops painting their squad cars pink and further footage of some youths setting fire to one of the squad cars after the cops had gone to find help, their radios and phones having been sabotaged, and their weapons stolen. Traffic had come to a standstill.

The chief of police blustered his way through the rest of the press conference, mostly repeating what had already been said, and calling again for calm. If you read between the lines it was clear that the LAPD had taken a very public spanking and had no idea what to do about it. The bikers had publicly threatened retaliation for any acts of recrimination against the community by the police, and parts of South Central were now a no-go zone to anything in a uniform. The word 'tinderbox' was being used a great deal, and there were more than a few references to Rodney King and the LA riots of 1992, the 2014 protests in Ferguson, Missouri, and, indeed, numerous other incidents all over the country. 'Bonnie and Clyde' were being hailed as heroes on the streets and denounced as possible terrorists by the press. Not exactly the most inconspicuous start considering Aberrant MC only got into town yesterday evening. They'd barely had time to unpack their bags and already there was chaos.

Which was all well and good, except that Dum Dum had absolutely no idea where to go or what to do next. The three of them, along with club president Mad John, had landed at LAX just as the sun was going down, but it was dark by the time they got through customs and baggage claim and out of the terminal. They'd been picked up by another motorcycle club, mostly younger guys on crotch rockets, all weaving in and out of traffic on the freeway at ridiculous speeds. Splitting lanes, they called it over here, and Dum Dum had done his best to keep up on the bike he'd been loaned, a tricked-out GSXR something or other. He'd been too busy trying not to get killed to pay any attention to where they were going. It had taken roughly half an hour to get from the airport to the clubhouse, but Dum Dum had no idea what part of town it was in. He saw signs for Firestone, which stuck in his mind because it sounded cool and reminded him of Motörhead, and for Manchester, which didn't, but beyond that he was clueless.

It didn't help that Dum Dum's sense of direction was like a compass in a magnet factory, so bad that he'd had to resort to following bus routes to find his way around London. It was his first time in Los Angeles, a place he'd always dreamed of visiting, but he had never imagined that it was so vast, sprawling out as far as the eye could see from the plane, and no less intimidating from the ground. Both Mad John and Numb Tongue had business to attend to in the morning, but thankfully a couple of guys from the other club offered to show Dum Dum the sights, first Venice Beach and the PCH, all the way up to Malibu, then on to the legendary Sunset Strip, where they parted company. He was supposed to meet Mad John, Numb Tongue, and Snow at the Rainbow in the afternoon, before they all headed out to the desert to meet a wizard, but, given that Aberrant MC now seemed to have rather more pressing concerns, it was unlikely that this was going to happen.

Fuck. What to do?

Dum Dum finished his beer and ordered another one. How long should he wait? He glanced at his watch and took a moment to work out what time it was. Thanks to some help from Vincent he was getting the hang of telling the time, although he already knew that the others were late. It was starting to get dark. Oh, what to do?

There seemed little point in heading back to the host clubhouse. If the place wasn't already crawling with cops then Dum Dum certainly didn't want to be the one to lead them there. And that was *if* he could find it again. On the other hand, he'd been told that he needed to work on his navigational skills, – or lack thereof – so maybe this was a good time to prove his worth. Since all the revelations about government agencies spying on everyone, the members of Aberrant MC had been forbidden from using cell phones or GPS, so it was important that they always showed up on time. Which made it all the more worrying that the other three weren't here yet. It also made it impossible to call them and find out what was going on.

So. What to do?

Dum Dum sipped on his beer. The bar didn't close until two so theoretically he could just sit here and get pissed while he waited for them to show up, but what if they never came? Obviously he could get a hotel room for the night, but then what? The news reports made it clear that neither Numb Tongue or Snow had been apprehended yet, but there was no mention of Mad John, who was also currently MIA. And no doubt the cops were coming down hard on anyone with two wheels and a cut, so it was going to be difficult to stay off their radar. Not to mention all the heat that this would be bringing down on all the local motorcycle clubs, who really could do without it. That in itself would be making Aberrant MC unpopular, especially on foreign soil.

Thankfully, there were many spells cast and woven into the patches that made up Aberrant MC's colours, protection spells and such, that made the cops look rather foolish when they forgot what they'd stopped you for. And, given their magical nature, there was no clear footage of the patches, – just enough to let the world know it was a motorcycle club – but Dum Dum couldn't help wondering if their powers had ever been tested in a full-scale manhunt. Well, and ladyhunt, as the case may be. The plod in England tended to get all flustered, apologise for bothering you, and wish you a nice day, but over here the police were a gang that hunted in packs, as proven by Numb Tongue's recent intervention. Cops in LA were known to execute people in broad daylight, and would quite likely take no prisoners if the situation were repeated. The cop that tazered Numb Tongue was lucky he only got his arm broken, but next time they might shoot first and ask questions later.

Fuck.

The TV screen cut to commercials, but promised to be back with more of this ongoing story after the break, despite the fact that there was nothing new to tell beyond dragging up the unrelated killing of nine bikers in Waco, Texas, in 2015. A couple of cop cars rushed by outside with sirens blazing.

Double fuck.

"Mind if I put the music back on, honey?"

"No, go ahead," sighed Dum Dum.

"I'll turn it up if there's an update," the bartender promised, sliding another beer across the bar.

She turned the music back on: Bad Religion, *Los Angeles Is Burning*. That seemed about right at the moment, and Dum Dum had no clue what he should be doing about it. You'd have to be psychic or telepathic or something, and while it was true that a couple of the club members did possess such powers, Dum Dum wasn't among them. It was size, not magic, that had always been on his side, but that wasn't really much use if nobody needed knocking out. Dum Dum was spectacularly good at that, but, so far as he could tell, he didn't have a magical bone in his body. Even the simplest of card tricks had him baffled. Indeed, a lot of people made the mistake of thinking that Dum Dum was stupid, a fool, but, as Mad John himself had pointed out, slow and stupid were not one and the same. Dum Dum may have been painfully slow at times, but he was nobody's fool.

So. What to do?

Before joining Aberrant MC he might have been at a loss, but with time and encouragement, not to mention a great deal of patience, he had learned to think outside the box. Granted, they'd also had to explain to him that no actual boxes were involved in this process, but still, every little helped. There were always clues, signs that would be otherwise missed if you didn't look at them in the right way.

Dum Dum finished his beer.

The news came back on, but none of it was news, just speculation, hearsay, and flat-out lies. Rather than focussing on the fact that Numb Tongue and Snow – who else could it be? – had apparently intervened in a vicious beating, the gist of the story was that bikers were all dangerous criminals who should be locked up on sight. They rattled out the usual suspects, Hells Angels, Bandidos, Mongols, failing, of course, to mention the many Christian biker clubs, the very worthy Bikers Against Child Abuse, or, for that matter, the growing number of cop clubs that were sprouting up all over the place and causing all manner of trouble, playing at outlaws whilst hiding behind their badges.

So much for the news. Dum Dum picked up his empty bottle and waved it at the bartender to get her attention. There was a business card stuck to the bottom of the bottle, and he peeled it off and examined it. 'Psychic', read the card, 'fortunes told, tarot and palmistry by Crystal Ball. Walk-ins welcome.' The address was less than two blocks away. Dum Dum didn't even have to cross the road.

CHAPTER THREE

The little silver bell tinkled when Dum Dum opened the door, but the small, glass-fronted shop appeared to be unoccupied. A red-bulbed lamp and the neon light in the window fell upon a red velvet sofa and a small round table covered with black lace. On the table was a crystal ball and a pack of tarot cards. At the back of the shop was a red veiled doorway.

"Hello?" called Dum Dum. "Anyone here?"

There was no reply, just the gentle tick of an ornate-looking clock mounted to the wall, the street outside strangely muted.

"Hello?" Dum Dum tried again. "It said walk-ins welcome on the card. I was hoping to, er,..." He trailed off, not entirely sure what he was hoping to do.

"Ah, sit down, Dum Dum, I've been expecting you," called a voice from beyond the veil.

Cautiously, Dum Dum lowered himself onto the sofa. It raised quite dramatically at one end but otherwise failed to protest his weight. If anything it was really rather comfortable, comfort*ing*. It had been a long day and the truth was that Dum Dum didn't really know what he was doing here, except perhaps grasping at straws. He gazed out of the window at the drunks stumbling past on the Sunset Strip, the sidewalk crowded and noisy with chatter, cars rushing by, and yet the shop was silent but for the ticking of the clock. He'd never been to a psychic before, but he took it as a good sign that he'd been expected.

In the back room, beyond the veil, Crystal Ball, née Margaret Torpin, adjusted the focus of her security camera and zoomed in on Dum Dum, searching for further clues. It didn't hurt to have a head start, or that he had his name on a patch on the front of his jacket. And it wasn't really cheating as such, merely a little something to impress the tourists. It was nothing she couldn't pick up just by observing someone and listening to their voice. But this one didn't seem like the average tourist coming in off the street for a laugh, or out of curiosity. This one was looking for something specific. "I was hoping to..." he'd said, in that thick English accent.

"Three sugars?"

"Pardon?"

"In your tea. Three sugars, isn't it?" He was a big fella, too, probably liked his sugar. And there wasn't a Brit alive who could resist a nice cup of tea.

"Um, yes please," said Dum Dum, suitably impressed. He had no idea psychics were so good.

There was the sound of an old-fashioned kettle boiling, the high-pitched whistle rising and falling, and eventually Crystal emerged from the back of the shop. She was a dainty lady, perhaps in her late eighties or early nineties, and seemingly as frail and delicate as the porcelain tea cup she had balanced on a wafer-thin saucer. Her hair was silver-grey and fashioned from a bygone age, not a hair out of place, and though she wore make up it wasn't crazy old lady make up, caked on to conceal the years, just a hint of mascara to highlight her startlingly green eyes. There was an air about her of a young spirit trapped in a body that was failing her in her later years. When Dum Dum stood up she looked tiny. But then, to be fair, most people looked tiny when Dum Dum stood up.

"There you go, dear. No, don't get up." Her accent was American, perhaps Southern, although Dum Dum was only guessing based on what he'd seen in movies. Her voice soft, but not weak.

Dum Dum sat back down and attempted to make room for the old lady, but the result was that the sofa raised far too high on one end, leaving Crystal with her feet dangling over the edge like a small child. One false move from Dum Dum would catapult her into the ceiling.

"Prob'ly best if I sit on the floor."

And so, with Dum Dum sitting on the floor, Crystal Ball began her reading.

Dum Dum had no idea how long the reading went on, only that time seemed to stop in that tiny, fortune teller's shop. The passers-by and traffic outside the window became a blur, and all that could be heard was Crystal's voice and the ticking of the clock. Her voice was soothing, hypnotic almost, just her and the tick, tick, tick of the clock, though Dum Dum was free to ask questions. She read his cards first, deliberating over each card, explaining its meaning, and asking Dum Dum what he saw in the card.

"The Fool is not as he seems," she said when Dum Dum groaned at the card. "The Fool is honest, child-like in his innocence, and yet he carries no malice and does not care what you say of him. Is he really such a fool?"

"He's about to fall off the cliff," noted Dum Dum.

"All journeys have their dangers, but no journey can be completed without the first steps. The Fool is unafraid to take those steps, he is happy in his travels and knows no fear."

Apparently, The Hanged Man wasn't quite as bad as Dum Dum had thought, either, and simply indicated that he needed to try a different approach in solving his problems, look at things from a fresh perspective. It was a card of sacrifice, but that could mean sacrificing outdated mindsets. Rather than clinging on to old ideas and fighting against the current, he needed to let go and see where it took him. Go with the flow. Likewise, The Page Of Swords was about looking at problems in a new way, expanding the mind and such. And the Death card didn't mean he was going to crash his bike.

By this time Dum Dum had finished his tea, and Crystal spent a good five minutes peering down her nose at the tea leaves in the bottom of the cup. She turned the cup this way and that, and said, "I see" a lot. All Dum Dum could see were some tea leaves, but so far, the fortune teller had been fairly accurate, if a little vague. Well, not so much vague, it was just that most of it could apply to anyone. Everyone had problems, everyone was looking for something. Then again, she had known his name.

Finally satisfied that there was no more to see, the old lady put the cup down. She gave Dum Dum a curious look, as if what she had seen in the tea leaves didn't entirely match up with the person who was sitting in front of her.

"Give me your hands," she said, taking Dum Dum's giant paws between her bone-thin fingers. The contrast in size reminded Dum Dum rather uncomfortably of the cover of the Dead Kennedys album *Plastic Surgery Disasters*, the photograph by Michael Wells of a white missionary holding the hand of a starving child. It also reminded Dum Dum that he didn't have a huge amount of cash on him.

"Is this going to cost extra?" he asked. "I mean, I've got money, but it might have to stretch a bit further than I thought."

"There is no charge for you," said Crystal. "Please, I must see your hands."

Half an hour later Dum Dum was back at the Rainbow with a great deal to think about. He ordered a beer, the bartender informing him that there was no further news about his friends on TV and asking if he'd had any luck himself.

"I'm not really sure," said Dum Dum. "Sort of."

"Well, you might want to keep a low profile, honey. The cops are down on anything with two wheels like a ton of bricks."

This was not helpful. Dum Dum now knew that he couldn't just sit here and wait for the others to show up, but he still had no idea where he should be going. That was one thing Crystal had been specific about.

"Your friends are safe, but you must not wait for them," she had told him. "This is your journey and you must begin it alone, and find your own path. They will find you in due time, but you must find your own way for now."

"But I don't know where to start," protested Dum Dum. "I was supposed to meet them in the Rainbow, and then we were going out to the desert to meet a wiz... ah, um, a friend."

"The answer is in your passion, Dum Dum, the thing you love the most," said Crystal. "Now, please, you must leave. I don't feel at all well. I've been suffering the most terrible headaches."

"But..."

"I'm sorry, you must go." Crystal clutched at her temples. "Be safe on your journey, Dum Dum, be safe. Now, please..."

Crystal hadn't charged him for the readings, which was nice of her, but aside from saving a few much-needed dollars it wasn't much help in solving Dum Dum's predicament. He was effectively back to square one, sitting at the bar, nursing his beer, and wondering what the fuck he should be doing.

"The answer is in your passion." What the hell did that mean? Dum Dum was fairly passionate about pizza, but, beyond hunger, he didn't see how it would solve any of his current problems.

Up on the TV screen the news was back on, subtitles running along the bottom of the screen, and a collage of images from today's disturbances, but they were just rehashing what had already been said: Firestone and the surrounding areas of South Central Los Angeles were still a no-go zone for the LAPD, and there were repeated calls for calm, meetings with community leaders, and various talking heads offering unnecessary opinions. Lots of experts, but no actual news. Which also didn't help.

Of course, there was always the possibility that Dum Dum's bike held some sort of magical powers, it wouldn't be the first time he'd encountered such things, but somehow he doubted it. Apart from the fact that it was a loaner from the other club, he would need to know how to activate such powers, if it had any, and then, presumably, he'd have to know how to control it. As it was, he could barely control the damn thing *without* any magic, and found himself clinging on for dear life as it tried to take off without him. Not that it didn't handle well, it was just so overly responsive and ludicrously fast, even carrying Dum Dum's weight. At least he could be fairly certain that it was capable of evading high-speed pursuit, but he wasn't so sure that he was capable of it himself.

And if Dum Dum was honest with himself, motorcycles weren't really his true passion anyway. Aberrant MC was more about brotherhood to him, family, and if riding a bike was what it took to be a part of that family then that was what he'd do. Deep down, it wasn't something he particularly enjoyed. Perhaps if he didn't have such an awful sense of direction and the constant nagging worry that he was heading the wrong way he might enjoy riding solo, but on club runs he was mostly just trying not to fall off his bike, or knock anyone else off theirs. It wasn't what you'd call a passion, more a necessity.

The music grew louder in the bar, with the growing amount of customers, and Dum Dum couldn't help smiling to himself as System Of A Down's *Lost In Hollywood* started playing. Yeah, that seemed about right. Except that, for once, Dum Dum knew exactly where he was, so technically he wasn't lost at all. And technically this was West Hollywood. The legendary Rainbow Bar And Grill on The Sunset Strip, previously The Villa Nova, where Marilyn Monroe and Joe DiMaggio first met on a blind date in 1952. If there was one thing Dum Dum knew it was his rock 'n' roll history. The Rainbow itself had opened in 1972, and soon became the hang-out for every rock band in town, a Mecca for every rock fan on the planet, and certainly up near the top of Dum Dum's bucket list. Hell, there was a statue of Lemmy in the bar, and before he died it had been his favourite watering hole. You didn't get more legendary than that!

But that didn't help much either. Dum Dum was a veritable encyclopedia of rock 'n' roll trivia, but, again, the knowledge that Iggy Pop had once overdosed on stage at the Whisky A Go Go, just down the road from here, wasn't going to be a great deal of use. Shame really, thought Dum Dum, I'm good at that. He even knew that the Black Sabbath song that came on next wasn't the original but a 1994 cover by the Bullring Brummies, with Rob Halford on vocals. That was his true passion, when all was said and done, heavy fucking metal. But how the hell was that going to help him find a wizard in the middle of the desert? Not that it wasn't a cracking tune, but seriously...

Think, Dum Dum, think... How is music going to help you find a wizard?

CHAPTER FOUR

Vincent and Stone stood behind the yellow line while they awaited their turn at customs. So far things were going well. Joker and Billy Toothless were through without any problems, and Andy One-Leg was all smiles with the customs official. His story was an easy one: He was a surfer – hence the missing leg – and he was out here to check out Surfer's Paradise. Australian customs were well used to people travelling all the way across the world for that sort of thing, and missing limbs were not exactly a rarity in shark-infested waters. Andy always looked more surfer than biker anyway, one of those older guys who'd been doing it their whole life, more Patrick Swayze than Keanu Reeves.

With the current draconian clampdown on the biker culture by authorities in Australia, it was important that none of them were discovered to be anything to do with an outlaw motorcycle club. That was game over, simple as that. They'd be held for several hours questioning and then unceremoniously fucked off back to where they'd come from, regardless of whether they had so much as a parking ticket. Bikers were not welcome, so Aberrant MC made themselves strangers, distancing themselves in the customs line, and doing their best to disguise themselves.

Vincent and Stone were the only two going through together, alleging to be father and son on a bonding trip to the outback following a death in the family. If one of the club were caught out and deported then it would be an inconvenience, a dent in their numbers, but it was imperative that Stone made it through, and if he was detained for any reason then it was important that he wasn't alone. As father and son they might be detained together, and Vincent could explain Stone's condition as one of deep mourning following the loss of his wife, Vincent's mother. The pair were journeying to Australia as part of the recovery process.

Andy One-Leg was still chatting away to the customs official, cheerfully recounting the tale of the tiger shark that mistook him for a seal, and, farther along the line, Smiler had stepped forward for his turn to be questioned. He was an MMA trainer, down here a few weeks early in preparation for the big UFC fight in Sydney, his flattened nose attesting to the fact that he'd been in the game for many years.

Vincent glanced behind him, fifteen or twenty people back. Even with a forged Australian passport Zig Zag McClintock was going to be a problem. He just had nasty little bastard written all over him, quite literally, as customs would discover if they decided on a strip search and saw the tattoo across his chest. True, it was written in Orcish, but Orcish calligraphy is surprisingly descriptive. In fairness, Zig Zag was one of the nicer orcs you could hope to encounter, which wasn't saying a great deal as they all tended to be rather unpleasant, but he was still a nasty little bastard thinly disguised as a cunt. Even in his own country he wouldn't be welcome.

On the plus side, at least Vincent had managed to slip a potion into his drink before they landed, so he looked vaguely human again. Zig Zag hadn't been too happy about that, but there really wasn't much choice. It was bad enough that he looked like a nasty little bastard, but he couldn't go through customs looking like a nasty little *orc* bastard. For fuck's sake, it was like dealing with Mr. T! I pity the orc fool!

Usually, when Zig Zag had to appear in public, he'd just keep his full face, dark-visored, crash helmet on, and his mouth shut, but since this wasn't an option in airports the orc had to resort to magic. And orcs hated magic. It didn't seem to matter that Zig Zag was a long-standing, full-patch member of a motorcycle club that actively endorsed magic, he wanted nothing to do with it. It simply ran too deep in his blood: Neither orcs or dwarfs trusted magic, and Zig Zag was both, ergo, magic could fuck off. Which left the problem of airports.

In the end, Zig Zag had agreed to apply the lotion to his skin – which led to a lot of Silence Of The Lambs jokes – but he refused to drink the longer lasting potion.

"At leascht thish way I'll schtill 'ave orc bollocksh," he grumbled, covering just the bare minimum, hands, face and neck.

By the time the plane began its descent into Sydney he was beginning to look unnervingly orcish again. He woke up with a stiff neck and a foul temper.

"Oh hey," said Vincent casually. "We're nearly coming in to land."

Zig Zag lifted the blind to look outside, and his face was lit by the morning sun. It was absolutely and unmistakably an orc face. It snarled something at Vincent in Orcish, which Vincent pretended to understand. Curiously, the orc tended to change language as he changed shape, more out of habit and convenience than a desire to be understood, and now to the point where it was automatic. There was not a hint of English in anything he'd just said.

"They've, er, they've been round with drinks already, but you were asleep, so I got you some water," Vincent offered. "And there's some peanuts."

He'd left the plastic glass and the nuts on Zig Zag's table.

Due to Vincent's ring the orc couldn't actually see him, and generally just aimed anything he had to say to him in vaguely the right direction. Much to both their annoyance, it didn't seem to matter whether the ring was working or not; it worked on Zig Zag all the time. The only exception, the one time Zig Zag had seen him, had been in a city where magic was forbidden, its iron buildings specifically designed for the purpose of keeping magic away. The rest of the time Vincent did his best not to startle the orc, or get accidentally sat on.

Zig Zag snarled in his direction again, and then went back to looking out of the window. For a moment Vincent thought he wasn't going to drink the water, but then, absently, he took a sip. And then another. He paused and looked down at the glass, then looked at Vincent, growling something that became, "...little bashtard! Why'sh thish water tascht funny?"

"I had to!" protested Vincent. "We're landing! You'll get thrown into quarantine!"

Even now the potion had yet to take its full effect, and Zig Zag kept pulling faces like he was in some world champion gurning competition.

"Sir?"

Vincent felt a nudge from Stone and he looked around to see the customs official gesturing him forwards. He resisted the terrible urge to say, "G'day", and an hour later they were checking into a large hotel overlooking the Sydney Harbour Expo Centre. They kept their distance in the airport in case they were being watched, travelling separately to the hotel, but Vincent could see a couple of the club loitering around the lobby. Although it was only midday, Smiler and Billy Toothless were already at the bar, where they appeared to be taking bets on who else had made it through customs. They looked relieved to see Stone.

The view from Vincent's room was quite spectacular, but the room itself was nondescript, with a mixture of colours and artwork that didn't quite go together. Which was kind of how Vincent felt right now. Since they were in disguise – all their cuts, the sleeveless leather vests sporting the club's colours, safely hidden away – they all looked like fish out of water, none more than Vincent himself, who felt like a lost little boy. He said as much to Stone when he joined them at the bar, and received a reprimand for his troubles.

"It's the man that makes the colours, not the colours that make the man," said Stone. "We're thirsty, if you wouldn't mind."

Vincent headed for the bar. At least he could be reasonably certain that he wasn't in any danger right now, since the bar staff could see him quite clearly, although the barman didn't believe that Vincent was old enough to drink, and asked to see his ID. Which wasn't at all humiliating.

But Stone was right: Vincent may have looked like some gimpy student type in his current disguise, but he was still the same person, the same man, with or without his cut. And in his time prospecting for Aberrant MC Vincent felt that he had become a man, rather than a boy. He'd learned the meaning of bravery and strength, and of friendship and honour. Bravery, he had learned, was not about being a tough guy but about overcoming your fear and doing what was right regardless of the dangers involved. Numb Tongue, for instance, wasn't being particularly brave if he faced down a roomful of football nutters, because he knew that he could dismantle them in seconds. Acting when you might lose took bravery. Likewise, strength wasn't simply about being able to bench-press a minivan, it was about mental strength, moral strength, fortitude, the desire to never give in.

Vincent spotted Andy One-Leg and Joker across the lobby, the surfer and the somewhat dodgy-looking used car salesman, and he ordered them drinks to save them the bother of telling him.

So that was everyone from their flight accounted for, apart from Zig Zag of whom there was still no sign. Vincent wondered if the potion was wearing off in some brightly lit interrogation room, and couldn't help chuckling to himself. The customs people would be in for one hell of a surprise when Zig Zag suddenly became all teeth and guttural snarling. But still, it was a worry.

Vincent had no idea why Aberrant MC were here in Australia, other than the fact that it was something to do with the headaches, but whatever was going on it didn't hurt to have a nasty little orc bastard on your side. Vincent hoped he'd made it through.

"So, are you down here for the convention?" asked the barman.

"What convention?" said Vincent.

"The comic book thing across the road. Comic Con, or whatever it's called. You get people from all around the world come down and dress up in all these crazy costumes. Bloody good, they are sometimes. Not that it's my thing, if ya know what I mean, but you should see the detail that goes into some of the costumes. Amazing! I mean, look at the fella over there. Bloody amazing!"

Vincent turned to where the barman was looking, over by the check-in area, and there stood Zig Zag McClintock, a nasty little orc bastard, having his picture taken with a herd of American tourists. He looked absolutely furious.

"Oh fuck!" gasped Vincent.

"Exactly," grinned the barman. "Bloody amazing! Can I get you anything else?"

CHAPTER FIVE

It would be a matter of seconds, just one more photo request, before Zig Zag exploded. Vincent was so afraid of the consequences that he thought he might start to flicker, as his invisibility ring sensed danger and decided that it was best if he wasn't around. Not that Vincent was in any danger from Zig Zag himself, but certainly there was a palpable danger in the air, a feeling that comes when you walk into a room where people have been arguing. Except this was more like walking into a murder scene.

As far as Zig Zag was concerned, cameras worked by magic, and magic – unless performed by a member of Aberrant MC and wilfully ignored by him – was very bad. Clearly he was freaking out under the focus of so much attention, desperate for a way out before he accidentally lost the plot and killed someone. Unable to make himself understood at the reception desk he then stomped over to the bar, hackles raised and ready to bite large chunks from the next American to ask for his picture. Joker, meanwhile, dashed over to the reception to attempt to check in for him. There was a big line in front of him, and only one receptionist in three doing anything approaching their job.

Stone joined Vincent at the bar. "Get him out of here," he insisted. "Take him to your room until Joker's sorted this out. Hurry," he urged, as another camera flash went off.

Vincent alerted Zig Zag of his presence and took him by the arm, quickly leading him away. They all but ran through the lobby towards the lifts, all of which were, inevitably, several floors away and in no rush to save them.

25

If anything, the lift area was even more crowded and public than the bar, all eyes upon Zig Zag and his "amazing costume". Vincent could have cried with relief when they were joined by Doctor Who, a very scantily clad Amy Pond, and a Wookie carrying several bags full of shopping. Thank fuck for comic book nerds!

The Wookie stood a little too close to Zig Zag, and Zig Zag growled at him. He wasn't going to the let the Wookie win.

The left-hand lift arrived on the ground floor, with a ding, and an elderly couple struggled out with their luggage. Agonizing seconds ticked past, and then they all shuffled into the lift – Vincent, a couple in their early twenties, Doctor Who, Amy Pond, a Wookie, and Zig Zag McClintock, a small and seriously pissed off orc. With another cheery ding, the lift door began to close. And then it opened again, as a last-minute passenger managed to wedge his foot into the remaining gap. It was another orc.

"Oh fuck!" gasped Vincent, not for the first time.

The orc got in, and the lift door dinged shut. Going up.

First floor. Second floor. Third floor. Fourth floor. Fifth floor.

Ding.

The twenties couple got out and everybody shuffled a little farther apart, while the door tried to make up its mind whether or not it was going to close. Doctor Who jabbed at the button for his floor in the hope of hurrying it up.

Ding.

Sixth floor. Seventh floor. Eighth floor.

Ding.

The Wookie got out.

Ding.

Doctor Who was shitting himself. It was like being inside some sort of cosplay pressure cooker, the air so thick with tension you could hang your Batman outfit on it. And then the orc spoke.

"Aka'Magosh," it said.

Zig Zag stared, open-mouthed, at the orc. The costume was fantastically well made, but it was still a costume. The Orcish had been real.

Ding.

Ninth floor. Tenth floor.

Ding.

Hurriedly, Doctor Who and Amy Pond got out and legged it for their TARDIS.

Despite his best efforts, Vincent had yet to understand more than a few words of Orcish, and could only understand Zig Zag in human form, when he spoke a rough approximation of English, albeit with rather too much spitting. A lot of Orcish words appeared to mean different things depending on how you said them, and, frankly, Vincent had difficulty producing enough phlegm. Coughing up greeners seemed integral no matter what language Zig Zag was speaking. By the time they got to the nineteenth floor, however, both the real orc and the cosplay orc were deep in conversation. It sounded like a couple of junkyard dogs arguing with a cement mixer full of snot. Half an hour later they were back in the bar, chatting away like long-lost brothers.

"Seriously," laughed Vincent, relating the tale to Smiler and Joker, "you should've seen Doctor Who's face. He was fucking desperate to get out of that lift."

"Beam me up, Scotty!" grinned Smiler.

"No, that's Star Trek," said Vincent.

"The one with the Wookie?"

"No, that's Star *Wars*!"

"Doctor Who's not in Star Wars."

"I *know* that," sighed Vincent, another story lost on them.

It was fairly obvious that Smiler wasn't ever going to pass as a comic book geek, or nerd, or whatever the politically correct term was. Zig Zag, however, was rapidly becoming a celebrity. Admittedly, he still wasn't too keen on having his picture taken, but so long as the flash was turned off he didn't seem to know that people *were* taking pictures, and he was happy to stand facing people as they waved their phones about. Vincent wasn't about to tell him that phones had cameras on them. There was every chance that Zig Zag had never seen a phone before and would think that they, too, worked by magic, if he found out what they did. Finding out might not improve public relations.

"He'll be signing fucking autographs next," muttered Andy.

"And what better place to hide an orc?" grinned Stone. "It's perfect. Who'd've thought some of them actually speak Orcish?"

"Summa they akk-sents is bladdy arfuw though," noted Billy Toothless, also introducing Mister Pot to Mister Kettle. "Cahn't unnerstan' a bladdy wurd they's sayun'."

Billy Toothless was a hobgoblin. Of course, that wasn't what it said on his passport, which, if they had a section for professions, would have claimed him to be an archaeologist, but he was a hobgoblin nonetheless. Apparently the smell of damp dog, decaying sofa, and mouthwash were quite normal for a hobgoblin, and, remarkably, Billy had the olfactory senses of a bloodhound. He was also damn near impossible to understand. West coast of England mixed with deep South American and Pakistani, possibly. Gibberish, certainly. But he always seemed to Vincent to be a nice enough fella, given the rough parameters of 'nice' in Aberrant MC. Yes, he was smelly and somewhat weasely looking, his terrible brown teeth belying his nickname, but when he wasn't on Aberrant business he also ran a business making driving aids for disabled people, and he was nice to cats.

Suddenly, Billy sat bolt upright, sniffing at the warm air like a rodent. His eyes locked onto a middle-aged man at the other end of the bar, alone at a table in a semi-hidden corner. Billy sniffed at the air again, suddenly deadly serious, and he gave Joker a nudge, whispering something into his ear.

"You sure?" said Joker.

"No doubt 'boutit," nodded Billy. "Bin af'er that'un fer years. 'E dunna fur stracth, 'bout a while 'go, then ge's 'isself put 'way in Ban'cock fer fiddlin' kiddies. Cahn't keep 'isself t' 'isself."

"Prospect!" called Joker, bringing Vincent to attention.

"Nah, 'e's too ole," said Billy. "'E loikes 'em a lat yunger 'n 'at."

"No, not for bait," said Joker. "We just need to know what room he's in."

And so Vincent spent the rest of the afternoon and early evening watching a rather uninteresting man in a suit and tie, who ate and drank alone. Cuts or not, he was a prospect, and he did as he was told by the full-patch members. And it could have been worse. At least they weren't using him as a fucking canary again, throwing him into potentially dangerous situations and then gauging said danger by whether or not he disappeared.

Aberrant did a lot of that sort of thing. In fact, he'd got so used to it in the past six months or so that he'd actually stopped being scared at one point, and found himself suddenly reappearing in the middle of a packed skinhead bar in Berlin. Thankfully, he'd vanished pretty promptly the moment the fists started flying, but, as with the skinheads, it was a close shave. This bloke just sat there, engrossed in some electrical device, a Kindle or some such. Since Vincent wasn't allowed a phone, he hadn't bothered looking into any new gadgets that might be trackable.

Eventually the bloke turned off the device and put it in his briefcase. Vincent followed him to his room on the seventh floor, and jotted down the room number. Then he went back to the bar and passed the information on to Billy and Joker.

"Good work," said Joker. "Take the rest of the night off."

Vincent went straight to bed. Jet lag was starting to kick in with a vengeance, and his mind kept trying to tell him what time it was in Berlin, and precisely how long he'd been awake. He showered and flicked on the TV, a news channel showing some sort of disturbance in Los Angeles, lots of aerial shots of flashing police lights, and then a black lady in her nightgown, presumably an eyewitness. He flicked through the channels looking for something more interesting, and settled on a rerun of Mad Max Beyond The Thunderdome, the lesser of the Gibson trilogy by far, but salvaged by Angry Anderson. It had been a while since Vincent had seen a TV that wasn't mounted to a bar, and he didn't miss them much, but it was an okay movie to fall asleep to.

He awoke the next morning feeling surprisingly fresh and alert, all the better for a good night's sleep in a nice comfy bed. The TV was still on, some local channel doing the breakfast news, and Vincent left it on while he showered and cleaned his teeth. He pulled blue jeans and a T-shirt from his bag, clean socks and pants. And then he stopped in his tracks and gaped at the TV screen, one leg halfway into his pants. There was a face he recognised on the screen. He hit the volume button.

"In a bizarre turn of events convicted paedophile, Michael Lynd, thirty-nine, was found dead this morning in the shark tank at Sydney Aquarium. Police officers say that Lynd's remains were discovered at around six o'clock this morning, and for the moment they are treating the death as suicide. Lynd served four years in Long Bay Correctional Centre for sexual assault, before moving to Bangkok where he was arrested and served an additional four years for child sex offences, before being deported back to Australia. Lynd was staying in a hotel near the Sydney Harbour Expo Centre and was suspected by police to have been on the lookout for victims at the nearby comic book convention this weekend. For more on this story we go over to John Joseph, live at Sydney Aquarium. What can you tell us, John?"

"Well, Howard, so far authorities say they have very little to go on as only Lynd's head has been discovered. The rest of the body, they say, was likely eaten by sharks."

"Holy fuck!" gasped Vincent.

Someone from the seventh floor had just checked out early.

CHAPTER SIX

Dum Dum felt like a fool; a fool for listening to some stupid fortune teller, a fool for heading off into the desert on his own and not waiting for the others, and, most of all, a fool for believing, even for a second, that music could talk to him. Seriously, what kind of fucking idiot, what kind of fool, would believe that?

He lay face down in the dirt, his hands and feet bound behind his back, hog-tied, The Hanged Man. There was a gun pushed into the back of his head. Death. Stuck to a nearby fence, flapping in the hot desert breeze, was a page from what proclaimed itself to be Blade Magazine. The Page Of Swords. And Dum Dum, The Fool, was under arrest.

And yet it had all seemed so logical, and, once Dum Dum had given in to the idea – looked at it from the upside down point of view of The Hanged Man – it had all seemed remarkably easy. The Bullring Brummies cover of *The Wizard* had been followed by The Who's *Pinball Wizard*, *The Black Wizard* by Electric Wizard, and, just to nail the point home, Motörhead's *Out Of The Sun*, which was about a wizard.

"Got it," Dum Dum muttered to himself, feeling like the point may be getting laboured, even for him. It was getting late, close to last call, and he really didn't want to hear any Uriah Heep. "But where the hell do I find this bloody wizard? At least point me in the right direction."

Dum Dum had smiled when he saw the signs for San Bernardino. So far so good. He'd found the 101 highway and was following signs for the Interstate

31

10, going east. Not that he had any idea *where* he was going, but that's where the music had told him to go. He stuck to what he guessed was the speed limit – a steady seventy miles an hour – and was frequently passed by faster moving traffic. He'd seen no sign of any cops, but, still, there was no need to be careless and give them an excuse to pull him over. If he was right then he had about another hundred and thirty miles to go.

The last song of the night had been unfamiliar to him, a ballad to let people know that the place was closing for the night. Dum Dum had listened for messages in the lyrics, but heard nothing that stood out as important or helpful. It was only when he discovered the title, *Zzyzx Road*, by Stone Sour, that he knew where he should be going.

"This Zzyzx Road," he asked the bartender. "Is it a real place?"

"Oh yeah," she smiled, and wrote down directions.

Having waited outside the Rainbow for a while after last call, in case the others showed up, Dum Dum had filled his bike at the petrol station opposite the Whisky A Go Go and bought himself a couple of maps that he probably wouldn't be able to read. There was a goth kid behind the counter, listening to Canned Heat, *On The Road Again*. Another sign, perhaps? The song changed to Eagles Of Death Metal, *San Bernardino*. Definitely a sign. According to Goth Kid, it was on the way.

The early morning sun was coming up when he finally came to Zzyzx Road, much welcome after riding through the desert overnight. He'd known it could get cold at night, but he'd been surprised to see snowcapped mountains, and the cold had bitten at him in the dark, slowing his pace, and forcing him to find warmth in the wake of big trucks. He stopped for breakfast in an old fifties diner, and was grateful for American portions, wolfing down steak and eggs, with a side order of everything. Every time he got halfway through his coffee, the waitress would come over and fill it up again for free. Eventually she just left the pot on the table.

It was at the diner, however, that Dum Dum first started to have doubts about what he was doing. He hadn't really noticed the music while he was eating, but it was Bob Dylan's *A Hard Rain's A-Gonna Fall* that was playing now, hardly relevant since he was in the middle of the desert and it wasn't raining. Dum Dum vaguely remembered that the song was about nuclear fallout, but, again, that didn't seem much use.

"I'm a-goin' back out 'fore the rain starts fallin'. I'll walk to the depths of the deepest black forest," crooned Dylan.

And Dum Dum looked out of the window at the start of a bright sunny day, with absolutely no sign of a forest, and not a cloud in the sky.

"And it's a hard, and it's a hard..." sang Bob.

You're not bloody wrong, thought Dum Dum. Bloody impossible.

Next was Blondie's *Atomic*: *"Oh, your hair is beautiful."* Dum Dum had a short cropped mohawk, a Chuck Liddell stripe, that could be called all kinds of things but beautiful. There were a couple of dents in his skull from an argument with a man with a hammer, but only because Dum Dum had been asleep when the argument started. Again, he failed to see the relevance.

It wasn't until the third song, *Enola Gay*, by Orchestral Manoeuvres In The Dark, that Dum Dum began to notice a pattern. Surely three songs back to back that referenced nukes couldn't be a coincidence? Dum Dum searched his mind, but found nothing. He even looked right at the back and under the cushions. And yet he had to be on the right path, somehow this *had* to be right. All he had to do was figure out how and why he was right.

The waitress came over to clear his plate and to tempt him with dessert. She was a kindly lady, fifty-something, with a warm smile, and a star tattooed on the back of her hand. Dum Dum had seen the same tattoo before somewhere, his mind locating it during a two-stretch in Wormwood Scrubs. And with that thought, so Dum Dum's mind came upon an old magazine article he'd seen while he was in that prison. It had been a gentleman's magazine, so some of the pages were missing, but he remembered the article as clear as day.

"'Scuse me," he asked the waitress. "Didn't they do some sort of nuclear testing out here in the fifties?"

"That was the Nevada Test Site, out in Nye County," said the waitress, that sunshine smile flitting across her eyes. She winked at Dum Dum, "You'll like Nye County, they have legal brothels there."

"Is it far?"

"Oh, it's a good three hundred miles or more from here," the waitress nodded vaguely out towards the road. "They did hundreds of tests up there, turned the sand to glass, they say. I believe they do tours these days."

Three hundred miles seemed like an awful long way to go on a hunch, but then Dum Dum had already done about a hundred and seventy miles with no real idea of why he was doing them. Doubt raised an eyebrow in his direction. Three hundred miles. On top of the miles he'd already done. What if the fool was supposed to have stayed in Los Angeles and tried to find his fellow club members instead of taking off on this hare-brained goose chase? What if they were in trouble...or more trouble than usual, anyway.

And yet the whole reason they were here in the first place was to see a wizard in the desert. Admittedly, Dum Dum hadn't expected it to be quite so vast and deserty, and he'd not really considered that there might be more than one desert, but in his guts he felt that he must at least be on the right path. Normally he was useless at directions, yet he'd found his way this far. That, in itself, *must* be a sign of something, if only that hell had got a bit chilly and Satan had invested in some skates.

Still. Three hundred miles. On a hunch. Fuck.

The radio was playing a commercial for the law firm of Hoo-Ha and So-n-So – Dum Dum didn't catch the name – some class action lawsuit against a drug company who'd manufactured an anti-depressant that made people suicidal. The next ad was for a drug that relieved back pain, but had the downside that it "may cause anal bleeding and leakage". Fortunately, the bike seat wasn't so uncomfortable that it had caused either. Quite a nice ride in fact, always ready to eat up the miles, and never once protesting Dum Dum's weight. He was a little worried that he wasn't supposed to be putting so many miles on it, but the host club had said to treat it as his own. He was tempted to see if it was for sale.

Dum Dum looked out of the window at the bike, its exhaust catching the sun in such a way that it lit up the security van that was parked alongside. Dum Dum looked closer. There on the side of the van was a painting of a wizard and the logo of a company called Money Wizard ATMs. The wizard, a cheery fellow in a green robe, was holding a wand in one hand and a wad of cash in the other. The licence plate said the van was from Nye County, Nevada.

"Well, I'll be..." said Dum Dum, finishing his coffee.

Dum Dum had followed the van for several hours until, eventually, there were signs for Nye County, and he followed those instead. Finally he'd pulled to a stop by a sign that welcomed careful drivers to the county. He asked the first passer-by for directions to "the atomic stuff" – they did tours of the place, after all – and he then drove vaguely in that direction for a while, not at all sure what he was looking for.

The battery on his iPod was long dead, so music offered no further clues. Instead, Dum Dum chose roads at random, hoping for the best, but quite aware that he might ride straight past whatever he was looking for and not even know it. Dusk was falling once more, and in a few hours it might be difficult to find what he was looking for even if he knew what that was. Eventually he found a cheap motel for the night and settled on reading some brochures about the local tourist traps. It was unlikely that the wizard was a tourist attraction, but they were better than nothing. At least now he knew where he could get his nails done and play a round of golf.

Awake at first light, Dum Dum ate breakfast at another roadside diner, taking full advantage of the endless coffee. Quickly back out on the road, he tried random directions again, anything that looked like it might head somewhere a bit remote and didn't have a Starbucks or Burger King at the other end. Some of the roads faded into dirt paths, the tarmac making way for dust and potholes, others seemed to take him around in circles. Once in a while there would be a house, but those few people who answered their doors knew nothing of wizards.

He reached the end of one promising-looking road to find it blocked by a tall wire fence that seemed to go on for miles through the scrub in each direction. There were several signs on the fence advising visitors that what lay on the other side of it was government property, and that trespassers would not be greeted with quite the same warmth as they could expect with their coffee refills. Dum Dum parked his bike and peered through the fence at nothing but desert. The day had grown warm, and the arid ground shimmered in the heat. Dum Dum tried his iPod again, now that it had been charged.

"The wind is cold where I live. The blizzard is my home. Snow and ice and loaded dice, the wizard lives alone..."

There was no sign whatsoever of any snow or ice, but there was the wizard reference again, leaping up and down and waving its arms about, going, "Look over here, you big oaf!" Dum Dum felt he was getting close. Fuck, he *must* be getting close. He'd seen snowcapped mountains, knew how cold it could get out here. Maybe there were more mountains hiding at the end of one of these roads? Maybe that was where he'd find a wizard?

"Trees are stone where I live, flowers made of glass. Cold and white and wrong and right and voices from the past..."

For just a brief second, no more than the blink of an eye, Dum Dum thought he saw a movement in the heat vapours, a flash of cold, white light.

"Life is death where I live, frozen grin my smile..."

With a mental apology to Lemmy, Dum Dum turned the music off. Nothing was moving, not so much as a rabbit, and yet he felt certain that something was out there. He pressed his face against the fence, watching for anything, finding nothing but dust and heat. He was still peering through the fence at nothing, shielding his eyes against the glare of the sun, when he heard the truck.

They were military, not cops, and remarkably unsympathetic to the fact that Dum Dum wasn't yet trespassing. They were nervous, too, Dum Dum could tell, and he didn't like nervous men pointing guns at him. One of them had his knee pressed into Dum Dum's back, while another pinned his face to the ground with an itchy trigger finger. With dust in his eyes, Dum Dum blinked into the hot midday sun. And there, not three feet away from him, on the other side of the fence, was a wizard. He was levitating.

CHAPTER SEVEN

"You're just going to let them do that, are you?" sneered the wizard.

Dum Dum could see the wizard as clear as day. He was a wiry little man, maybe five foot seven, not including the nine inches or so he was hovering above the ground. In case this – and the ludicrously long white beard – wasn't enough evidence that he was a wizard, he carried a wooden staff and wore a long, hooded, white robe. He produced, from his robe, a sturdy wooden pipe, which he lit with a click of his fingers. His pupils were milky white, as if he were blind, but he watched them like a hawk.

"I didn't really think I had a lot of choice," said Dum Dum.

"Always got a choice," shrugged the wizard. "These three, for instance," the wizard nodded at the men in black uniforms, "have the choice to go away before I turn them into something unpleasant. Or they have the choice to stay around and find out exactly how unpleasant."

Dum Dum could sense that the men were unsure of themselves, the knee in his back offering a little less pressure, but they stood their ground, two of the three now aiming their weapons at the wizard. The wizard blew a large smoke ring that smelled like skunk.

"Of course," he added, "they won't have that choice for very long."

"You know your magic doesn't work on this side of the fence," said one of the military, the one with his knee dug into Dum Dum's back. He didn't sound completely convinced.

"And your guns don't work on my side," said the wizard, blowing another smoke ring. "Thing is," he coldly stared them down. "What if I'd moved the fence?"

There was a flash of cold, white light, and suddenly the wizard was floating on the other side of the fence. He winked at Dum Dum. And the men in black uniforms turned and ran for their lives.

Dum Dum snapped the zip ties that were binding his wrists and ankles, and clambered to his feet. It was more of a courtesy thing that he'd kept them on. That and the gun that had been pointing at his temple. The wizard continued to hover above the ground, eyeing Dum Dum with some curiosity.

"Where's Yeshua?" he demanded.

Dum Dum dusted himself down, unintimidated. The wizard was by no means friendly, more like someone who'd had a good poo interrupted by some trivial business, but Dum Dum caught a whiff of amusement about him, too. He'd enjoyed fucking with the military, showing off his power, and leaving no doubt which side of the fence he sat on – both literally and metaphorically – but he hadn't actually hurt anyone, just frightened them off. This suggested to Dum Dum that the wizard *could* have hurt them if he'd wanted to. The wizard was a powerful man, for now just having a bit of fun.

"Don't know," said Dum Dum.

He blinked in the sunlight. He could have sworn the wizard had moved closer, like some spindly, weed smoking, weeping angel.

"And what else don't you know, I wonder?" pondered the wizard. "Where's Reprobus?"

"Don't know."

"Don't know who or don't know where?"

Dum Dum had to think about that for a moment. Honesty was clearly the best policy right now, but he wasn't sure that he fully understood the question. "If they're places then I don't think I've been to them, and if they're people then I don't think I know them," he said slowly.

"Not a good answer," scowled the wizard. Any hint of amusement had gone from those white eyes that now seemed dark and menacing, and Dum Dum found it difficult to look directly at him, like he was trying to stare at the sun, but without any of its bright light. "Who are you?" demanded the wizard. "What do you want? Who sent you, bridge troll?"

"My name is..." began Dum Dum.

"I know your name," snapped the wizard. Without appearing to move, he was close enough now to poke at the name patch on Dum Dum's cut. "It's right there on your jacket. *If* this is your jacket."

Dum Dum would later confess, if only to himself, that, just for a moment, he'd felt what it was like to be vulnerable, what fear felt like. He was a big fella by anyone's standards, and it wasn't a familiar feeling. During his time in prison Dum Dum had faced down nutters on E Wing armed with crude shanks, and he'd worked as a bouncer on the outside, in some of London and Manchester's toughest clubs. He'd even taken on full-grown orcs in a godforsaken hellhole called Fero City, back when Aberrant MC had to battle their way out of a cage fight. And not once had he felt fear. But he felt it now.

But, still, it was his cut, and no one touched his colours. No one.

"It's *mine*," said Dum Dum firmly. "Take your hands off."

Damn right it was his. It had taken Dum Dum four years to earn his colours. Even some of the biggest and most respected outlaw motorcycle clubs only expected their prospects to serve a year. But then, Aberrant MC were different in that they weren't looking to expand. There were thirteen full-patch members, and there would always be thirteen. The only way in was by way of dead man's shoes, which, given that some of the club members were immortal, could mean a considerable wait. In that context, four years was a comparatively short time to prospect for Aberrant, but, nevertheless, no one could say that Dum Dum hadn't earned his right to wear their colours. He was willing to die for them. The wizard seemed to sense this, and his manner softened just a touch, more curious than angry or suspicious.

"Yours but you don't know Yeshua?" he pondered. "So, who *are* you, bridge troll that doesn't know Yeshua?" This time the wizard didn't say "bridge troll" like it was an insult.

Dum Dum explained, as best he could, that he was on a vague mission to find a wizard who lived in the desert. He had no idea why, other than it had something to do with a couple of his fellow club members getting headaches in Berlin and then flying to Australia. He'd been rather hoping that the wizard would know more about why he was here, or, better still, that his president or sergeant-at-arms would be here already.

"And what do they look like, this president and sergeant-at-arms?" asked the wizard.

Dum Dum described them: President, Mad John, was about five foot ten, dark skin, like a tan that never fades, piercing blues eyes, dirty blonde hair.

Numb Tongue was seven and a half feet tall, shaved head and goatee beard, face full of scars, like he'd dived head first into a combine harvester.

"Well then, bridge troll," said the wizard. "I suppose you'd better come with me. This motor-bicycle of yours, will it take two?"

"It will," nodded Dum Dum. "But I ain't giving you a ride unless I know your name."

"Is that so?" said the wizard. "In that case, bridge troll who doesn't know why he's here, my name is Merlin."

CHAPTER EIGHT

Vincent poured himself a small glass of orange juice, drank it down in one, and poured himself another. He balanced this, and his coffee cup, on a flimsy, red plastic tray, and headed to a vacant table, trying not to spill either fluid on his breakfast of scrambled eggs and toast. It was probably going to be a long day and he didn't want to face it on an empty stomach. He placed the tray on the table and began buttering his toast. At which point he heard raised voices from the hotel lobby, and he knew for a fact that it was going to be a very long day indeed.

"I've never been so insulted in my life!"

"I find that incredibly hard to believe! Do you stay at home a lot?"

The second voice belonged to Flashback, Aberrant MC's vice president and resident loose cannon, which was saying a great deal when you considered the competition. Not that he was a violent man particularly: Flashback enjoyed a good bar brawl every now and again, although he was often more of a danger to himself than anyone else, throwing wild haymakers that had less than a fifty-fifty chance of connecting with anything. But, on the whole, he would rather be buying drinks for everyone than swinging punches at them, it was just that fights had a strange habit of breaking out around him.

More concerning, however, was Flashback's tendency to show off his magic when he was drunk, which was most of the time. It was one thing to pull a coin from a child's ear, but quite another when Flashback produced a live rabbit from the same ear, and then got all indignant when the worried parents

41

of said child pulled him or her away from the strange man, and refused to let the child keep the rabbit.

Vincent left his breakfast and hurried to the lobby, where, inevitably, he found some angry parents, a crying child, and Flashback stumbling around drunk clutching a large white rabbit. He was dressed as a chef, complete with apron and fluffy white hat, and sported a badly drawn moustache.

"Ah, there you are, Prospect," he said, spotting Vincent and lurching towards him, brandishing the rabbit. "Here, take this. 'S a rabbit."

"I can see that. What am I supposed to do with a rabbit?"

"Fuck should I know?" Flashback slurred. "Deal with it. I'm going to the bar while you check me into my room. Make sure the minibar is fully stocked and tell them that I am not to be disturbed under any circumstances."

A little late for that, thought Vincent. "It's that way," he said, pointing Flashback at the bar and feeling not a little sorry for whoever was in there. At two o'clock in the morning, when you weren't ready to call it a night, Flashback was a hilarious adventure. At seven-thirty in the morning, when you were stone-cold sober, had possibly assisted in the murder of a paedophile, and just wanted breakfast, not so much. It was a miracle he'd made it through customs in that state, particularly since he didn't appear to have any luggage.

When he got back to the bar with Flashback's room key, Vincent wasn't in the least surprised to find that a couple of the club had kept it open all night and were still there. Smiler looked rather the worse for wear, several empty shot glasses suggesting that it might be nearly bedtime, but Andy One-Leg and Stone were drinking slow beers and appeared relatively fresh. There was no sign of Billy Toothless, Joker, or Zig Zag.

"Ah, Prospect, there you are," said Andy. "Take this idiot to his room." He nodded at Smiler. "Make sure you put the Do Not Disturb sign on the door, and get him a wake-up call for seven o'clock this evening."

"I thought I told you to deal with that rabbit," mumbled Flashback.

Vincent had tried to deal with the rabbit, but, hardly surprisingly, the hotel staff weren't particularly helpful, informing him that since "some idiot Pom" called Thomas Austin had released just twenty-four of them into the wild in 1859 they'd bred, as one might expect, like rabbits, and become a serious pest, now numbering around three hundred million. They had no use whatsoever for another bloody rabbit.

Vincent steered Smiler down the long corridors to his room and helped him to bed. Then he called the front desk for a wake-up call. The rabbit found some lettuce on a plate that Smiler had left on the floor and decided to help itself. Vincent was tempted to leave the fluffy bastard to shit all over the carpet, but decided to leave it in his own room until he came up with a better plan. He took the lettuce and the rabbit, not forgetting the Do Not Disturb sign on his way out. If he hurried, he might still get breakfast.

"Ah, there you are, Prospect..."

Vincent had almost made it to the breakfast area when Chaos spotted him across the lobby and wanted help with his luggage. Unlike Flashback, he seemed to have packed perhaps everything he had ever owned – including, but not even slightly limited to, the kitchen sink – and, naturally, Vincent had to carry it all. Their arrival also meant that Apples and Mental had landed at Sydney airport and would doubtlessly be making equally unreasonable demands of him just as soon as they arrived.

With both Stone and Flashback suffering from the same crippling headaches it made sense to put them on separate flights, arousing a little less suspicion should they take a turn for the worse. Given Flashback's complete inability to blend in, it also seemed best if just a few of the less conspicuous club members went with him. In regular clothing, Apples could pass as a cab driver, a lie easily substantiated by his encyclopedic knowledge of London streets and his fluency in Cockney rhyming slang. Chaos, too, could pass under most radars, a seasoned traveller in Hawaiian shirt and shorts. Even Mental, with his flaming red hair and beard, managed to clean up well enough that he didn't attract any awkward questions or rubber gloves at customs. Flashback, again, not so much.

"Ah, Prospect, there you are," he called, when Vincent finally got back to the bar. "Loafing again, I see."

Mental had sent Vincent on a cigarette run, and then vigorously complained about the price of the cigarettes and the fact that they all came in a black packet, with a picture of someone dying on the front. Then Apples had wanted help with his luggage and some rather unpleasant suits taken for dry-cleaning. It was almost midday and Vincent still hadn't had any breakfast. He was beginning to think they'd be able to use his picture on the cigarette packets if he didn't get fed soon. As the only prospect on duty, he couldn't actually recall the last time he'd done any loafing.

"I need you to go to this address and pick up a vehicle." Flashback handed Vincent a piece of paper on which a drink had been spilled making some of the ink bleed. "Tell them Mister Smith sent you, and make sure the air conditioning works. And no GPS."

"Yes, Flashback," said Vincent.

"Oh, and, Prospect, I need you to deal with this." Flashback took off his chef's hat to reveal a small rabbit sitting on his head.

And so it was that some hours later Vincent was driving across Sydney, somewhat lost, in a stretched Hummer, with two white rabbits on the passenger seat. They were starting to look like breakfast, but instead he sufficed with a packet of mixed nuts he found in the bar at the back. It was that sort of vehicle – full bar, sound system and all – and Vincent was terrified that he'd crash it into something. The thing was fucking huge! And it certainly didn't help that Vincent had never driven anything bigger than a Mini before, three years ago, in a car park. Having inched across an unfamiliar town, he gave up trying to park when he finally got back to the hotel, and had it valeted.

"Sir, you know you've got a couple of rabbits in your passenger seat?" the valet ventured cautiously. Clearly Sir was a wealthy man, and if Sir wanted rabbits in his passenger seat then that was Sir's business.

"I don't suppose you want them?" Vincent asked hopefully.

"No, sir. Your best bet, if you want to get rid of them, is to let them go. There's hundreds of them over by Coogee Beach. Bloody pest, they are. Shall I get your vehicle, sir?"

Thankfully, the valet printed out directions, but still it took over an hour to get to Coogee Beach and back. Sure enough, there were rabbits all over the clifftop overlooking the beach, and now there were two more. Vincent's breakfast had long gone cold. It was nearly dinner time.

Vincent made his way to the bar, where, at last, he was able to sit down and look at a menu. Apples, Chaos, Billy, Joker, and Stone were lounging around the bar on comfy, black leather sofas, happily chatting away, the tables in front of them littered with empty glasses and bottles. The fish and chips looked good. The soft-shelled crab looked like a fucking spider, so not that. Vincent turned the menu over in case he'd missed something, but it was just the wine list. Yes, fish and chips, you can't go wrong with fish and chips. Vincent could almost smell it.

Suddenly Billy Toothless sat bolt upright. He sniffed at the air, nose twitching, eyes darting from person to person around the packed bar. His gaze stopped on a man in his mid-thirties, trimly built but already balding, gangly, like his arms and legs were too long. Billy sniffed intently in his direction, then nudged Joker and whispered in his ear.

"Another one? Are you sure?"

"Cahn't say uz Oi recernize 'im, but Oi cun smull 'im roight inuff. Kiddie fid'ler."

"Prospect!" called Joker.

Vincent never did get his fish and chips.

CHAPTER NINE

For the second time in as many hours, Dum Dum awoke in the darkened room. His head was pounding and his mouth was dry, and he felt like he might throw up. He lay still for a moment until the feeling passed, and then, slowly, he hauled himself upright, and swung his legs over the edge of the bed. On the bedside table was a fat candle, burned almost to the end, and beside it a handwritten note, Dum Dum's sunglasses, and a jug of water. 'Wear these. Drink this', said the note.

Dum Dum drank some water, careful not to gulp it all down in one. The candle flickered a warning that it was about to die. His head thumped like a drum soundcheck. He closed his eyes. Thump, thump, thump, like some terrible industrial machine. The candle died.

In the pitch dark, Dum Dum felt for his sunglasses and put them on, as instructed. Carefully, he got out of bed and shuffled around, hands outstretched, to the door, which, like the walls, appeared to be made of thick, black glass and was cool to the touch. The door was unlocked and Dum Dum opened it just a fraction. No light came into the room from outside, so Dum Dum risked removing his sunglasses for a moment and peered through the crack in the door. All was in darkness.

"Hello?"

"Hello? Hello? Hello? Hello?..." Dum Dum's voice echoed from everywhere, but there was no reply. He waited and tried again, but still there was just his own voice bouncing back at him. Dum Dum put his sunglasses back

47

on and crept outside, feeling his way along the wall. He'd gone about fifty feet when his shin cracked into something very solid.

"Ouch! Bugger!"

"Ouch! Bugger! Ouch! Bugger! Ouch! Bugger! Ouch! Bugger!..."

"Ah, there you are, bridge troll," said a voice in the darkness. "Awake at last. You can remove the sunglasses, it's late."

Merlin's voice had no echo, and it was impossible to say from which direction it came or at what distance. Dum Dum removed his sunglasses, and the wizard lit a candle, the room suddenly coming alive with gentle light, like he had somehow turned on the stars in the night sky. The room was the size of a ballroom, empty besides a few glass statues dotted along the walls, one of which Dum Dum had walked into. Merlin was on the other side of the room, standing by another entrance.

"Wow!" said Dum Dum.

"Wow! Wow! Wow! Wow!..."

"How are you feeling?"

"Better now, thank you."

"Better now, thank you. Better now, thank you. Better now, thank you..."

"Good," said Merlin. "And the eyesight is fine? It would be a shame if my first visitor in seventeen years were to go blind."

Dum Dum nodded. In truth, he still felt a little queasy and even in this low light he could see dots in front of his eyes. He felt weak, and it was an unpleasant and unfamiliar sensation, his legs like jelly when he climbed out of bed. The first time he'd tried to get up he had all but toppled over, so he'd laid back down, eventually falling back to sleep. But, waking a second time, he had grown impatient for news of his friends and eager to get on with whatever his mission might be. He had no idea how long he'd been out, only that it had been several hours.

"You have been asleep for some time," Merlin answered the unspoken question. "I was on my way to wake you. Yeshua is coming."

Dum Dum followed the wizard along endless corridors, all of them made of glass and glittering like fireflies as they passed by with the candle. Gradually it grew light, the corridors ahead appearing a cool, moonlight silver, until finally they reached the top of the wizard's tower. The view was quite the most astonishing thing Dum Dum had ever seen, miles and miles of desert turned to glass, flat like a calm sea, and glistening with reflected stars.

"It's beautiful," said Dum Dum.

"Yes, quite beautiful, I'm told," the wizard responded, melancholy in his voice.

It was only then that Dum Dum realised that Merlin could barely see past the end of his nose.

"Your friends will be here within a few hours," continued the wizard. "They have a girl with them, faerie-kind. You did not speak of her."

"You did not ask," said Dum Dum bluntly. Years of dealing with police interrogation rooms had left him reluctant to reveal any more than was absolutely necessary. Just because they'd been coming here to visit this wizard didn't mean he was a friend to the club, not until Mad John said so. Aberrant MC had encountered wizards before who had cheerfully tried to kill them, and, sadly, they had succeeded on one occasion, those being the dead man's shoes that Dum Dum now wore so proudly, if not literally. Damn right, he wasn't giving too many secrets away.

"I'm asking now," said Merlin just as bluntly. "I've a right to know who's coming to my home."

Dum Dum shrugged: "Fair enough. That'll be Snow, she's Numb's... Reprobate's girlfriend."

"Repro*bus*," the wizard smiled. "Although I'm sure you're right. Has he spoken to her yet?"

Dum Dum couldn't help but laugh: Whatever name he went by, Numb Tongue was not exactly known for his conversation, speaking barely more than a few words in a day – this despite the large amounts of cocaine he shoved up his nose. And Snow wasn't much better, quietly spoken on the rare occasions she felt the need to say anything at all. Somehow they were perfect for each other, golden in their silence and all but inseparable. In fact, it had been noted that Numb Tongue had become almost chatty since their romance began, sometimes managing a full sentence, and even a smile.

"Well, maybe, not a smile," chuckled Dum Dum. "I'm not sure he remembers how to smile, but he's definitely happier."

"Well, I'll drink to that," said Merlin. "Forgive me, it's been a long time since I had visitors. Would you care for some wine?"

Dum Dum and the wizard made themselves comfortable. The entire place seemed to be built of glass or stone, sometimes both blending together, but cushions were not in short supply, and if Merlin was right they had a few hours to wait before Mad John, Numb Tongue, and Snow arrived. Even though he'd been passed out for many hours, Dum Dum was grateful for some time to recharge his batteries in the cool night air. He'd never had heat stroke before, and being from England he'd certainly never considered that the sun could kill him, until today.

It was already starting to get hot, this morning, when Merlin had hopped onto the back of his bike. The wizard weighed barely nothing, but his bony knees dug into Dum Dum from behind, and he clung on with a grim determination, clearly rattled by the experience. Dum Dum felt a twinge of guilt that he'd got a kick out of it at first, scaring the all-powerful wizard, but it hadn't lasted long. And then Dum Dum, too, would admit that he was scared.

Merlin had magicked a gate in the fence, and they'd set off at a gentle plod, no more than fifteen or twenty miles an hour, on a long-lost desert road that had become little more than a dirt track. Twenty minutes later, however, the path began to sparkle with fragments of something, and Dum Dum saw exactly why the wizard was so rattled. The path ended abruptly, and beyond it were those miles and miles of velvet smooth, glass desert. Except that it wasn't smooth at all.

Dum Dum stopped the bike. It was like looking at a booby-trapped Bonneville Salt Flats, the perfect drag strip if it wasn't liberally dotted with glass spikes sticking out of the surface. The stone trees might be a bit of a hazard, too, although they were much easier to spot. Off in the distance there was a lone mountain that Merlin called home, all jagged peaks like the end of a broken bottle, rising up from the glass desert perhaps two thousand feet or more, and perhaps only visible if Merlin wanted it to be, since Dum Dum hadn't seen it from beyond the fence.

"You're not serious?" said Dum Dum, his eyes on the spiky minefield ahead.

"There is a path," said Merlin, "but we must hurry. In just a few hours the sun will make it impassable and there is no turning back. It would not be good for you, bridge troll, to get caught in that. It will burn you alive, or possibly turn you to stone."

At first the ride wasn't too bad, Dum Dum maintaining a steady thirty-five, easily able to pick his way through the jagged obstacles. But then, clearly against his better judgement, the wizard began to urge Dum Dum to go faster. And faster. And faster. Fifty, sixty, seventy miles an hour... ninety, one hundred, with shards of glass like razors threatening to tear at the tyres the moment Dum Dum strayed from the path.

"Faster, bridge troll, faster! The sun is coming!" Merlin bellowed. But Dum Dum didn't need telling. Already he could feel the rising heat, and the glare of the glass desert was making it difficult to see straight, or even see where the ground ended and the sky began. Every instinct told Dum Dum to slow down before he and the wizard were puréed, but at the same time he could see now why there was no turning back. They had passed the point of no return.

Dum Dum shuddered at the memory. He could have sworn that his tyres were starting to melt by the time they'd got close to Merlin's mountain tower, and then came the sickness, the sudden nausea, and the terrible feeling that he was about to pass out. The chrome dials on the bike, even the key in the ignition, were dazzling, and waves of heat from the engine hit Dum Dum like he was free-falling into a furnace. Sweat stung his eyes.

"Faster, bridge troll, faster!"

They had reached the great doors at the entrance to the mountain only just in time, Dum Dum staggering as he got off his bike and almost dropping the machine on its side. At which point, according to Merlin, Dum Dum had buckled at the knees and fallen flat on his face. Quite how the scrawny wizard had got him to bed was anyone's guess, but at least it explained the bruise on his cheek. Hours later they waited in the tall tower, built into the top of the mountain, and Dum Dum couldn't help wondering if the ride was any safer at night.

"Safe?" said Merlin. "No, of course it's not safe. They'll be lucky if they get here without being torn to pieces. Why do you think I never get any visitors?"

CHAPTER TEN

It was long into the night, the early morning catching up fast, when Dum Dum at last heard the sound of motorcycles. Merlin had nodded off in his chair, his feet – with those curious curly-toed boots – resting on a stone and glass table, an empty wine bottle hanging from his hand. Dum Dum scanned the horizon until he spotted what looked like three shooting stars, headlights moving across the desert. He nudged the wizard awake.

"Huh? Whassat?"

"They're here."

Merlin leapt to his feet and, ignoring Dum Dum, charged over to a glass desk and began furiously scribbling on a piece of paper.

"He's on the move," said Merlin urgently.

"Who's on the...?"

"Be silent!" snapped the wizard. "I must concentrate."

Dum Dum waited. Being so tall, he couldn't help but see that Merlin was hastily writing his notes on a map of Australia. They were directions, coordinates of some sort, but there were a lot of question marks on the page. Eventually the sound of bikes grew loud enough that Dum Dum felt obliged to interrupt.

"What? Damn needle in a haystack," Merlin muttered to himself. "Oh yes, here, take the keys. Let them in yourself."

It took Dum Dum half an hour just to find the front door, and as he arrived there was a hammering on the other side.

"Merlin!" Thump, thump, thump. "Merlin!" It was Mad John's voice.

"You took your time," called Dum Dum. "Just a minute. Damn wizard's got more keys than a jailer."

"Dum Dum?" Mad John sounded confused, which had to be a first. "Is that you?"

"Yeah," said Dum Dum. "Merlin's upstairs talking to himself and writing on a map of Australia."

"But how on earth did you get here? How did you find him?"

"Dunno," shrugged Dum Dum, finally selecting the right key and swinging the door open with a big smile. "Magic, I think."

When the four of them – Mad John, Numb Tongue, Snow, and Dum Dum – reached the top of the tower, the wizard was still hunched over the map, writing notes. He held up one hand for silence, and they waited. And waited. And waited some more. Numb Tongue started chopping out lines of coke on the glass table. Not many people got away with making Aberrant wait, especially not Numb Tongue, but Merlin did. Eventually he turned to face them. His expression suggested that he'd forgotten they were there.

"Yeshua, Reprobus," he said, greeting them with a nod and ignoring Snow.

"Merlin," Mad John nodded back.

"Any luck finding that grail of yours?"

Mad John smiled: "Not yet. But that is not why we're here..."

"I know why you're here," Merlin said curtly. "Your bridge troll told me."

"I did?" said Dum Dum.

"You did," said Merlin.

And apparently Dum Dum had.

The sun began to rise and they adjourned to a room deep inside the mountain. Long before midday it would be too bright, too hot upstairs, and cool minds were needed to think. From what Dum Dum now understood, there was an Aboriginal man in Australia, named Derain, who had been kidnapped and badly beaten by dwarfs. Since Derain was capable of telepathy he had sent out a psychic SOS, a distress signal so strong that Flashback and Stone had picked it up in Berlin. It was known that the pair had telepathic abilities, indeed it was Derain who had taught Stone, but never had they received a signal at such distance, and never with such urgency. They had no choice but to follow.

"And you can talk to this Derain person too?" Dum Dum asked.

"It's not so much talking as sending mental pictures, but yes," said Merlin. They were sitting around a long glass table, the room lit by many candles, the map of Australia spread out in front of them. "I've been attempting to track his movement by the stars, but the dwarfs have been moving him underground a lot, and I'm afraid he has been drifting in and out of consciousness."

"Needle in a haystack," said Dum Dum, looking down at the map.

"Precisely," Merlin nodded. "They appear to be somewhere around here," – he pointed at the map – "heading west, but that's about all I can tell at the moment. Unfortunately, I think the dwarfs may have caught on: They have him blindfolded now."

Mad John, it transpired, was an old friend of Merlin, as were many of the members of Aberrant MC, even if he seemed to know them all by different names. That was why Merlin had been so suspicious of Dum Dum, wearing the club's colours, but apparently unfamiliar with its president. It had been a while since Merlin had seen any of them – seventeen years, to be precise – and Dum Dum wasn't with the club back then. Knowing that Merlin could communicate with Derain – even played psychic chess with him – Mad John had come here searching for help.

Of course, it would have been better if Stone or Flashback could have made the journey to see Merlin, and better still if they'd been able to converse with him telepathically, but they were unable to communicate at such great distance, and in any case, Derain's signal was so strong, so overwhelming, that they could barely hear themselves think. They may as well be whispering to each other from opposite ends of a rock concert for all they could hear above his din.

"But why would the dwarfs kidnap him in the first place?" asked Dum Dum.

"Gold," replied Merlin. "What else? Australia has some of the richest gold mines on earth, and no one knows the land like Derain. He *is* the land. Unfortunately, he is also underneath it at the moment, so I'd suggest we adjourn for the time being. There is food and hot water, should you need to bathe, but for your own good I would ask that you don't go into any of the outer rooms before sunset."

Dum Dum didn't need telling twice about that. Any longer out there and he and Merlin would have been like ants under a magnifying glass, and he now understood why the others had tackled the perilous journey at night. You'd have to be insane to try it in daylight, and Dum Dum said as much to Merlin.

"It was that or leave you to be picked up by the military and taken away for questioning," explained Merlin. "They are not so hospitable to my guests."

Dum Dum was still feeling out of sorts from heat exhaustion so he went for a nap. Now that Mad John – Yeshua – and the others were here, he didn't have to worry that he was on the wrong path. And with this Aboriginal fella, Derain, being out of range, either underground or unconscious, there wasn't much else they could do but wait. It seemed they might be here for a few days.

But sleep never came. Dum Dum lay awake in the dark room, a fresh candle his only light, his mind a whirlwind of chaotic thoughts. Since joining Aberrant MC he'd become almost used to the unusual, the extraordinary becoming almost mundane. He'd met faeries, elves, orcs, trolls – a bridge troll *and* a cave troll – and at least half a dozen wizards, not to mention several characters from the Bible, all of which he had somehow managed to take in his stride. But in this case he couldn't help being a little star-struck.

Of course, Dum Dum had played it cool, no big deal, just Merlin, wizard to the court of King Arthur, but the child inside him couldn't help being terribly overexcited. As wizards went, Merlin was pretty much a fucking rock star! The uber-wizard! Which had made it all the more remarkable, last night, when he'd complemented Dum Dum on his magic. Dum Dum hadn't been entirely sure he was even doing magic.

"Oh yes," nodded Merlin, as they'd polished off the second bottle of wine and about half an ounce of skunk. "Beginner's luck, of course, but there's no denying you have some skills in divination. You'd be surprised how few people can successfully utilise the medium of music these days, and even then they would need an entire library of music to achieve what you did today."

Ever honest, Dum Dum had explained to Merlin what an iPod was, an entire library of music, but still, the wizard insisted that finding him just by music alone was no easy task.

"All the same, you did well, bridge troll, especially for one so young. Many have tried to find me and very few have succeeded."

"How did you know?" asked Dum Dum. "About me being part bridge troll." Dum Dum had only found this out himself fairly recently. And that was only because Mad John had told him. Though he was something of a giant, most people didn't look at Dum Dum and immediately think, bridge troll.

The wizard gave him a peculiar look: "You are ashamed of your bloodline?"

Dum Dum thought about this. The only bridge troll he'd ever met was called Cunt, a name he unfortunately lived up to, not least because his bridge was in a dreadful state of disrepair and he wanted far too much for crossing it. Dum Dum had knocked him out. Then again, he'd met a very nice cave troll, and since cave trolls were generally considered to be cantankerous and violent he had to assume that they weren't all the same. Perhaps not all bridge trolls were Cunts. "No," said Dum Dum. "Not ashamed, just curious. It's not the first thing most people say to me."

Merlin puffed on his pipe, blowing another impressive smoke ring. "You walk with a slight stoop, a trait common in most trolls from generations of banging their heads on low ceilings. Also, your head and hands are too big, acromegaly they call it, but it's not uncommon among troll kind, especially younger trolls. You'll be quite a force to be reckoned with when you are fully grown."

"Fully grown?" grinned Dum Dum, a man who made people nervous when he got into a lift. "I'm six foot eight, I don't think I've got any more growing to do!"

Merlin laughed. "Believe me, you still have some growing to do. You'll outgrow that jacket of yours, that's for sure."

"But I'm forty-two!" protested Dum Dum.

"Perhaps in human years, but you, Dum Dum, are not human, at least not entirely. Troll years are different to human years."

"So how old am I in troll years?"

"Ah, well, I, er..." said the wizard, suddenly becoming visibly flustered, like he was having to explain about the birds and the bees and where babies come from. "Well, as I say, still some growing to do. Growing lad, and such. Has no one spoken to you about this before?"

"How old?" demanded Dum Dum.

Dum Dum lay awake now, in the dark, dark room, but he was unafraid. Only kids were afraid of the dark, and Dum Dum was no kid. Even if he was only four years old.

CHAPTER ELEVEN

Hot-dog in hand, Vincent weaved his way across the crowded convention centre floor. The hot-dog was disgusting, barely edible even after he'd drowned it with ketchup, but due to the massive lines it was the only thing he'd been able to pick up as he followed his target. Now that he thought about it, it wasn't a good sign that there had been no line for the hot-dog stand, but it was that or nothing. He dared not risk losing his mark, who was currently browsing through some old sci-fi magazines.

"Pssst. Prospect."

Vincent looked around to find himself standing beside Darth Vader.

"Joker?"

Vader nodded. "What's the news?"

"Nothing so far," shrugged Vincent. "He got here a couple of hours ago, but he's just been wandering about looking at the stalls."

"No weird behaviour?"

"Weirder than dressing up as Darth Vader, you mean?"

"You know what I mean," snapped Vader.

"Nope." Vincent shook his head. Given that he'd spent the morning surrounded by people dressed as superheroes, the bloke he was following seemed positively sane. It was unclear whether Joker was wearing a cunning disguise or just had a Star Wars fetish, or, for that matter, why he hadn't come dressed as the Joker, but when you considered that Zig Zag had won a prize for the best costume, sane was pretty relative. Flashback, it transpired, had arrived in Sydney dressed as a chef because he'd been drunk at the meeting where they'd discussed the club travelling incognito and got the wrong idea. This also explained the badly drawn moustache. So, no, baldly bloke wasn't behaving weird.

"Well, don't let him out of your sight, even for a second," said Vader. "He's got a clean record, but Billy's certain he's a nonce."

"He's hardly gonna doing anything in broad daylight, in the middle of a convention centre!"

"You underestimate the power of the dark side," said Vader, who had clearly been dying to say that. "Don't take your eyes off him."

The convention was huge and Vincent followed the man for several more hours, the endless crowds long becoming tiresome, constantly shuffling forwards and never seeming to get anywhere. Unless it was a line for food stands or the toilets, there never seemed to be anything the other end, just more convention centre and more bloody Ninja Turtles. The event had been sold out for months and Vincent could only imagine how Aberrant had managed to get tickets and hotel rooms so close to the venue, especially at such late notice. It wasn't like they appeared to have planned a trip to Australia, they just grabbed the first available flights out of Berlin.

Not that Vincent minded too much. It had been snowing when they left Berlin, a bitter wind cutting to the bone, long before ice turned the roads into a skating rink. Even Chaos, a man not easily discouraged by the worst of weather, had locked his bike away for the duration. On top of that, they'd spent several months infiltrating some bonehead neo-Nazi group – hence Vincent suddenly appearing in their midst in a packed bar – only to discover that these weren't the boneheads they were looking for. It wasn't helpful that Aberrant had also aroused the unwanted attention of another motorcycle club who took exception to the fact that they seemed to have set up shop in their territory.

Since they'd been staying with friends and had no clubhouse in Berlin, it was unclear if Aberrant MC had moved onto their turf or not, but, regardless, the other club had proved themselves to be a nuisance. One night a couple of them had jumped Smiler outside a bar and, undeterred by the beating he gave them, they then tried the same thing on Mental, with much the same result. It was only a matter of time before they got lucky and someone from Aberrant got hurt.

It wasn't like they were the top dogs around here anyway, just puppies, who were maybe looking to get themselves patched over by a bigger club, notably the Hells Angels, who would already have expressed an interest in them if they were actually interested. Still, with the German authorities also coming down on patch clubs like a ton of shit, even banning colours, it really wasn't what anyone needed. Numb Tongue put four of them in hospital, but surprisingly that didn't seem to dampen their enthusiasm, and before Aberrant left for Australia there was talk of the rival club buying guns, old Russian hardware, to even the score. Vincent, of course, vanished every time they were near, but he might not be so fortunate if they started taking pot shots. All things considered, following a suspected nonce around a comic book convention wasn't so bad.

"Psst. Prospect." Vader was back. "What's he up to?"

"Nothing," shrugged Vincent. "Same as before, just poking around the stalls, buying a few comic books."

"Well, we need to hurry this along a bit," said Vader. "Stone and Flashback have started getting headaches again, so we'll be on the move in a few hours."

"What am I supposed to do about it?"

"I dunno," said Vader. "Go and chat him up or something."

"Chat him up? Even if he goes for it, it only proves he's gay, not that he's Jimmy fucking Saville!"

"True," Vader nodded, "but we haven't got time to piss about. Get him back to the hotel and we'll do the rest."

Prospects did as they were told, so Vincent didn't argue, but there was a great deal of muttering under his breath as he walked away. Seriously, he was bait now? As he'd already pointed out, even if the bloke did take the bait then it was no indication that he was up to anything wrong. Vincent may look young, but he didn't look underage. Well, not unless you were that idiot barman back at the hotel, but even then it was obvious that Vincent was no child. Hell, the bloke might not even like boys! And, come to think of it, Vincent, having spent a great deal of his life invisible, wasn't particularly adept at chatting up girls, let alone flirting with balding comic book nerds. What the fuck was he going to say?

Vincent sidled up the the stall where the man was flicking through an issue of *Creepy* magazine. The man looked at Vincent and smiled.

"You've been watching me all morning," the man winked. "I've been watching you, too. My name is Sebastian."

Ten minutes later the two of them were back at the hotel, Sebastian having taken the bait, hook, line, and sinker. The pair headed to the bar where Vincent had to show his ID again before ordering a pint, which he sipped on, urgently scanning the bar for any familiar faces. Joker said they'd be waiting, but there was no sign of him, no sign of anyone. If anything there were even less people around than usual because they were all at the convention centre.

And then Vincent felt sick to his stomach as the realisation dawned on him that this was quite possibly one of Joker's pranks! It had Joker written all over it! Either that or they'd abandoned him with a dangerous paedophile! Except that Vincent would have disappeared if he was in any danger, which, again, led back to one of Joker's oh-so-hilarious pranks. There was every chance that the man was just gay and thought he'd got lucky. Why else would *none* of the club be in the bar or loitering around the lobby? He'd expected someone to be here to give him the nod. Where the hell were they? Shit!

Sebastian made polite conversation – Where was Vincent from? How long was he visiting Australia? – and Vincent did his best to appear relaxed, all the time becoming increasingly more agitated. If this was supposed to be a joke then it wasn't at all funny.

"There's no need to be nervous," said Sebastian, giving Vincent's knee a little squeeze. "I don't bite...unless you'd like me to."

"I've just not done this before," Vincent said honestly, his eyes still flitting around the bar and lobby area. Seriously, guys, he thought, any time you feel like showing up and taking over. Sebastian smiled at him. He had a nice smile.

"I'll be gentle," he promised. Such a nice smile.

Eventually Vincent could make his pint last no longer, a decision made final when the barman took his glass.

"Can I get you another one, gents?"

"Yes, ple..." began Vincent, before Sebastian cut him off.

"No, thank you. Just the bill," smiled Sebastian, before turning to Vincent and waving his room key. "I have a minibar in my room."

Vincent scanned the area one last time, hoping against hope that Joker would leap out from behind one of the pot plants. He began to think that maybe he should make his apologies to Sebastian and tell him that he'd changed his mind. After all, there was still no proof that the man had done anything wrong, other than barking up the wrong tree. And yet, somehow, Vincent felt sure that the club wouldn't joke around where matters like this were concerned. They certainly hadn't been joking around when they'd fed that other bloke to the sharks, and while no one had mentioned the incident, Vincent was in no doubt that it had been their doing. He really had no choice but to go to Sebastian's room with him and pray that they were waiting there.

Not for the first time Vincent endured an uncomfortable ride in the lift, Sebastian smiling all the way. They stopped outside his room on the fourteenth floor and Sebastian slid the plastic key into the slot and stepped inside. The curtains were drawn and it was dark. Sebastian turned on a small table lamp. He looked at Vincent, confused, the smile frozen upon his face, a rictus grin, and then he looked back at the person dressed in black sitting in the chair by the lamp.

"I've been waiting for you," said Vader.

The smile vanished.

CHAPTER TWELVE

Vader had not been alone in the room. With him were Zig Zag McClintock and Billy Toothless, McClintock waiting behind the door to block Sebastian's escape when he attempted to flee, which, of course, had been his first instinct. Terrified and confused, Sebastian had then begged that they take anything they wanted and leave him unharmed.

"We're not here to rob you," said Vader. "We're here to stop you."

The following hour had not been pleasant.

Now, with Smiler at the wheel, the club were all crammed into the stretched Hummer, which seemed considerably less spacious when you put eleven bikers inside it. Flashback had been quite upset about this, but easily distracted by the fully stocked bar, as they headed across town to exchange vehicles. Apparently Vincent was supposed to have picked up some sort of tour bus instead of the Hummer, but Flashback's note had been rather difficult to read.

"I still say we should've killed him," Joker muttered darkly.

"But you said yourself that he was innocent," said Flashback, furnishing himself with a large whisky and knocking it back with a handful of painkillers. The headaches were back with a vengeance.

"Oh, he was far from fucking innocent," Joker growled.

"True," nodded Flashback, "but he has committed no crime."

Vincent doubted that Sebastian would ever get so much as a parking ticket for the rest of his days. The implications, were he to do so, had been made abundantly clear. Zig Zag had been holding his nuts in one hand and a knife in the other hand at that point, and looked, it had to be said, a lot less like a cosplay character and a lot more like a nasty little orc who was looking for any excuse to relieve Sebastian of his testicles. But still, while it was debatable that the man had much innocence to protest, he had indeed broken no laws, and had harmed no one.

As Vincent understood it, being a hobgoblin gave Billy Toothless the dubious ability of being able to tell a paedophile by smell. Schizophrenics, too, Vincent was told, gave off a distinct odour, particularly when they were nearing a psychotic episode. It was like how dogs could smell fear. The difference with Sebastian was that he had yet to act on those urges. Billy was sure of that, too, although there could be no question that he had suffered a terrible trauma in finding out. Vincent had never seen a man look so sad, so devastated. He could only imagine the horrors that Billy had seen, and he would happily drive nails into his eyes to stop his imagination from doing so. Billy Toothless could also read minds.

It wasn't a talent that Vincent envied for a moment, and Billy himself found it all but insufferable, using it only as a last resort, such as when they were about to part a man from his genitals. In fact, it was a talent that Billy had only discovered in the past year, having taken acid for the first time and found it to be a disturbing side effect that lasted pretty much the duration of the trip. It was always best to do acid when you were among friends, but for Billy it was essential. And even then, the nicest of people, the closest of friends, had some darkness inside their minds that in some way made them a monster. What had started as a neat party trick had lasted no more than an hour before Billy got as far away from everyone as possible.

Today Billy had only taken a small dose, just enough to peek into Sebastian's mind, but it had damn near broken him. Sebastian, should he ever turn his thoughts into actions, was left in no doubt that it would take him years to die an extremely painful death.

The Hummer swung a left at some lights, and Vincent tried not to think about any of it. Stone had once told him that, while telepathy was possible, no one he knew of was capable of reading minds. He and Flashback could send and receive mental images, but they couldn't invade each other's personal mind space. And, like most people, Vincent wasn't at all keen on the idea, if only because his own mind space tended to be cluttered with rather foolish thoughts, stupid questions, and self-doubt. He didn't like the notion of anyone poking around inside his head, and he tried not to think about that, too, but found it almost impossible. The more he tried not to think about something, the more he thought about it. It was no wonder that Billy Toothless was crying.

They made another left and Vincent began to recognise some of the streets from when he'd picked the vehicle up. At least in a tour bus they'd be able to spread out a bit, dilute the mood a little. Stretched though the Hummer was, it was also accustomed to rather a more cheery atmosphere, wedding parties and the like, and it was no place for such mean tempers. Vincent was relieved when they finally pulled up at the rental place and tumbled out into the early evening sunshine, where Flashback expressed his displeasure to the owner, with considerably more swearing than was necessary. Clearly the place was just about to close.

"What the fuck are you trying to pull here, Michael?" Flashback demanded, still clutching his drink. "Do you take me for some sort of cunt?"

"No, Mister Smith, of course not!" said the owner, a plump and heavily tanned man in his early fifties. "It's just that I thought your note said seven people and..."

"Eleven people!" yelled Flashback. "Eleven! Can't you fucking count?"

"No, Mister Smith. I mean, yes, Mister Smith," stammered the man. "I just thought..."

"You thought? Who the fuck told you to do any thinking?"

It was a rhetorical question but Michael tried to answer it anyway, and Vincent couldn't help feeling a little sorry for the bloke. Despite Flashback's appalling handwriting he'd provided a perfectly good vehicle, perfectly air-conditioned against the heat, and luxurious in every way. But, drunk and foul-tempered, 'Mister Smith' wasn't about to throw him any bones. He might, however, throw him in the nearby canal.

"I just thought that anything bigger might be difficult to get around town in," explained Michael, almost breaking into a jog as Flashback strode across the lot towards a gigantic white tour bus that looked like a jumbo jet with the wings missing. "It says on the form that you booked it for a skirmish and the paintball centre is..."

"Paintball?" snapped Flashback. "What are you talking about, you silly man?"

"Skirmish," repeated Michael, pointing hopefully at the form that Vincent had hurriedly filled out only yesterday morning, already a lifetime ago. Vincent had, in fact, meant to tick sightseeing.

"Skirmish, yes, yes, that sounds about right. Could be quite a bit of that," said Flashback. "We'll take this one!" he added, kicking at a tyre on the gleaming white behemoth and almost falling flat on his backside. "And make sure the bar is fully stocked!"

Michael was obviously beginning to have visions of waving goodbye to the pride of his fleet and never seeing it again, but it was equally obvious that he was desperate not to further antagonise Mister Smith and his ten scary friends.

"Of course, Mister Smith," he said nervously. "It's just that last time..."

"That was an accident!" protested Flashback. "Could've happened to anyone!"

"Yes, I remember that's what you told the police, Mister Smith. It's just that this bus is more for long distance touring and..."

"Yes, yes, that's fine," snapped Flashback. "We'll be travelling a long distance. Just have the paperwork drawn up. We're going," he added, pointing dramatically into the distance, his hand still clutching the now empty whiskey glass, "to the bush!"

"Er, the bush is that way, Mister Smith," said Michael.

CHAPTER THIRTEEN

At the top of Merlin's tower, the fire crackled in the fireplace. Or, more precisely, the fireplace crackled in the fire, which was a little disconcerting because it meant that the glass fireplace was cracking due to the heat. In places the glass was actually melting, and Dum Dum lost himself for a few moments watching it bubble and glow, the entire fireplace reshaping itself over time so that even the mantle looked liked something Salvador Dali might have made. It was among the most beautiful things Dum Dum had ever seen, and he'd seen quite a few of them in the last couple of days.

Outside a light snow began to fall, and, hunched over a glass table, pen and paper in hand, Dum Dum carefully ticked off 'ice/rain/snow?' from his checklist. At least two of the songs that had played a part in leading him here had mentioned wintry weather of some kind, and while Dum Dum understood that sometimes it was just a word or two, whatever stuck out from the songs, that was guiding him, he felt pleased to have made another connection and joined a few more dots together. It was remarkable how far the temperature fell overnight.

On the paper in front of him was a list of every song he could remember hearing since they'd landed in Los Angeles, every snippet of lyrics he could remember, sometimes a whole song, and sometimes just a few words or a title. It was astonishing how many of them related to his journey, even songs that he'd just heard in passing, and he was tempted to turn the iPod back on and see what it had to say, but wary of the battery running low. It usually gave him eight to ten hours before it died and right now it was about half-charged. Since Merlin had no electricity it seemed wise to save what power remained and try to fathom meanings from what he'd already heard.

He heard the echo of footsteps long before Mad John came into the room.

"I'm not disturbing you, am I?" he said.

"Not at all," smiled Dum Dum, happy for some company. He was beginning to think that everyone had fucked off and left him here on his own. "You get some sleep?"

"Yes, thank you. Much needed, too. We had quite the adventure getting here, thanks to Numb Tongue."

"Yeah, I saw the news," noted Dum Dum. "Can't say I blame him though."

"No, not in the least," Mad John agreed, "but I'm afraid we really can't afford to be the focus of so much attention. It's hard enough to stay out of the eyes of authority without them launching a nationwide manhunt. Still," Mad John sighed, sitting himself down, "what's done is done. If we lay low for a few days it may blow over."

"I wouldn't be so sure," said Dum Dum. "Last thing I saw was him and Snow had kicked off a riot and half of L.A. was going up in flames. They had artist pictures of them and everything. Said Numb Tongue was a terrorist. Well, they didn't say his name, like, but the picture looked just like him."

"What's done is done," repeated Mad John. "I see you've been busy."

"Yeah," said Dum Dum, rather proud of himself for having written something legible, even if his tongue had been poking out in concentration for most of it. Some of the spelling was quite creative, and he'd alternated between one and two Z's in wizard, but, generally speaking, most of the letters were in roughly the right place. "I haven't figured out how it works yet, y'know, the magic and stuff, but I thought this might help."

"And does it?"

"Dunno," shrugged Dum Dum. "A bit, I think. It's just a bit weird, y'know. I never knew I could do this before."

"I'm sure you have many talents that are yet to be discovered," Mad John smiled. "But it may be best, for the time being, if you kept this one a secret."

"Okay, John," said Dum Dum, never one to question his president's judgement. "Er, who from?"

"From everyone, Dum Dum. Just for the time being."

"I told Merlin," admitted Dum Dum.

"That's fine," said Mad John. "Merlin can be trusted, as you can trust the club, but beyond them it may be wise to keep it quiet. I've said it before, Dum Dum, but a lot of people make the mistake of believing you to be a fool. It may be in our interests if we allow them to continue to do so. Call it a secret weapon."

Dum Dum nodded. A year ago he might have believed those who thought him a fool – and he still had his doubts on occasion – but Mad John had a way of bringing out the best in people, finding their strengths, building their confidence, and encouraging them to blossom.

Dum Dum had got left behind at school, not one teacher waiting for him to catch up, and there was little chance of an education in borstal. By the time he went to prison for the first time he'd resigned himself to being a bit thick and relying entirely on his size to get by. Even the members of Aberrant underestimated him at first, but while they tried to help as much as possible – albeit while taking occasional bets on how stupid he could be – it was Mad John who really made him shine, made him feel like a valued member of the club. Dum Dum wasn't about to let him down.

"Any news from Merlin?" he asked.

"Not much," Mad John told him. "The dwarfs are on the move again, but mostly below ground. Merlin is resting for now, so our best bet is to stay where we are until we know more."

"Is it safe?"

"Safe?"

"They nuked him, didn't they? Merlin, I mean. That's what turned this place to glass. I thought it might still be radioactive or something."

"I'm impressed," admitted Mad John. "I'm guessing Merlin didn't tell you this? You worked it out for yourself?"

"I think the songs told me," said Dum Dum, gesturing to his notes. Ringed in black ink was the word 'Atomic'. "Some of it sort of fits into place after, if you know what I mean. Like, it only makes sense later."

"I would imagine that makes things quite difficult," said Mad John, getting to his feet and moving closer to the fire. The snow outside was falling heavily now, and snowflakes drifted in from the open balcony, the wind whistling around the top of the tower.

"But, yes, you're right," Mad John continued. "October 1951 they dropped the bomb on him. We're safe so long as we don't stay more than a few days, but poor Merlin has been a prisoner here ever since."

"The soldiers, you mean? They seemed more scared of him than he was of them."

"I don't doubt that," Mad John concurred. "And not without good reason. But ever since the bomb his magic no longer works beyond the fence. Theoretically he can leave whenever he wants, assuming he got past the guards unnoticed, but then what? An old man riddled with cancer is all he'd be. Dead within months if they didn't catch him first."

"So this is a prison," said Dum Dum.

"A prison like no other," Mad John nodded, "but a prison nonetheless. And most of his time served in solitary."

Dum Dum glanced down at his notes, as another few pieces of the jigsaw fitted into place, his tongue inadvertently poking out in anticipation. Monster Magnet's *Bored With Sorcery* seemed a little less vague, not just another song about wizards: "*I put my head on the atomic pile, and I did it all for you.*" And there, in the chorus, perhaps a reference to being held captive: "*Bored for a thousand years, you've gotta get me out of here...*"

Obviously, Merlin hadn't been here for a thousand years, but it must surely feel like it, locked away for the rest of time in this mountain tower, his only diversions being psychic chess with a man on the other side of the world, and his cat-and-mouse games with the military. What use was all the magic in the world if he would never be free? It was a wonder he hadn't completely lost his mind.

Outside, the wind picked up its mournful cry, and with it came a single snowflake, dancing gently across the room as if tugged by some invisible thread. It came to a halt directly above where Dum Dum was sitting, held for a brief moment in suspended animation, before drifting down to land on his notes, like the loneliest of tears. The ink bled as it melted, drawing Dum Dum's attention to a particular lyric near the end of Motörhead's *Out Of The Sun: "Frozen and insane, I alone remain..."* Dum Dum took his pen and drew a line to the lyric. At the end of the line he wrote 'Merlin'. There was no question mark.

CHAPTER FOURTEEN

It was quite likely that the Sturt Highway passed through some spectacular scenery, but driving through the night there was precious little to see beyond the wide beams of the bus. Vincent sat up front, navigating for Smiler and keeping him company, partly in case he fell asleep on a road that didn't require much navigation. They passed some exotic sounding places, names like Gumly Gumly and Wagga Wagga, but still there were endless miles of bugger all. Vincent was hoping to see a kangaroo.

At the back of the bus there was quiet. Vincent had been back there a few hours ago to fetch some smokes and a bottle of water for Smiler and he'd found most of the club asleep in their bunks. Only Apples was awake now, reading a book by the light of a small table lamp. It was probably for the best, what with Billy's sobbing, and both Flashback and Stone in agony from the headaches. Stone was known as the club's 'doctor' and he had medicated those who needed a little help, which meant they could be out for hours, but it was better than being awake. Quite where he'd hidden these drugs, given the intimate nature of his search at the airport, was anyone's guess, and Vincent preferred not to think about it, which meant, of course, that he thought about it. It really was for the best that Billy Toothless was asleep.

And still the endless miles went by, the town names becoming fewer and farther between, under the millions of stars that carpeted the pitch night sky. For a while there was dark forest to their right, The Berry Jerry State Forest, if the map was to be believed, and through it – and for miles in either direction – ran the spookily named Old Man's Creek. Vincent smiled to himself as he pondered the map, the white lines of the highway stretching out in front of them. Already this was beginning to feel like the start of a new adventure.

Not that adventures ever seemed to end for Aberrant MC, but somehow this seemed rather more magical than following boneheads around Berlin in the snow. Here might be dragons, thought Vincent, or wizards, or, at the very least, a fucking kangaroo, and not just some knucklehead with a swastika tattoo on his neck.

That had been an adventure, too, of sorts, but it hadn't really felt like one at the time. Before going to Berlin the club had visited far-off lands; Vincent had been to a cage fight in an orc city and a strip club run by faeries; he'd heard ravens talk and he'd helped to bring down a bridge troll. Berlin was just boneheads and snow, and, to be fair, some pretty good bars. In Australia it felt as if they were in some magical land again, the sheer enormity of it suggesting all manner of possibilities.

"I'm gonna pull over for a shit at the next services," announced Smiler, rather breaking that train of thought.

The service station was about another thirty miles on, and Vincent got himself some coffee and a few snacks. The sun was starting to come up, the sky was awash with pinks and deep purples, soon to turn the clearest of blues. Vincent paused to take it all in, but it was impossible to comprehend the vastness of this country even after you'd driven through the night, mile after mile, and then stood, open-mouthed in a run-down old petrol station, staring at the most spectacular sunrise on earth. Oh yes, there was magic here! Vincent could feel it all around.

Not that there hadn't been magic in Berlin, especially in the older parts of the city, but this was different, this was steeped into the earth beneath his feet, like a charge coming up through his boots. And the funny thing was that not much more than a year ago he'd have laughed at the very idea of magic existing at all. Faeries and elves, cave trolls and orcs, magic rings and wizards... Seriously, who'd believe in that sort of crap?

It was only sixteen months since he'd started prospecting for Aberrant MC, since he got his cut and his prospect patches, and took the first step to fulfilling a childhood dream and what he knew to be his destiny. *Only* sixteen months! Fucking hell, it had been a lifetime, and yet it had flown past in the blink of an eye. And it had been relatively normal for the first nine months or so, too. Vincent had been one of four prospects, and together they'd done prospect things, cleaned bikes, stood guard, cleaned more bikes, cleaned the clubhouse, run errands and cleaned more bikes. Most clubs only expected their prospects to serve a year before getting their full patch, but it wasn't exactly tough, like some other clubs, just long hours and not much sleep. He'd never had to fight anybody.

And then, right out of the blue, their long-lost president, Mad John, had turned up, having been missing for five years, and the world Vincent once knew had been turned completely upside down and inside out. Mad John had not only turned out to be his father, which was a headfuck in itself, but also rather famous in the biblical department, what with getting himself nailed to a cross a couple of thousand years ago. His hands were still scarred to this day. Which made Vincent the son of the Son of...

Once you'd got your head around that – and Vincent wasn't sure he would *ever* get his head around that – everything else was positively normal. Orcs, elves, invisibility rings, all of it. Oh how he would have laughed at the notion of magic, and now he would swear he could feel it through his boots.

"What are you pissing about at, Prospect?" Smiler called from the bus, spoiling the mood yet again.

Vincent climbed back on board the bus with his coffee and crisps. So much for magic. Sleep was what he really needed, but it seemed as if Smiler was intent on driving non-stop until they reached wherever the hell it was that they were going to. As usual, no one had bothered to tell him, and he strongly suspected that none of them knew. He sipped at his coffee and stared down at the map, which was almost at the point of having to be folded again. Holy shit, this country was vast! Other countries could hide here and never be found again! Given that Flashback appeared to be in charge of directions this was a bit of a worry, particularly since he didn't seem to know where 'the bush' was. So far as Vincent could tell, Flashback had pointed in the only direction that *wasn't* the fucking bush!

Hours later the bus was still heading west with no end to the highway in sight. New South Wales became South Australia, and some of the club had stirred from their bunks, although Flashback, Stone, and Billy Toothless were not among them. The temperature outside was nudging one hundred degrees, heat vapours rising from the road ahead. Vincent still hadn't seen a kangaroo.

"Piss stop in ten miles!" Smiler announced to a chorus of muttering from the back of the bus, most of the club being of the opinion that lunch was well overdue, and that the toilet on the bus would serve rather better as a sauna. Since none of them could aim straight and he had to clean it up, Vincent was of the opinion that it was a blessing that the air conditioning was broken in the toilet and deterred them from going in there. He could only be thankful for the 'no solids' rule, particularly since a diet of drugs and alcohol was unlikely to produce anything that was actually solid.

Presently the bus pulled into the dusty car park of a roadside diner. Next door to the diner was a small, white stone church, a handful of people outside dressed in their Sunday best. They looked over at Aberrant, piling off the bus in various states of disarray, and they hurried inside the church. It was an irony not missed on Vincent. Admittedly, Aberrant MC wasn't what came to mind when most people thought of the twelve disciples, but that's exactly what they were! Not the original twelve, granted, but disciples nonetheless. Only Stone remained from the original twelve, better known as Thomas Didymus, or Doubting Thomas, and currently passed out in his bunk. A couple of the others had retired over the years and the rest had passed away, but, like a band that had replaced its members, it was still the same group.

That had also come as something of a surprise to Vincent when he found out, particularly when Judas Iscariot – latterly know as Loud-As – had tried to stab him in the neck. Judas was dead now, killed by a powerful curse in a poisoned tattoo, and ultimately by an improvised bomb, but just as many of the club had been disciples for longer than the original members. People always go on about the original line-up. As the churchgoers scurried inside, the apostles went for lunch. Some of them were quite hungover.

With predicable timing Aberrant emerged from the diner at the same time as people were starting to leave the church. Again, there were worried looks in their direction. Even in 'civilian' clothes Aberrant MC looked like a motley bunch, and since farmers in these parts were likely to have guns, and equally likely to shoot an orc on sight, Zig Zag had stayed on the bus, out of sight. But still, the rest of them looked like off-duty criminals, perhaps scouting for future burial plots.

They climbed on board the bus – Joker taking over driving duties – and were just pulling away when an old man stepped into their path, his hand raised to stop them. He wore shorts and hiking boots, but no shirt, and beneath wild, white hair, he was so tanned that he seemed to be made of leather. He stood staring up at the bus, a troubled look on his leathery face.

"Go and find out what he wants," ordered Joker.

Vincent got off the bus. "What do you want?" he said.

The old man looked at Vincent, as the bells in the old church began to toll.

"I have a message from Jesus," he said.

CHAPTER FIFTEEN

"Do you think it worked?" asked Mad John.

"Only time will tell," said Merlin. "I've done all I can for now, and you should not wait here much longer."

"We will leave at nightfall," affirmed Mad John.

For the past many hours Merlin had been searching for a suitable mind in Australia, a mind that was capable of telepathy. Moreover, a mind that was roughly along the path that Aberrant MC were travelling, and wasn't crippled by headaches. Needle in a haystack was an understatement! At least Derain was actively sending a signal, so they had some hope of pinpointing him; the mind that Merlin was searching for might not even know what it could do. The mind's owner, when they suddenly started receiving odd messages, might think that they had gone insane.

Eventually, more by luck than judgement, Merlin had stumbled across such a mind. It belonged to a long-retired firefighter named Joe Myrtle. Unfortunately, while completely sane, Joe's mind wasn't accustomed to telepathy, and thought it might be having some sort of religious experience. Which, in a way, it was.

"If I hear back from our new friend Joe, then I will try to send a message to you," said Merlin. "But I'm sweeping a huge area."

As Dum Dum understood it, Joe's mind was powerful enough to receive messages, but getting anything back was rather like trying to find a radio station that had a feeble signal and that was broadcast in random directions.

And the radio station had moved. For now, though, their hopes lay with luck and with Joe, who had never done this sort of thing before. Either way it was nearly time to leave.

By sunset, Mad John, Dum Dum, Numb Tongue, and Snow were packed and ready to go. Already the heat of the day had gone and there was a chill to the air, a bitter night laying in wait. Dum Dum was thankful for his wargskin jacket, but he could have done with some better gloves, and possibly some long johns.

They said their goodbyes to Merlin.

"Any time you are near," said Merlin hopefully. "I get so few visitors."

The image of the wizard standing alone in his doorway watching them leave made Dum Dum's heart grow heavy. There could be no greater loneliness than this, no harsher sentence than life in prison for a life that would never end unless he were to escape. And then what? *"Just another sad old man, all alone and dying of cancer..."* Dum Dum had found the lyric in his head, a line from Pink Floyd's *Dogs*, and he tried to pretend to himself that he didn't know why it was there, tried not to think about it.

His task was made easier by the treacherous path ahead. At night the glass slithers and spikes that littered the smooth desert floor glittered like fool's diamonds, waiting to slice the first fool that strayed near them. At first the path had been easier to see by night, without the glare of the sun. But then a light snow began to fall and with it the visibility. Since they didn't want to ride straight into a bunch of trigger-happy soldiers the route was longer, too, than the one Dum Dum and Merlin had taken. Merlin said he would cause a diversion when they got near the fence. He said they'd know it when they saw it.

And so, for hour upon increasingly cold hour, Mad John, Dum Dum, Numb Tongue, and Snow stuck to the jagged path. They kept a slow, steady pace, no more than fifteen or twenty miles an hour, eyes scanning for anything that might puncture their tyres, or worse. The cold bit into them, tearing at them as sharp as any glass, and still they rode on through the night, knees tucked in tight to catch any warmth from their engines, and to keep them from being accidentally shredded.

The jukebox in Dum Dum's head played *No Fun*. Now that he thought about it, it always played him songs, and he began to worry that his new talent might be more of a curse than a blessing. What if he could never listen to music again without hearing some sort of hidden message or prophecy? He'd have to listen to nothing but instrumentals! Inevitably his mind tried to find one, and went back to his Pink Floyd collection, thumbing its way through *Meddle*. It started playing the opening track, *One Of These Days*, and then it paused. Oh wait, that one had lyrics. Dum Dum kept his eyes on the path, and unplugged his mental jukebox.

At long last the sun began to rise, the sky glowing a bright orange beneath dark and moody clouds. The glass began to thin as it made way for sand once more, the odd hint of green here and there indicating that some desert shrub had found enough nutrients to survive. Soon they were back on a dirt track, a bitter wind blowing dust and sand across their path. And then, out of nowhere, there was a streak of something up into the dark clouds off to their left, like backwards lightning, thought Dum Dum, or the trail of firewo...

BOOOOOM!

The noise came first, and then the light of the explosion in the sky, which was curious unless you were deliberately trying to distract a group of people to whom explosions might be commonplace. Even to those people this would not be considered a normal explosion. Dum Dum smiled to himself, his heart a little less heavy. Lighting up the morning sky, one hundred feet high or more, were two musical notes, two Ds separated by a lightning bolt.

Merlin was saying farewell.

He'd grown close to the wizard in the few days that they'd stayed with him, perhaps more so because they both understood prison. At least Dum Dum hadn't done his time in solitary with no chance of parole, and no end in sight. He promised himself that he'd visit the wizard again someday. Maybe bring him a cake with a file inside it. Merlin had that sort of sense of humour.

They spotted the fence up ahead, no sign of any guards, and no sign of any gate until they drew nearer. Merlin had been fucking with the fence again, moving it during the night so there was always a danger of his foes ending up on the wrong side, his side. It wasn't supposed to have any gates at all. And, now that Dum Dum thought about it, how the hell was the wizard getting all the way out here in the first place, if he wasn't walking? Oh yeah, duh, he's a wizard. Which probably explained why, after they'd passed through the gate, there was no sign of it from the other side.

There was a strange sensation, stepping from a place of great magic into the so-called 'real world'. Dum Dum had experienced it before, like a slight popping of the ears due to a change in altitude, but until now he'd not known what it was. And until a few days ago, having never flown before, he'd had nothing to compare it to. But yes, that was it, a weird pressure in the ears and a need to swallow to make it go away. That was how you could tell if you were entering or leaving a place of great magic.

Ironically, the first time Dum Dum had noticed it had been in reverse, when Aberrant MC went to a place called Fero City, deep inside orc territory. Magic was illegal there, punishable by death, and its complete absence in the city made the popping sensation all the more noticeable when you left. Dum Dum had noticed it in other places since then, not just magical places like Vernon Wells, but in the older parts of Berlin, the parts of Kreuzberg that hadn't been gentrified. There was sometimes the feeling that just beyond this or that door lay a magical realm, home to faeries and elves and giants and dwarfs.

It was funny what you noticed once you thought to look for it, thought Dum Dum, pleased with himself for having solved another puzzle. And the more you thought to look, the more you noticed what had been in plain sight all along. It was like when he found the card for the psychic in the Rainbow, and then all of the songs piecing together to lead him to Merlin. The more you noticed, the more you noticed. Unfortunately, what Dum Dum, Mad John, Numb Tongue, and Snow all completely failed to notice, as they hit the road, was the police helicopter that was following them.

CHAPTER SIXTEEN

Vincent awoke in his bunk and lay for a while, listening to the gentle rhythm of the road. He had no idea how long he'd been asleep, or how many miles they might have covered, or even whether it was day or night. Joe Myrtle had delivered his message and then driven off in his beaten-up station wagon, and Aberrant had got back on the road. It was dark outside his bunk, and the doors to the front and back lounges were closed, a low-pitched snoring indicating that someone else was still sleeping. Vincent was tempted to go back to sleep, but his bladder insisted otherwise. Fuck it, he thought, may as well see what's going on out there.

He found Apples still reading his book by lamp light, with Mental and Andy One-Leg sitting in the opposite booth playing cards. Billy Toothless was sitting on the couch.

"Oi'd cahl 'im if Oi wuz you, Mental," said Billy.

"Oh, come on!" protested Andy.

"He's bluffing," said Mental, calling the bet.

"Free uv a koin' beats 'is two purr, dunnit."

"Oh, for fuck's sake!"

Both players threw down their cards and Mental started dealing another hand.

"Oi 'eard that!" muttered Billy.

Clearly the acid hadn't worn off yet, but the fact that Billy was up and about suggested that the worst of it was over. The mood in the lounge was deliberately mellow, just a card game and some reading, no drinking or rowdy behaviour. A couple of incense sticks were burning to mask Billy's ever-present body odour. Chaos was in the driving seat, sticking to the speed limit, the clock on the dashboard telling Vincent that it was 2:45 am. This country never seemed to end.

And still no sign of a kangaroo, thought Vincent, as he gazed out of the window at darkness. Well, there could be kangaroos. Could be thousands of them hopping around out there, but you'd never see them at night.

Billy Toothless raised a finger to his lips. "Shhh."

"Sorry," said Vincent, and tried not to think too loud, which, frankly, was as ridiculous as it was impossible.

He wasn't at all keen on having Billy poke around inside his head, and clearly the feeling was mutual. The alternative, however, was whoever was awake in the back lounge, which could be Stone and Smiler discussing literature, or, just as easily, Flashback and Smiler having a drinking competition. Or Flashback and Mental having a drinking competition. Or...

"Pra'bly woize," said Billy, when Vincent decided he'd rather not venture back there and find out.

Vincent got up to have a poke about on the magazine shelf when suddenly he was sent flying down the aisle as the bus swerved and Chaos slammed on the brakes. Chaos looked down at him lying in the aisle.

"Fuck! I think I just ran someone over!"

Vincent was first off the bus, terrified by what he might see, but instead there was nothing, just darkness and the gentle chirruping of crickets. They were in the middle of nowhere. He looked under the tyres of the bus expecting the worst, but still there was nothing, not even skid marks. By this time Chaos, too, was outside.

"Anything?"

Vincent finished his inspection of the rear tyres. "Not that I can see," he said. And then he straightened up, and looked straight into the face of a very, very black man.

"Fucking hell! You made me jump!" exclaimed Vincent. "Are you all right?"

The man smiled at him, a beaming, friendly smile, full of large and impossibly white teeth.

"Yes, boss," he said.

The man, perhaps in his early twenties, wore dirty jeans, an old Pepsi T-shirt, and no shoes. He was, if Vincent were ever asked to describe him, Aboriginal. And, if Vincent were ever asked, he would swear that he felt a charge of magic.

"What's going on?" asked Chaos, joining them.

"Er, there's a bloke..." Vincent began stating the obvious.

"I can see that. Is he okay? Are you okay?" Chaos addressed the man.

"Yes, boss," the man smiled.

"You're not hurt or anything?"

"Yes, boss."

"Ah," said Chaos. "Do you speak English?"

"Yes, boss."

"Other than that?"

"Yes, boss."

"I'll take that as a no," said Chaos turning to Vincent. "Go and wake up Stone, he speaks some of the lingo."

When Vincent and Stone returned, the man was looking rather puzzled as Chaos attempted some mime.

"Is it a book or a film?" Stone grinned.

"There you are, Stone," said Chaos. "You speak some Aboriginal, don't you? Ask this bloke if he's okay."

Stone looked momentarily confused. "There are over two hundred Aboriginal languages and I only speak three of them, but I'll give it a go," he said.

Stone gave it a go.

"Yes, boss," smiled the man.

Stone tried again, a different language, and suddenly the man began babbling away, speaking rapidly, and apparently quite serious.

"What's he saying?" asked Chaos.

"I've got no idea," said Stone, a curious expression on his face. "But if I'm right then he's speaking a language that's supposed to be extinct."

And so it came to be that the Aberrant MC tour bus had an extra passenger. He seemed to expect to be invited onto the bus and happy to go with them. Not that he said much, except when Stone spoke to him in that one language, and then he'd babble away in a dead tongue, an intent look upon his face. Billy Toothless tried to read his mind but to no avail, at first because there were too many people crowding the lounge and he could hear all of them, and then because he simply didn't understand the man because he wasn't thinking in English. It was somewhat ironic that Billy only spoke English when he spoke it so badly.

Surprisingly, Apples had then made some small progress with the traditional English method of saying things louder and waving his hands about.

"Apples," he said, pointing to himself. "A-pples."

"Yes, boss."

"No. Apples. A-pples."

"A-pples," repeated the man.

"That's right," beamed Apples, pointing to himself again. "Apples. And you are?"

"Yes, boss."

Eventually it was established that the man's name was Balun. But that was all. Why he'd been wandering barefoot along the side of the highway at three o'clock in the morning, apparently expecting them, remained a mystery.

"You hungry?" said Apples, miming the motion of eating. "Hungry, yeah?"

"Yes, boss."

"I wish he'd stop saying that," complained Andy One-Leg. "We're not his boss. It's sounds really racist."

"I'm afraid this country doesn't have the best record in that department," Stone said grimly. "The indigenous peoples were slaughtered in their thousands, not even recognised as human beings. One of the most advanced races on earth and they were used for target practice, hunted like criminals, an entire culture decimated."

"You want a sandwich? Sand-wich?"

"Yes, boss."

It wasn't long before things on the bus returned to normal. Apples went back to his book, Mental and Andy to their card game. Some of the club went back to their bunks, while a few returned to whatever nefarious activity they'd been up to in the back lounge. Balun just sat there looking vaguely expectant. Vincent went and sat up front with Chaos, watching the sunrise for the second time in as many days. Or was it the third time? He'd already lost track. The dawn gave way to yet more spectacular scenery, a veritable paradise, and, up ahead, another roadside diner.

"Breakfast?" suggested Chaos.

"Breakfast," agreed Vincent.

Forewarned that they had an extra passenger on board, Zig Zag stayed in the back lounge, where he was said to be going slightly stir-crazy. It was too hot for his usual crash helmet disguise, and, besides, who wants to eat breakfast wearing a crash helmet? Instead he was growing increasingly hostile, which was another good reason to keep him out of sight. Stone had threatened to dose him if he didn't calm down. The rest of the club trooped inside the diner, taking Balun with them.

The diner was empty, an old wooden structure that had seen far better days, and, with it, an old wooden waitress who seemed none too pleased to have customers. With the eyes of a hawk, she spotted Balun's bare feet under the table.

"No shoes, no service," she scowled.

"Prospect, go and get Balun some shoes," Flashback said calmly, which was possibly a bad sign depending on his mood and how drunk and/or hungover he was.

Sensing that he might be about to turn the waitress into a toad or something Vincent hurried outside and was surprised to see a young man sitting on the ground near the door of the bus. He was perhaps in his late twenties, with dark, shoulder-length hair, and he wore jeans and sneakers, but no shirt. He was also, if Vincent were ever asked to describe him, Aboriginal. He looked at Vincent expectantly.

"Can I help you?" asked Vincent.

"Yes, boss."

"I think you'd better come with me," said Vincent.

He glanced back at the diner, at the sign in the window: No shoes, no shirt, no service.

"I'll get you a shirt."

CHAPTER SEVENTEEN

They were somewhere around Barstow, on the edge of the desert, which would have thrilled Dum Dum a great deal more if he read a good book every now and again. Instead he gestured to Mad John that his bike needed fuel, something the president tended to forget since he never refuelled his own bike. It was Zen, apparently. And only a few of the club could do it, so Dum Dum didn't feel too bad that he wasn't among them. Whatever bike he was riding seemed to do around four hundred miles to a tank, way more than its normal range, which was a damn good start considering he'd only had his full patch for six months. He was still learning.

That, in itself, was also a big step for Dum Dum. He'd never really thought of himself as much of a learner and, to an extent, he hadn't been bright enough to be bothered by it. He could lift heavy things, after all, and, should the occasion arise, he could knock most men out with one punch, which solves most problems. Admittedly, being able to count higher than ten without taking his socks off would be useful, but other than that he didn't feel like he was missing out on much. And, truth be told, he still couldn't count without using his fingers, but thanks to Mad John he'd started to discover that he possessed other talents.

It wasn't like the rest of the club hadn't tried to teach him, often until they felt like beating him repeatedly with a stick marked 'stupid'. But it was no use, he remained steadfastly clueless, resigned to being the brawn, only now all the more frustrated because he'd actually tried to learn something. Big, stupid,

Dum Dum, who gets lost all the time and has to follow bus routes just to find the clubhouse. Dum Dum by name and Dum Dum by nature. And then Mad John had showed up, and somehow everything changed, everything started to click into place. Slow, not stupid, Mad John had told him.

"Sometimes if you drive the mind too fast you will miss your exit," he'd explained it one time. "A rushed decision is not always the right decision."

Dum Dum knew he was slow, but thanks to Mad John he was also beginning to believe that he wasn't entirely stupid. Mad John actually asked his opinion about stuff. It didn't matter that Dum Dum couldn't count, or that the workings of the internal combustion engine continued to baffle him. He had *other* talents. Bartering and negotiation skills second to none, Mad John had told him. An ability to communicate. Those were skills. And now there was this thing with the music, the predictions or whatever they were. Another talent to explore.

The strange thing was that Dum Dum was pretty certain that he could feel it happening, feel himself getting smarter and missing fewer of life's exits. In fact, for a bloke with no sense of direction, he'd performed a small miracle in finding Merlin. But it was more than that, it was actually seeing the dots connected for himself, and, more and more, joining those dots for himself. He was never going to be a brain surgeon, but increasingly that was because he didn't want to be a brain surgeon. Well, all right, not a brain surgeon, thought Dum Dum, but maybe one day he could be a wizard, just like Merlin. Well, no, not exactly like Merlin, obviously, but... Well, who knew? If working out the mind was like going to the gym then Dum Dum could swear he was starting to see some muscle. Of course, it still didn't hurt that he could knock people out with one punch. Except for the people he knocked out. It hurt them quite a lot.

The four bikes peeled off the road into a busy service station, Dum Dum and Snow waiting for an empty pump while Mad John and Numb Tongue went to find seats in the restaurant. Dum Dum was glad he wasn't the only one who needed fuel, particularly since Snow was a prospect of just one month's standing, but, to be fair, being a faerie did give her a few advantages in the magical department. For a start, they could alternate between human size and faerie size at will, and in faerie form they could fly, which Dum Dum thought was really cool, apart from all the nudity when their clothes didn't change with them. He found that rather embarrassing, especially when he'd been foolish enough to ask her about it.

Apparently, faeries could change their form whenever they liked, apart from once a month, when, for a few days around their, um, lady time, they became human-sized for the duration of, um, things.

It was dreadfully sad really; there had been a bounty on faeries back in the olden days, and what they'd do is they'd catch faeries and put them inside these iron cages that stopped their magic from working. They'd be tortured in there for days, weeks, on end, and then, when the time came for their, er, monthly change, they were given the choice of repenting their evil ways and living out their lives as outcasts in human form, banished from society, or another month of torture.

Thousands died rather than submit, their bodies now pinned like so many butterflies in some underground vault, but just as many were broken, their wings crudely castrated. Those who were caught often got wings tattooed on their backs as a grim act of defiance and, according to Snow, the bounty still stood to this day, although few were ever caught, partly because faerie numbers had been so depleted, and partly because they'd got a lot better at hiding.

Given that Snow rarely spoke unless spoken to, it was the longest conversation Dum Dum had ever had with her, and he kind of wished he hadn't asked, what with all the lady stuff. It did have the effect of making him feel more protective towards her, but it wasn't like she needed protecting. She could ride a bike faster than most of the club, so you'd have a job catching her, and – as if being Numb Tongue's girlfriend wasn't enough – she seemed to have a sponge-like ability to soak up Numb's knowledge of mixed martial arts, already holding purple belts in ju-jitsu and aikido. If you did catch her, she'd likely kick your arse. As a prospect, she was given no quarter, treated the same as any other prospect.

The SUV that had been taking its sweet time in front of them finally pulled away, and they filled their tanks from the same pump before parking alongside the other bikes. They were just about to head inside the restaurant when Snow stopped in her tracks, her eyes cast up at the sky.

"We can't stop here," she said. "This is bat country."

"Huh?" said Dum Dum, who really should read more.

"Up there," Snow nodded. "Police helicopter."

"I think they call them Ghetto Birds, not bats," said Dum Dum, squinting into the sun. "You think they're following us?"

"I'm almost certain of it," said Snow.

Dum Dum sent Snow inside, realising as he did so that this was the first time he'd told a prospect to do something, the first time he'd given an order. Admittedly, "go and tell the others," wasn't much of an order, but it still felt strange after so many years of doing what he was told. Sometimes, even now, he had to remind himself that he wasn't a prospect anymore, and that, as a full-patch member of Aberrant MC, he was expected to put the prospects to task. Nicely asking Vincent if he'd mind making a cup of tea probably didn't count.

Mad John and Numb Tongue emerged from the restaurant with Snow a few paces behind, all three of them inadvertently glancing up at the cloudless sky. The helicopter was still there.

"I hear we have company," said Mad John.

"Looks like it," confirmed Dum Dum. "There's not much else out here that they could be watching."

"Just one?" asked Numb Tongue.

"So far as I can see."

Numb Tongue nodded to himself, as if coming to a decision. He glanced up at the sky again. Just because there was only one helicopter didn't mean that the entire state police force wasn't waiting up the road, out of sight. Oddly enough, Snow appeared to reach the same decision at the same time.

"How fast do you think that thing goes?" she asked.

"Not as fast as that," replied Numb Tongue, gesturing towards her bike.

"Exactly what I was thinking."

Indeed, the Suzuki Hayabusa, when it was released in 1999, was the world's fastest production motorcycle, and, due to a 'gentleman's agreement' between the major manufacturers, remains pretty much unsurpassed to this day. There were faster bikes, but not by much. Snow's bike, however – on loan from the L.A. club – had been heavily modified by someone named Subway, who most certainly wasn't a gentleman, and when asked how he got his nickname liked to reply, "cos my dick's a foot-long." He wasn't much for polite conversation, but he was a genius when it came to brake horse power.

"You think they'll take the bait?" Mad John asked.

"They can't follow all of us," Snow pointed out, "and they'll probably go after the one that's running away. I'll let them keep up for a while..."

That was the thing about Snow; she was so softly spoken as to barely speak at all, dainty almost, with her porcelain skin and slender frame. And yet, you stuck her on a motorcycle and she turned into Valentino Rossi, easily capable of evading a high-speed pursuit. Mad John and Numb Tongue both rode Harleys, which were too slow for the job, and even on the powerful loaner bike Dum Dum would struggle with such a pace, but Snow could leave a helicopter for dust.

"Meet us here tonight," instructed Mad John, hastily writing an address on a piece of paper. "Ten o'clock. And try not to get on the news."

And with that, Mad John, Numb Tongue, Dum Dum, and Snow got on their bikes and headed back out on the road, the black speck of the helicopter in their mirrors. They rode in formation at first, sticking to the speed limit, and then, with a kiss blown at Numb Tongue, Snow lowered her visor and took off like a bat out of hell. This was bat country, after all.

CHAPTER EIGHTEEN

The back lounge of the Aberrant MC tour bus was almost as cramped as the front, and Vincent stumbled to maintain his balance as he poured Flashback a drink. They were on a dusty dirt track somewhere in the bush – or if not in the actual bush then definitely in the shrubs – and the bus had slowed to a crawl, Chaos up front doing his best to avoid the sort of craters that are usually associated with the extinction of dinosaurs. The sun was setting on another long day, and the discussion in the back was centred on their guests in the front lounge, seven of them now, all chatting away in a language that Stone insisted was similarly extinct.

"Could be an old Thuggee trick," suggested Mental, "but they'd generally pretend not to know each other."

"They've definitely picked the wrong bus if that's their plan," Flashback snorted dismissively. "As I recall, the Thuggees would wait for their victims to go to sleep before they robbed them. Besides, they don't have the numbers yet to overpower us."

"No, but the odds are getting more even," noted Mental, "and some of them are solid looking lads. At least none of 'em's armed."

"Couple of them are," Stone chipped in. "Balun and the second one we picked up, Uwan. I noticed that both of them kept their chicken bones back at the diner."

"Did they now?" Flashback raised an eyebrow. "Difficult ritual, but perhaps we should keep a closer eye on them."

The bus rocked quite suddenly, hitting another deep hole in the track and causing Flashback to spill his drink. His chef's whites were becoming increasingly stained and unpleasant, but his mood had improved. Apparently the headaches had subsided, not gone, but no longer crippling, just a nagging reminder that they had a path to follow. Vincent refilled his glass.

"Um, why are chicken bones dangerous?" he asked.

"Kurdaitcha," explained Flashback. "Powerful Aborigine curse, if it's done right. The method varies from tribe to tribe, but the result is the same." He ran his finger under his throat.

"What would they want with us?" said Vincent.

Flashback shrugged. "Who knows? I shouldn't worry too much, you'd have disappeared if they were dangerous."

"Not if..." began Vincent, and then found himself sitting in Zig Zag's lap as the bus lurched through another large pothole. Zig Zag wasn't at all happy about this – particularly since he couldn't see Vincent – and tried to bite him. The bus had come to an abrupt halt.

"Sorry, Zig Zag." Vincent picked himself up and backed away sharply. "I'll go and find out what's going on."

He came back with a worried look on his face.

"Chaos wants you up front," he told Flashback. "There's bloody hundreds of them out there!"

Moments later they were staring out of the dusty windscreen at something that looked unnervingly like a scene from a low-budget zombie movie; hundreds of dark silhouettes were all heading in the same direction, in a haze of dust and sand turned orange by the setting sun. Vincent was unlikely to be asked to describe them, but they were, without doubt, Aboriginal. It was difficult not to notice that some of them were armed with spears and even a rifle here and there.

"So much for not being outnumbered," grunted Mental.

The bus plodded on, barely faster than walking pace as Chaos tried not to get stuck or run anyone over. Thankfully, the people outside parted for them, falling into place behind the bus as it passed, but still, as the sun finally dipped over the horizon, visibility was down to a few yards, and every bump felt like it might potentially be fatal. If there was a path out here then it had long fallen into disuse and vanished into the desert.

"How much further?" asked Flashback.

"Five, ten miles, if the coordinates are right," replied Chaos. "It's not on the map so I was going by the stars until all this sand kicked up, but I'd say we're on the right path."

"Yeah," said Flashback, "but what's at the other end?" He turned to Vincent. "Go and get me a drink, and tell Stone to start handing out the cuts."

Vincent felt more like himself again once he was back in biker attire, like he'd been in disguise when he was wearing civilian clothes, which was exactly the point. But at the same time Aberrant MC would never knowingly go into battle without their colours, and there was no mistaking what it meant when Flashback gave the order to put them on. So far their guests had been nothing but friendly, albeit rather difficult to communicate with, but it didn't hurt to be cautious. The club were, after all, heading farther and farther into the middle of nowhere, based only on the word of a retired firefighter called Joe who said he had a message from Jesus, but had no idea what any of it meant. Which sounded, to Vincent, like most people who said they had a message from Jesus.

Instead, Joe had given them a handwritten note: 31°30'45.6"S 121°40'51.7"E Ruin

"At first I thought it was a reference to Bible verses," he'd said, matter of fact, like it wasn't at all weird getting psychic messages from the son of God that told him to meet up with a bus full of bikers. "But then I realised it was map coordinates. I'm guessing there's a ruin there."

After Joe left, Chaos had found the coordinates on the map, some miles east of an abandoned mining town called Widgiemooltha. There was a large lake nearby, but not a great deal else, just shrubby outback with the Coolgardie-Esperance Highway running through the middle of it. And now they were getting close to their destination. Even without the coordinates that was pretty obvious. It felt, to Vincent, like that moment when you're going to a rock show or a festival and suddenly all the crowd are heading in the same direction, all with a common purpose. Except that metalheads weren't generally armed with spears and rifles.

The curious thing was that, as Flashback had mentioned, Vincent should have vanished by now if they were in danger. That was what his invisibility ring *did*, sometimes even when he wasn't in any danger at all and just thought he was. Frankly, it could be a pain in the arse. And yet Balun and his friends could clearly see Vincent, which left him with the question of whether he might have disappeared but everyone could still see him.

So far as Vincent could tell, the ring worked best in areas of high magic on people who weren't particularly magically inclined, but that was never a certainty. Zig Zag, of course, couldn't see him at all, even when he wasn't supposed to be invisible. Everything else was a crapshoot: Dum Dum was a good gauge for when it *was* working, Smiler too, every now and again, but several of the Aberrant crew could see him regardless. As could wizards and faeries, but not bridge trolls – which probably explained Dum Dum's difficulties – and, annoyingly, most bartenders. Vincent strongly suspected that the ring was broken, but so far a great deal of research into its origins had turned up very little.

There was every chance, then, that Vincent had technically 'disappeared', but that the Aborigines could see him anyway. Certainly, he was sure he could feel magic about them, and, even more certainly, he was beginning to get nervous enough that the ring should have worked either way. Outside the bus a stream of silhouettes – spread out in ones and twos but seemingly endless – appeared in the dusty haze of the headlights, then vanished into the gloom and growing darkness behind them.

"It should be around here somewhere," said Chaos, peering out of the windscreen. "I can't see more than a few yards though, so I don't know how we're supposed to find any ruins. Just keep following this lot, I suppose. What do you reckon, Balun?" he called back.

"Yes, boss," beamed Balun.

"Yeah, that's what I thought," said Chaos to himself.

Eventually, out of the gloom, they saw some lights not far up ahead, a nebulous glow that was completely failing to illuminate the outside of a building, but doing a reasonable job of making the large crowd that was waiting there look rather intimidating. Well, that and the spears. Vincent, by now, was pretty sure he had disappeared, which was a little disconcerting since Balun was smiling at him.

When the bus stopped, the crowd parted to let them off, opening a human corridor to the building. There was silence apart from the whistle of the wind and the rusty squeak of a wooden sign on metal hinges flapping back and forth.

The Roo Inn.

A pub, thought Vincent, peering out of the window. Of course it's a pub. Every other building in Australia is a pub!

Alone, Stone stepped down from the bus, and he was greeted by a huge Aboriginal man, built like an oak cabinet and carrying a spear. Words were exchanged as the rest of the club stood by, ready for action if anything went wrong. They talked for a few minutes outside and then Stone turned and headed back to the bus. So far so good. He wasn't dead.

The door hissed open and Stone stepped back inside, all eyes upon him. "Gentlemen," he said. "It looks like we've got ourselves an army!"

CHAPTER NINETEEN

It wasn't until Subway showed up that Snow was sure she was in the right place. The address had looked strange – 1621 1/2 N. Cahuenga Blvd – like it would be between railway station platforms in a Harry Potter movie, but it turned out to be a dimly lit dive bar just south of Hollywood Boulevard. There was an art gallery next door, all pin-ups and punk rock, a run-down hotel, and another bar, a sports themed place with big open windows facing the busy street. With none of them clearly numbered, Snow had waited outside on the busy sidewalk, arriving a full hour early. When Subway showed up, they headed inside and found a booth at the back of the dive bar.

Even though it was night-time, it was darker inside than it was out on the street, and Snow's eyes took a while to adjust to the gloom. At first the place was all but empty, just the bartender cleaning glasses, and a couple of customers, young punk-looking types. The bartender glanced at Snow's prospect patch when she arrived, nodding as if he recognised it, but he made no comment. He placed a Newcastle Brown Ale on the table, evidently knowing Subway well enough not to ask him what he wanted to drink. Snow asked for water.

And now they waited, Snow with her eyes cast to the door every time someone came in. The doorman was tall, about Dum Dum's height, six-eight or so, and although the bar was small the ceilings were high, so at least there was plenty of head clearance. Somehow that seemed important. If Numb

Tongue didn't bang his head on the way in then he might be in a better mood when she told them the news. Which was not good news.

For starters, Subway's Hayabusa was completely written off, damaged beyond all repair. He'd been cool about it, remarkably cool considering, but that didn't change the fact that she'd wrecked someone else's bike and in doing so had let Aberrant MC down. What's more, Snow's prospect patch, only a month old, was now tattered and frayed and covered in oil, having been run over by several trucks. The W on her name patch had suffered particularly badly and now looked more like a T.

But it was worse than that, oh so much worse.

"You're all in one piece, that's all that matters," insisted Subway. "The bike's insured an' we've got alibis out the ass. It was stolen, is all. I'm just glad you're okay."

Obviously he failed to grasp the gravity of the situation, his 'footlong' perhaps taking some of the blood that should have been going to his brain. Okay, that's not entirely fair, thought Snow. If it weren't for his fear of Numb Tongue then he'd be all over her like a rash, trying to get into her knickers, but without that distraction Subway was a stand-up guy, the kind who would drop anything to help a friend. Admittedly, he'd also sleep with that friend's girlfriend given half a chance, but as far as Snow was concerned that was as much the girl's fault for giving him that half a chance. And, not that it would ever come down to it, but, ex-Navy Seal or not, Snow could kick his arse.

Instead Subway had made a call to a lady friend to get Snow some shoes, for which she was extremely grateful, even if they were stripper heels and not something she could actually walk in. But lost footwear, frankly, was the least of her problems. What really worried Snow was that Mad John had specifically told her not to get on the news. That was the real problem.

Just as expected the police chopper had given chase when Snow pulled away from the others, allowing them the opportunity to slip off the highway and onto the back roads. She'd toyed with the cops at first, sticking to a steady hundred and ten miles an hour and easily passing any slower moving traffic. And then, when she was sure the others would be a safe distance away, Snow had taken off like something out of Cape Canaveral, greased lightning with gears to spare!

The Hayabusa was phenomenally quick, a bottle rocket with handfuls of unrestrained power, and Snow hunched low over the tank as the long, sweeping bends became hairpins. Thankfully the road was wide and relatively empty, but at nearly two hundred miles an hour there was no room for error. There was certainly no room for hitting a big dip, where the road went over a sand dune, and getting airborne! Not at those speeds. The bike came down hard and went into a ferocious tank slapper, Snow doing her best to lie on the tank and power through it, but simply running out of road. A hundredth of a second before the bike crashed into the centre divide, flipping end over end and spreading itself liberally across four lanes, Snow disappeared.

Or at least that is what the eye in the sky for the local news station had caught on tape. In fact, Snow had just a millisecond to transform to faerie size before the crash, and while she was probably the first of her kind to achieve such speeds, she was lucky not to have had her wings torn off, and luckier still not to have been squished all over a car windscreen. It was hardly surprising that the news crew found themselves baffled by the sight of Snow apparently vanishing into thin air, her helmet, boots, jacket, and jeans suddenly becoming empty.

Snow had found herself battered and bruised and naked in the central divide, while around her the traffic screeched to a chaotic halt. Unseen, she managed to sneak back to the scene of the crash, where her cut was lying in the road, and in all the confusion she managed to retrieve it without being noticed. From there she had dragged the leather vest nearly two miles before thinking it safe to return to human size, which left her all but naked at the side of the road. And indeed all butt naked, since the vest didn't leave much to the imagination.

She should probably have been thankful that she was able to change at all, a day later and she'd have been stuck in human form and killed for sure, but, all things considered, it had not been her best day. It was only stubbornness that prevented tears, especially when she'd walked past the CNN building on Sunset Boulevard and seen herself on TV. So much for "try not to get on the news."

Gradually the dark bar began to fill up with customers, and Snow was introduced to a couple more of Subway's friends, the girl who'd brought the stripper shoes already on her way to being quite drunk and somewhat annoying. Then again, the girl probably thought Snow was a stuck-up bitch, sitting there in a stolen tracksuit, cut, and stripper heels, sipping on water, and not really speaking to anyone. It wasn't like Snow could tell her that her wings hurt and that she might have just popped up on the radar of a thousand bounty hunters. Snow was rarely one to curse, but really, fuck today! Today could fuck off, and then fuck off some more when it got there!

And then Mad John, Numb Tongue, and Dum Dum showed up. Numb Tongue banged his head on the way in. They didn't see her at first, their eyes taking a moment to adjust, by which time the bartender had greeted them and set about pouring drinks. He didn't have to ask Mad John or Numb Tongue what they wanted. Apparently they'd been here before. Snow waited until Numb Tongue had knocked back his shot. He was unquestionably a violent man, but it wasn't like he would hit her, it was just that she felt she had let him down so badly, let all of them down. He didn't notice her at first, what with the bar being so dark and him being so tall. Feeling like a stupid child, she tugged on his sleeve and he looked down at her with what passed, on his face, for a smile.

"Evening, Snot," he said. "Had a bad day?"

At which point Snow burst into tears.

CHAPTER TWENTY

By midnight the bar was packed and the music was cranked up loud, with a number of inebriated punk rockers singing along. Snot had stopped blubbing and was now rather pleased with her new nickname. She'd had a little talk – or shout, given the volume of the music – with Mad John, who'd explained, quite gently, that some of the club would relish the idea of a thousand bounty hunters trying to find them, just so they had someone to mess with. There were *already* a thousand bounty hunters looking for various members of Aberrant MC, and those unlucky enough to actually find them were given the opportunity to spend many years regretting it. It saved Aberrant the bother of looking for them.

And that wasn't to mention the assorted oddballs, archaeologists, theologians, conspiracy theorists, and even the occasional misguided Satanist, who devoted their lives to following rumours of the club and its members. A few more wasn't going to make a lot of difference.

Admittedly, getting on the news wasn't good no matter how you looked at it, but already the story had been relegated – as had the story of the burning cop cars and police brutality – by a bomb scare at LAX and some celebrity or other getting arrested for driving drunk. One good thing about Hollywood was that news didn't stay news for very long. If anything, Snot's accident may have thrown the cops off their scent a little because they'd still be poking through the wreckage trying to figure out where she went.

Mad John was being kind, of course, and Numb Tongue had even given her hand a squeeze in a rare display of public affection, but that served just as well in getting her to pull herself together. She didn't need special girlie treatment, she was a proud prospect for Aberrant MC, and she said as much when she refused Mad John's offer of the rest of the night off.

"In that case, Prospect," Mad John smiled, "the bar is that way and I'd rather like a White Russian. If they don't have fresh cream then I'm sure you'll be able to find some."

It was a menial task, deliberately so, but Snot appreciated the gesture. It wasn't a drink that was ordered often, and few bars had fresh cream. Mad John was just giving her a moment to go off and collect her thoughts while feeling useful and independently resourceful at the same time. She'd have found the task a lot easier without the stripper heels, and easier still if there was anywhere to buy fresh cream within easy walking distance of the bar. Instead Snot tottered off towards Hollywood Boulevard, hoping for the best.

The streets were alive with people, tourists, party people, homeless people, and just plain crazy people. No one paid much attention to Snot, and she felt a moment of excitement wandering these brightly lit streets. Granted, Hollywood wasn't nearly as glamorous as she'd expected, not glamorous at all in fact, but it was still something of a thrill to be here amongst the hustle and bustle. The stars on the Walk Of Fame might have been grubby, but this was a long way from the woodland faerie village where she'd grown up, and although not the first time she'd been alone in a big city, it was certainly a new and exciting experience.

As an avid reader of anything and everything, she recognised these streets, The Pantages Theatre, The Capitol Records building, The Frolic Room, an old Bukowski haunt, all of it lit by street lights and headlights, moonlight, and neon signs, the delicious smell of food poisoning drifting from a curbside food vendor.

Home for Snot, until she took a wild flight of fancy and ran away with Aberrant MC, had been rather a dull place in the middle of nowhere, picture-perfect but oh so boring. There was a pub a few miles away, The Dragon's Head, and, to be fair, they put on decent bands every now and again, but beyond that there was nothing to do. At all. Essentially they were in hiding, cut off from the outside world like so many of faerie-kind these days, afraid of living in case they should draw the attention of death.

Snot had always dreamed of running away, going out into the big wide world and finding her destiny. She'd even had a motocross bike secreted in the woods in preparation for the big day, which was where she'd developed her talent for riding, but somehow that big day had never come. Twice she'd got as far as Cardiff, but mostly she rode to the library, just twenty-five miles away, devouring books about a world she would never see.

And then along came Aberrant MC, all dirt and thunder, daring the world to come and have a go if it was hard enough, and in a moment of madness she'd got swept along with them. And madness it was, even now, but it was better, oh so much better, than hiding. The world was Snot's oyster, so to speak. Which, funnily enough, looked exactly like the thing that someone had coughed up on Perry Como's star on the Walk Of Fame. Hell, Hollywood was far from glamorous, but it was living, it was alive, and it wasn't hiding!

As she waited for the lights to change at Hollywood and Vine, Snot felt a moment of regret that she hadn't done this sooner, hadn't taken the plunge into the pool of life. But she'd had good reason to be cautious. No doubt about it, this was madness!

In fact, Snot had known some of the Aberrant members for many years, but a long time ago her friend, Sunshine, had taken this exact same path before her, and it had not ended well. Sunshine had run off with Numb Tongue and wound up getting herself killed, and now Numb Tongue had... issues. It was complicated. Sunshine had treated him badly, perhaps not going so far as to cheat on him, but nonetheless doing more damage, hurting him more, than all his fights ever had. Slowly she had destroyed him, that destruction made worse by her own death.

That was the trouble with giving your heart to a faerie – you could never get it back, even after it had been broken.

In fairness, that part wasn't Sunshine's fault; it was a curse upon faerie-kind that once you had given them your heart, it was theirs forever. But Sunshine had always known this and had always been careless with love regardless of who she hurt. Numb Tongue's was not the only soul she had crushed, and eventually he had ended up hating himself, just like all the rest. The difference with Numb Tongue was that he was immortal, stuck with that pain for eternity. It hadn't exactly made him pleasant company.

They'd been friends, Snot and Numb Tongue, before all this happened, and maybe could have been more if Snot hadn't been so shy. But Sunshine had got there first – knowing but not caring – and then after Sunshine died he would have nothing more to do with faerie-kind. Instead, he went back to his go-to pain release of fighting, all the time hoping to get himself killed and be done with it. Even immortals could be killed if enough damage was inflicted upon them. He'd nearly succeeded a couple of times, too, the last time being when he took on an orc berserker in a cage fight at the so-called Orc Olympics in a place called Fero City. He nearly bled to death, and it had been Snot who nursed him back to health, and slowly, she hoped, back to life.

Even before then she had loved him from afar, wanting so badly to ease his suffering, and the cruel irony was that she could end the curse if only she could get close to him. The one thing that could break the curse was the love of another faerie, but Snot could never tell Numb Tongue that she loved him because he wouldn't have anything to do with faeries. It wasn't until he nearly died that she could finally try to make him truly well again, and she knew there was still a long way to go in his recovery.

He loved her, in his own way, but it was not unconditional, and he had never given her all the pieces of his heart, always holding something back. In short, Sunshine had really done a number on him, and the only people he would ever fully trust were members of Aberrant MC. No one else. Theirs was not a love he would die for, but he would willingly give his life for any member of the club. By prospecting for the club Snot hoped to show that hers *was* a love she would die for, and that she would never hurt him, never be careless with his heart. And then, one day, maybe he could truly love her back.

"Hey, baby!"

Snot stepped sharply back out of the road as a car swept around the corner, ignoring the cross sign and quickly bringing her mind back to the here and now. That was twice today she'd nearly been run over, twice she could have been killed, and yet she had never felt so alive. She was actually in Hollywood, for goodness sake! Eventually she found a convenience store where she bought fresh cream and a postcard with a picture of the Hollywood sign on it. Maybe she'd send it to The Dragon's Head.

Snot found her way back to the bar on Cahuenga Boulevard, the sidewalk outside cluttered with smokers and passers-by. She showed her ID to the door-man, who waved it away.

"You've been in already, pretty lady," he said. "You're with brother John and brother Numb Tongue, right?"

"Yes, that's right," replied Snot, somewhat surprised since they hadn't gone into the bar together.

"Yeah, brother Numb Tongue's told me all about you." The doorman smiled a big friendly smile. "A blessing on you both. He's very proud of you, and..."

"Numb Tongue said this?" said Snot, completely dumbfounded.

The doorman was an amiable man, almost as black as he was tall, and clearly friends with all the locals, but the idea of Numb Tongue standing out here sharing his feelings with the guy was preposterous. Numb Tongue wasn't a talker, he didn't do *feelings*. Not that he didn't have them, of course, probably more than most, which is why he buried them so deep, but he'd no more share them with anyone than he'd ride his bike off the edge of a cliff.

"Oh yes," the doorman beamed happily. "You make a great couple. He's such a funny guy, cracks me up..."

"Numb Tongue?" repeated Snot, realising that she probably sounded a bit stupid. "Sorry, it's just that he's..."

But Snot never got to finish her sentence. Suddenly the night was alive with flashing red and blue lights as dozens of cop cars descended on Cahuenga Boulevard, coming up from Sunset and down from Hollywood to block off the street and surround the bar. In fact, with the bikes parked outside the neighbouring sports bar, the cops had blocked that off, too. Inevitably they were joined by police and news helicopters, bright spotlights glaring down from above. There could be little doubt why they were here. Quickly the doorman ushered Snot inside.

Again she was momentarily blind upon entering the bar, but thankfully the other three were still in their booth at the far end, chatting to the bartender while he collected glasses. She squeezed and bumped her way through the throng of people to reach them. That was good at least; even LA cops were unlikely to charge, guns blazing, into a packed bar. The bad news was that there was only one way out of here. Her significant other would not be alone in vigorously resisting arrest, but, still, they were trapped like rats in a cage. Hurriedly, Snot explained the situation.

"Look lively," said the bartender. "This way." And they crossed the bar to what looked like a small storage cupboard. The bartender unlocked the door and ushered them inside. It *was* a storage cupboard. There was a broom and some cardboard boxes, and, with Mad John, Numb Tongue, Dum Dum,

Subway, and Snot all crammed in there, very little room for anything else. Snot attempted to transform to faerie size to give them breathing space, but realised she was too late. Or rather, that she was not late at all and would be stuck in human form for a couple of days. On the other side of the door they heard the music come to an abrupt halt. They were surrounded.

CHAPTER TWENTY-ONE

Vincent vaguely remembered that the terminal velocity of a skydiver was somewhere in the vicinity of two hundred miles an hour if they adopted what was known as the 'bullet position'. He had no idea why he knew this, but he was pretty sure that Chaos was approaching those speeds as he hurtled past them with an exhilarated "Whoooo-hoooo!". Vincent looked down between the bars of the cage, waiting for the canopy to open, but Chaos simply vanished into the darkness below.

"You know there's gonna be a horrible mess down there if he doesn't pull the chord in time," said Joker, following Vincent's gaze.

"And there'll be a horrible mess down there if you keep shaking the cage," Stone added tersely.

"What, like this?" grinned Joker.

"I'm serious," snapped Stone. "Unless you'd like to spend a few months exploring the joys of anal incontinence I strongly suggest you stop doing that."

"All right, I'm sorry," smirked Joker, unable to resist another little wiggle of the cage. "How far down do you reckon it is?"

"About two thousand feet, I'm told," replied Stone, looking rather pale about the face, like he was going to throw up. It wasn't unusual for him to talk with his eyes closed, but they were clenched tight shut, a light sweat gathering on his forehead. Vincent hadn't been particularly scared when he stepped into the cage, but he was now. Stone saw his worried expression. "Sorry," he said. "I'm sure it's perfectly safe, I'm just not very good with heights."

"Depths," corrected Joker.

"I'm warning you! You'll be walking around with a bucket tied to your backside!"

"Sorry, Stone."

The Roo Inn had turned out to be no ordinary pub. It was an old building of stone and wood, beams running high across the ceiling, and a smell that was somewhere between stale beer and piss. There were black and white pictures of its heyday on the walls, and once there were houses nearby, and a post office now long gone. When the mine closed down so did the town, and any customers these days were usually lost and had happened across it by accident. In the dirty kitchen at the back of the pub, however, was a trapdoor leading to a dimly lit basement, and in that basement was a large hole in the ground, beside which sat a metal cage big enough for three people. Or one Dum Dum. The hole looked down into a gigantic cave, on top of which the pub had been built in order to conceal it, and the cage was, until now, the only way to the bottom, a journey that took around half an hour and passed through actual clouds on its descent.

Chaos had been unimpressed. "Don't look very safe," he'd said, inspecting the worn-out pulley system that lowered and raised the cage, and then sending Vincent back to the bus to get his parachute. Of course he has a parachute, why wouldn't he have a parachute? thought Vincent. He also had a point about the cage not looking very safe, the teeth on the cogs were worn almost round, but since Vincent had no idea how to operate a parachute there was no other choice. Chaos said he'd send his chute back up in the cage should anyone else fancy a leap into the unknown. Joker, Stone, and Vincent were about ten minutes into the descent when he flew past, a big, shit-eating grin plastered across his face.

Even without Joker's help, the cage swayed disconcertingly, and it was cold as they inched down through the clouds, a single oil lamp giving everything an eerie glow. It was a while before they could see the ground, but at least the welcoming committee at the bottom explained why the army of Aborigines at the top had looked somewhat smaller in the light of day. While Aberrant slept one last night on the bus, the cage had been in use all night, three people at a time, with two people operating the winch. On the floor of the cave, the army looked huge, perhaps a thousand strong, and it was something of a relief to see some friendly faces when Chaos and Balun let them out of the cage. Stone looked as if he might kiss the ground.

Slowly the cage went back up into the darkness. What little light there was in the cave came mostly from fire torches dotted around the crowd, but it lit no more than a handful of very dark faces, and the few battery torches in evidence fared no better. The cave seemed to suck the light out of everything. It was cool at the bottom, perhaps fifty degrees, and smelled quite strongly of bat poo. Vincent was not unaware that he might be standing in quite a lot of it.

It was some time before all of the Aberrant crew were on the ground, although some arrived sooner than others, Andy One-Leg, Mental, and Smiler all opting for the faster descent. Unfortunately, about halfway down, Smiler had managed to get the parachute tangled up in the cage, tearing a hole in the canopy, and leaving him dangling precariously until he reached the ground and was cut free, but otherwise the hours were without incident. Vincent was put to work stitching up the hole in the parachute. And at last, when everyone was safely on the ground, Aberrant began their journey on foot, following at the tail end of a small army.

In one or two places the cave thinned to not much more than a sharp, narrow crack, and they walked in single file, feeling their way along the smooth walls, but for the most part there was a sense of great space about them. Either way, the torches were next to useless, the darkness always close by, and always the foul stench of guano and a horrid rustling noise, like the sound of millions of insects hidden and writhing in the pitch-black shadows. Vincent had no idea how long or how far they walked, but it felt like many hours and many miles. Certainly it was long enough and far enough that his feet were starting to complain as much as his stomach.

At long last they stopped to rest, and Vincent was relieved to see Balun begin making a campfire, even if it was no more than a few twigs. Quite where he'd found any firewood at all down there was anyone's guess, but the warmth would be welcome, and it would feel safer with a fire burning, as if it was warding away evil. The flames probably wouldn't provide much light, just enough to illuminate a few nearby faces, but it was a lot better than nothing.

Vincent had never known such darkness, or rather such an absence of light. When they were walking, the flicker of a nearby torch was enough to see the person in front of you and the ground, so long as you paid attention to where you were going and what you were stepping in, which was definitely bat shit. Now that they'd stopped it seemed as if the darkness became all the more enveloping, like the walls of the cave were made of coal. Even coal had a shine to it though; in here the light was simply gone, absorbed. There was a sense of vastness about the cave, but Vincent could no more see the roof than he could see the person sitting five feet away from him. The horrid rustling of insects grew louder and closer.

Still, at least Vincent could rest his weary legs and cook up some beans over the fire, and he set about doing this, whilst trying not to imagine what might be lurking in the darkness. The floor of the cave was really quite disgusting, but thankfully didn't smell quite as bad as it might, which, again, suggested that they were in an extremely large cave. And it turned out that bat shit was highly flammable – Balun only using the twigs to get the fire started – so it was soon hot enough that Vincent's beans were bubbling away in their tin. It had been a long time since Vincent's backpack didn't have at least two cans of Heinz finest tucked away inside, just in case. It wasn't unknown for Aberrant MC to stray from the beaten path to the kind of places that even McDonald's had failed to discover, and it wasn't even the first time they'd spent the night in a cave. Assuming it was night; it could be the middle of the afternoon, for all Vincent knew.

He spooned beans into his face, pleased that he had also thought to bring a spoon. Around the now roaring fire were Balun and his friend Uwan, along with Andy One-Leg, Stone, Joker, and Billy Toothless, whose acid trip had thankfully worn off. Vincent could hear Flashback's voice not too far away – it was difficult sometimes not to hear his voice if you were in roughly the same country – but there was no sign of him, no sign of anyone beyond the few faces in the flickering light of their own fire. Balun and Uwan were chatting away in their dead language. It was a nice sounding language, gentle and rolling, but Vincent had no clue what they were talking about, only that they seemed excited, agitated even.

"You want some soup?" Andy interrupted them. "Soup, boss?"

Both Balun and Uwan erupted into fits of laughter.

"What?" said Andy. "What did I say?"

"Probably the bit about "soup, boss,"" grinned Stone.

"What?" said Andy, still baffled. "They keep calling me boss."

"Yes," said Stone. "I felt just as uncomfortable as you about that, so I had a word with one of the elders. Turns out it's an old Aboriginal name. In English it would be spelled with four Zs and a U, 'Yezzbouzz'." Both Balun and Uwan stopped laughing when he spoke the word.

"Oh," said Andy. "And what the fuck is a Yezzbouzz?"

"Not what," said Stone. "Who? Who the fuck is Yezzbouzz?"

"All right, who the fuck is Yezzbouzz?"

"Yezzbouzz," said Stone, "is a dragon. And it looks like we're going to meet her."

CHAPTER TWENTY-TWO

The boxes in the storage cupboard suddenly began to move as if pushed from behind, where there was nothing but a brick wall. There was another great shove, the wall definitely moved, and the uppermost boxes fell on Dum Dum's head. Luckily they were mostly empty.

"Sorry!" said a voice from behind the boxes. And then, with a final push, a face appeared. "Sorry about that," repeated the man, stout and heavily tattooed. "We haven't used this door in years. This way! This way! Hurry! Watch your heads."

And with that, Mad John, Numb Tongue, Dum Dum, Snot, and Subway followed the man into a dusty corridor lit by equally dusty bare light bulbs. The ceiling was low and there was not a little cursing from Numb Tongue and Dum Dum who both failed to mind their heads. There was also some confusion as to why Subway was with them, since he wasn't actually wanted by the authorities and appeared to have followed them out of habit.

"Shut the door, hurry," urged the man. "That's it. Don't worry, it doesn't look like a door from the other side. This way." The man scurried off down the long corridor almost leaving them all behind.

"Where are we going?" Mad John asked as they hurried after him.

"Away from the police," said the man over his shoulder. "This has been here since Prohibition in the twenties. They used it to move booze from bar to bar. You'll be pleased to know that it comes out in another bar."

"Well, that's good," Mad John smiled. "Lead the way."

It was quite a long walk to the other bar, a good twenty-five minutes or so, and a great many swearwords. Both Numb Tongue and Dum Dum were hunched double as they walked, and Dum Dum had rather a large welt on his forehead by the time they got to the other end, where the corridor ended and a ladder led up to a trapdoor. The trapdoor opened into a small, cluttered office, with pictures of bands and old gig flyers on the walls. The walls of the office rattled to suggest that one of the bands was currently on stage.

"Sorry, about the mess," said the man. "We weren't expecting anyone. I'm Matt," he proffered his hand for shaking. "I'll er, go and get the manager. Just knock on the hatch if you want a drink."

There was indeed a small hatch in one of the walls, and when Mad John knocked, the hatch slid up to reveal a bar on the other side that serviced what appeared to be a modestly sized night club. Suitably furnished with adult beverages, they waited for the manager. Mad John even got his White Russian at last, Snot having brought the cream with her, and Dum Dum was in his element checking out all the band flyers.

They waited a long time and ordered more drinks. Eventually Mad John grew impatient and sent Snot to find out what was going on. She was back five minutes later with a rather embarrassed expression on her face.

"I think I might be a bit overdressed," she said. "There's a lot of people not wearing very much out there."

It turned out that the club – a place called The Dragonfly – was holding some sort of fetish event, and since there was still no sign of the manager they went outside to explore. They found a crowded smoking patio out the back, fairy lights twinkling upon assorted fetishists, goths, and punk rockers. Of course, they weren't *real* fairy lights, which Snot knew to be rather more beautiful, but everyone seemed friendly enough and the place was unlikely to be crawling with cops. Indeed, the cops would still be crawling all over the bikes parked on Cahuenga, and since that left them with no transport, Subway went off to make a few calls. He was gone for some time and looked worried upon his return.

"Not good," he told Mad John. "Most of Hollywood's shut down, cops everywhere. Luckily the tunnel's thrown them off, but we're still too close for comfort. It's gonna be difficult moving you very far, at least until shit dies down. There's a couple of no questions motels nearby, might be a good idea to lay low overnight, then we can get you guys out of here tomorrow."

"Thank you, yes," said Mad John. "That might be for the best. We can get a fresh start in the morning."

"Might have to be a van rather than bikes," Subway added. "Anything on two wheels is a target right now."

"For which you have my sincere apologies," said Mad John. "We've drawn far too much attention and brought you all unnecessary trouble."

"It'll die down," shrugged Subway. "The video might be more of a concern."

"Video?"

"Snow's little off on the freeway, the video's gone viral on YouTube."

"It's done what on who?" Mad John looked utterly perplexed so Dum Dum stepped forward to explain as best he could. Though he'd had the insight to forbid the club from using trackable devices, cell phones and GPS, the internet was largely a mystery to Mad John, and while Dum Dum was no webmaster he knew enough to know that nearly four million hits and counting wasn't good news. Snot's accident was fast becoming an internet sensation.

"It's news we could do without," said Mad John, "but we'll deal with things as they arise. For now we just need to avoid the attentions of the law."

"We can get a van to you first thing," nodded Subway. "All legit, you won't get pulled over."

And so it was agreed that Mad John, Numb Tongue, Dum Dum, and Snot wait out the night in the nearest cockroach motel, and Subway hurried off to make the arrangements. An outsider might think he was trying to impress them, perhaps with a view to getting himself patched over, but more likely he was simply being helpful. It hadn't escaped Dum Dum's notice that a lot of people seemed to owe Mad John and Aberrant MC favours that they could never return, and favours they were not expected to return but nonetheless felt obliged to repay in whatever way possible. Snot was sent to fetch a round of drinks.

"How's the music in here?" Mad John asked Dum Dum.

It seemed like rather an odd question at first – Mad John could clearly hear the music for himself – but then Dum Dum caught his meaning. He hadn't really been paying attention; it was just background music, a mixture of pop and dance music, and he'd been rather distracted by two girls who appeared, despite the improbability, to be flirting with him from across the patio.

"Dunno," said Dum Dum, cocking an ear to a nearby speaker to find a somewhat repetitive chorus about "bedroom eyes". If there was a hidden message in the song then it was lost on him, but he had already learned that sometimes the clue was in the name of the song or even the name of the band.

"*Oh, I need your bedroom eyes,*" went the song. "*Oh, I need your bedroom eyes.*" And now that he was fully aware of it, it did kind of seem that the girls across the patio might be flirting with him. Nah, he thought to himself, don't be daft. Still, it didn't hurt to be sure, and there was another girl dancing nearby, apparently familiar with the tune, so Dum Dum asked her who the song was by. And she told him. And he told Mad John.

"In that case," Mad John smiled, "I'd suggest you go and buy those ladies a drink, and I shall wish you a pleasant evening."

And Dum Dum had a very pleasant evening indeed.

"Dum Dum Girls," he grinned, walking away. "Well, I never..."

CHAPTER TWENTY-THREE

Vincent awoke in a mild state of panic, startled until he remembered that they were still very much at the bottom of a gigantic cave that was filled with bat crap and cockroaches. He'd found out about the cockroaches when Billy Toothless had snuck off into the dark to catch some for his supper. Apparently, the roaches lived on the crap, and the bats ate the roaches, a perfect circle of life interrupted briefly by a hungry hobgoblin who would happily eat either. You got used to Billy's disgusting habits after a while, but it didn't make them any less disgusting.

The campfire was burning bright, tended by Balun while they slept, to keep the cockroaches at bay, and Vincent edged closer, needing its light more than its warmth. Still the foul reek of guano permeated everything, insinuating itself into his nostrils and up into the back of his skull like he'd snorted some horrible toxic chemical. Which, thinking about it, was exactly what bat shit was.

That was the thing about adventures, thought Vincent, they could be really gross sometimes. His mind took him back to Fero City, an Orcish metropolis with no toilet facilities and a penchant for decorating buildings with severed heads. Such was the violence associated with the place that it was said to have been where the word 'ferocity' was born, although Vincent later found out that it was more to do with someone not understanding the Orcish language, and trying to make it into English. Fero, when pronounced correctly in Orcish, sounded rather like a badger belching snot, and it was a slang term meaning 'city'. Due to a mistranslation, technically, Fero City was City City. But, oh the terrible smell! It may as well have been Shitty City for all the orcs crapping in the streets, not to mention the dead dogs, vomit, and, frankly, the orcs themselves, whose fragrance was nothing if not original. The smell had followed him around for months afterwards, a foetidness like no other on earth, and right now bat shit was running a close second. Maybe, thought Vincent, that's where the term 'bat shit crazy' comes from.

It was a rather bigger creature that was worrying Vincent, however. A dragon, to be precise. A very old and very, very large dragon, who, by all accounts, wasn't at all keen on white people. Understandably so, given that white people had this idiotic fetish for slaying dragons, but concerning nonetheless since Aberrant MC were, for the most part, white, even if it would take a bath or two to prove it. Not that there weren't other skin tones mixed in – almost grey in the case of Billy Toothless – but they'd all look the same to a dragon. Aborigines, on the other hand, had lived in harmony with dragons for centuries, millennia even, and were considered friends, particularly since they had no interest in gold and would happily divulge its whereabouts if they found any.

The good news was that Stone was well known among the Aborigines, a friend to many, and obviously close to Derain. He had known none of those present until just yesterday, but still they would vouch for him. The not so good news was that Yezzbouzz might not give a crap, and could, if she so decided, turn them all into kebabs. And the tricky part was that none of the Aborigines present had ever met Yezzbouzz in person – or dragon as the case may be. They were friends of a friend, vouching for other friends of that same friend, but at least able to speak the dragon's tongue. Only an idiot would assume that the dragon would be called Cedric and speak with an English accent. Safe passage through the dragon's lair was not guaranteed.

Oh, and there was a small possibility that Yezzbouzz may have recently given birth – or laid an egg, since that's what dragons do – which meant she would be feeling particularly protective, and that Mr Yezzbouzz could very well be in the vicinity. And while, admittedly, 'in the vicinity' to a dragon could be anything up to five hundred miles away, it was certainly another concern.

Vincent put a small pan of water on the fire, grateful when Stone woke up and demanded coffee. Balun was taking his turn to sleep and it didn't do to be sitting alone in the dark for too long with just your fears for company. Unfortunately Stone wasn't much better, and his own fears merely served to amplify Vincent's worries.

Stone usually had this Zen-like calm about him, like he already knew the outcome of any given situation, and most of the time he was right; just let it wash over you, be still and know; ask the right question and you will find that you already know the answer. At the bottom of Bat Poo Cave, however, Stone seemed unsure of himself, afraid of the journey that lay ahead. Quietly, he was of the opinion that they were all going to be burned alive.

As if on cue there was a distant roar, the sound of something huge.

"She's closer than I thought," Stone said in hushed tones. "Can't get to us from this side of the cave, they tell me, but we'll be seeing her soon enough. She knows we're here."

Vincent almost asked if they could simply take another route and go around the dragon if she was feeling uncooperative, but obviously they couldn't or they would have. It was one thing to dream of seeing a dragon, but quite another to actually meet one, especially if you hadn't been invited. To make matters worse, it had been explained to Stone, who now told Vincent, that the cave grew exceptionally narrow where it entered the dragon's lair, single file only for over a mile. Yezzbouzz, should she take umbrage at their presence, could fry the lot of them alive and there would be nowhere to run, nowhere to hide. Even the immortals among them would perish if they were turned to charcoal.

"What if I went first?" Vincent heard himself say. "The dragon won't be able to see me cos of the ring, and maybe I could sort of do the introductions or something, like talk to her or something?"

"I admire your courage," said Stone, "but I fear you'll find no surer way to get us all killed. More than a few dragons have encountered invisible thieves, and they tend to burn first and ask questions later. Dragons have a keen sense of smell, too. She'll know you're there even if she can't see you. On top of that you don't speak dragon's tongue, and even if she could see you she's unlikely to want to play charades."

They both chuckled at the idea, but it was nervous laughter. If things went wrong it would wipe out most of the club, not to mention the hundreds of Aborigines who were guiding them and hoping to travel the same path, all of them on a perilous mission to rescue one man. Now that Vincent thought about it in those terms it seemed a little crazy, so many lives at stake to save just one. It reminded him of a scene from Saving Private Ryan where the troops were complaining about their mission, questioning whether it's really worth the risk. What's so special about him?

Instead, he said, "He must be pretty special, this bloke we're rescuing."

"I like to think that everyone is special in their own way," replied Stone. "But, yes, Derain is certainly what you'd call special."

Vincent waited for Stone to elaborate, but as was often the case he'd become distracted by rolling a joint and seemed to have forgotten the conversation.

"Er, special how?" ventured Vincent. "Is he a wizard?"

"Derain? Oh yes," said Stone, lighting the joint. "The oldest wizard of them all, proper earth magic. If he dies then that magic dies with him, lost forever. If he dies... Well, let's just say we can't let that happen. Not by the hand of a bunch of gold greedy dwarfs, and not to the oldest man in the world. Not on my watch." And with that, Stone was suddenly on his feet. "Now, let's get these buggers up and go and have a word with this dragon, shall we?"

"Yes, boss!" said Vincent.

CHAPTER TWENTY-FOUR

Hours passed and still they seemed no closer, still there was no sign of a dragon, just endless miles of bat crap and roaches crunching underfoot. There was the sound of running water at one point, a slow running stream perhaps, but no sight nor sound of Yezzbouzz. And while Vincent knew enough to be careful what he wished for, it was reaching the point where getting turned into beef jerky might be favourable to this. *Anything* had to be better than this. They promised us dragons, he thought to himself, where's the fucking dragons?

But Vincent was wrong, anything wasn't better than this. Moments after he'd started complaining to himself, they came to a dead halt and he walked into the back of Joker. They had finally reached the narrow point in the cave that led to the dragon's lair, and from now on it would be single file and no going back. Soon enough there would be dragons – or at least one dragon – but as he took his first steps into the tunnel, no more than a crack face of the earth, it occurred to Vincent that if negotiations didn't go well then he would never get to see one. The last thing he'd ever see would be the back of Joker's head and, presumably, a huge fireball. And as much as he liked Joker, he really didn't want the back of his head to be the last thing he ever saw. And he certainly didn't want the last thing he ever saw to be a fireball. Not that he'd given it a huge amount of thought before, but Vincent rather hoped that the last thing he ever saw was some boobs. Preferably many, many years from now.

It was unclear whether or not Vincent ranked among the number of immortals: Obviously his father had a somewhat extended lifespan, what with predating the Bible by several decades – as did Numb Tongue, Stone, and several other members of Aberrant – but no one seemed to know if it was a hereditary condition, so to speak, and there was really only one way to find out, which, if it turned out not to be the case, would be fatal. There was also the small fact that getting turned to ashes would kill them all regardless. It wasn't just a flesh wound.

If anything the light was a little better inside the tunnel, but claustrophobia set in almost at once. In the cave there had been a feeling of vast space even if it couldn't be seen, but here you could see the walls, and they seemed to close in on them with every step. Despite the coolness there was sweat running down Vincent's forehead and into his eyes, making them sting. Fear took the breath from him, making him gasp for air, panic rising in waves that he had to fight to control lest it should overwhelm him completely.

No one talked.

And then, at last, the long procession came to another halt, and they waited in the dim, grimy light of their torches, hoping that it didn't suddenly become a lot brighter.

More hours passed, or so it seemed, and Vincent did his best not so much to keep his composure as to not completely lose his shit and scream like a girl. It was horrible in here, a living tomb with no escape, not even enough room to turn around and run. Not that it mattered, but he was damn sure he was in enough danger that his ring had rendered him invisible. But fire doesn't need to see you to burn you.

Still they waited.

And waited.

And then, as suddenly as they had stopped, they were all on the move again, one after the other, all groping along trying not to crack their heads. Somewhere up ahead it appeared that Yezzbouzz the dragon had agreed to let them pass without torching them. In a strange way it was somewhat anticlimactic – they saw and heard nothing of the negotiations, they simply started walking again, sighs of relief spreading down the line as the news travelled back to them – but anticlimactic was fine as far as Vincent was concerned. Anticlimactic meant not getting incinerated.

As it was, the temperature rose quite dramatically, growing increasingly warmer and more uncomfortable, dry and dirty and stifling, as they continued forward along the narrow path. Even the bats and roaches didn't venture this far, occasional bones on the ground suggesting that Yezzbouzz wasn't always so welcoming. Vincent was sure that some of them were human bones. It was probably for the best that he couldn't see very well.

And then there was light, and Vincent was blinded more completely than he had been when he was in the dark, like staring straight into the midday sun. He was reminded of stepping out of a nightclub, unaware that morning had broken and was on its way for lunch, except this was brighter than that, oh so much brighter, and so very, very gold. For a moment he was unable to move.

"Beautiful, isn't she?" whispered Stone.

"I can't see," said Vincent.

"Ah yes," said Stone. "I should have mentioned sunglasses. It'll pass. Come, we must keep moving."

Stone grabbed Vincent's sleeve and led him onwards into the golden glare of the dragon's lair. Real gold, too, according to Stone, but not, as legend has told, hoarded in greed, but rather because gold, when heated to the right temperature, is perfect for incubating dragon's eggs. That's why they tend to get a bit stroppy when people steal it from them.

With predictable timing, there was a sound like a small avalanche of coins, and something moved in the blinding glare, something huge, like a two-story building having a bit of a stretch. There was a rumbling noise like, well, like a dragon breathing. It moved again and there was another cascade of coins.

"Quite magnificent," breathed Stone. "Quite, quite magnificent."

Typical, thought Vincent, we walk through miles and miles of bat shit and cockroaches, risking life, limb, and fuck knows how many revolting diseases, and now I can't see a bloody thing! Here be a great big blurry thing! It moved again, and Vincent knew somehow that it was watching them intently, capable at any moment of turning them into human candles. Well, mostly human; there had been some debate about how to explain a hobgoblin and a dworc to a dragon, but it had been thought best not to complicate matters. They were all snacks to the dragon if she so decided. Besides, Zig Zag still hadn't taken his crash helmet off for fear of freaking out their Aboriginal friends. Instead they walked in a reverential silence, even Flashback knowing when to shut up.

Vincent worried at first that his eyesight might be permanently damaged, and then that it wouldn't have fully recovered before they'd passed through the dragon's lair, and he might never get to see the beast in all its glory. But it was a long way across the dragon's lair, airports were smaller, and gradually the great big blurry thing began to come into focus, and with it the rest of this incredible golden cavern.

"Holy..." Vincent gasped.

The cavern was vast, like the inside of a football stadium if Wembley were made of solid gold, and there in the middle sat Yezzbouzz, gleaming like a well-polished office block. At first it seemed as if she, too, were made of gold, but when she moved, those great scales showed black as night, reflecting the golden gleam of the cavern. A flicker of blue flame came from each of her wide nostrils, a warning, if it were needed, that she might still roast them like so many potatoes. Here and there the precious metals were bubbling, made liquid by her fire. Her head was the size of a reasonably priced family saloon car.

Now that, thought Vincent, is a fucking dragon!

CHAPTER TWENTY-FIVE

The pilot was praying as they taxied down the short and rarely used desert runway, unaware that the person he was praying to was sitting right beside him, with Numb Tongue's knees pressing rather uncomfortably into his back. Again, the small plane swayed in the heavy crosswinds, a lone orange windsock flapping furiously, ragged and torn. The single propeller engine revved, and Dum Dum checked for a third time that his seatbelt was tightly buckled. It was going to be a very bumpy ride.

Dum Dum was no aviation expert, but even without the pilot's prayers it was fair to say that a four-seater plane carrying five passengers didn't exactly inspire confidence, particularly since the pilot had insisted on weighing each passenger before they squeezed on board. He'd been somewhat distressed when Dum Dum broke the scales, but now, with those great gusts of wind trying to throw it sideways from the runway, it seemed as if his bulk might be the only thing keeping the damn thing anchored to the ground.

"Christ be with me," muttered the pilot, still less than blissful in his ignorance.

Dum Dum checked his seatbelt again. His mental jukebox kept trying to play Buddy Holly and Lynyrd Skynyrd songs, with the occasional Randy Rhoads solo thrown in, and he did his best to ignore it. That was the problem with his new gift; any song that popped into his head immediately started to take on some deep significance and lead him down false paths towards overthinking everything. The whole point was not to overthink it. Probably.

Certainly he had been thinking about it too much, trying too hard to find meanings that weren't there. He did, for example, have a fondness for large bottoms and an inability to lie about it, as one of the songs he'd heard last night had suggested, but he wasn't really the type to *"get low when the whistle blows"*, or indeed to back his not inconsiderable ass up. Sometimes songs were just songs. And since Dum Dum couldn't seem to completely shut the songs off, he mentally selected something less bothersome than a bunch of musicians who'd died in plane crashes.

"Ain't a hope in hell/Nothing's gonna bring us down..."

Ah yes, Motörhead's *Bomber* should do the trick.

"The way we fly/Fives miles off the ground..."

Except the chances of them getting five feet off the ground, let alone five miles, seemed fairly remote. Exceeding its payload by over fifty pounds, the plane sat lower on Dum Dum's side, both he and Numb Tongue bent double just to fit into their seats, while Snot sat on the floor. A bomber this was not. Despite their proximity to the Mexican border it was, however, their best chance of getting to Mexico City in a hurry – without the inconvenience of customs officials – from whence they could get a flight to Perth, Australia.

With Subway at the wheel of a white van that advertised pest control, they had left Los Angeles early in the morning, Dum Dum waving a cheery good-bye to his two friends, the Dum Dum Girls. Already the streets were busy with traffic, an accident on Santa Monica Boulevard slowing everything to a crawl, and then the freeway was at a standstill for no apparent reason, mile upon mile of angry commuters making things worse by trying to change lanes, and none of them giving each other space. The van was noisy and the air conditioning didn't work, but it went unnoticed by any passing cop cars, blending into the morning madness, until at last the traffic cleared.

They drove east for a couple of hours, the city giving way to desert once more, crosswinds growing in strength and buffeting the van. On top of the hills and alongside the road, great white wind turbines picked up speed, Dum Dum getting a kick from seeing signs for Whitewater, the name of which was also a Kyuss tune. Perhaps Sky Valley was nearby, but disappointingly he saw nothing of the infamous sign for the place.

Presently they'd pulled off the freeway and taken back roads and finally a dirt path to the abandoned runway, where the pilot was waiting beside his plane. He was a thickset Mexican man in his late fifties, and apparently only spoke English if it was in the form of a prayer, but he was nonetheless deter-mined to get them where they needed to go.

And so, here they sat as he tapped again at all the dials and gibbered under his breath. "Holy Mary, Mother Of God..." Tap, tap, tap. "Pray for us sinners, now and at the hour of our death..." Tap, tap, tap. Until finally he seemed resigned to his fate and revved the engine for take-off. Dum Dum waved goodbye to Subway out of the window and, just for good measure, checked that his seatbelt was buckled.

The small plane seemed frightfully slow as it took off, like sticking your feet out of the bottom and running along like The Anthill Mob would make it go faster. It shuddered and pitched in the wind, but take off it did, just moments before they ran out of runway. There was a collective sigh of relief from all on board.

"Gadzooks! That was a little close for comfort!" said Mad John, and they settled in as best they could for a seventeen-hundred-mile roller coaster ride.

Moments later Numb Tongue tapped Mad John on the shoulder.

"No one says gadzooks anymore," he said.

"They don't?"

"No."

"Oh," said Mad John disappointedly. "That's a shame. I rather liked gadzooks."

Dum Dum looked down at the tiny buildings and ant-sized cars, until, despite the uncomfortable ride, he found himself nodding off. It had been a long night, after all, and not that he was complaining but he'd slept for an hour at most. In a regular passenger plane it would take about five hours to get to Mexico City, but in this thing they would have to stop to refuel a couple of times, particularly since it was carrying less fuel than usual in an effort to lose weight. Best to take sleep where you could find it.

He awoke with dribble on his chin, momentarily confused by the smooth ride and the lack of engine noise until he realised that they were on the ground. He wiped the sleep from his eyes and the slobber from his chin, and peered out of the window, but the light was fading and there was nothing much to see apart from the others stretching their legs, Numb Tongue smoking a cigarette while the pilot was in discussion with two other men. He clambered out to join them. Clearly they weren't in Mexico City yet, just another disused runway, but at least the vicious winds had died down, and the air was pleasantly warm.

There was a van parked alongside the plane, no doubt the source of their fuel since there was nothing but an empty field here, and it occurred to Dum Dum that they were probably taking a route that was more often frequented by drug dealers. Certainly, the two men whose van it was looked the part, Mexican cartel maybe, tough-looking, and entirely un-fazed by the sight of Numb Tongue and Dum Dum. They worked in silence, strictly business, load up and leave. Half an hour later the little plane was back in the air, flying low in the darkness.

Dum Dum was wide awake now, cramped and somewhat bored, since there was nothing to see outside. Mad John was engrossed in the writing of a letter, and Numb Tongue and Snot weren't much for conversation, so he dug out his iPod and headphones and stuck it on shuffle. It played *Freebird* so he turned it off and sat in silence. Whatever the future held in store, he hoped it wasn't bloody *Freebird*.

CHAPTER TWENTY-SIX

It was night-time when they stopped to rest, of that much Vincent could be sure. Leaving Yezzbouzz to her gold, its warm gleam fading behind them, they had returned once more to darkness, fire torches leading the way for several miles. And then, quite suddenly, there was light up above, a million stars twinkling down upon them through a great hole in the sky. Or so it seemed for the moment it took the brain to adjust. In fact, it was a hole in the roof of the cave, and below it, black and bathing in faint silver light, lay a lake perhaps two miles wide.

"Wouldn't get too close to that if I was you," Stoned warned as they made camp. "Just fill your water bottles quick and get out."

"Why? What's in there?"

"I've no idea," said Stone, "but Balun and his friends are keeping their distance, so I'd suggest you do the same."

Vincent didn't need telling twice. Only this morning – or possibly afternoon – he'd been looking at a dragon that was roughly the same size as their old London clubhouse, and not more than a year ago he'd been on board a ferry boat that was attacked by a kraken. There was not a ripple on the surface of the water, but who knew how deep those waters were, or what strange creature might lay beneath? They might be a long way from Loch Ness, but that didn't mean there wasn't a monster.

Thankfully, the floor of the cave here was empty of bats, bat poo, and cockroaches, and Vincent longed to dive into the cold, clean water, and wash the smell away, but instead he filled his water bottles at arm's length and moved quickly to what he hoped was a safe distance away from the edge. He sufficed with brushing his teeth, saving the rest of the water for drinking. His next concern was of a more intimate nature so he went behind one of the bigger rocks, thankful that he'd remembered to steal some toilet paper from the hotel.

Small campfires were built, and after so long in darkness it seemed positively bright under the hole in the sky. For the first time Vincent was able to properly see the army of Aborigines they'd been travelling with. Up until now it had mostly just been a long line of the backs of people's heads and a few faces around the campfire, but now he could see that whatever this was, it was definitely no army. For a start, there were far fewer of them than he'd previously estimated: He wasn't about to hazard another inaccurate guess, but it was undoubtedly less than a thousand, and probably nearer half that number, most of them far from fighting fit. True, there were some solid looking blokes here, warriors even, but just as many were too old or too young, too ill-fed. Vincent was no warrior himself, but he knew what they were supposed to look like and he could only hope that whatever foes they might be expected to face weren't heavily armed. Or awake. The kid sitting opposite, handsome and scrawny, with thick black hair and arms like pipe cleaners, looked like he might work in a 7-Eleven if he were old enough.

The kid saw him looking. "G'day," he said with a broad smile.

"You speak English?" said Vincent.

"Yeah," the kid nodded. "Name's Sam, but everyone calls me Tike. How are you liking all the bat shit?"

"Oh, loving it, mate," Vincent grinned. "I was tempted to go for a swim just to get rid of the smell, but apparently there might be something nasty in there."

"Probably freshies," shrugged Tike.

"Freshies?"

"Freshwater crocs."

"Vincent," said Vincent by way of introduction, shaking Tike's hand. "You have a lot of crocs out here?"

"Oh yeah, fair few. Freshies are pretty harmless though, long as you don't bother 'em. This your first time in Australia?"

Vincent nodded. "First time seeing a dragon too!"

"Yeah, me too," grinned Tike. "Huge fucker, wasn't it? I've gotta admit I was crapping myself when we walked past. I kept thinking, any second now..."

Vincent laughed. "Yeah, any second now we're all gonna be toast! Although, from what I've seen on those wildlife documentaries, most things in Australia will try to kill you if you sit still for long enough. Even the plants will have a go!"

"Nah," Tike shrugged again. "You leave them alone, they'll leave you alone, mostly."

"Mostly?"

"Well, you'd be wise to steer clear of any funnel-web spiders, them fuckers will come after you if you piss them off. Nasty bite on them."

Tike, it transpired, did indeed work in a convenience store, and like nearly everyone else here he had received and had no choice but to follow a psychic SOS, its signal so strong that it caused them to get headaches. They were from all walks of life – a couple of school teachers, social workers, mechanics, a few homeless – and most had never met before, at least not in person. It was just whoever received the signal and was close enough to show up. For the most part they didn't really know what they were doing here, and were desperately underprepared.

"You and me both, mate," said Vincent. "My lot never tells me anything. All I know is two of them started getting headaches and we flew straight here from fucking Germany. I think we had to wait around when the signal stopped, but we've been on the move ever since. Apparently it's something to do with a bloke getting kidnapped by dwarfs."

"Yeah, I gathered that much," said Tike. "Fuckin' heigh-ho! I had no idea they even fucking existed like that, but by all accounts they're vicious little buggers and we're seriously outnumbered."

Others would follow, explained Tike, those who had received the SOS and had taken longer to get to the coordinates, but Yezzbouzz would let no more pass. In order to stop anyone who followed from getting fried, the path had been blocked behind them. For now, at least, they were on their own, just over four hundred in number, and up against at least ten times that number. There was no going back.

"The little dwarf buggers are a couple days ahead of us on foot," Tike continued. "Fuckin' heavily armed, and they probably know we're coming, which don't sound too promising."

Vincent had been to a dwarf city before, even made a few dwarf friends after he'd accidentally stumbled into a gay dwarf disco, but going into battle against them was an entirely different proposition. Most of the dwarfs Vincent had encountered were barrel-shaped and as strong as five men, often nearly as wide as they were tall. They'd fought bitter wars with the orcs over the centuries, some of them *for* centuries given that dwarfs live so long, and not only had they survived but frequently they'd given the orcs a good kicking. A height advantage doesn't stay so for long when you have some bearded maniac swinging a mining axe at your knees.

Vincent thought back to his time in the dwarf city of Grun Mar, all those endless tunnels and endless levels below the mountain. He'd only visited the upper reaches of the city, no more than a few floors below ground, but the tunnels went on for miles. There could be no doubt that the dwarfs would have the advantage underground, they *lived* underground, some of them rarely seeing daylight. They had better eyesight, for one thing, and didn't bang their heads on the ceiling, but more than that, as the orcs had found out the hard way, it's very difficult to fight someone when you're hunched double.

Vincent looked about him at their own small and woefully unready army, lacking in everything but enthusiasm, some of them lacking even that and just wanting the headaches to stop so they could go home and get a decent night's sleep. They were no match at all for an army of dwarfs.

"So," said Vincent, "what's the plan?"

"Plan?" snorted Tike. "I thought you lot were the fucking plan! There is no fucking plan! Just try not to die!"

CHAPTER TWENTY-SEVEN

Morning came through the hole in the sky, azure and cloudless, as the desert above them turned into an oven. Down below, Tike was helping Vincent with cooking duties. It seemed that sometime during the night Chaos and Billy Toothless had got bored and gone hunting, the result being crocodile steaks for everyone. Not to mention new boots. No part of the creature was wasted, even the bones being fashioned into crude weapons for those who were unarmed. Flashback had made himself a hat from the crocodile's head.

Vincent had talked to Tike for several hours before they slept and at least had a better idea of what was going on, if not where they were going or what the hell they were going to do when they got there. He was fascinated to learn that many Aborigines were capable of telepathy, and shamed to learn that it had been commonplace before white folks turned up and started slaughtering them all. Tike was saddened but not surprised to see how few had showed up, and how many were unemployed, homeless, or alcoholic. Even now the damage done was far from repaired.

Still, the small army looked a little more robust after a decent breakfast, a little more like they might actually stand a chance. They'd made it this far, after all, and it was remarkable how many of them knew each other without ever having met in person. What had been a ramshackle crew, blindly following the few who seemed to know what was going on, now started to become a more cohesive unit, exchanging ideas and preparing themselves for what lay ahead. Between them they had many skills, and it was time to start putting them to use.

For starters, all the Aborigines present possessed the gift of telepathy to a greater or lesser degree and, despite some speaking different languages, they could all communicate well with each other. Quite a few spoke English, but those who did not, like Balun and Uwan, did not need words. Indeed, now that the headaches were gone, Stone and Flashback were pleased to discover that they could communicate rather more easily if they used their minds instead of their mouths.

"Stupid of me not to think of it before, given how we all got here," said Stone, rather embarrassed. "I've been struggling to remember what little I know of their languages and it seems that we don't need language at all."

"Built in walkie-talkies, this lot," grinned Joker, tapping the side of his head with his finger. "Could come in handy later."

It turned out that about two dozen or so of the Aborigines – the warrior-looking guys who had spoken to Yezzbouzz and seemed to know more about what was going on – were from a nomadic tribe. They knew the land and would lead the way. They would also be able to find water, which, again, would come in very handy. Better still, they had friends coming, a couple of hundred of them from Northern Australia. By all accounts there were three or four thousand dwarfs, so they'd still be outnumbered, but at least it evened up the odds a bit, and with their telepathic abilities it would be easy to set traps and cause diversions, perhaps feign an attack from the north while sneaking in from the south.

While it was important to catch the dwarfs and release Derain, it was also important to have a rough idea of how they were going to achieve that. Where might it be best to set a trap? Where might they gain the advantage? Below ground the dwarfs had the upper hand, but they would have to surface at some point or dig tunnels in order to continue. Tunnels took time, but the dwarfs would be vulnerable above ground. The Australian outback would not be kind to them during daylight hours, not in leather and chain-mail outfits with the desert heat beating down on them.

Flashback and Stone were now able to receive messages from Derain, and they spent the morning in council with the nomads, working out how best to proceed. It was good to see Stone back to himself now that they were safely past the dragon and, for once, Flashback appeared to be relatively sober, treating the nomads with respect. They were deep in discussion for some hours, sometimes without anyone talking, which was rather strange to watch, especially when, as one, they all turned to look at Vincent.

Here we go, thought Vincent, fucking canary duty again. This was the part where they told him he'd be tiptoeing around in the dark, hoping to fuck that his invisibility ring was working. It was amazing what you got used to, how quickly you could adapt if you had no choice but to sink or swim. It's like this, kid: You thought you were joining an outlaw motorcycle club, but instead you're prospecting for a crew that has, quite literally, been around since the Last Supper. Oh, and by the way, your dad's Jesus, your sergeant-at-arms is Saint Christopher, trolls, orcs, faeries, hobgoblins, and wizards are all real, and that ring you're wearing sometimes makes you invisible. Good luck!

That's pretty much how they'd broken all the news to him – although not necessarily in that order – and Vincent had been winging it ever since, always out of his depth, but somehow still not drowning. He could leave whenever he wanted, but the thought never once crossed his mind. And go back to what exactly? Having virtually grown up in their clubhouse he'd spent his whole young life dreaming about joining Aberrant MC, even to the point of running away from home when his mother had moved the two of them to the countryside. Sure, it had turned out to be no ordinary motorcycle club, if there even was such a thing, but they were *his* motorcycle club, *his* destiny.

Besides, where the fuck else was he going to go? It wasn't like he could ever go back to what people considered a normal life; not from here, not after seeing all the weird shit that he'd seen. As Dum Dum's own mother had found out the hard way, people tended to get locked up fairly sharpish when they started talking about how the father of their child was a bridge troll who lived in a magical land, far, far away. Yeah, right. Medication time. Screw that. Vincent would rather be in this asylum than that one any day. The jacket fit better for a start.

And one day that jacket – in Vincent's case a wargskin jacket given to him by an elderly witch called Bertha – would bear the club's full colours, which he would wear with pride, so, no, there was no thought of leaving, no thought of doing anything else with his life. If being a human canary was what it took, then so be it. Hell, apart from the threat of imminent death every other day, it was a lot of fun most of the time. Well, some of the time. Usually after they'd just survived the threat of imminent death. And how else did you get to see a real-live dragon?

The council looked over at him again, and Flashback said something to Stone, who nodded in agreement. Any minute now, thought Vincent. But it felt good to be important, a vital link in the chain, integral to the plan. Who else among them could sneak about unseen behind enemy lines? Stone turned to the others, who also nodded. A decision had been made.

"Prospect!"

"Yes, Flashback!" Vincent grinned a knowing grin to himself as he hurried over. "What can I do for you?"

"Put the kettle on, we'll be here for a couple more hours. And when you're done I want the bat shit cleaning off these boots."

CHAPTER TWENTY-EIGHT

It was raining hard in Mexico City, giant, dirty raindrops bouncing up from the pavement and into the running stream of the gutters, which Dum Dum could really have done without stepping in. Not that he wasn't soaked to the skin already, but after many, many hours crammed into a seat the size of a postage stamp it was possible that he was reaching the end of his usually limitless sense of humour. Travelling, he'd decided, was largely crap.

Thankfully, the current monsoon had held off long enough for the pilot to bounce the little plane to a halt in a field that had been recently emptied of cows, if not cow shit, but the dark grey skies broke before they reached the waiting car, not fifty feet away, and the heavens had opened with biblical force. From there they'd driven for over two hours with the windows steaming up and the rain beating down, a constant drumroll on the roof of the car to accompany the irritating squeaking of the windscreen wipers.

The car was too small, some ancient Italian thing, perhaps even less comfortable than the plane, and it clunked heavily through potholes, the suspension ready to collapse at any moment. The driver had a Jesus tattoo on his arm and probably would have driven with more care if he'd noticed that the bloke in the backseat was completely bone dry. Instead he aimed the protesting vehicle at non-existent gaps in the heavy traffic, while Dum Dum jammed his foot into the floorwell on the passenger side, heavy on the imaginary brake.

To make matters worse, Dum Dum wasn't entirely convinced that the driver wasn't lost and driving aimlessly, if far too rapidly, through the same run-down streets over and over again. Surely no city could have this much ghetto? Finally they'd screeched to a halt outside one of the sketchiest looking bars Dum Dum had ever seen, and, tired, soggy, aching from head to foot, and, despite himself, leaning increasingly towards grumpy, he'd stepped straight into a huge puddle.

"Oh for fuck's..." he swore. "I hope they've got some decent food in this place."

They didn't have decent food; they didn't have any food at all, unless you were Billy Toothless and enjoyed a good cockroach every now and again, but since he wasn't here, Dum Dum settled for a beer that tasted, against all probability, like cleaning fluid. Everything else in the bar was filthy, or would be if it were visible under the dull twinkle of Christmas lights from about 1972 that hung from the ceiling, an electrical fire waiting to happen.

"Well, I did say 'off the radar'," noted Mad John, as they found themselves a corner booth.

"More like off the map," said Dum Dum huffily.

To be fair, Aberrant MC had made no secret of the fact that they were a nomad chapter, claiming no territory and growing no roots. It's just that Dum Dum hadn't expected them to be quite so, well, quite so nomadic. His time as a prospect for the club had been spent almost entirely in London, where they'd had a clubhouse for twenty-something years, and despite the NFA on their bottom rocker – meaning No Fixed Abode – it seemed as if they were fairly settled in their ways. Numb Tongue ran a mixed martial arts gym; Billy Toothless made driving aids for the disabled; Joker was married... Half of them had jobs and businesses, wives and girlfriends, responsibilities and shit to take care of. Well, maybe not many responsibilities, but certainly shit to take care of. And, true, some of the club would disappear for months on end, travelling far and wide, but they always came back to the clubhouse eventually, always treated it as home.

That had all changed when Mad John showed up after his five-year absence. Within months of his return the clubhouse was abandoned – boarded up and protected by powerful spells – and Aberrant MC were on the move. After a long and dangerous journey – during which Dum Dum had finally got his full colours – they'd wound up in Berlin where they'd stayed long enough that Dum Dum's hopes grew high that they might find a new clubhouse. Instead they were in a dodgy bar in Mexico waiting for a bloke to bring them forged passports, while the rest of the club were thousands of miles away following a bunch of dwarfs across Australia. They were getting some air miles, that was for sure.

It wasn't that Dum Dum wouldn't follow them to the ends of the earth, it was more that he wished it wasn't so damn far and with such uncomfortable seating. He'd follow them to hell and back if he had to, but he'd really rather not; he'd rather they were back at the clubhouse drinking a few beers and having a laugh. The beer in this place was horrible and no one was laughing. And Dum Dum's bottom was wet.

"I did warn you," said Mad John, always able to read him like an open book.

"You did," nodded Dum Dum. "I'm just tired is all."

Mad John had warned him that he might start getting homesick after a while, which was stupid really since he'd never had much of a home to feel sick for, unless you counted Her Majesty's accommodation. According to Mad John it was partly due to the fact that his dad was a bridge troll: Trolls were not, by nature, prone to wandering too far once they found a nice bridge to live under – or in the case of cave trolls a suitably sized cave – and to this day there were relatively few of their kind outside of Norway, where they were said to have originated. On top of that Dum Dum had spent most of his life in prison and had grown accustomed to it. Institutionalised, they called it. He was used to having his little space, his routines, and when it had suddenly become a huge space, with no routines, he'd found it at times rather overwhelming, almost like he had too much freedom, too many options.

Then again, his mother had been human, and obviously something of a free spirit given that she'd slept with a bridge troll, so it wasn't like he'd never been outdoors. He remembered her taking him to hippy communes when he was young and when she wasn't in a mental hospital. And since she'd frequently kidnapped him from foster homes in order to do so, they'd spent quite a lot of time on the run.

Just as likely he was thinking too much on a tired mind. And the truth was that he hadn't exactly been one of life's great thinkers before he joined Aberrant MC, so he wasn't really used to it. He'd relied on his size to get by and, aside from spending most of that life behind bars, it had worked out all right for the most part. Certainly, he hadn't been afraid to drop his soap in the shower. Since meeting Aberrant, however – specifically Mad John – Dum Dum's horizons had been considerably broadened, and he wasn't always sure how to deal with it. He just had to get used to it; he certainly didn't want to spend his life locked up and missing all that it had to offer. Thinking may lead to overthinking, which, frankly, made his brain hurt, but it was better than not really thinking at all. Besides, he enjoyed flexing a little mental muscle now that he actually had some.

And then it suddenly dawned on Dum Dum why he was feeling so out of sorts. It wasn't that he was homesick, or tired, or overthinking everything, it was, well... He didn't really want to admit it, but it was this lot. With the rest of the Aberrant crew there was always someone to talk to, someone to have a bit of a laugh with. Numb Tongue and Snot, while he cared for them both dearly, were neither. And Mad John was...different. Friend, mentor, saviour even, but at times very distant, like he had the weight of the world on his shoulders and he'd drop it if you bothered him.

Outside the rain kept pouring, while inside they waited in silence. Some days were just like that. Some days you just had a wet bottom.

CHAPTER TWENTY-NINE

"**Y**' gunner reet tha'?"

"Pardon?"

"Oi sed, 'y' gunner reet tha'?"

"I know," said Vincent. "I just don't know what it means."

"Tha'," Billy gestured.

"Oh," said Vincent, his mind finally joining the dots. "No, I'm not going to eat that. Knock yourself out."

Or indeed poison yourself, thought Vincent, given that the delicacy in question was a bright orange centipede about the size of his arm. He'd been backing slowly away from it, hoping that despite its many legs it wasn't a fast runner, but it wouldn't be the last deadly creepy-crawly to find itself giving Billy Toothless little more than mild indigestion. It really was quite amazing what hobgoblins could eat; disgusting, but nonetheless amazing. And never with any sign that it was anything less than delicious, especially when garnished with belly button fluff, snot, or earwax. He even had his own recipe for toenail soup. A bright orange centipede stood no chance.

And revolting though he was, it had to be said that Billy Toothless was the only one not going hungry. The nomadic Aborigines, of course, could find food and water, their people having survived in one of the harshest environments on earth for hundreds of thousands of years. But they were not used to feeding so many, and resources were scarce.

They had walked for many more miles underground, mostly in darkness but for the light of the torches, which occasionally revealed stalagmites and stalactites, like jagged teeth in some giant's mouth. The thought crossed Vincent's mind for a moment, but he dismissed it as foolish; it wasn't like anyone was keeping their voices down so as not to wake the sleeping giant, and even those who were silent were engaged in their own private conversations, of which Vincent found himself envious.

"You're not missing much," Tike told him. "Gave me a rotten fucking headache."

It turned out that Tike had been aware of his own telepathic abilities, but only insofar as he could communicate with his grandmother who lived in the same village, no more than a mile away. No one else in his family shared their abilities, so it had come as something of a shock – not to mention a blinding headache – when he'd picked up Derain's distress signal, particularly since he'd no idea who Derain was.

"Well, I say 'picked up'," explained Tike, "but it was more like getting hit around the head with a fucking mallet! I honestly don't see the point of a signal so strong that it fucking floors you, but I suppose he was trying to reach as far as possible. Pretty amazing that your guys picked it up from so far away."

It was nothing less than astonishing, agreed Vincent, but then it was fair to say that Vincent never stopped being astonished by what some of them could do or, indeed, who some of them were. It wasn't something you got used to easily, being in the company of... these people. Vincent dared not even think of it sometimes for fear that it was all some wild hallucination or, worse still, that he had gone completely insane. And it wasn't something you could tell anyone else about, for obvious reasons. "Hi, my name's Vincent, and my dad's Jesus." Vincent didn't believe it himself sometimes. Most of the fucking time, frankly.

Zig Zag had finally taken his crash helmet off – although not before everyone had been warned – but, all things considered, even an orc wasn't the most unusual member of Aberrant MC.

Eventually the ground had started to rise quite steeply, and they marched on heavy legs until at last the caves ended, and there, up ahead, was the bright glare of daylight. The mouth of the cave emerged from the side of an arid, grey stone mountain, into parched and seemingly barren desert. It was mid-afternoon, the fierce sun beating down from up high, so they would wait until it was falling before moving on. Billy Toothless jabbed the unfortunate centipede with a pointed stick, removing its head with one satisfied bite.

Vincent had learned to make the most of any rest he could get. Soon enough they would have to press on into the unforgiving desert if they wanted to catch the dwarfs, who were apparently still below ground and taking a different route. Understandably the dwarfs were avoiding the surface at all costs, although not just because it was too hot during the day, but because it was impossible for Derain to send anyone his coordinates if he couldn't see the stars. It was uncertain if the dwarfs had figured out that that was what he was doing, but he'd been blindfolded for some time, his hands bound behind his back. Either way, the dwarfs could do very little about Derain's capabilities as a human GPS beyond keeping him unconscious, which they were not doing at the moment.

So far, that was all they really knew for sure. It would've helped if Derain spoke Dwarfish, but even then it would have been of limited use. Aside from Stone and Flashback, only a few of their small army – mostly the nomads – could understand Derain's messages, and to the rest it was so much white noise. Those who'd even been aware of their abilities were used, like Tike, to communicating no more than a few miles, and this, by all accounts, was positively deafening, but from a far greater distance.

"We can only really talk to each other when he's asleep," said Tike. "The rest of the time it's too loud and you have to try and block it out."

When the sun began to set they moved on, but after a few hours their pace was slowed by those who were either too old or too unfit to keep up, and the party became spread out. The nomads could keep this pace – and faster – all day, but just as many people were struggling and would be in no fit state to fight an army of dwarfs, if and when they ever caught them. On the plus side, the dwarfs would almost certainly have to come above ground at some point, which they'd be ill-equipped to deal with, and which would quite likely deplete their numbers. But unfortunately those numbers were quite considerable, perhaps as many as four thousand. As Mental had put it: "Even if half the beardy little buggers die of dehydration there'll still be a fucking handful."

For hours they walked into the chill night, but for each hour they walked so the line became longer and thinner. Occasionally someone would lose their footing in the darkness, trip and fall, or twist an ankle, until finally they came to a halt, waiting for people to catch up. When they moved on, they changed direction, turning left, or possibly west. Not knowing Orion from Uranus, Vincent could only guess.

"What's going on?" he asked Tike.

"Change of plan. There's water not too far from here."

"There is?"

"Apparently," Tike nodded. "It's a bit of a detour, gonna cost us a few hours, but we should be able to make it up later."

Vincent looked around him, and behind at the long line of stragglers, already falling behind again and near total exhaustion. They looked more like marathon runners completing their last few yards on jelly legs than an army ready to take on four thousand dwarfs. One or two were helping each other to walk.

"How the fuck are we gonna do that?" said Vincent. "No offence, mate, but some of this lot aren't going to be 'making it up later'."

"That's why we're leaving them behind," announced Tike. "One of the guys who knows the land is gonna stay with 'em, make sure they're okay, but we'll be faster without them, might have a better chance of catching these dwarf assholes. Trouble is, there'll be quite a few less of us when we get there."

"How many?"

Tike shrugged, like an ill-fitting suit on a hanger: "Three hundred."

"Sparta!" Vincent let out a hollow laugh.

"What's that?"

"Oh nothing," said Vincent. "Some crappy movie about three hundred Spartans taking on a fuckload of Persians in their underpants."

"Never seen it," said Tike. "Did they win?"

"No."

CHAPTER THIRTY

"Sir."

It was to be expected that at least one of them would get pulled apart at customs. You couldn't put Numb Tongue and Dum Dum on the same flight – or even in the same room – without attracting nervous attention, and neither one of them was easily forgotten. People who didn't know them tended to vacate said room quite rapidly, if it wasn't flying at 37,000 feet above the Pacific Ocean. Since there was no way of hiding them it had been decided that they travel together, sticking to the same cover story they'd used to get into the US, that they were actors travelling for work. The correct visas had been arranged.

"Sir!"

Numb Tongue carried on walking, a determined look on his heavily scarred face, but you could only ignore the 'sirs' for so long before it became obvious that you were doing it deliberately in the hope that they'd go away. This bloke obviously wasn't going to go away.

"Sir!"

For fuck's sake! His passport was stamped, he had his luggage, he could see the exit! Just keep walking...

"Sir!" The voice was more urgent.

Numb Tongue stopped and swore under his breath. He was not a man who was used to people stopping him from going about his business, and he was already in a dangerous mood, it being difficult to answer stupid questions from customs officials about whether or not you were carrying products made of wood when you could just as easily bite the man's nose off and spit it in his face.

"Sir!" The man – a customs official of some sort – had caught up with Numb Tongue, but his approach was tentative now that Numb Tongue had stopped. He was a big fella, after all, and as menacing as a junkyard dog with no leash. Except that a dog might bark before it bit you.

"Sorry to er...." the man blustered. "Don't I know you from somewhere?"

Numb Tongue shook his head. He was a man of very few words and a great many scars.

"Yeah, I know I've seen you somewhere," the man insisted. "Now, don't tell me."

Numb Tongue wasn't about to tell him. Numb Tongue was about to apply pressure to a point on his neck, rendering him unconscious. And not because the man might well have seen him on America's Most Wanted and would alert the authorities the moment it dawned on him, but simply because he was in Numb Tongue's way, and Numb Tongue didn't like people being in his way. Besides, it wasn't like he could be mistaken for anyone else. It wasn't every day that you encountered a man who was over seven feet tall, with a face like a kitchen chopping board. It was not a face that people forgot in a hurry, no matter how hard they tried.

"It's on the tip of my tongue," persisted the man, blissfully dotting the i's and crossing the t's on his own death warrant.

Thankfully, Dum Dum chose this precise moment to show up and blunder into the very one-sided conversation.

"Cabs are out that way," he said.

"Game Of Thrones! That's it!"

"What?" said Dum Dum, apparently noticing the customs man for the first time.

"Game Of Thrones," repeated the man. "I was just telling your mate here that I knew him from somewhere. You *are* actors, right?"

Moments later the pair of them had signed autographs for the hapless customs official and reluctantly had their pictures taken. He'd be disappointed when he went online later and couldn't find either of them, but not nearly as disappointed as if he'd woken up bound and gagged in the trunk of a car in long-term parking. And although Dum Dum had been lying when he said he'd had a part in The Lord Of The Rings, he wasn't lying when he said he was a bridge troll. The customs man wished them a pleasant trip.

At least Mad John was safely through customs, that was the main thing. Dum Dum had seen him collect his bag from the carousel and leave the airport, his suit, tie, and cover story telling of a mining consultant here in Perth on business. Ironically, after all the worry about getting Numb Tongue and Dum Dum into the country, it was Snot who'd had the most hassle so far, and that was before they'd even left Mexico City.

They'd waited a long time in the dim and dirty bar, switching to tequila because the beer was so foul, and for the most part drinking in silence until, eventually, a Mexican man named Jose showed up with their documents. He apologised profusely for being late, but he had been thorough in his work and seemed to know exactly who he was dealing with. Along with new passports there were visas, official papers, phone numbers, and hotel details, and from the bar Jose drove them to a different part of town for a change of clothing.

It was late when they checked into the airport hotel and early when they checked out, sunrise on another dark and cloudy day. There was only a small line for check-in. Unfortunately, when Snot got to the front of it, there were immediately problems.

"Uh, hold on a second Miss Farman," said the man behind the counter, reaching for his phone. "It seems you've come up on the no-fly list, er, I... Let me just make a quick call."

The man explained the situation and listened to the reply. He looked at Snot.

"Yes, I'm sure she's female," he said into the phone. "No, of course I haven't checked!"

There could, in fact, be no doubt whatsoever that Snot was female. Now in a knee-length floral dress and flats instead of a track suit and stripper heels, her long, black hair pulled back in a ponytail, she looked as dainty as a daisy, and quite astonishingly pretty. Still, this didn't stop her from being detained at gunpoint for nearly an hour because her name was similar to that of a known terrorist. This despite the fact that the real terrorist was a man, and was unlikely to be using his real name if he was attempting to board a plane. Obviously it was a mistake, pure coincidence, but it put Snot's fake passport through extra scrutiny that they could have done without. Thankfully, Jose had done his work very well.

Numb Tongue and Dum Dum stuffed themselves into a cab and headed for their hotel, a place called The Northbridge about twenty-five minutes away, where they found that Mad John and Snot had already checked in and adjourned the adjoining bar. They pulled up chairs and attracted the attention of a waitress.

"Ah, gentlemen," Mad John smiled. "You made it. What are your thoughts?"

"My thoughts are that I'm fucking starving," replied Dum Dum, turning the menu over in the hopes of finding another page of food. "Is this the only menu?"

"With the best will in the world, Dum Dum, you are far from starving," said Mad John. "But I'm sure we'll all think better on full stomachs."

Built in 1898, the Northbridge was a modestly sized hotel, just forty-eight rooms, with an ornate balcony running along the outside, overlooking a busy street. It was not even midday, but the bar and restaurant were starting to fill up, a warm breeze blowing in through the open doors as people enjoyed a late breakfast or an early lunch. On the other side of the room were glass doors leading to the lobby and reception area, a long wooden desk facing two comfortable looking sofas, and a table littered with tourist brochures. Beyond that was the lift up to the rooms, and opposite that a gold ornament in a glass display case.

The waitress cheerily went through the specials and took their orders, happy in her work. It was nice here, relaxed and mellow, carefree. Their drinks arrived quickly and with another warm and friendly smile. The food was excellent.

"So," said Mad John, when they had finished eating. "How exactly are we going to rob this place?"

CHAPTER THIRTY-ONE

The fire alarm sounded at precisely 4:01am, but it took a few minutes and cries of "Fire!" before the guests emerged from their rooms, bleary-eyed and confused. Thick smoke was already filling the hallway.

"This way! This way!" urged a calm voice in the murky haze. "Take the stairs. Carefully now, don't run."

Visibility was down to nothing in the lobby, and as the guests groped their way down the stairs they were surprised but nonetheless relieved to find Dum Dum coming the other way to lend a hand. It was remarkable how, in times of emergency such as this, a very large biker was suddenly a welcome sight and not a horrid thug after all. Dum Dum even carried one elderly gentleman who was lagging behind, gently depositing him on the pavement, where another gigantic biker kindly helped him out of harm's way. Dum Dum had then bravely run back into the smoking building, only to emerge five minutes later, coughing and spluttering, all but dragging Mad John, who was barefoot, wearing just his suit trousers and a crumpled white shirt.

"I think there's someone still in there," Mad John gasped, and again Dum Dum dashed into the building.

Soon enough there were fire engines, all gleaming red and chrome, their flashing lights casting over a cluster of dishevelled looking hotel guests. Dum Dum and one of the hotel staff had been the last out, bringing with them a Miss Farman, who had apparently managed to sleep through the alarm.

Still there was no sign of any fire, no bright flames flicking from any windows, but anything past the front door was wrapped in a blanket of smoke. It would be nearly an hour before the fire department determined that there was, in fact, no fire, and, surprisingly, a further two hours before anyone noticed that the gold ornament in the lobby was missing from its display case.

Of course, questions would be asked and statements would be taken, but the question most asked would be, "Why would anyone go to so much trouble to steal a plaster replica of a gold nugget from a hotel lobby?" Dum Dum had asked the same question of the police officer who'd knocked on his door the following morning.

"Hell if I know," shrugged the cop. "Everyone knows it's a bloody replica, says so on the case. You don't mind if I, er..." The cop looked a little embarrassed as he nodded towards Dum Dum's room.

"No, go ahead," Dum Dum waved him in.

The cop poked about a bit, but without much enthusiasm. If you were going to go to that much bother to steal something, replica or not, you probably wouldn't just stick it in the drawer of your hotel room. Besides, Dum Dum was something of a hero, running several times into what he thought was a burning building to rescue others.

"I feel a bit stupid really," Dum Dum told the cop, "what with there being no fire. They told me someone let a smoke bomb off in the lift."

"Yeah, brave all the same," acknowledged the cop. "Between you and me, we reckon it was college prank or something that got a bit out of hand. Either that or we're dealing with idiots. The thing's basically worthless."

The cop took another cursory glance around Dum Dum's room. "Well, sorry to have bothered you. Here's my card in case you remember anything that you think might be important."

"I will," promised Dum Dum, closing the door and throwing the card in the bin, smiling to himself as he heard the cop knock on the next door along. And then he went downstairs for a hearty breakfast.

By ten-thirty the four of them had checked out of the hotel and were heading north in a nice air-conditioned van. No one at the hotel had seemed remotely suspicious, and the waitress even made jokes about 'the crime of the century'. In the back of the van sat a large gold nugget wrapped in a hotel blanket. Crime of the century, indeed. They'd even given Dum Dum his breakfast for free.

At 4am Snot had called the lift up to the top floor and dropped in a couple of smoke grenades, the ingredients for which had been picked up that afternoon from various stores. Numb Tongue, meanwhile, was down in the lobby summoning said lift. Given that he and Dum Dum were so conspicuous – not to mention the obvious suspects – it was thought best to keep Numb Tongue out of the picture as much as possible and leave the heroics to Dum Dum.

In broad daylight Numb Tongue frightened the crap out of pretty much everyone, with the curious exception of little old ladies, who thought he was a good listener. Looming out of the smoky gloom he would be absolutely terrifying, so as soon as the lift door opened, smoke billowing out into the lobby, he'd alerted a member of staff and left the building to wait outside. People would remember him being outside the whole time. "Yes, officer, the tall bloke with a face like a blind cobbler's thumb..."

Dum Dum, on the other hand, while equally unforgettable, had a more genial approach, like a bouncy castle come to the rescue. Sure, he was big and scary, but he was in many ways a gentle giant, and certainly a reassuring sight when you think the hotel is on fire, particularly when Mad John's calm and kindly voice had already guided you towards him.

On top of that, Dum Dum was rather better at dealing with the police than Numb Tongue, who generally reserved his right to remain violent. Doubtless they'd want to ask a few questions, and Dum Dum could bullshit the cops all day, make them laugh. He was good at that. Numb Tongue, in fairness, was getting better at not beating the shit out of them. But only because he tried really hard. Yes, best if he waited outside in plain sight.

When Dum Dum ran 'heroically' back into the hotel, he felt his way around in the smoke until he found the display case, smashing the glass with a gloved hand and grabbing the gold nugget. He then made his way to the top floor, where he and Mad John lowered Snot – aka Miss Farman – and the gold out of the window to a waiting van. Then he 'rescued' Mad John, before dashing back one last time to pull Snot back up and save her, too.

Quite the hero, indeed.

Dum Dum politely declined an interview with a local TV station, saying that he didn't want to appear foolish, what with there being no fire. He was getting rather adept at playing the fool – big, thick Dum Dum – but where once it had been because, frankly, he *was* a bit thick, more and more these days he found himself playing a part. Fool, eh? They'd just pulled off one of the biggest robberies in history and it was being dismissed as a prank!

When it was discovered on Thursday the 15th of January, 1931, The Golden Eagle Nugget was the largest of its kind ever to be found in Western

Australia and it had caused a national sensation. It remained one of the largest solid masses of gold ever found on earth. Today, even melted down, it would be worth over a million dollars. Intact it would be priceless. Certainly it had felt heavy, maybe 70lbs, when Dum Dum lifted it from the glass display case, and Snot had struggled getting it into the van after they'd lowered her to the ground.

The sun was bright and warm, not a cloud in the sky, as the van cruised along smooth highways. Dum Dum leaned forward and put the radio on, and of all the random things it could have offered it gave them a tune called *Get A Bloomin' Move On*, better known as *The Self Preservation Society* from The Italian Job. Even Numb Tongue smiled, although he was still a long way from singing along with Dum Dum. It made robberies so much easier when people thought you were stealing a plaster replica.

They went thataway!

CHAPTER THIRTY-TWO

Something like seventy per cent of Australia is desert, and Vincent felt like they must have walked across at least half of it, although he knew that in reality it was probably no more than twenty miles at most, perhaps five miles since they'd changed direction. It all looked the same, just mile after mile of sand and rocks and spiky things, and yet somehow their nomadic guides seemed to know the land like the backs of their hands, able to navigate this barren land with ease, always finding water where there seemed to be none. Without them they would all be wandering in circles and facing certain death, of that much Vincent was sure. As it was, they walked on near empty stomachs, even Billy Toothless struggling to find anything edible beyond the occasional beetle. This wasn't just a hostile environment, it was hateful and vindictive and downright spiteful!

But still, by all accounts they were making good time, slowly creeping up on the dwarfs, slowly making progress. Thanks to his telepathic abilities Tike was rather better informed than Vincent, who, as usual, was told next to nothing by the club. Well, Joker had tried to tell him to watch out for drop bears – so called because they'd drop out of a tree and land on your head – but of all the unpleasant things lurking out there, that was not one of them. There weren't any trees, for one thing. Instead it was Tike who kept Vincent up to date with whatever titbits he'd picked up from the others.

"They're above ground," he told Vincent sometime during the night. "They've still got him blindfolded, but they're definitely above ground. They've stopped for a rest. Sounds like there's been some arguing going on."

"And you can hear that?"

"Oh no," said Tike. "It's still just a bunch of noise to me, but some of the guys are in touch with this Derain fella. He says the dwarfs have been bickering, but he doesn't speak Dwarfish so we don't know what they're pissed about."

"Probably got blisters from all this walking," complained Vincent. "My feet are fucking killing me."

"Yeah, me too," said Tike. "I think we're stopping for a break soon, too."

Sure enough the party had come to a halt, and small fires were built to cook what little food was left. At least here there were desert shrubs of some kind, predictably spiky and vicious, but nonetheless flammable. It was a shame they weren't also edible, but more importantly there was water, a thin running stream that came out through a crack in the earth and was above ground for no more than six inches. Water where there seemed to be none. And there were tall rocks – if not enough for all of them – that would provide some protection from the murderous heat when daylight came.

Having waited his turn and refilled his two plastic water bottles, Vincent sat himself down beside one of the rocks, grateful to take the weight off his legs. He was tempted to take his boots off, but wary in case he couldn't get them back on again. He knew there were big blisters on both heels.

"I wouldn't get too settled if I was you, mate," Tike warned. "Looks like we're just stopping for a couple of hours before we leave the others behind. Here, put some of this on your lips."

The pair sat in silence for a moment, Vincent picking something thorny out of his backside and hoping it wasn't poisonous or turned out to be some sort of venomous stick insect. He didn't trust anything not to bite him. Including the rock.

"So this gang of yours..." began Tike, clearly with something on his mind as he gestured to Vincent's prospect patch.

"Club," corrected Vincent, dabbing ointment on his dry lips.

"This club of yours, they're bikies, are they?"

"Yeah," Vincent nodded. "Except they're called bikers in England, not bikies. Bikies sounds a bit silly."

"No offence, mate, but your lot wouldn't last five minutes against the bikies we've got over here."

"Have they got a bridge troll?"

"Have you?"

"Yeah," grinned Vincent, rather proud of the fact. "He's six foot eight and he can bench-press a Harley. And I wouldn't let him hear you say that when he gets here, if I was you."

"No offence," repeated Tike, in the manner of one who has just caused it.

To be fair, Vincent could see his point; some of the club didn't exactly look match-fit, and unless you knew that Flashback, for instance, was a powerful wizard, you'd think him to be little more than a drunken acid casualty. Stone, too, with his dreads and half-asleep eyes, resembled something that might have just crawled out of a tent at Woodstock, perhaps unaware that the sixties had come to an end some time ago. But while it was true that he was no fighter, he was a supremely capable chemist, with a penchant for dosing his foes with concoctions of his own making that would make them weep like children. Or bark like dogs, depending on his mood and how much said foes had pissed him off. And some of that shit wasn't going to wear off until you asked him really nicely for an antidote.

Violence wasn't always the first option for Aberrant MC, but when it had to be, there was Numb Tongue. He was sergeant-at-arms for a reason, a black belt in just about every form of unarmed combat known to man, and owner of his own mixed martial arts gym. Smiler, Mental, and, of course, Zig Zag and Dum Dum, were all pretty tasty in a brawl – particularly the orc and the bridge troll – but anything they had learned about the true art of fighting they had learned from Numb Tongue, the master.

"It's okay," said Vincent. "Some of them can get a bit tetchy if you disrespect the club. I'm probably supposed to have punched you or something, but I'm too fucking tired."

"Sorry," said Tike. "I didn't mean anything by it. Fucking bridge troll, eh? That's mad, that is! I never even knew they existed!"

"Me neither until last year," admitted Vincent. "And it came as a bit of a shock the first time Zig Zag took his helmet off, I can tell you. Believe me, you don't want to get on the wrong side of him. He might be small, but he's hard as fucking nails."

"He's the orc, right?"

"Yeah. Well, half dwarf, half orc, but it's recommended that you stick with orc. He doesn't really like dwarfs much."

"Came to the right fucking place then, eh?" Tike laughed.

"To be fair, he doesn't really like anyone much," Vincent added with a smile. "But he's a good bloke once you get to know him."

Calling Zig Zag 'a good bloke' was probably stretching things somewhat, but it wasn't like he was a bad bloke, all things considered, just different. And best kept at arm's length unless you didn't particularly like your arm.

"They all seem like good blokes," acknowledged Tike.

Again, good was relative; at least half of the club enjoyed a good brawl, but they'd never actually start one, and while they were frequently on the wrong side of the law – they were an outlaw club, after all – there was rarely a victim when they broke those laws, paedophiles notwithstanding. Most who encountered them tended to think of them as bad boys and good people. Even Zig Zag.

They sat in silence for a while longer, the fire crackling and spitting sparks. Even the campfire was fucking hostile, but daylight was breaking, the sky a deep, bruised blue-purple, and soon a fire would be the last thing they needed.

"So, this club of yours," Tike cautiously ventured further. "What have you gotta do to get in?"

Just then there was the familiar cry of "Prospect!" from somewhere in the semi-darkness. Flashback was calling.

"That!" sighed Vincent, clambering wearily to his feet. "I hope he's got a fucking rabbit!"

Flashback didn't have a rabbit, but at least this time he didn't want any bat shit cleaned off his boots. Vincent found him with Mental and Chaos and a couple of the nomads, crouched low on a sand dune that looked over yet more desert, the light of morning coming fast. Chaos was peering into a pair of binoculars, and there, not five hundred feet away, was the unmistakable glow of a campfire.

"What is it?" Vincent whispered.

"It's a fire."

"I can see that. Whose is it?"

"A dwarf."

"A dwarf? What, just one?"

"Far as I can see," said Chaos.

"I thought we were still miles behind them. What's he doing out here in the middle of nowhere?"

"Don't know," said Flashback. "It could be a trap. Quite possibly a trap. That's what you're going to find out. Off you go!"

CHAPTER THIRTY-THREE

There were times, thought Vincent, as the dwarf wildly swung a heavy battle-axe at his kneecap, when it would be nice to know in advance if his invisibility ring was working or not. It was working now, obviously, because he'd just come within inches of becoming an amputee, but, nonetheless, it would have been nice to know that it wasn't working before. Vincent took a few hasty steps backwards, and, cursing aloud, the dwarf swung again, this time at nothing.

"Cut that out!" yelled Vincent.

This time the dwarf jabbed his axe in Vincent's general direction, attempting to cover a wide area with the weapon rather than aim it directly at him. Vincent moved again.

"I said, cut that out!"

The dwarf spun on his heels, eyes darting left and right. He spoke in Dwarfish, possibly still swearing quite profusely, although to be fair much of the language sounded like profanities. There was fear in the dwarf's eyes, and now that Vincent got a proper look at him he looked exhausted, barely able to hold the heavy axe. Unfortunately, the sight of this caused Vincent to reappear, and the dwarf charged!

The funny thing was that as an adolescent Vincent had always thought that he was a naturally gifted shoplifter; he had no idea that his fear of getting caught was the very thing keeping him from getting caught. Likewise, when Vincent kept getting knocked off his bike he'd assumed that he was just really unlucky, rather than considering that his ring might have rendered him invisible because he was in danger. Hell, he hadn't even been aware of the damn thing – slipped onto his finger when he was eleven years old – until he was twenty-one, and nine months into prospecting for Aberrant.

Since then he had learned to control it, to a degree, or at least use it to his advantage, but he still never knew for sure whether it was working or not. It wasn't like in the movies where everything went all fuzzy and this or that character vanished, he simply had to hope for the best. Which was something of a problem when an angry dwarf was coming at you with an axe.

Vincent stepped neatly aside, backing away a few paces, and the dwarf stopped in his tracks, swinging blindly at the air. He was definitely swearing; Vincent thought he recognised one of the words, and had a vague idea that it rhymed with punt. The trouble was that the dwarf was more scared of Vincent than Vincent was of him, which was making it difficult to stay invisible. Catch-22: the dwarf would lunge at him and Vincent would disappear and get out of the way, only to reappear moments later because he wasn't in danger anymore. And as his confidence grew, so Vincent stayed visible for longer. The dwarf simply wasn't very scary – especially all alone out here in the desert – and fear was another key to how the ring worked, perceived danger as much as real danger. Vincent wasn't remotely afraid. Whatever this was, it was no trap.

The dwarf attacked twice more under the rising sun before giving up and taking a defensive stance, the axe clearly growing heavier by the minute. Vincent raised his hands, a placatory gesture to show that he was unarmed. The dwarf was uneasy, still muttering and cursing, but for the first time he didn't try to hack off any of Vincent's limbs.

"That's it, calm down," Vincent said gently. "I'm not going to hurt you."

The dwarf swore at him again.

"Do you speak English?"

More swearing.

"That'll be a no, then."

Vincent had to admit to himself that he hadn't really thought this part through. At first he had intended only to creep as near to the dwarf as necessary to report back to the others, but, realising that it wasn't a trap, he had then strayed a little too close, assuming that he couldn't be seen when in fact he was clearly visible. It was foolish and he should have known better. Hell, it wasn't just foolish, it was Cartman crawling butt naked across the school stage in South Park, thinking he was wearing an invisibility cloak! He may as well have been accompanied by a brass band! But what was done was done, and now he just had to figure out what to do next, knowing as he did so that Chaos was watching through his binoculars, and would give a brutally honest critique when he got back. Typically, they hadn't given him any instructions beyond, "Go and see if it's a trap."

Behind long hair and an unkempt beard, the dwarf's eyes were tired and afraid. His forehead and the end of his nose were horribly sunburned, and his lips were cracked and dry. He looked near to collapsing, but nonetheless ready to go down swinging, even if that wouldn't be very far, perhaps a little over four feet.

Vincent tried to recall what little Dwarfish he had learned in Grun Mar, but like most people learning the basics of a new language in a bar, he'd only picked up a few phrases, most of them useless or downright offensive. "Can I have large beer, please?" wasn't going to be much use, but it was better than, "Your mother's beard has many sheep ticks," which Vincent had been assured was among the most insulting things you could ever say to a dwarf, and was guaranteed to start a fight. It was then that it occurred to him that he may, in fact, be dealing with a lady dwarf.

"Vincent," he said, tapping his chest. "Vin-cent."

"Feenat," the dwarf said warily. The axe was still raised – the weapon slightly taller than the dwarf – but his or her manner had become less hostile, especially now that Vincent had stopped disappearing, which even he had to admit must be disconcerting.

"Are you thirsty?" he asked, miming the action of drinking. "Thirsty?"

He reached with deliberate caution into his jacket pocket and pulled out a water bottle, tossing it to the ground in front of Feenat. Thirst overcame suspicion and the axe was lowered if not discarded. Feenat seemed perplexed by the plastic bottle, but drank greedily and gratefully. He – or possibly she – offered the bottle back to Vincent who gestured for him – or her – to continue drinking. Soon the bottle was empty and the dwarf said something that Vincent took to be "Thank you."

Vincent looked about him, as if to take in the vastness of the desert. The sun was rising fast and already the heat of the desert was coming. The sense of emptiness was omnipresent, and with it the knowledge that death was a certainty if you didn't know what you were doing. Even vultures didn't live in Australia, but there was plenty more out here to worry about. Shit, there were spiders in Australia that were nearly as big as the dwarf, not to mention snakes, scorpions, centipedes, poisonous ants, and, should they ever get near the coast, sharks, jellyfish, and the blue-ringed octopus, one of the most toxic sea creatures on the planet. Alone and without water, Feenat would be lucky to see the end of the day. Sunburn would be the least of his or her problems.

On the plus side, leaving Feenat here would mean one less dwarf to fight – one down, three thousand nine hundred and ninety-nine to go – but somehow that seemed terribly cruel, just walking away knowing that the dwarf would die. It wasn't the Aberrant way; you had to have actually done something to deserve it. And what if this wasn't one of the baddie dwarfs? Certainly, if this was some sort of trap then it was about as effective as a chocolate frying pan.

"You hungry?" Vincent made the appropriate motions. "Hungry?"

Feenat nodded, still cautious. Now that Vincent had stopped with the disappearing act he was far from threatening – twenty-two going on seventeen and build like a coat hanger – but, as far as Feenat was concerned he could do magic, which probably made him a wizard. And, technically, Vincent could do magic, he just didn't know how to control it very well.

"Hungry?" Vincent repeated, gesturing for the dwarf to follow him.

Feenat hesitated, but what else was there to do? Where else was there to go? In truth, the dwarf had been lost and wandering for three days, barely surviving and lucky to last this long. The water was all gone, those last drops dripping from the flask long before Vincent had showed up.

"Come on," encouraged Vincent. "Come with me."

Finally Feenat relented, and Vincent turned to lead the way. He stopped and looked about, left and right, a sickening feeling rising in his stomach. It was then that he realised his footprints were gone and he had no idea which direction he should be going. It was astonishingly easy to get lost in the desert, as easy as that.

CHAPTER THIRTY-FOUR

The jet lag didn't really kick in until they pulled into the service station and Snot was left to guard the van. It was hot outside, over a hundred degrees, and the nozzles on the air conditioning were aimed into her face. A truck went past on the road, swaying the van, and she found herself nodding awake. She rubbed at her eyes, yawning and shaking her head. It wouldn't do for a prospect to be found asleep on guard duty, especially not with a large chunk of gold to be keeping an eye on. The clock said it was four-thirty-five in the afternoon, but she had no idea what day.

Not that she wasn't always wiped out at this time of the month, preferring whenever possible to stay in bed with a large amount of chocolate and a hot water bottle, it was just that losing an entire day on the journey here had thrown her even more off-kilter. They'd barely had time to touch down in Perth before she'd been sent out to get a van and assorted smoke bomb making ingredients, and within less than twenty-four hours they pulled off one of the biggest robberies in history. And all the while she was bleeding like a slashed artery, with her body trying to tell her that it was three o'clock in the morning. Numb Tongue had promised to bring her coffee.

Another big truck went past, the swaying motion of the van threatening to lull her back to sleep. She opened the door to step outside and the heat hit her like she had stuck her face into an oven, made worse by the fact that they were now wearing their cuts again, the leather vest sticking to her skin. She felt faint for a moment, cramps kicking in as if someone was stabbing her ovaries with a coat hanger, and she reached for the side of van to steady herself as she got out, burning her hand on the hot metal. She felt quite sick.

"Cheer up, darlin', it might never happen!"

Snot looked over to the four blokes who were returning to their pickup truck. She had long ago learned not to judge people by their appearance, so she tried not to think of them as toothless hillbillies. Another wave of nausea washed over her, and with it the feeling that she might have diarrhoea.

"I said, 'Cheer up, it might never happen'," the man repeated, and Snot gave him a smile whilst deciding that she'd be better to shit her pants than leave the van unguarded. The smile was supposed to convey polite acknowledgement of the man's comment and the desire to be left alone, but apparently it did not. The hillbilly grinned a predictably gummy grin, every other tooth either missing or rotten, and nudged one of his friends. "Watch and learn, son. Watch and learn."

The man ambled across the car park, taking his time, clearly thinking himself to be cooler than a six-pack on ice. He was around six feet tall, a solid frame carrying the extra weight of regular beer drinking, but not without some muscle.

"All right, darlin'," he grinned another disastrous grin, already standing too close. He smelled of beer and body odour.

"Fine, thank you," said Snot.

"Not seen you around here before," noted the man. "You live around here?"

"No, I'm just passing through," said Snot. "Just waiting for my boyfriend." She nodded towards the diner.

At this point the man should have taken the hint and left her alone. He did not.

"Boyfriend, eh?" he loomed over her. "Not much of a fuckin' boyfriend if he leaves you out here."

"I'm fine, thank you," Snot repeated. "I was just feeling a bit sick. Got my period," she added pointedly. If mention of a boyfriend didn't get rid of the bloke, then that should do the trick.

It did not.

Instead the man looked at her with disgust, like she'd just uttered some profanity, and his manner became openly hostile.

"What's with the patch?" he demanded, breathing stale beer at her. "Reckon yourself some sorta bikie?"

Snot said nothing.

"Fuckin' dykes on bikes over here," the man called across the car park to his three friends. They smiled back at him, two of the three revealing mouths that were also dentally challenged. So much for not judging by appearances. Then again, Snot didn't really look like the type who would break a man's wrist in three places when he made the monumental mistake of trying to grab her boobs.

Relying on her ju-jitsu she performed a standing arm lock that took the man completely by surprise, and he lay now in a crumpled heap on the ground, cradling his right arm in his left hand, surprise and pain written across his face. Up until a few moments ago he'd also had brawler written all over his face, a hard man as well as a bully, but it was remarkable how quickly and how easily Snot had taken him down.

"I *did* say I was on my period," she growled.

"Fuckin' bitch! You've broke my fuckin' arm!"

"You should learn some manners."

"I'll teach you some fuckin' manners!" the man spat at her. "Fuckin' bitch!"

He clambered to his feet, still cradling his arm. By this point his three friends had wandered over to better assess the situation, unsure how far they should get involved. The bloke with the broken wrist was the bigger of the four men, heavier set and tougher looking, used to throwing his weight around. In normal circumstances he was their backup and not the other way around, and yet he had just, in a matter of seconds, been dismantled by a small girl who was still wearing a floral dress under her cut.

"Should teach you a fuckin' lesson," snarled the man, proving himself to be rather a slow learner.

"I wouldn't if I were you."

"Are you fuckin' threatening me?"

"Yes," Snot snarled, a small vein making itself visible on her temple.

It was undoubtedly for the best that Mad John, Dum Dum, and Numb Tongue returned when they did. Best for the hillbillies, at least, who were about to get their arses handed to them. But, irreparably stupid though they were, the hillbillies were not completely suicidal and they hurriedly backed away to their pickup truck.

Snot was expecting a pat on the back or some comment from the others as they got back into the van, but they acted like nothing had happened. Dum Dum took over driving duties, with Mad John in the front passenger seat with the map spread across his lap. Numb Tongue climbed in the back beside her, silently handing her coffee and a couple of packets of sugar and creamer. She took off the plastic lid and dumped both sugar and creamer into the coffee, looking around for something to stir it with. Her cramps were kicking back in with a vengeance, and the vein on the side of her head was throbbing. Numb Tongue handed her a knife, a vicious looking switchblade, which, in the circumstances, was probably not particularly wise. He nodded to her coffee and she stirred it with the blade and handed the knife back. Numb Tongue wiped the blade on his jeans and put it back in his pocket.

And then, as suddenly as it had come, her rage subsided and she felt rather proud of herself. For months she'd been training with Numb Tongue, soaking up his knowledge of martial arts – if not marital arts – but aside from offering Numb Tongue a small amount of backup against the LA cops, this was the first time she had used any of those skills for real and, frankly, she'd kicked ass. Was it really too much to ask that one of them had at least noticed? But, no, instead they drove in silence.

Finally Numb Tongue spoke: "Good job," he quietly rumbled.

"Was that a compliment?" Snot smiled.

"Maybe," allowed Numb Tongue. "But next time break both his wrists."

CHAPTER THIRTY-FIVE

It was just as well that Vincent was being watched, otherwise he and Feenat would have been up a rather smelly creek and noticeably lacking in the paddle department. Instead there was a cry of "Oi! Numbnuts! Over here!" and the two of them traipsed back to camp, Vincent already aware that he'd never hear the end of this, while Feenat had to be coaxed every step of the way. Since then the frightened dwarf had been fed some rat soup – an old dwarf recipe – and given fresh water, before being gently questioned by Stone, who spoke fluent Dwarfish.

"I think she's a girl," he said finally.

"You think?" said Chaos.

"Well, Feenat's a girl's name," Stone shrugged. "But I'm afraid the language is like nothing I've heard before. I don't know if she's just got an unusual accent or she's making it up as she goes along, but most of it's gibberish so far as I can tell."

"You've tried your telepathic thing?"

"Yes," Stone nodded. "Nothing."

"Could get Zig Zag to have a word," suggested Chaos.

"No, I don't think that's necessary," said Stone. "She's already terrified and the sight of an orc won't improve things. I think a gentle approach is best for now. From what little I can tell she may have been lost for some time. I've given her a little something for medicinal purposes, but she's severely dehydrated."

"Yeah, you're probably right," conceded Chaos. "But we need to find out what she knows, and Zig Zag's not gonna stay hidden for the benefit of a dwarf."

"Well, warn him to play nice or she might run away."

Not that there was anywhere for Feenat to run away *to*, unless she was feeling suicidal and wanted to wander aimlessly around the desert again. Vincent was given the job of keeping an eye on her, but having been fed – dwarf delicacies, no less – and watered, she showed no signs of wanting to escape. In fact she seemed quite pleased to be with them, and eager to make new friends, happily babbling away in a language that no one could understand.

"I reckon you've got an admirer there," Tike winked at Vincent.

"Bloody nuisance more like," grumbled Vincent.

They were preparing to move on into the heat of the day, leaving behind those who were too weak or too slow to keep up. White sheets were distributed from various backpacks, including two that Vincent had stolen from his hotel room in Sydney. He'd wondered at the time why he'd been told to steal them, but now the sheets were tied to the ends of spears and long sticks to provide shelter as they walked. Feenat seemed to have a lot of questions about this, and it didn't seem to matter that no one knew what she was saying, less still that she was constantly in the way.

"It's a tent, okay?" Vincent finally snapped. "Spear, sheet, tent," he pointed at each item in turn.

The dwarf looked at each item in turn, but barely paused for breath.

"Fuck's sake," moaned Vincent, "doesn't she ever shut up?"

"Seems happy enough though, eh?" observed Tike.

"Yeah, that's because Stone fucking dosed her up with happy pills," explained Vincent. "He was trying to get her to calm down a bit."

"Calm down?" laughed Tike. "She looks fucking loved up! You reckon he's got any more?"

And so it was that, not an hour later, Tike, Feenat, and Vincent found themselves traipsing across the Australian desert, merrily tripping their tits off beneath a giant white caterpillar. Vincent was pretty sure that it was a caterpillar, but he was also fairly certain that he wasn't usually aware of his hair growing. He felt a vague sense of euphoria and had to keep resisting the urge to skip.

"You ever notice how useful fingers are?" said Tike.

"Fingers?"

"Yeah, fingers," said Tike, examining his hand like it was an unfamiliar object. "We'd be fucked without fingers."

"Fingers," Vincent smiled. "Fin-gers. It's a funny word, when you think about it, isn't it? Fin-gers." He waved his hand at Feenat, wiggling his digits, and the dwarf said something that sounded like "potatoes".

"Fin-gers," repeated Vincent.

"Fin-gers," said Feenat, waving back at him.

"That's right," beamed Vincent. "See, we're making progress!"

"Fingers," agreed Feenat happily.

And in a strange way they were making progress. The dwarf never seemed to shut up, always chattering away nineteen to the dozen, and now throwing random English words into the conversation, which reminded Vincent of Japanese pop music, and showed a clear indication that she didn't understand a word of it. But more to the point, she wasn't frightened anymore, she was bonding with them, making friends, which, at the end of the day, meant one less enemy. Stone was no fool when it came to drugs and, although it appeared otherwise, he rarely dished them out on a whim. It had been extremely cheeky of Tike to even ask him, and Vincent had only suggested it as a joke – he didn't think Tike would actually do it – but Stone had just smiled and said, "Yes, of course. Excellent idea!"

Vincent recognised the feel-good factor of MDMA, but there was every chance that they had also ingested some sort of truth serum, a little something to get the dwarf talking. The thought of this gave Vincent the giggles. Feenat was still babbling away, her sentences now including the word 'fingers' for no apparent reason, and the idea of giving her drugs to make her more talkative was preposterous, like giving speed to an Ewok. It was getting her to *stop* talking that would require drugs, and even Stone might not have anything that debilitating. By now Tike was also giggling uncontrollably, and their laughter became infectious, spreading along the line like ripples in a pond. Most of them didn't even know why they were laughing.

That was the genius of Stone, thought Vincent; he could dose three people and lift the morale of three hundred. When they'd left the others behind there had been a sense that they were losing a large part of their army, the mood quickly growing dark in stark contrast to the wide-open sky. Now, as they walked, there were smiles all around, and a couple of the older Aborigine guys even broke into song. It was quiet at first, a low whisper trying to find a breeze to make it fly, and then a few more voices joined in to give it wings. Gradually it grew until there must have been fifty voices carrying the song. The great white caterpillar was happy.

Vincent had no idea what the song was about, only that it was beautiful and soothing, and seemed to resonate through the ground, drifting like the desert sands. At one with the land, the song seemed to rise with the waves of heat, and then catch on the gentlest of breezes, a melody a thousand years old or more, a song as old as time.

"It's a rain song," explained Tike when he caught the look on Vincent's face. "They're singing to bring us rain."

Above the white caterpillar there wasn't a cloud in the sky, and yet somehow Vincent didn't doubt for a second that the song would bring rain. Of course it would bring rain. He listened to the harmonies, the voices intertwined, and it took a few moments to notice that there was an extra voice among them, lower than all the rest in more ways than one. Vincent looked down, and there beside him was Feenat, merrily singing along to the old Aboriginal song at the top of her voice.

CHAPTER THIRTY-SIX

Snot felt a sense of rising panic, a shock of anxiety, and a wave of nausea. Things were about to get very bloody, very quickly. The two cars that had been following them for the past twenty minutes were joined by a familiar looking pickup truck, now with added hillbillies in the back, seven of them in all, which, including the occupants of the other cars, made fourteen total. Fourteen against four.

"Guys," Snot urged desperately.

"I know," said Mad John. "Dum Dum, put your foot down."

"I am!" Dum Dum protested. "It's just not a very fast van."

"Guys, really," Snot pleaded.

"I'm doing my best," grumbled Dum Dum.

The pickup was joined by a third car, some big old American thing that had enough room for another five hillbillies. Nineteen against four. Well, eighteen really since the one with the broken wrist, now a passenger in the pickup, wouldn't be much use in a fight. Still, there could be no mistake that things were going to get bloody. The man with the broken wrist stared at her through his windscreen and ran his finger under his throat. Snot nearly vomited.

"There," said Mad John, pointing. "Just up there on the left, pull in there." He turned to face Snot. "When we get there," he said, "just run, don't look back, run."

Snot nodded, a grim look of relief written across her face. Eighteen against three. "I'm really sorry," she said.

Dum Dum pulled the van into the car park and Snot ran. When she returned it was all over. Even without Snot, the men had been hopelessly outnumbered. Eighteen against three, what the hell were they thinking? They stood no chance.

"Everything all right?" asked Mad John.

"Yes, thank you," said Snot, mortified. "I really am very sorry, I..."

"No need," Mad John hushed. "These things happen."

In fairness, Snot had warned them that she needed the toilet a good five minutes before anyone noticed that they were being followed, so it wasn't like she was trying to duck out of a fight. And it wasn't like the hillbillies ever had a hope in hell of winning, it just looked bad for a prospect to be seen running away, even if they were actually dashing for the toilet. A few of the hillbillies were back on their feet by now, standing on unsteady legs, and one or two were crawling around on their hands and knees, dazed and confused. A couple of them were missing teeth they could scarcely afford to lose. The evidence suggested that it had been an incredibly brief and one-sided fight. They often were when people were foolish enough to take on Aberrant.

The four of them climbed back into the van, Mad John taking a moment with the map before they set off. Again, they acted as if nothing had happened. A punch-up with some morons in a car park really wasn't a big deal when you'd faced down full-grown orcs, more like a gentle workout. And while Mad John was usually quite adept at talking these situations down, preferring to avoid a fight altogether if possible, he was also surprisingly adept as a pugilist when words failed, quick on his feet, and with a deceptively heavy right hand. Dum Dum, meanwhile, tended to pull his own punches in case he seriously hurt someone. Even without Numb Tongue they'd have had little trouble dealing with these idiots. Thankfully, they were gentlemanly enough to let her dash off and deal with her own issues, knowing that she'd have been there if she were actually needed. And Dum Dum, bless him, would fight to the death before hearing anything about periods, which, frankly, should have finished by now.

According to the display on the dashboard, the van was heading northeast. There was little traffic on the two-lane highway, but they passed a few roadside pubs, always with busy car parks, and here and there was the occasional farm or off-the-beaten-track tourist attraction. The radio began to lose its signal, the songs fading or distorted until Dum Dum turned it off and they sat in silence.

Snot lost herself in thought as they drove, part of her – quite a large part, if she was being honest – still wondering what on earth she thought she was doing. Not the first time, she had the bizarre feeling that she was watching someone else do all this, like someone else had taken control of her body and she was merely a helpless passenger, dragged along on a crazy joyride. She considered, for a moment, digging her book out of her bag, but then changed her mind. It was a book about Australia, a fascinating read, but it seemed a bit redundant reading about the place when she was actually here. She could just look out of the window and see it for real. And yet there was a strange sense that by doing so she would be somehow validating this other person, this rough and tumble biker chick.

It was a foolish thought and, not for the first time, Snot dismissed it. Of course, she was still her; it was just that her old self, Snow, would never have dared to do anything so outrageous as visiting the places she was reading about, and she certainly wouldn't have committed a robbery within hours of getting there. Admittedly, her old life had not been without danger, the most common cause of death among faeries being the common cat – she still bore a scar on her wing after an encounter with a particularly vicious tomcat – but certainly there had been no robberies, no high-speed police chases, no brawls in car parks. Then again, the old her didn't know mixed martial arts.

Snot had been worried, at first, about the violence associated with Aberrant MC, and with outlaw motorcycle clubs in general, but she'd found that for the most part they were simply a reflection of their surroundings. If you treated them well, they treated you better, and if you treated them badly, they treated you worse. It wasn't rocket science. For the most part they were a friendly bunch even if they didn't look it, and those who weren't tended to keep to themselves. You'd generally have to go and find them if you wanted to bother them, and if you didn't like the consequences then that would be your own stupid fault.

Despite all the lurid tales of motorcycle clubs going to war with each other, the most common cause of death among motorcycle clubs was still motorcycle accidents. And that, in itself, was a misnomer; her little off on the freeway notwithstanding, nine times out of ten it wasn't motorcycle accidents, it was car accidents that were the problem.

Snot spent the next few hours staring out of the window at Australia, until the sun dipped spectacularly over the horizon, the endless sky awash with the deepest reds and purples. If there was one thing Australia did well, it was sunsets, huge, fantastic sunsets.

It was a lot less interesting after dark, however, the road dragging on and on, with nothing to see but trees and blackness. By now she was used to not knowing where they were going – prospects were rarely kept up to speed with what was going on – but it would have been nice to know how long it was going to take to get there. A toilet break seemed way overdue. Instead they turned off the main road and onto an intolerably bumpy dirt path that really wasn't doing her bladder any favours at all. And from there they drove for several hours. It was unlikely that there would be a clean lavatory at the other end.

CHAPTER THIRTY-SEVEN

The great white caterpillar had come to a slow halt, bunched up in the middle where all eyes were on Feenat, the other voices dying down until she sang alone. It really was quite an extraordinarily deep voice for someone so small and so, well, female, and perfectly in pitch, the bass in any male voice choir. The small army watched in astonished awe until Feenat reached the end of the song.

"Well, if that doesn't make it rain I don't know what will," said Tike.

By all accounts it was a miracle that the song had worked at all, way out here under the mid-afternoon sun, and it was barely a shower when it came, but rain it did, a light pattering that was enough to wet their faces and raise their spirits further. Since they'd stopped walking for a moment to take in Feenat's song, it was decided that they should rest for a while. Besides, what was the point of singing a rain song and then moving somewhere else?

Unfortunately, while it was unanimously agreed that Feenat's rendition of the song was quite magnificent, it was also quickly established that, as far as anyone could tell, she didn't really know what the song meant. At Stone's request Vincent sat in while Feenat was questioned again – this time in the language of the song – but the best that could be established was that the dwarf recognised just four words of it, and possibly thought that the song brought good luck.

This, in itself, was a remarkable breakthrough, and led to a great deal of speculation about how and where she might have learned the tune, but it didn't really help much beyond that. Communication with her was still almost entirely based on sign language, mime, and guesswork.

"Maybe we're not looking at this right," said Vincent, when they'd all but given up.

"How do you mean?" Stone asked.

"Well, you said yourself there were hundreds of Aboriginal languages, what if she's speaking one of the other languages? Just because she doesn't understand this one doesn't mean she won't understand one of the others."

It was just as well that Feenat liked to talk. She spent the next several hours engaged in the equivalent of speed dating, blathering away to each of their party for five or ten minutes in turn in the hope that they might recognise some of it, which, so far, none of them did. When the sun began to set the walking continued, as did the speed dating. The dwarf was even introduced to Zig Zag, though, curiously, she showed no sign of fear, or even that she knew what an orc was. To Feenat, the orc was just another in a long line of people who couldn't understand a word she was saying, she just didn't have to look up so far when she was talking at him. If all else failed then Vincent had been instructed to teach her to speak English, like that was no big deal when you were having mild hallucinations and got the giggles every time you thought about fingers. He rather hoped it didn't come to that.

That said, the drugs were fast wearing off, and it was clear that Vincent was back on prospect duty. Party time was over. If Stone wanted you to trip for a couple of hours then that was exactly how long you tripped for. He considered it terribly bad manners if you got a comedown from his drugs, so it was an easy return to whatever passed for normality around here. Of course, had they wronged him, he could make people suffer the torments of hell, with trips that went on for weeks and comedowns that lasted an eternity, but unless you'd pissed him off the drugs simply wore off. Vincent noticed that his legs were aching, but more than likely that was from all the walking than from Stone's pharmaceuticals. Otherwise, he felt remarkably fresh. The desert heat was fading with the sun, and the great white caterpillar was back to being some bedsheets tied to sticks. Back to the business at hand. Possibly avoiding fingers in case he got the giggles.

But the walking continued until long after fingers had stopped being funny, and still there was nothing but desert. And the depressing thing was that Vincent knew full well that they were barely making a dent, little more than ants in a sandpit. He shrugged the thought off, aware that it led to dark places. Now was not the time for pondering the insignificance of mankind, now was the time to figure out how to gather information from a very talkative dwarf whose vocabulary consisted of 'ground', 'sun', 'sky', and 'luck'. Or possibly 'dirt, sand, or earth', 'sun', 'sky' and 'hope'. Both 'sun' and 'sky' were certain since Feenat had pointed at them when saying the Aboriginal words, but 'luck or hope' was a guess after watching some enthusiastic but very poor mime on the dwarf's part. What they really needed to know about were words like 'army' and 'how many?'. Useful information would also include stuff like 'where' and 'the fuck are they going?'.

Still they walked. And walked. And walked. On through the cold night, mile after mile.

Vincent's lips were dry and beginning to crack, and his piss – what little there was of it – was frothy and almost orange. Surely that couldn't be good? Morning was upon them, already uncomfortably hot, and they stopped, at long last, to rest by the shade of a cluster of trees, the land now showing a few more signs of life, which hopefully meant that there was water nearby. Everything out here depended on finding water. Orange piss meant you weren't drinking enough of it. On the plus side, Vincent couldn't remember the last time he'd wanted a cigarette, so at least if they all didn't die of thirst he might have kicked that habit. Exhausted, Vincent went to sleep.

When he awoke it was to a late breakfast of monitor lizard, and some rather muddy looking water that he was assured it was safe to drink. The sun was high in the sky, unrelenting in its attempts to kill them, and they would wait until it gave up for the day before moving on. Vincent swatted a fly away from his face. It was too hot to think. Every time he tried to bring his mind back into focus he found it drifting and thinking of nothing. It's hot, he thought, so stupidly, stupidly hot. He went to swat the fly from his nose and realised that it was a bead of sweat. Fucking stupid place! Whose stupid idea was it to make a place this fucking hot? The fly came back and landed on his nose.

"Fuck off!" He batted it away.

"Fuck off!" repeated Feenat.

"And now you think a fly is called a 'fuck off', don't you?" Vincent sighed to himself.

He recalled reading somewhere that the literal translation of 'kangaroo' was 'I don't know', but he wasn't sure if it was just an urban legend. Certainly, it was easy to see how words changed their meanings over time through mispronunciation or misunderstanding, or even sometimes just because people started using them differently. It was a conversation he'd had many times with various members of Aberrant MC, mostly when one of them used a phrase that was long out of date. His father, Mad John – probably the worst offender – had this weird habit of cocking his head to one side when you told him, like you were tipping this new information into his ear. Mental just got grumpy about it, insisting, despite the evidence to the contrary, that he was quite happy being gay, but that it had meant something entirely different until about fifty years ago.

The fuck off fly landed on Vincent's knee and he watched it crawl around on his jeans, too lazy to brush it off. How long had the dwarfs been here? he wondered. It was a question that no one seemed to have bothered asking, but surely four thousand dwarfs hadn't just flown down here on Quantas with a bunch of axes and battle armour? And what if Feenat *was* speaking an Aboriginal language and not Dwarfish? That meant they must live here. It was a slow thought at first and had trouble wading its way through the treacle of his mind, but what if...?

Vincent climbed wearily to his feet and wandered over to Stone, who was engaged in what looked like a serious discussion with Flashback. He hesitated, lurking awkwardly, not wanting to interrupt the conversation and get a bollocking if he was wrong. But if he was right then they needed to know as soon as possible.

"Yes, Prospect? What is it?" Flashback demanded irritably.

"Er," said Vincent, unsure of himself. He would rather talk to Stone alone than deal with the possibility of Flashback flying off the handle, as he was prone to do if you interrupted something important. He nearly started his sentence with "I've been thinking", but Flashback would undoubtedly beg to differ. Instead he said, "What do we actually know about these dwarfs we're chasing?"

"Short, bearded, heavily armed," snapped Flashback. "What are you getting at?"

"I mean," said Vincent, "that Australian customs would probably notice four thousand dwarfs, and they would certainly frown upon chain-mail and battle-axes. If Feenat's speaking an Aboriginal language that means they probably live here."

"Meaning?" said Flashback, who, for an immensely powerful wizard, could be frightfully slow on the uptake.

"Meaning," said Vincent, "that they might be a lot better adapted to the desert that we're giving them credit for, and there might be a lot more than four thousand of them!"

CHAPTER THIRTY-EIGHT

After what seemed like an eternity of bouncing around in the van, Mad John, Dum Dum, Numb Tongue, and Snot were greeted, at the end of their journey, by the business end of a shotgun. The man with his finger on the trigger – solidly built, and wearing shorts, T-shirt and flip-flops – looked to be in his mid to late fifties, certainly no younger, but he also had the look about him of someone who might surprise people by announcing that he was, in fact, eighty-something. Assuming he didn't shoot them first.

To be fair to the man, there had been plenty of warnings of the 'trespassers will be shot' variety, and the signs grew increasingly more hostile as the van neared his farmhouse home, the last one simply reading, 'I mean it'. No one could say that they hadn't been warned. And no one came here by accident.

"Show yourselves and state your business!" the man demanded.

Beside him sat an Australian shepherd dog, grey and white, its long, pink tongue lolling from one side of its mouth, its eyes alert and keen, ready to obey any command.

"Stay here," said Mad John, stepping slowly and carefully from the van, his hands raised above his head. Around him the night was alive with a madness of moths, attracted by the headlights of the van, and, to a lesser extent, to Mad John himself. He'd once told Dum Dum that it was, in fact, an aura that surrounded him, not a halo, and that everybody has one, but to the dive-bombing moths it made no difference, his head may as well have been a light bulb.

"I said state your business," the man repeated firmly.

For a long few seconds there was silence, broken only by the flapping and buzzing of insects, which were actually rather loud. Mad John batted at something winged and furry that seemed intent on flying up his nose.

"A cup of tea would be rather nice," he said at last. "And then I thought we might attend to business over a rematch."

For an even longer few seconds it seemed as if the man might shoot him stone dead where he stood, but then, as slowly and cautiously as Mad John had stepped from the van, the shotgun was lowered as recognition inched its way across the man's dark, tanned face.

"Mahjong?" he said questioningly, part of his expression suggesting that he wasn't at all sure, and was more than ready to blast large holes in someone if they were playing silly buggers.

"I believe the score still sits in my favour."

At this the man's face lit up with a smile that might itself attract bugs, and he let out a short whistle, at which another two sheepdogs appeared from the darkness, and hurried to his side, attack mode cancelled. Mad John lowered his hands and stepped forward to greet an old friend.

"Well, fuck me sideways with a cricket bat!" the man exclaimed happily, his arms extended in welcome, his Australian accent thicker than treacle. "It is you, isn't it? Strewth, it must've been about twenty-five fuckin' years!"

"Thirty-five," corrected Mad John as they embraced.

"Fuckin' thirty-five! Well, it's been too fuckin' long, that's for damn sure! What the fuck brings you all the way out here to the middle of fuckin' nowhere? I'm guessing you didn't come all this way just so I could win me fuckin' money back, eh? Let's get inside and put the fuckin' kettle on, and then you can tell me all about it."

"I'm here with friends," Mad John motioned back to the van.

"Well, what the fuck are they doing sitting in there like a bunch of fuckin' idiots?" beamed the man, apparently forgetting that he'd recently been pointing a loaded shotgun at them. "Fuckin' get 'em inside an' we'll see what's what, shall we? Fuckin' thirty-five fuckin' years, eh? Fuck me, you haven't changed a bit, you old bastard..."

The man continued to excrete enthusiastic expletives, as Mad John signalled to the others to come out of the van. Evidently he was a man to whom swear words were merely punctuation, sometimes to be used in the middle of words, such as, abso-fuckin'-lutely. On seeing Snot, however, he stopped mid-sentence, and indeed mid-swear word.

"My apologies," he said, looking rather startled. "Please pardon my language, I had no idea there was ladies present. Don't often get visitors around here," he added, as if this was something of a surprise, and more to do with the remoteness of the farm than the several miles of signs telling people to go away.

"George, this is Snot," Mad John introduced them. "She is faerie-kind. And this is Dum Dum, descendant of bridge trolls. Reprobus, I am sure you know by name."

"Honoured, I'm sure," said George, shaking each of them by the hand.

He offered his left hand, which immediately drew attention to the fact that most of his right hand was missing, just a thumb and a badly scarred forefinger remaining. There were terrible burn scars all the way up his right arm, too, and onto his face, the remnants of a melted ear not quite hidden by his dark and unkempt hair. "Bit of a fire," he explained, as the three of them pretended not to notice.

They followed George into the ramshackle farmhouse and along a short, cluttered corridor into the kitchen, where he lit a wood-burning stove to boil some water, before excusing himself while he went in search of chairs. Both Numb Tongue and Dum Dum were hunched so as not to bang their heads on the various pots, pans, and miscellaneous objects that hung from the ceiling, the one chair in the room – a sturdy wooden thing that was obviously George's special spot – respectfully unoccupied. All four of them remained funereally silent until George returned, as if letting the house get used to having guests. Few words had been spoken here in some time, other than George talking to himself or to his dogs.

George returned a few minutes later. "Well, there's one," he said proudly. "I'll be back in a tick."

There was a moment when all eyes were upon the chair. It was once purple, now grey, and had poofed dust into the air when George put it down beside his lone kitchen chair. There was a strong chance that he'd found it in one of the barns. Possibly there was something living in it. Ticks, presumably.

"After you," grinned Dum Dum, relieved, for once, to see a chair that couldn't take his weight.

"Oh, age before beauty, I think," Mad John winked at Numb Tongue, who was his senior by several decades.

Even Numb Tongue let out an unaccustomed smile: "Ladies first," he nodded to Snot.

"Um," said Snot.

Thankfully, she was rescued as George reappeared, carrying what appeared to be a milking stool and another wooden chair to match the first.

"There," he grinned, proudly depositing them on the stone tile floor. "Just need one more." He glanced at Dum Dum, sizing him up. "I'll be right back."

George was gone for a long time, a few minutes becoming several. Still the four of them remained standing, an unspoken rule suggesting that it was rude to take a seat before their host, like starting a meal without waiting for someone. It was a decent-sized kitchen, with room enough for everyone around the long oak table, but it had been many years since it had been used for more than one person. Even when George was out of the room it felt as if he was still there, his presence infused into the very foundations of the building. It never surprised people to learn that he had built it himself.

Several minutes became five or ten, during which time one of the dogs came in, sat itself down, and let rip the most obnoxious stench. In moments it filled the entire room, eye-wateringly pungent, a taste as much as a smell. There was no pretending it wasn't there; it hung so heavy in the air that you could almost see it. The dog seemed rather pleased with itself. And still they waited, all four doing their best not to breathe.

Eventually George returned. He was carrying a medium-sized tree trunk, which he plonked down next to the other mismatched furniture.

"Ah, strewth, that's disgusting!" he announced, waving his good hand in front of his face. "Get out of here, Bingo, you little fuc..." – he glanced at Snot, ladies present – "fur-ball. Sorry, the poor fu-fella's not been well lately. Go on, out you get," he gently nudged the dog out of the kitchen. "Please, sit yourselves down. Sorry, about the log. I don't really get much call for extra chairs."

They waited for George to take his preferred seat, and then, unnoticed by George, the four of them played the fastest and quietest game of musical chairs in history. When the imaginary music stopped, Snot was still standing. Dum Dum had taken the log, a natural choice since the other chairs would break if he sat on them, and Mad John had taken the milking stool, leaving the other wooden chair to Numb Tongue. There was only one chair left; it was formerly purple and a possible carrier of the plague.

"Er," said Snot. "Do you mind if I use your toilet."

CHAPTER THIRTY-NINE

"Well, that's a bit of a game changer, eh?" observed Tike by way of massive understatement.

The rain was falling harder now, far from torrential, still just a gentle pitter-patter, but it was rain nonetheless, fresh and warm, and oh so sweet. Feenat had been singing again, leading the choir in their magical song, those who didn't know the words doing their best to at least make the right noises. Vincent had felt rather like someone in church, mumbling along to unfamiliar hymns. But although the rain was significant and much needed, it wasn't the game changer that Tike was referring to. If only it were that simple.

In fact, to all intents and purposes, they were still playing the same game, it was just that the rules had changed rather dramatically, and their chances of winning seemed exponentially slimmer. They might possibly have to cheat.

Before she began her song again, Vincent had spent several hours with the dwarf, and around them, now disappearing into the falling rain, were dozens of drawings etched into the sand. They'd given up trying to communicate verbally with Feenat – not that that stopped her from talking – and since she seemed to be happiest talking at Vincent, he was put in charge of trying to find out as much from her as possible.

They were both rubbish at mime, and English was ruled out when it became clear that Feenat failed to grasp that you couldn't use the new word to apply to just anything. She understood, for instance, that the word 'fingers' meant the wiggly digits on the end of her hands, but then she'd just say it for no reason, adding new English words as she learned them. Vincent was pretty sure that "fingers jacket stick" was just meaningless gibberish.

So, stick drawings it was. And while Banksy had very little to worry about, the same could not be said for Aberrant and their friends. After a lengthy meeting with Flashback and Stone, Vincent had just broken the news to Tike.

"Well, on the bright side," he said, "we never had a Plan A, so Plan B couldn't be any worse. I'm guessing we don't have a Plan B?"

"Fucked if I know," shrugged Vincent. "But it's certainly a game changer, like you said. I mean, look at this," Vincent pointed to the fading sand etchings. "This is a big city that goes miles underground, not some ill-prepared bunch of..."

He left the sentence unfinished; he didn't know what they were a bunch of, apart from being dwarfs, obviously. But his hunch had been right, and there were a hell of a lot more of them than previous estimates suggested. Four thousand dwarfs had become four hundred thousand, probably more, with their own city and their own army. Even up against four thousand they had little hope unless they came up with a spectacular plan. Against an entire city – an underground city no less – all hope was surely gone. Clearly it was written on Vincent's face.

"We've got this far," said Tike, always the optimist. "I mean, well, we weren't exactly gonna charge in there mob-handed in the first place, not against that many; there had to be a plan really. All we need is a better plan."

Vincent let out a long sigh, poking at the last of the drawings with a stick. "I've got a feeling I'm the fucking plan," he said sullenly. "Plan A *and* Plan B. And I don't much like my chances."

"You mean that ring of yours?" Tike gave him a dubious look.

"Yeah," Vincent glanced down at it, like always. He couldn't get it off.

"About that, mate," Tike ventured cautiously. "I've been wanting to tell you something."

It was then that Vincent found out he'd recently acquired a new nickname. It didn't help. It didn't help at all. For starters, he'd only just shaken the last one, Turtle, which came about because his jacket was far too big, making him look like a turtle. It had fizzled out when he finally made some adjustments with a very large needle and thread, wargskin being as tough as old boots. The new moniker, however, had come from the Aborigines, and it was rather less humorous. In the Yolngu Matha language it was 'Nhama nhuna yukurra', and Vincent had trouble saying it. The distressing thing was it meant 'I see you'.

"What, *all* of them?" asked Vincent when Tike told him about it.

"Yeah, pretty much, mate, sorry," said Tike. "Out of all of us there's four or five who reckon they've seen you disappear, and there's a couple more said you might have flickered a bit, like, but the rest of us can see you clear as day."

"Seriously?"

"Yeah, sorry, mate."

"Fuck's sake..."

For all its failings – and there were so many that Vincent didn't even know where to start – the one thing his stupid ring could be relied upon to do was make him vanish when he was truly terrified. That was the one time he knew, the one time he felt it, and now here was Tike telling him that as far as the Aborigines were concerned he'd not once been invisible on the entire journey.

"I don't wanna be rude, mate," insisted Tike, "but I watched you go and talk to that Feenat the first time, and you just walked up to her right out in the open, it wasn't like you were hidden or anything. I did wonder what you were doing."

"What about in the dragon's cave," Vincent persisted, "that bit in the tunnel before we saw the dragon? I must have..."

"No, mate." Tike shook his head. "It was pretty dark in there too, and you were a little bit in front of me, near Stone and your other mate, what's his name...? The one that keeps trying to tell everyone to watch out for drop bears."

"Joker."

"Yeah, Joker, that's the one. You were behind him, mate. Sorry."

Tike looked disappointed for his friend, embarrassed for him, like he wanted so much for Vincent to be able to do his little magic trick. Vincent just felt fucking stupid, and again it seemed written on his face.

"No, really, mate," Tike said. "I'm sure you can do it and all, and you said it worked on Feenat..."

"Who can obviously see me now."

"Well, yeah, but, like you said, it only works..." Tike was doing his best, he really was, but he'd be lying if he said he'd witnessed anything at all in the disappearing department. He was just trying to be kind. "It only works if, uh..."

Tike struggled so hard to find the right words, stumbled so much, that Vincent burst out laughing.

"What? What did I say?"

But Vincent couldn't stop laughing and, inevitably, it started Tike off, too. After all they'd been through, all the caves and cockroaches and bat shit and dragons, all the miles trekking across the desert, and crapping behind rocks that had gigantic insects lurking behind them, the heat, the cold... After all that, Tike was telling him that his magic ring didn't work. If that wasn't funny, then what the hell was?

But more than that; Tike was telling Vincent that he was a friend, there until whatever the end may be. He wasn't much more than a bag of spanners, but then neither was Vincent when all was said and done. They'd be lucky if they weighed three hundred pounds between them, and that was with all the sand that had found its way into their boots and underpants. And yet, here they were on some great adventure together, often down, but never out, both laughing their arses off. Neither of them would have swapped it for the world.

"So this name," managed Vincent, when the giggling finally died down to a level where they wouldn't asphyxiate with laughter. Tears were streaming down their faces, and Vincent's cheeks hurt. "This name," he tried once more, "how do you say it again?"

"Nhama nhuna yukurra."

"Fucking hell, mate, I'm never gonna get that right. Say it again."

Tike said it again.

"Narayan..."

"No, it's nhama nhuna yukurra."

"How about Nhama for short?"

"Fuck it, why not?" laughed Tike. "We're going after dwarfs, after all."

"Tike," said Vincent.

"Yes, Vincent," said Tike.

"That joke was shit."

CHAPTER FORTY

The old kitchen slowly warmed to its guests, although the stench of Bingo lingered for some time. George kept apologising – ladies present, after all – but they were used to having Eau de Billy Toothless following them around. Dog farts were nothing compared to the everyday perfume of a hobgoblin, even one who was forced to take a bath at least once a month, whether he liked it or not. It had been a stipulation of him getting his full patch.

George had dusted down an old bottle of rum and some glasses, and poured them large shots, which had restored a bit of the colour back to Snot's face even if it hadn't stopped her screaming inside. She was never going to the toilet again. Never. And we will never speak of this again. Just a Huntsman? *Just* a Huntsman? The damn thing was the size of a dinner plate! The only reason she hadn't seen it straight away – sitting there on the shower head – was because she thought it *was* the shower head! And then its legs unfolded! Snot shuddered at the memory and knocked back the rest of her drink.

According to George, it was good luck having a Huntsman spider around the place because they kept crickets and cockroaches away, but Snot was having none of it. Huntsman. Hunts-man. There's a clue right there in the name. What the hell did they think it would do to a faerie?

Ironically, she had been checking, when she spotted the spider, that she was done with her special time and could adopt faerie form again. Without being too graphic, certain things had to be removed, because three inches of cotton wasn't going to fit inside three inches of faerie, and Snot was just about to transform for a moment to stretch her wings when she saw that *thing* in the shower. She would now be remaining fully clothed and human-sized until they were safely on a plane leaving the country.

George, though, turned out to be quite a wonderful character, his misplaced chivalry and his ability not to swear in front of "a lady" almost as amusing as it was touching. Snot wasn't much for swearing herself, but she was a prospect for an outlaw motorcycle club nonetheless, and quite a few of them had mouths you wouldn't kiss your mother with. George however, was on a completely different level, a professor of profanity, an expletives expert. So far she'd heard fuck become fur-ball, furniture, f'r instance, function and, of course, fudge, and another word had become cunning, cunctative, and a near miss with countryside. It made him sound he had a stutter, and Snot frequently had to bite the inside of her lip to stop from laughing.

The funny thing was, the minute Snot left the room he was straight back to fuck this and fuck that and countryside the other, barely missing a beat. He was a warm soul though, and she liked him, felt safe in his house, if not in the toilet. She could tell that, swearing aside, he treated everybody the same no matter who they were, kitchen staff or king. He also wasn't shy about how he got his burns, and preferred people to "have a good fu-fulfilling look and get it over with" rather than keep trying to stare when he wasn't looking, which was weird and annoying. Apparently he was something of an authority when it came to dragons, but not enough that he hadn't been "fu-furnaced a couple of times."

"Anyway," he said at last. "Listen to me go on. I'm sure you didn't come all this way just to hear about my fu-fiery f- er, f- f..."

"Frights?" offered Mad John.

"Frights, yes, frights," said George, grateful for any port in a storm. "I'm assuming this isn't just a social visit?"

Much of what was said by Mad John in the next few hours was news to Snot, too. She knew about the gold, obviously, having had to dangle out of a hotel window in order to help them steal it, but how and why it got to be in a hotel lobby was new information, as was the fact that they intended to use it to pay a dragon for some security work. Any dragon would do, the bigger the better.

"I might have known that ba-bachelor Merlin had something to do with this," said George when Mad John was done, his tone implying that there was no love lost between him and the wizard. "I thought they'd melted that gold down years ago, and you're telling me it was f-fortuitously hidden in plain sight in some fu-fancy hotel?"

"So it would seem," said Mad John. "Merlin had intended to come back and get it, but given the circumstances that won't be possible, so he wanted to use it to help his friend."

"Circumstances? What circumstances? And since when has Merlin had any f-friends?"

"Uh," said Mad John, not usually at a loss for words. "He rather gave the impression that *you* were his friend."

"Did he?" said George incredulously. "Cheeky fu-f-f-falsifier. We might have been friends still if he hadn't run off with my f-f-f-phenomenal gold!"

Nice save, thought Snot, as George continued to rant, but evidently he was fuming, and desperately trying not to visit the countryside in the company of a lady. For a moment she thought he might ask them to leave – and there was another close call with the swearing when he referred to Merlin as a "f-f-freelance cun-conjurer" – but eventually he calmed down enough for Mad John to tell him what had become of the wizard, so lonely in his radioactive prison of glass and stone. The gold was useless to him now.

"Well," said George, his temper slowly subsiding. "That's as may be. How do I know it's not one of his tricks?"

"It's no trick," Mad John assured him. "Besides, why else would he tell us to bring the gold to you? Perhaps it's his way of apologising. After all, he told me what you'd want to do with the gold."

"Just didn't tell you that half of it was mine in the first place!"

"No, he didn't," Mad John conceded, "but the fact remains that you wanted to give your share to a dragon, and now you have your chance. His share too, should you wish."

Mad John let this sink in for a moment. It had quite a long way to sink.

"And it's just sitting outside in your f-four-wheeled van?" George said, as if assuring himself.

"Yes."

There was some further sinking. It had been some time, after all. Snot later discovered that the last time George had seen Merlin was on Saturday the 22nd of January, 1931, just one week after the Golden Eagle Nugget was said to have been discovered. The pair of them had stolen it, replacing the original with a copy made of fool's gold, liberally coated with spells to stop anyone from noticing. They'd been escaping, north-east towards Darwin, when they were stuck by a terrible storm in which the wizard had vanished along with the gold, never to be seen again.

A long wait at their rendezvous point in Darwin was followed by an even longer search for the "ba-back-stabbing wa-wizard", after which Merlin was last seen in New York in October of 1939, a black and white photograph showing him standing alongside President Roosevelt.

"By the time I got to New York he was gone," said George. "And then the war broke out and I never heard of him again."

George poured out the last of the rum and lifted his glass as if examining the contents. He was lost in thought for a moment, alone in the room as if they weren't there. During the course of the evening Bingo had snuck back into the room, and he chose that precise moment to let rip again, a creeper this time, slowly rising up to assault the nostrils and bring tears to the eyes.

"Oh, for f-f-f-for the last time, Bingo, that's disgusting! "How did you get back in here, you f-fleabag?"

George got to his feet, his mind dragged violently back to the here and now. "Well," he said, "I'd best find somewhere for you lot to get some rest, unless you want to sleep out there with the gold. We've got a fu-fantastically early start in the morning if we want to rescue this mate of yours. I'll send the birds out tonight, see what they can find out."

Relieved to get out of the kitchen, they trooped outside to get some air, and George went to make arrangements. The night sky was alive with glittering, twinkling stars, and, as it turned out, moths and weird flappy insects, so Numb Tongue and Snot quickly decided to sleep in the van, leaving Mad John and Dum Dum – since George had no spare rooms – with the choice of a barn full of rats, or a kitchen full of Bingo.

Rats were probably preferable.

CHAPTER FORTY-ONE

"Y ou can't be bloody serious? Tell me he's not bloody serious!"

"He's serious, I'm afraid."

"That'll take half the fuckin' day just to get there. It's fuckin' miles out of our way."

"Nonetheless," said Mad John, "I think it would be wise."

"Well, of course it's wise" said George. "Course it's fuckin' wise, but it would've been a lot fuckin' wiser to bring some fuckin' boots in the first place."

Dum Dum had woken from quite a comfortable night, in a relatively rat-free barn, to find that Mad John was already up and about, helping George to load up his battered looking Land Rover. The sun was barely risen, but they were almost done, most of the essentials strapped to the roof rack to allow more space inside.

"Er, John," he said, "can I have a word?"

Which was when he'd told Mad John about Black Sabbath sending him messages.

Mad John hadn't questioned him for a second, just nodded and went to tell George that they needed to take a detour to get Snot some boots. Since there was no connector in the van, Dum Dum had been saving the battery on his iPod, but he liked to hear a few tunes before he went to sleep. He'd stuck his earphones in and selected shuffle mode, but it hadn't shuffled very far. Snot and Numb Tongue were still asleep in the van, and Dum Dum felt a little guilty for getting her in trouble before she'd even woken up, but the song – repeated three times – couldn't have been more clear. *Fairies Wear Boots.* Unfortunately, the nearest shoe shop was a long drive in the wrong direction.

"Oh well," said George. "If my auntie had a dick she'd be my uncle. But if they want any fuckin' breakfast they'd better get a f-f-f-f-..."

"Fork?" suggested Snot.

"Ah, fork, yes," blustered George. "Good morning, Miss. Didn't see you there. You slept well, I hope?"

"Yes, thank you," said Snot, who'd barely slept at all thanks to her new-found terror of spiders. She had also heard all the cursing about her footwear, and felt, once again, like she'd let the side down. George was right, it was bloody stupid to come out here without any boots, although, in her defence, she had been rather too preoccupied with robbing a hotel. Ingredients for smoke bombs were on the shopping list when she was gathering supplies, not boots.

After breakfast, they moved the gold – still wrapped in a hotel blanket – to George's Land Rover, and set off along the dusty trail back to civilisation. They drove with the windows down because George had insisted on bringing his dogs. It took several hours to get to the nearest road.

The mood in the Land Rover was upbeat and cheerful, George chattering away happily, always throwing in questions to keep the conversation flowing and make everyone feel included. Granted, most of his sentences sounded like they should have a question mark at the end, just because that's how Australians talk, but he seemed genuinely interested, and he was never intrusive, only inquisitive. He talked bridges with Dum Dum for a while, and even managed to get a few words out of Numb Tongue on the subject of mixed martial arts. And all while stuttering like an outboard motor so as not to swear. Snot found it very f-f-funny.

Evidently, George and Mad John went back years, old friends who saw far too little of each other, and it was rare to see Mad John so relaxed, so defence-less. It didn't do for everyone to know who he was, and for obvious reasons he could be quite guarded at times, private, and, with that, rather lonely. You'd really have to trust someone to tell them you were Jesus.

Except that he wasn't; at least, not as people thought. For one thing, there wasn't a J in the alphabet back then. It wasn't even the same alphabet or the same language. But more than that, people tended to make enormous assumptions based almost entirely on a book that was written long after he was supposed to have died, by people who had never met him, and then revised numerous times to suit political needs. They didn't know his real name, but they were convinced they knew all about him, and would even go so far as to argue with him about it. By all accounts, some of them got quite irate. It didn't seem to matter what he said, just what they had chosen to believe, and they got particularly angry when he suggested that virgin births were a ludicrous idea, and that he might, in fact, lean towards atheism.

Today, however, Mad John was just Mad John, or Mahjong, as George called him, a nickname acquired after a particularly heavy night of drinking. There could be no question that George knew his true identity, but he treated him the same as anybody else, no pretence and no b-bull-b-bullhorns. George was what you'd call 'down to earth'.

"So tell me, Snot," he asked over his shoulder. "What's the top speed of a faerie? If you don't mind me asking?"

Snot didn't mind him asking at all.

"Well, I found out a few days ago that it's about a hundred and eighty miles an hour, but it wasn't on purpose. I fell off a motorbike."

"Strewth!" said George. "Where y' hurt at all?"

And Snot, who was usually so quiet, went on to tell him all about her chase with the police helicopter and her subsequent crash, and how she'd retrieved her cut from the highway...

"Cut?" asked George.

Snot explained, telling of how she'd dragged her cut for several miles before adopting human form, and how she'd then had to steal clothes from a department store because she was virtually naked. They even had a bit of a laugh about how Snot got her new nickname, and how she had repaired her name patch but left it as Snot instead of Snow. From then on George would only call her Snow, the only person to call her by that name, and, in an unspoken way, the only person allowed to do so. She never asked him why, it was just the way things were. By nightfall he was an old friend.

And by nightfall they had all learned a great deal more about what was going on and where they were going. According to George there were twenty-seven different species of dragon living in Australia, all of varying size, colour, and temperament. George had been responsible for relocating some of them when civilisation got too close; still was, in fact.

"See, they hibernate for hundreds of years," George explained, "and then some stupid ba-b-builder comes along and tries to build a f-f-freeway over their home. Back in the old days, we had a few of 'em wake up before anyone knew they were there, and a lot of people got killed," George shook his head. "Lots of people. And y' can't go blaming the f-flaming dragon when the dragon got there first."

George had worked with the Aborigines in gaining the trust and respect of the dragons, first having to gain the trust and respect of the Aborigines. The former, he said, was more difficult, because if a dragon didn't trust you it just set you on fire. Between them they had saved hundreds. Hundreds of what, George never said, but presumably people, since dragons, as mentioned, tended towards incinerating people who pissed them off. Indeed, the dragon that George was taking them to see had once burned down an entire town.

"Didn't need to relocate that one, obviously," George said cheerfully. "He still lives up by the coast, and they never tried to build there again. Quite a sight, too. You'll see when we get there. About all that's left of the place is the f-f-forsaken signpost. Everything burned to the f-foundations, and then there's this sign without a scratch on it, 'Welcome To Honali'."

"How do we know the dragon won't set us on fire?" asked Dum Dum not unreasonably.

"Big slab of gold in the back of the f-f-f- van."

The conversation moved on, George asking Mad John about someone who had passed twenty years ago, which was followed by the strange sort of numb grief when it's too late to mourn.

"Bummer," said George. He was allowed that one.

They drove late into the night and Snot drifted off to sleep. Numb Tongue sat, as ever, in silence, staring out at the darkness. In fact, for now, they all sat in silence, but it was not uncomfortable. George and Mad John were intent on the road, and Dum Dum was lost in thought. He had a really annoying song in his head.

"Little, something, something. Something by the sea..." Dum Dum sang in his head, struggling to remember the lyrics.

And then suddenly it hit him.

Dum Dum shook his head. Nah, couldn't be. Then again, it doesn't hurt to ask.

"George," he said, breaking the silence.

"Yes, Dum Dum?"

"Can I ask you a question?"

"Yes, Dum Dum."

"This dragon you're taking us to see, does it live by the sea?"

"Yeah, I told ya, up by the coast. Best place for him, too, if you ask me, Dum Dum. He's the f-f-fella that burned me. Quite a way to go yet, though. You'll be pleased to know there's a pub on the way."

"And you said that place that got burned down was called Honali, right?"

"Yeah, that's right," nodded George.

"Um, George."

"Yes, Dum Dum?"

"This dragon," Dum Dum persisted. It seemed a bit foolish now, but the song had popped into his head out of nowhere. "It wouldn't by any chance happen to be a *magic* dragon, would it?"

CHAPTER FORTY-TWO

There is something to be said for a pungence so revolting that it wakes people up from the deepest of sleeps – a sleeping potion in reverse, like smelling salts dipped in rotten eggs – and in this case it was another of Bingo's farts that did the trick, Numb Tongue, Snot, and Dum Dum all spluttering back to consciousness at the same time, each of them wearing the same expression of horror.

"For the love of God!" coughed Dum Dum. "That's rotten!"

They were on a deserted road somewhere, George and Mad John on driving and navigational duties, although Mad John seemed to be providing company more than directions as George already knew where he was going. It was long into the night, the Land Rover's headlights revealing a narrow, two-lane road lined with sparse, white trees that seemed to glow in the dark. Dum Dum wouldn't have been surprised to learn that they were called Ghost Trees, but instead he asked if Mad John might wind the window down a bit further. Something wasn't right with that dog's arse.

"Not far to go now," George assured them. "Couple of miles."

"What time is it?" asked Dum Dum.

"Dunno," said George. "Three-ish?"

Dum Dum groaned: "Won't it be closed?"

"F-f-fortunately not," grinned George.

Sure enough, the pub was just a few miles up the road, and just as George had promised it was open. Not that anyone would have known from the outside, just a dull glow above the sign hanging outside the pub to show that the place had *ever* been open to the public, but, nonetheless, after George had knocked on the door just so, it was answered by a buxom lady in her mid-forties, fully made-up, and dressed as it were mid-afternoon. On quite a hot day, given that she was wearing very skimpy jean shorts and an unusually revealing T-shirt.

"Friend or foe?" she said.

"Stop f-f-fooling around and let us in."

"Oh, it's a f-f-friend," grinned the lady, ushering them inside. "Well, this is an unexpected surprise, George. How have you been? Who are your friends?"

"Jeanie, this is Mahjong," George introduced Mad John. "He's an old friend of mine, trust him with my life."

"The pleasure is mine, Jeanie," said Mad John. "George has told us all about you."

"He has?" said Jeanie, evidently quite surprised.

"Actually, not a word," Mad John smiled, "which is rather odd considering how much he likes to talk. Jeanie, this is Numb Tongue, Dum Dum, and Snot."

"Well, I've heard stranger names in my time, but not by much," Jeanie winked. "Let's get you all a drink, shall we? It is a pub, after all."

It was, in fact, quite a nice pub, once you got inside. On the outside it appeared to be boarded up and ready for demolition or collapse, but that was because it was one of a very special chain of pubs, thirty-eight in all, spread out around Australia, all of which were cunningly disguised as complete shit-holes. Even the name, The Roo Inn, was designed to be off-putting, a dump with a wacky sense of humour. The interior, however, was clean and welcom-ing, with not a speck of dust on the oak wood bar, nor the frames of the many ship-themed paintings that decorated the walls. There was a ship's wheel mounted on one of the walls, too, and the air outside tasted curiously salty considering they were still inland and nowhere near the sea, but, besides that, there was nothing remotely unusual about the place. If anything, it felt like an old English pub, and, more to the point, the bar was incredibly well stocked.

"I'm sure it's been a long journey," said Jeanie, "so if any of you are hun-gry I'm sure I can find you something to eat."

They were all hungry.

"Is she the only one that works here?" asked Dum Dum, when Jeanie headed off to the kitchen.

"Yeah, she's run this place for f-f- a fair few years," said George. "Caretaker, so to speak. She keeps the place safe."

"From what?" Dum Dum asked.

"Everything," said George.

Dum Dum was sure that there were some serious spells protecting the place, as his ears had not yet fully recovered from the weird popping sensation when he came through the door. It was stronger than he'd ever felt before, and he yawned to try to get rid of it. Mad John handed him some chewing gum.

"Thanks," said Dum Dum. "How did you know? Stupid question..."

He knew it was a stupid question the moment he asked it; he'd been asleep in the Land Rover for hours, so he was unlikely to be tired. And now that they weren't in such a confined space with Bingo's rancid backside, he felt reasonably fresh. It was also quite nice to find that his mental jukebox had turned itself off for a while, and he quite deliberately didn't turn it back on again.

"I'll tell you later," said Mad John, suggesting that it hadn't been such a stupid question after all.

They found themselves seats in a booth, roped off and heavy on the ship motif.

"All salvaged," George told Dum Dum, noticing that he was taking it all in. "All the wood, the rope, everything from the sea. I hope you like f-fish."

Tomorrow they would journey to the coast and meet a famous, albeit not particularly magical, dragon called Puff. At least not magical in the sense that it could perform any spells, it was more that Puff was protected by magic. George had told Dum Dum this earlier, and Dum Dum was rather excited about it. He knew that dragons were real – Mad John had told him so – but he had never seen one in the flesh, never expected that one day he'd be introduced to one, least of all a dragon that he'd actually heard of.

Over his time with Aberrant MC, more so as a full-patch member, Stone had taught Dum Dum to appreciate the moments every now and again. And this was definitely a moment; not a life-changing moment, but a moment to reflect upon those life-changing moments. It was a life that was enjoyable at this particular moment, and he'd been taught to enjoy that more. So he enjoyed it now.

He'd met Merlin, for one thing, which was pretty cool, and while multiple journeys in seats that were far too small were beginning to get tiresome, it was also pretty cool to have pulled off a robbery and not have anyone looking for him. His previous attempts, all three of them, had led to him being the prime suspect within hours, sometimes minutes. It was a totally new experience to have got away with it. And now he was going to get to meet a dragon, which, again, would be pretty damn cool. Or, if it went wrong, pretty damn hot!

But George seemed fairly confident that wouldn't happen, and, despite the burns, Dum Dum had every confidence in him. If Mad John trusted him, had faith in him, then that was good enough for Dum Dum, when all was said and done.

"So how are those new boots treating you, Snow?" George was asking. "Got any blisters yet?"

"Not yet," she smiled. "But I don't doubt they're coming. The last pair took forever to wear in."

Dum Dum listened contentedly as George gave her advice on softening leather with olive oil. Small talk. Idle chit-chat. It was nice, sometimes, to talk about nothing much, things that didn't really matter. And if the truth be told, Dum Dum got a bit lost with some of the big talk. Boots, he could understand.

Jeanie began to bring out food, baskets of bread, and then fish, potatoes and vegetables, all home-grown. Apart from the fish, obviously, which tended to grow themselves. She laughed at her own joke, doubtless told a thousand times, but it was genuine nonetheless, a warm and some might even say sexy laugh. Certainly Dum Dum would say so, and though he didn't like to flatter himself, he could have sworn there was an exchange of glances between them, a hint of flirtatiousness. Probably not. Hollywood motels notwithstanding, he wasn't very good at that sort of thing, and it wasn't right to make assumptions just because someone was nice.

"That was f-fabulous," said George, when they had finished eating. "Thank you, Jeanie."

"Yeah, thanks, Jeanie," agreed everyone at once.

"My pleasure," she smiled that sexy smile.

Plates were cleared – with Snot put on dishwashing duty – and short drinks were poured all around, just a nightcap. Casually, Jeanie asked a few details about why they were here, why they were going to see the dragon. Her tone suggested that she was merely making conversation, but Dum Dum had been inside enough police stations to know otherwise, so he kept his mouth shut. He knew 'good cop' when he saw it.

It also explained the flirting, which was a bit of a shame.

CHAPTER FORTY-THREE

Vincent had no idea how far he'd imagined they would be walking. It seemed, at times, like they would never stop, like they'd just keep walking forever, always with miles of endless desert ahead of them, miles and miles of fuck all. When they did stop it was only to hide from the worst of the sun, they were never 'there yet'.

Of course, he was aware that at some point they'd either catch up with the dwarfs or the dwarfs would reach their own destination, and there would be some kind of showdown; they couldn't just keep following the little buggers in circles around Australia. It was quite another thing, however, to find out that the little buggers only lived about twenty miles away in a small range of mountains that had seemed forever distant. Suddenly it all seemed a lot more real.

And suddenly plans were being hatched, weapons readied, and messages sent. Vincent had seen Stone talking to a huge black raven for the good part of an hour this afternoon, before the bird took off heading presumably east, and the occasional odd look or vacant stare indicated that much was being said with telepathy, not just within their small army. This was confirmed when it became known that more help was on the way from the north, more Aboriginal warriors, nearly a hundred in all, who were converging with the other group of two hundred or so that they already knew about. They were nowhere near enough, and still two days away, but every little helped.

A day's walk, that's all it would take to reach the dwarf city now known to be called Badger. At least, it sounded like Badger, and when Vincent repeated it back to Feenat she seemed to understand. He had no idea how it was spelled, but Badger would do for now. And it was in the underground city of Badger that Derain was being held captive, now confined to an iron cage to stop him from using magic. Derain's final message to them had come about four hours ago.

For now the small army waited, preparing as best they could, an air of nervous anticipation about them. They were well hidden behind a steep, rocky terrain, an almost-cliff face, with giant boulders and skeletal trees, but look-outs were posted in case of any stray patrols. The patrols would be in for a hell of a surprise if they ran into this lot, but it wouldn't do for anyone to get back to the city and raise the alarm. Should the circumstance arise, prisoners were to be well treated.

Vincent was having a well-earned rest from talking to Feenat duty, when Stone came over to join him by the small campfire. There was coffee and soup of some description, although Vincent found it was best not to ask what was in it, one man's delicacy being another man's disgusting creepy-crawly thing.

"Hey, Stone, how's things?"

"Good," said Stone, helping himself to coffee and rolling the inevitable joint. "Well, mostly good."

Stone stared at the fire, puffing on the joint. He blew on his coffee, even though it wasn't particularly hot, took another puff on the joint, and handed it to Vincent with a nod of his head that said it was safe to smoke. It was like a poker tell, and Vincent had never mentioned that he did it. If he shook his head, the slightest of movements, it meant you were in trouble and likely to have a really bad trip. Thankfully, he had never done so with Vincent.

As ever, Vincent waited for Stone to continue. You got used to the long pauses after a while; he seemed to drift off, only half there, pausing in the middle of conversations sometimes, and not say anything for a few seconds, even minutes. And then he'd sort of snap back to whatever you'd been talking about. Before Vincent had known about the telepathy he had always just assumed Stone was really, really high. Now he just assumed that Stone was really, really high *and* talking to someone else. He also had a good idea of what was coming next, and no doubt that it would involve him sneaking about trying to be invisible.

"Mostly?" Vincent ventured.

"Yes," nodded Stone. He took the joint, took a puff, exhaled and watched the smoke dissipate.

Vincent waited.

"Yes," Stone eventually repeated. "Yes," he nodded to himself.

"I saw you talking to the raven," Vincent prompted.

"Yes, yes," said Stone, inhaling deeply. "Mad John is bringing reinforcements if all goes well. We'll be moving a bit closer to the city..."

"Badger."

"Badger?"

"It's the name of the city," said Vincent. "Sounds like Badger, anyway."

"Yes, well, we'll be moving a few miles closer tonight," Stone continued, "but otherwise we're to sit tight and formulate a plan. We don't know exactly where they're holding Derain, but we have a rough idea."

"And, let me guess," grinned Vincent, "you want me to go in there and find him?"

"Absolutely not!" Stone frowned, looking, for a moment, unreasonably surprised that such a thing would even be suggested. "Well, not yet anyway, it's far too dangerous until we know a bit more about the place and where they might be keeping him. No, it's Flashback, I'm afraid."

Stone took another hit on the joint and handed it back to Vincent. Some time passed.

"Flashback?" Vincent prompted again. "Is he okay?"

"No, not really," said Stone. "It's certainly not the best timing, that's for sure."

Another long pause.

As much as Vincent liked Stone, it could get somewhat frustrating trying to talk to him when he clearly had his mind in two places. And in many ways it was a rhetorical question asking if Flashback was okay. The man was a lunatic, a drunken, drug-addled maniac! He was *never* okay!

"For what?" Vincent asked patiently.

"Hmm?"

"Not the best timing for what?"

"Timing?" Stone seemed to have momentarily forgotten what they were talking about. "Ah, yes, Flashback," he added, apparently back in the here and now, if not the why. "I've done what I can, of course."

For fuck's sake, it was like pulling teeth!

"About what?"

"I do wish you'd pay attention," Stone said somewhat irritably. "About Flashback. He's going through withdrawals. Like I say, I've given him something for now, just to take the edge off, but it won't last long. He's in quite a bad way."

Vincent gave Stone a questioning look. If Stone didn't have anything strong enough to deal with Flashback's comedown then nobody did. The man could dose entire armies – sometimes with only three pills – and while it was true that Flashback had a drug tolerance that made Keith Richards look like a lightweight, if Stone didn't have it then it probably hadn't been invented. Between the two of them they were so toxic that they needed some kind of warning that you could get wasted just standing near them.

But Stone took breaks every now and again, recharged, did a little meditation and yoga, while Flashback continued with medication and vodka. A lot of medication and a lot of vodka! It wasn't just about partying and having fun, it was about shutting something out, shutting something *off*. And for Flashback it wasn't lost loves or heartache he was hiding from, it was magic, so deeply ingrained in him that it never gave him a moment's peace unless he was wasted. Of course, they were all used to him being something of a stranger to sobriety, but no one had realised until now how deep he was hiding. According to Stone, Flashback was now a gibbering wreck, hallucinations, the whole deal. He had no idea where he was, and what's more he'd started spouting what sounded like rather unpleasant spells. It was difficult to tell, because he wasn't speaking English anymore, nor a language that anyone could understand.

"To be perfectly honest," said Stone, "we're a little worried that he might accidentally turn someone into a toad or something. He's more than capable. He won't tell anyone where he's getting all those rabbits, but you can thank him for the soup."

"Right," said Vincent, still somewhat perplexed. He nearly asked what exactly this had to do with him, but that might have got him into trouble. It was all about the wording. As a prospect for Aberrant MC it had *everything* to do with him that his vice president was going cold turkey, it was just that he wasn't in possession of anything stronger than a couple of aspirin, possibly not even that.

"I'm sorry, I don't see how I can help," he said.

Stone took a long hit on the joint, watching the smoke again as it drifted from his lips. He moved his mouth and blew a smoke ring, just so.

"Well," he said, "it's like this. We need you to go and get him a drink."

CHAPTER FORTY-FOUR

Of course, there couldn't be a conveniently located off-licence or a pub around here, that would be far too easy, far too bloody convenient. It had to be a five-mile walk across pitch-black bloody desert towards what may or may not be a dwarf outpost of some kind, where said dwarfs may or may not have some booze.

Actually, it was quite likely that there would be booze there if it was a dwarf outpost, since dwarfs, rather like Australians, liked to accompany all of their meals with beer before getting on with some proper drinking in the evening. It was devastatingly strong, too, from what little Vincent could remember of when he'd tried a few pints. The first beer was rather refreshing, enlivening almost, making you think it might be a good idea to sing a song or two. It was sweet-tasting, like honey, but with a curious hoppy aftertaste. Halfway through the second beer you generally fell over and passed out. Dwarfs could drink extraordinary amounts of the stuff before they passed out.

Now that he got closer, Vincent could see that it was indeed a dwarf camp, and around the campfire that had acted as his desert lighthouse, he could see four dwarfs, all of them wearing chain mail and armed with heavy axes worn across their backs. He crouched in the darkness, scanning the area for more of them. Two more were asleep a little distance away from the fire, easier to spot now that his eyes had adjusted. He could see no sign of any booze.

Vincent edged a little closer, aware of every sound, every crackle of the fire, every footstep. The dwarfs were talking amongst themselves. They seemed to be angry about something, disgruntled, but Vincent was just guessing from their mannerisms and the tone of their voices. He'd never encountered dwarf soldiers before so perhaps they were naturally angry and disgruntled. Certainly they looked a fearsome bunch, stout barrels of muscle on legs like tree trunks.

Vincent nurtured his fear and let it wash over him. It was a good idea to be afraid, the more scared the better, since it helped him to become invisible. And it was a fucking good idea being invisible if you were going to sneak into a dwarf camp and steal their beer. For a horrible second it occurred to him that, given his new nickname, his magic ring might have stopped working completely, its power finally gone, and that he'd just stroll right up to his death. He let that fear wash over him too, and threw in funnel-web spiders for good measure.

Sufficiently terrified he crept forwards.

Closer still, he paused again, watching and listening, his senses charged. He took a breath and crept on. The soldiers around the campfire were still grumbling, and there was some sort of cricket nearby, a lone chirruping sound in the darkness. And then, all of a sudden, Vincent heard an unmistakable groaning noise and he froze in his tracks. Not two feet away, previously unnoticed, was a dwarf squatted down behind a bush, taking an apparently very gratifying dump. He was looking straight at Vincent.

Vincent stared back at the dwarf. If he reached out his arm he could touch the dwarf, poke the little bugger in the eye, and yet the dwarf continued to look straight at him, straight through him, as he unabashedly dropped his load. Which was good news and bad news; the good news being that Vincent's invisibility ring was working fine, the bad news being that he'd have to watch a dwarf taking a shit.

An evil part of his mind thought about giving the dwarf a good shove, but now was no time for childish pranks, perfect though the timing might have been. He allowed himself a smile at the thought of the dwarf rolling arse over end with his trousers around his ankles, but he did not move and he made no sound. There would be nothing funny about an angry, shit-covered dwarf charging at him with an axe.

Instead Vincent waited.

And waited.

Seriously, mate, what have you been eating?

Finally, the dwarf gave another satisfied grunt and rose from his crouched position, yanking his trousers back up without feeling the need for any more than a cursory wipe with an old rag. Then he headed back to the campfire, with Vincent following close behind using the noise of the dwarf to mask any that he might make himself. It was something Vincent felt he'd got down to a reasonably fine art, walking to someone else's pace to disguise his own steps, and it was best done with some degree of confidence, though not so much that you forgot to be scared.

Thankfully, Vincent was also confident that he'd be in a world of pain and misery if he got caught, which helped with not forgetting to be scared. Something just below a level of complete terror was best where that was concerned. Any more was a debilitating fear, paralysing, which was no use at all unless you wanted to stay rooted to the spot, like the proverbial deer in headlights.

The tricky part now was to sneak around going through their stuff. Vincent had learned that if he picked something up when he was invisible then it would also disappear, as did his bike when he was riding it, but his task would still not be easy. He still left footprints, still made sounds. In a crowded bar his biggest problem was not getting stepped on, but out here every noise seemed amplified. Was he breathing too loud? Was his heartbeat too loud? It sounded to Vincent like Philthy Animal Taylor playing *Overkill*, but that was a good sign, that was the blood pumping around his veins, and it meant he was still alive.

It would have helped if the dwarfs themselves were making a bit more noise, perhaps getting stuck into a few drinking songs, but instead they fell into silence, all just standing around looking vaguely pissed off. One of them poked at the campfire with a stick – because where there's a campfire there's always someone with a good stick – but he said nothing, lost in thought.

Vincent was out in the open by now, scanning the area for anything that looked like it might contain alcohol. There was a wooden cart with some supplies on the back, Hessian sacks tied with rope, but without opening them it was impossible to say what they contained, and Vincent would not be popular if he returned to Flashback with a sackful of dirty laundry.

He considered, for a moment, throwing a stone into the bushes to create a distraction, but, as he'd learned the hard way in previous similar situations, this tended not to have the desired effect. One or two of them might go and check it out, but the others would stay behind, all the more alert. If he was going to distract them he was going to have to be quick, in and out before they knew it, not rummaging through sacks on the back of a cart. What he needed was less a distraction and more a diversion.

It was then that Vincent had what he thought to be quite a clever idea. Or possibly a monumentally stupid idea. He thought it through again. It might actually work. Of course, if it didn't work then he might have all seven of them – Dopey, Grumpy, Sleepy, Oliveri, Hewho, and all – angrily waving axes about, but then that would be the time for a distraction, wouldn't it?

But, no, seriously, of all the fucking stupid ideas...

Ever so slowly, Vincent tiptoed his way over to the two sleeping dwarfs. They both slept under thick blankets, using their kit bags for pillows. Both slept with their axes. Vincent inched closer and closer still, until he was standing right beside one of them. Absolutely sound asleep. Up close he looked quite old, but dwarfs often did. They lived a long time. This fella could be three hundred years old, wise and proud, and steeped in ancient tradition.

Got any better ideas? Nope...

Vincent bent down and flicked the dwarf hard, on the end of the nose.

As plans went, it really wasn't that bad. In fact, it took two flicks to the bulbous proboscis to rouse him, but according to plan the dwarf woke up – aptly, a little grumpy – and, after an accusatory glance at his friends, headed straight for the beer, which was indeed on the wagon.

So far, so brilliant. And it didn't hurt that the dwarf was stomping about having a minor tantrum, all the better to cover Vincent's tracks. There were several large clay jugs inside the sacks on the wagon – five gallons or so – and Vincent was able to steal one as easily as simply lifting it up and walking away with it.

What wasn't so brilliant was that he walked away in completely the wrong direction.

CHAPTER FORTY-FIVE

Dum Dum opened his bedroom window and took a great big lungful of fresh sea air. He could taste the salt on the morning breeze, hear the cry of gulls. Stretched as far as the eye could see was a golden coastline, shimmering blue seas, and the cloudless blue sky that marked the start of another baking hot day. Which was extremely odd, because none of it had been there before he went to bed.

"Hmm...that's extremely odd," said Dum Dum, and went downstairs.

In the kitchen, Jeanie and Snot were preparing breakfast. They shooed Dum Dum away when he offered to help, so instead he went and sat with a mug of tea, over by the back lounge window. It really was the most glorious coastline, gentle waves breaking in flecks of white against the warm, golden sand, and beside it an empty road lined with palm trees, not a soul in sight. Paradise.

Yes, extremely odd indeed.

Dum Dum sipped on his tea. It had been dark when he'd looked out there last night, but not so dark that he couldn't tell land from sea, not so dark that he couldn't make out half a dozen or so trees that were now rather conspicuous in their absence. Last night, aside from the trees, there had been nothing but desert out there, outback, as they liked to call it. Today it was... different.

By the time breakfast was ready Mad John, Numb Tongue, and George were all up and about, and they joined Dum Dum at his table, overlooking the view that hadn't been there yesterday.

"Well, fine day for it," acknowledged George.

"It's a different view," said Dum Dum bluntly. "There was trees out there last night."

"One of Jeanie's little tricks to keep f-folks away who shouldn't be here," said George, tapping his nose to indicate secrecy. "What they can't see can't f-f-fully interest them."

"What, like a magic spell?"

"I told you," said George, "all these pubs are protected by magic. Only a few of them even... Oh, thank you, Jeanie, that looks f-f-fabulous," he broke off as breakfast began to arrive. "I was just telling Dum Dum here about... Sorry, let me move that for you. There we go."

There was some rearranging of plates and utensils, salt and pepper shak- ers, a couple of bread baskets and butter dishes, a jug of iced water, and George never did get back to what he'd been saying about the Roo Inns. This was more to do with a sharp warning look from Jeanie than an absent mind, a reminder that loose lips may have been responsible for the ship-themed décor of the place, and that furtively tapping one's nose before revealing a secret did not guarantee the keeping of said secret.

As Dum Dum understood it, the chain of pubs – the Wetherspoons of witchcraft, so to speak – had lots of branches dotted all over the country, each of them, as George had carelessly revealed, guarded by magic. He now suspected that many, if not all of them, might have hidden landscapes in their backyards, oceans where there should be desert, perhaps mountains where there should be lakes or forests. Either way, he hoped that Mad John had brought enough chewing gum.

"Well," said George, when breakfast was finished, "I suppose we'd best be making tracks. Tide and time wait for no man. Let's just hope the f-f-f-f-..."

George floundered. Two ladies present, after all, and he'd gone far too deep into the sentence without thinking it through.

"Fu-f-f-..." he tried again.

"Fortunes?" offered Snot.

George paused, looking at once immeasurably grateful and not a little confused. You could see the cogs moving as he tried to fit this new word into a space that was clearly designed for "fucking". Let's hope the fucking van starts, let's hope the fucking dragon doesn't set us on fire, let's hope that George can finish his fucking sentence...

"Fortunes," he grasped, all eyes upon him. And then suddenly there was a moment of relief written upon his face. "Yes, let's hope the fortunes shine upon us," he managed finally, triumphantly.

"Yes," agreed Jeanie. "Let's. Otherwise you're all fucked."

With the Land Rover still packed and ready to go, they bid Jeanie farewell, and left her chuckling to herself as she went back inside the pub. George was obviously rather embarrassed about Jeanie's foul language, and they drove in silence. It was difficult to say how the giggling started, but it was probably Snot's fault.

"Yeah, alright, alright," George said at last. "You try to show a bit of f-respect, and that's what you get."

After that they drove in a more comfortable silence, no words to spoil the beauty of the scenery, just miles and miles of paradise, until, out of nowhere, paradise was lost. Suddenly the land began to look scarred and blackened, scorched palm trees lining the road, some no more than charred stumps. No one needed to be told what had happened here. The sign was just as George had described it: 'Welcome to Honali', unscathed by fire, if not by time and seagulls. And beyond it the remains of a town turned to ashes.

The song came into Dum Dum's head, *that* song, but it played at the wrong speed, all slow and mournful, a funeral dirge. So this was what Puff the magic dragon had done? It looked more like the work of Puff the psychopathic dragon! Puff the completely insane. Nothing had been left standing.

Presently they came to a fork in the road, and George turned left, driving the Land Rover a few incinerated blocks, before parking close to what would once have been a pier. Perhaps once there was a gift shop here, and a penny arcade, but now there was nothing but ruins.

"Best if I go in alone," said George. "I'll leave the keys, just in case."

He stepped down out of the vehicle and closed the door, and then, with a nod to Mad John, he set off along the beach, walking with a purposeful stride. His words seemed to hang in the air; just in case. Just in case he didn't come back. Not half a mile away were the caves that led to the home of the dragon, the town of Honali inadvertently built right on the doorstep.

The town had stood for thirty years, happy and prosperous, a charming picture postcard, until, one day back in 1802, a couple of teenagers decided to do some exploring. People didn't really go in the caves because the high tide could sneak up and trap them inside. A kid had drowned in there once. But these two teenagers thought they knew better, thought they'd see just how far these caves went. From where the pier used to be, the mouth of the cave looked like no more than a dark shadow cast against the rocks at the end of the beach. It was months before anyone really noticed it, and a while still before anyone went inside. But when the tide went out it was possible to climb down and explore, and that's the kind of thing that teenagers do.

It was late when they came back, the sun long gone over the horizon, and at first their tales of dragons were dismissed as nothing more than lies, adolescent fantasies invented to get them out of trouble. It wasn't until two nights later that the sheep started disappearing, and then one of the farmers. Within two weeks Honali was burned to the ground, the dragon turning land and sky to fire and ash.

Today they watched from the Land Rover as George made his way along the beach, repeating the journey he'd first made in 1802. Even though it had been three months since the fires, there were still bodies in the streets, still funerals to arrange and relatives to inform about the terrible "mining explosion". And there was still a dragon to confront. George paused now, as he must have paused then, taking one last backwards look, one last breath. The tide was on its way out.

"Balls," said Numb Tongue quietly. "Must've taken balls."

George climbed down into the entrance of the cave and was gone, once more to meet his dragon, if not to meet his maker. There were no words, nothing that could be said.

It was Dum Dum who broke the silence. "Can you crack that window open a bit, John. Bingo's let one loose again."

CHAPTER FORTY-SIX

Meanwhile, behind some rocks in the middle of the desert, Vincent was taking a very well-earned rest, basking lizard-like in the glory of his success, and tucking in to roasted wild boar. Flashback was saved, and so was the day. Hurrah! Mostly...

The truth is that a five-gallon jug of dwarf beer weighs nearly fifty pounds, so stealing it hadn't been nearly as easy as Vincent thought it was going to be. He'd lifted it from the wagon without too much trouble, but he hadn't got more than a hundred yards before his arms gave out and he all but threw the jug to the ground. Thankfully, he didn't alert the dwarfs with all his racket, but this was also when Vincent realised that he was probably, almost certainly, going the wrong way, on account of the fact that he didn't know which way was the right way. That's the thing about desert, it all looks the fucking same.

Vincent had paused to get his bearings and his breath. He'd done his best to leave markers along the way, a cigarette packet here, some silver foil there, but he could have done with some paint to mark his trail. There were a million wrong directions in the desert and only one right one. Miss by six inches, then walk for five miles – even assuming you walked in a straight line – and you'd end up in a whole world of lost.

He'd come into the dwarf camp from the other side, but carrying the jug back through the middle of the camp wasn't going to work. Vincent was unlikely to make it all the way without putting the jug down, or at least making some sort of grunting noise. And, worse still, if he let go of the jug then it would suddenly reappear like it had popped out of thin air, which would inevitably make the dwarfs freak out. The last thing Vincent wanted to deal with was a bunch of freaked out dwarfs.

He would have to go around, try to find the dwarf turd to use as his first marker, and go from there.

Realising the enormity of his task, Vincent took a deep breath and hauled the jug onto his shoulder, already uncomfortable with its weight. He steadied himself, a look of determination upon his face. Even without the fifty-pound jug, five miles was a hell of a long walk across inhospitable terrain. On the way here, Vincent had stumbled on rocks and tripped on roots, twice almost falling. It wasn't like the desert was all flat sand the way Vincent had imagined it, there were rocks and boulders, cracks and dips in the earth, and horrible spiky plants to land on.

Soon it would be getting light and he wouldn't have to rely on the flashlight he'd borrowed, but full sunrise was still a way off, and there was nothing quite as dark as middle-of-nowhere dark. With people so used to light pollution in the cities it was easy to forget what real dark could mean. It was bitterly cold, too, when the wind picked up, but he'd made it this far, and he'd damn well try to make it back again. If the weight got too much to bear he could always tip some of the liquid out: Flashback would never need to know that the jug had been full.

Vincent staggered off into the desert.

Of course, Aberrant MC wouldn't leave him to die out there, not intentionally at least, but it might be a while before they thought to send someone to look for him, by which point the search radius would be pretty wide. They put too much faith in him sometimes, gave him far too much credit for knowing what the hell he was doing. Vincent could see the constellations, the Big Dipper and whatnot, the other one, but he didn't know what any of it actually meant. Come to think of it, he didn't even know which particular cluster of stars was the Big Dipper. He could no more navigate by the stars than he could tame a lion.

Were there lions in Australia? Oh, fuck, please don't let there be lions.

Vincent strained under the weight of the jug, shifting it on his shoulders. Surely five gallons couldn't weigh this much? It was like carrying a suitcase full of...

Vincent stopped in his tracks. Something was moving towards him in the darkness.

...bricks.

Vincent didn't move a muscle. Something was definitely coming, but it sounded more like a person than a lion. He stayed frozen to the spot, the jug growing heavier by the second now that his momentum was gone. If he dared to put it down he would inevitably make too much noise and give away his position, but if he didn't then he would eventually be forced to drop it. He didn't dare to breathe, didn't dare to blink.

And then Vincent heard a familiar voice in the night.

"Nhama nhuna yukurra."

"Tike?"

"You want a hand with that, mate? It looks like it might be a bit heavy."

So the truth was that Vincent hadn't been entirely alone in his beer heist – the beer run from hell, as he now thought of it – and without Tike's help he might still be getting increasingly lost. It was something he was going to have to work on, this whole astrology thing. Or was it astronomy? Either way, it was thanks to Tike that he made it back to camp in one piece.

Vincent helped himself to another slab of wild boar. Apparently there were hundreds of thousands of them running around loose in the Australian outback, wild, as the name suggests, which would have been useful information to know before setting off looking for beer. He said as much to Tike, who was perched on a nearby rock.

"For what purpose?" Tike asked with a cheeky grin.

"What do you mean, for what purpose? They're fucking dangerous, aren't they? *Wild* boar!"

"Yeah, but they can either see you or they can't," reasoned Tike. "If they can't see you then you've got nothing to worry about, and if they can see you then you're fucked anyway. It's not like sneaking about is going to make any difference."

"Yeah, fair point, I suppose," Vincent conceded. "Are there lions in Australia?"

"Only in zoos."

"Good."

Vincent had no idea whether or not he'd be visible in the presence of lions, and even less desire to find out. Certainly he was visible in the presence of Tike, who had taken it upon himself to follow Vincent all the way out to the dwarf camp, and had apparently nearly wet himself laughing when Vincent flicked the dwarf's nose.

When asked why he'd followed, Tike had shrugged it off as, "just what mates do," but Vincent was nonetheless extremely grateful, not just for the help carrying the heavy jug and with finding his way back to their camp, but for the company and the friendship.

Not that Aberrant MC weren't his friends, his brothers, his family, but as a prospect Vincent was constantly expected to prove his worth to the club, to act independently while doing pretty much as he was told. Sometimes it was nice to just hang out with one of your mates, and Tike was such a mate, expecting nothing but friendship in return. It was kind of a weird feeling, something that Vincent had never really experienced before, having a best friend. Most of the time his face hurt from laughing, and he quite liked his new nickname, Nhama. It was kind of cool that Tike could see him, and not just literally.

Once again, the heat of the desert began to rise. By midday it would be nudging triple digits, too hot to do much more than hide beneath makeshift shelters and try to rest as best they could before whatever was coming next. By the sound of it they would be here for a couple of days until reinforcements arrived, and there wasn't much else they could do but wait. According to Stone they'd be moving camp tonight, but only a mile or two, just a little closer to the dwarf city.

At last Vincent felt he had time to take his boots off and inspect his growing collection of blisters, perhaps even use a splash of water to wash his feet, or at least put a clean pair of socks on. Oh, the luxury, the bliss, the...

"Prospect!"

...fuck do they want now?

Vincent let out a long sigh. Not for the first time he was tempted to feign deafness or pretend to be asleep, but the thought only lasted a moment. Aside from anything else, whoever was yelling – and it sounded like Smiler – would only shout louder or come to wake him up. As a prospect Vincent was never really off duty unless he was told otherwise.

"Prospect!"

"Yeah, yeah, I'm coming," Vincent muttered.

He clambered to his feet and headed towards the yelling, which did indeed turn out to be Smiler. With him were Stone, Chaos, Andy One-Leg, and Zig Zag, and in front of them was a sheet of paper on which a crude map was drawn.

"Sit yourself down," said Smiler.

Vincent sat.

"So, this is a rough map of the area, roughly to this scale," Smiler explained, pointing to the map and to the measurements on the left side of the paper. "There's a valley here, a dried-up riverbed here, we're here, and this bit in the middle, this big hill-mountain thing, is where we reckon the dwarf city is. We want you to go and have a word with your dwarf and see if you can find out where the entrances are."

"My dwarf?" Vincent protested. "She's not my..."

"She is now," snapped Smiler. "Take the map and go and see what you can find out."

There was no point in complaining. Besides, apart from the fact that baby-sitting a dwarf wasn't exactly difficult, just mildly annoying, it was always vaguely flattering when the club gave him a task because they thought he was the best man for the job, rather than just being too lazy to do it themselves.

Unfortunately it took less than five minutes to discover that Feenat was missing.

CHAPTER FORTY-SEVEN

There were two openings to the vast cavern that Puff called home, the larger of the two accessible only by sea and only if you happened to be a dragon. It took a couple of hours to reach by the route that George had taken, so Dum Dum decided to go for a wander around the remains of the town. Mad John was engrossed in his writing, and Numb Tongue and Snot had gone for a walk on the beach, so there wasn't really much else to do.

It was fucking depressing. Dum Dum could only guess how many people had perished on that fateful day, but among the ruins he found a child's toy, a small wooden horse, charred at one end, and it made him realize the full extent of the horror that had descended upon the seaside town of Honali. Men, women, and children, no one had been spared.

Carefully, Dum Dum placed the toy back where he'd found it. He felt as if a moment of silence was in order, but his mental jukebox decided that it wanted to listen to *Firestarter*. Shut up, he told it, but twisted firestarter was about right. No matter what odds the club were up against, it didn't seem right to enlist the help of such a cruel and vicious beast as Puff the psycho dragon. Regardless of the outcome, there was some help that was never welcome.

Dum Dum expressed his concerns when he returned to the Land Rover, interrupting Mad John from his writing.

"I sincerely hope that it won't come to violence," said Mad John, setting aside his pen and paper to give Dum Dum his full attention. "All we want is for Derain to be released and to ensure that the dwarfs don't kidnap anyone else, but it would be foolish to think that our demands will be met so easily when we are so few in number. Even with a dragon on our side we will be vastly outnumbered."

Mad John went on to explain that in the dragon's defence it had never encountered humans before those two teenagers went exploring the caves, and may still not have done so for hundreds of years if they hadn't woken it. Humans were just food until they started fighting back, after which they were dangerous food. And all creatures who hibernate tended to wake up hungry, especially those who hibernate for so long. There was no malice in the dragon's actions, no more than when humans hunt. Indeed, humans were often more of a threat to dragons than dragons were to humans, which is why George had taken it upon himself to mediate whenever possible.

"Yeah, but still," said Dum Dum. "What if it goes nuts again and burns everyone? Including us!"

"I'd be lying to you if I said I wasn't concerned," Mad John admitted, "but George knows what he's doing. There's more than one dragon in Australia, and he wouldn't have brought us here if he didn't think we were safe and that the dragon would help us."

If he was honest with himself, Dum Dum still had his doubts. He'd been keen to meet the dragon, excited even, until they got to Honali, but that was before he'd seen the place. Though he'd been told about it by George, the true extent of the devastation never really sank in. Now it seemed as if they might be bringing guns to a knife fight, unnecessary firepower that could wipe everybody out whether they were part of this or not.

Then again, Dum Dum was also having trouble getting his head around how any amount of dwarfs could be much of a problem. Orcs were a different matter; they were big buggers even by Dum Dum's standards, and vicious as a pack of hyenas, but the biggest problem with dwarfs was trying not to accidentally sit on them. Granted, they'd be armed, but they'd be getting in each other's way if they all attacked at once, likely doing as much damage to their own side as they did to any foes. Dum Dum had seen enough of that in bar fights and in prison; ten guys would jump one, and they'd all end up punching each other by mistake. Being surrounded just meant you could attack in every direction.

Still, if Mad John thought it was necessary to bring in reinforcements then Dum Dum wasn't about to argue. In fact, he should never have doubted his president – and had never doubted his judgement before – it was just that seeing the child's toys made him realize that the dwarfs probably had children of their own. And you don't mess with children. Ever. In prison, very nasty things happened to people who messed with children, and Dum Dum had done some of those nasty things.

"It's okay to have doubts, Dum Dum," said Mad John, always able to read him like an open book. "As the philosopher Bertrand Russell once said, 'the fundamental cause of trouble in the world today is that the stupid are cocksure while the intelligent are full of doubt'. Don't ever be afraid to ask questions. How else are we expected to learn?"

Dum Dum wasn't entirely sure what a philosopher was, but he wasn't about to ask that particular question. He knew it was something to do with stones, but that wasn't important right now. The main thing was that he understood what Mad John was saying, and, once again, he felt a little less stupid for asking. It was okay not to know, so long as you were trying to find out.

There was one question that was burning on his mind, however, something that Merlin had told him, but the more he thought about it, the less he knew how to ask. And perhaps it was more of a puzzle than a question: How the hell could he be forty-two and four at the same time? Okay, so troll years and human years were different, but he still had one birthday every year, and he'd certainly had more than four of them. He'd been a prospect for Aberrant longer than four years, done longer stretches in prison. And that wasn't including all his years in school, which, again, had been considerably more than four.

True, age was just a number, when all was said and done, particularly if you were a member of a club whose combined age needed to be added on a calculator, but what worried Dum Dum was that he might, as Merlin had suggested, still be growing. And if he was, then just how much would he grow? He was used to being bigger than everyone else, over six feet tall by the time he was thirteen years old, and it had been something of a relief to find someone taller than him in Numb Tongue. But Numb Tongue was built like a basketball player, long and thin, all knees and elbows, whereas Dum Dum leaned more towards sumo wrestler. It had been a while since he'd been weighed or measured with any accuracy, but he now suspected that he was rather more than 350lbs and inching ever closer to seven feet tall. And if Merlin was right then he was basically still a toddler!

But, again, it wasn't a question that Dum Dum felt he could ask, not least because there was no answer that was any better than an educated guess. Bridge trolls, by all accounts, tended to grow according to the size of their bridge, some of the smaller bridge trolls reaching no more than four feet or so, but since Dum Dum didn't have a bridge, the sky was the limit. That was what worried him! What if he never stopped growing? What if....?

Dum Dum had tried asking his music, so to speak, but he'd found that if he used that talent, or magic, or whatever the hell it was, too often then it had a tendency to play games with him. First there was the Ramones version of *I Don't Wanna Grow Up*, then the UK Subs *Teenage*, followed by *Silly Kids Games* by The Damned, at which point he turned it off to save his battery. Maybe if he asked again later it would stop messing around.

"You know," said Mad John, breaking his train of thought, "worry is a waste of a good imagination."

"Sorry, John," said Dum Dum, and stopped picking his nails.

They sat in silence for a while, watching as Numb Tongue and Snot practised some sort of mixed martial arts by the water's edge, kung fu or tai chi or some such, Dum Dum didn't really know the difference. They made slow, graceful movements, gentle waves lapping around their feet, and Dum Dum was reminded of snakes getting ready to strike. Certainly, those two were as dangerous as snakes, and it was always inspiring to watch them train, although today, for some reason, it felt slightly voyeuristic, more like they were making love than training for combat.

And then, once more, the spell was broken.

"For fuck's sake, Bingo, that's disgusting!"

CHAPTER FORTY-EIGHT

Afternoon passed into evening, the sun dipping below the horizon in the most breathtaking fashion, and then there was darkness, and yet still no sign of George. The wind picked up, moaning and wailing around the Land Rover, like the ghosts that doubtless haunted Honali, and still they waited, no one wanting to speak the inevitable truth that George might not be coming back. Minutes passed as hours. Tension made way for tedium.

Snot dug out her book about Australia and tried to lose herself in it, reading by torchlight now that the sun had gone, but she found herself unable to concentrate, reading the same paragraph over and over. It probably didn't help that it was about spiders. It also didn't help that Dum Dum was snoring rather loudly.

Mad John was sleeping now, too, and beside her Numb Tongue stared out of the window at nothing. He did quite a lot of that sort of thing, and sometimes it was best not to know what was going through his mind, best not to ask. Indeed, sometimes Snot couldn't help wondering how she had fallen for such a damaged human being, but the truth was that beneath all that scar tissue there was a very wonderful man, and, perhaps one day, a wonderful father.

She worried, sometimes, that she was merely following the path taken by so many women who made the mistake of thinking that they could change their man, that perhaps she was seeing something in him that wasn't there, but at the same time she had witnessed his kindness first-hand, the extent to which he'd go to help a friend, or even a stranger. They had been friends once, a long time ago, and it was not for no reason that he was known as a saint. That person was still in there somewhere, even if he was bricked up behind the wall he'd built around himself.

If nothing else, Snot was sure that she wasn't causing him any further harm. Unlike his former wife, her one-time friend, Sunshine, she could be trusted not to betray him, not to take his love for granted. Many was the time that Sunshine would flirt with other men, careless of the consequences, no matter that it would make Numb Tongue hate them and hate himself. It said a great deal of his character that he knew better than to beat them up, knowing that it was her fault and not theirs. Allowing Snot even the slightest trust was a big step forwards. The rest would follow in time. Instead of asking if he was okay, Snot gave his hand a gentle squeeze, and joined him in his silent contemplation.

Inevitably her thoughts turned to the journey ahead. Even if George did come back their journey was far from over, and there was a strong chance that they would have to do battle with an army of dwarfs at the end. Before that they would have to somehow find the rest of Aberrant in this vast country, which itself seemed like an impossible task.

Of course, Merlin had sent a message to them, but she had no idea whether or not they'd received that message, and, as a prospect, it was not her place to ask. She could only hope that some sort of plan was falling into place. George had sent out ravens before they left his farmhouse, presumably with further messages for the others, but, again, she could only guess whether those messages had been received. What if none of them had got through?

Moments later that last question was answered by a loud tapping on the windscreen that almost made Snot jump out of her skin. Perched on the hood of the Land Rover, and looking not a little angry, was a large, black bird.

"John," said Numb Tongue, roused from his reverie and nudging the president awake.

"Hmm?" said Mad John, somewhat bleary-eyed.

"Bird."

Mad John wound down the window and spoke to the raven in a strange gurgling croak, rising in pitch, and coming from the back of his throat.

The raven regarded Mad John, for a moment, its head cocked to one side, and then, in a voice that sounded remarkably like George said, "Fair dinkum, mate, your accent's not too fucking shabby, but we can speak English if ya like. Wouldn't mind getting out of this fucking wind for a bit."

"Of course," said Mad John. "Please, come in."

The raven came in through the open window and perched itself on the dashboard, poking and preening for a moment at its ruffled feathers.

"Sorry," it said. "Fucking long flight. I see George isn't back yet."

"No," replied Mad John, concern written upon his face. "We're getting a little worried."

"Shouldn't if I was you," said the raven. "Takes a while to deal with drag-ons. Slow as shit, half of them. You're basically talking to dinosaurs! And he'll have to wait for the tide to go back out before he can get out of the caves."

"I thought that might be the case," Mad John nodded, "but still, it's been some hours. What news do you bring?"

"Well, I found yer mates," said the raven. "That Stone fella's an all right bloke. Had a good old chat with him. They're not far from the dwarf place, asked me to go and have a scout around, but I couldn't really tell him much. Every time I got close they'd fucking shoot arrows at me. Lucky for me they can't aim for shit. Place is pretty heavily guarded though."

"You think they're expecting us?"

"Couldn't tell ya, mate," the raven appeared to shrug. "Didn't hang around too long. I wouldn't wanna be you if they are! Your mates are basically wait-ing for you lot to show up, but you'll need more than a big fucking lizard if..." The raven appeared to notice Snot for the first time. "Shit, ladies present," it said, apparently unaware that this meant it was supposed to stop swearing, and more of an observation. "Anyway, like I say, yer mates are doing okay, pleased to hear you were coming to join 'em."

"Good," said Mad John. "Thank you for your help."

"No worries," said the raven. "Don't s'pose you've got any food? I'm fuck-ing starving."

It was some hours later when George finally returned, the dim glow of his torch moving slowly along the beach from the cave mouth. It seemed to take an age before he reached the Land Rover, all of them eager for news. George looked tired and a little grubby, but otherwise unharmed.

"Well, that's done," he said, as he climbed into the vehicle. And then, spot-ting the raven, added, "Oh, hello Bramwell. You the first?"

Given the vast area they had to search, George had sent out all but two of his eight ravens, one of the two remaining being too old for long journeys, while the other had stayed behind in case George needed alerting of any-thing from his farmhouse. The rest were presumably still searching or en route back to Honali, their designated meeting point. Indeed, at that very moment another raven arrived, landing on the driver's side mirror of the Land Rover and demanding to be let in. It seemed rather annoyed to see Bramwell back already, particularly since its own search had been fruitless.

With these distractions out of the way, George told them about his meeting with the dragon, which had gone exactly according to plan. They would leave at first light in the morning, and, since flying was faster than driving, Puff would catch up with them later. Payment for the dragon's services would be made in advance.

"What if he just takes the gold and doesn't show up?" asked Dum Dum, still harbouring doubts that Puff could be trusted.

"Don't you worry about that," replied George. "Dragons ain't like people; if they give you their word then they f-f-f-find a way to keep it. Besides, if he wanted to do that, then he'd have done it already. I had to tell him where you were so he could come and get it."

"Come and get it?"

"Well, I'm not carrying that bloody thing all through those caves. Weighs a f-f-f-frightful amount."

"Come *here* and get it?"

"Well, where the f-f-...?" George gave up. "Yes, here, Dum Dum."

"Oh," said Dum Dum. "Right."

And so it was that the five of them, George, Dum Dum, Mad John, Numb Tongue, and Snot settled down as best they could, with three dogs and two ravens, in what was fast becoming a rather cramped Land Rover, awaiting dawn and the arrival of the dragon. Not for the first or last time they wished that Bingo had waited outside.

CHAPTER FORTY-NINE

Vincent poked his head up from behind the rocks, and got a face full of sand for his troubles. He ducked back down again, cursing to himself. How the fuck were you supposed to be a lookout when you couldn't see past the end of your nose?

It was long into the night, many hours since Feenat had disappeared, and still there was no sign of any horde of angry dwarfs coming to slaughter them all. Not that there was any sign of anything at all on this pitch-black night, but it seemed like even the angriest of dwarfs might wait until these bitter winds died down before coming to get them. Only an idiot would venture out in this.

And maybe there was no horde; maybe Feenat had simply gone home and was now tucked up in a nice warm bed, which would be the sensible thing to do. Or, just as likely, she was lost and wandering around in circles again. Either way, at least no one was blaming Vincent for her absence. It wasn't his fault that she had run away. Frankly, he'd be more than happy if he never saw her again, and happier still if they could all just fuck off back to civilization, a hot bath, and a good night's sleep.

Instead, they waited. Once in a while Vincent would stick his head back up over the rocks and see nothing, then he'd hunker down again, trying to dig himself deeper into his wargskin jacket, burying his hands in the pockets. He was thankful for that at least, especially since he'd loaned his sleeping bag to Tike. Some of their party weren't quite so lucky, wrapped in just hotel bedsheets against the bitter cold. At this rate half of them would freeze to death long before any hordes arrived.

Eventually Vincent was relieved of his watch – just one of several lookouts posted around their camp – but try as he might he couldn't get to sleep. And then, much to his surprise and acute disappointment, he woke up, apparently having slept after all. It was still dark and the wind was still blowing like Satan's backside, and now, on top of everything else, he felt entirely unrested and even more uncomfortable than before. Surely this had to be the longest night in history.

Vincent thought back to his previous adventures, like a tongue poking around a mouth looking for a rotten tooth, but he couldn't think of a more miserable night than this. And that was including the night he'd spent in a cannibal-infested cave, watching one of their former club members die. Which was a terrible thing to think, but nonetheless true. He'd ridden through terrible storms, soaked to the skin and clinging to his handlebars for dear life. He'd fought for his life on a boat that was attacked by a kraken. He'd fought his way out of an orc city. He'd infiltrated skinhead gangs in Berlin. And none of it had ever been as crappy, as miserable as this. During those dark times, if nothing else there had been an end in sight.

Vincent closed his eyes, trying to will himself to block out these negative thoughts and look to the positive. If he was homeless then he'd be out in this every night. But you *are* homeless, his treacherous mind reminded him. You don't actually live anywhere, you just get to stay in a fancy hotel every now and again, but more often than not, you sleep on the sofa or the floor of some club-house. Tomorrow the sun will rise, he tried again. Yeah, and it'll be too fucking hot. And you'll still be in the middle of this poxy desert, waiting for an army of dwarfs to show up and hack you all to pieces. And – guess what – if the dwarfs don't come to you, you'll be going to them on some doomed rescue mission.

Oh, woe is me, thought Vincent, and then allowed himself the merest of inward chuckles, because nobody actually thought that. Except, perhaps, his father, Mad John, who seemed to have trouble letting go of phrases that were no longer in use. But then, he'd also been nailed to a tree for six hours, and then jabbed in the chest with a spear to make sure he was dead, so he didn't tend to sit around wallowing in self-pity. There were worse things in life than freezing your tits off.

As if reading his mind, the wind redoubled its efforts and changed direction, giving the parts of Vincent's face that weren't covered another sandblasting. He cursed to himself, as the wind howled like a mean-tempered ghost, playing tricks on him now, calling his name.

"Veen-sent! Veen-sent!"

He sat bolt upright, straining to hear.

"Veen-sent!"

That was no wind. Someone really was calling his name.

"Tike," he hissed. "You awake?"

"I'm hardly gonna sleep in this fucking weather, am I," grumbled Tike.

"You hear that?"

"What?"

"I heard someone calling my name."

They both sat and listened as the wind continued to howl, but there was nothing but the mournful cry of the desert. Until...

"Veen-sent!" There it was again.

"I heard that!" said Tike. "It's that fucking dwarf!"

They sprang to their feet, and once more peered out over the rocks at darkness, but, again, there was nothing to see, and nothing that could be seen with eyes full of sand and grit. There was no mistaking the voice though...

"Veen-sent!" There was a note of desperation about it.

"You think it's a trap?" asked Tike.

"Doubtful," shrugged Vincent. "It's not exactly subtle if it is. I think it's more likely that she wandered off and got lost again. I suppose we'd better go and find out."

In fact, it didn't take very long at all to find the dwarf, but although there was no trap, it turned out that she was not alone. With her was another dwarf, slightly taller, slightly stouter, and almost certainly male. The two of them stumbled out of the blustery darkness, all but blown off their feet by the wind, Feenat's face breaking into a broad smile as soon as she saw Vincent, while her companion looked wary and somewhat nervous. Feenat began babbling away in her usual gibberish, and then, quite unexpectedly, the other dwarf stepped forward.

"My name is Gilgin, son of Norgrim," he said with a bow. "Do I have the honour of addressing Veen-sent the wizard?"

"Yes, I mean no," said Vincent, somewhat taken aback. "It's pronounced Vincent." And I'm not a wizard, he thought to himself, but didn't say aloud.

"My apologies," said Gilgin solemnly, his accent sounding vaguely Germanic. "I did not mean to offend. My friend Feenat has told me much of your greatness, but I am afraid she does not speak your tongue. I owe you much gratitude for saving her life, a debt I would hope to repay if I can be of some assistance. I am at your service."

"Oh," said Vincent. "Right. Well, I suppose you'd better come with us then."

The short journey back to camp was made shorter by the wind at their backs, pushing them on, and Vincent left Tike with the dwarfs while he went to find Stone. When they returned, Feenat began babbling again, apparently explaining something to her companion.

"Gilgin, son of Norgrim," said Gilgin, with another bow. "And you are the great apothecary I have heard so much about."

"Stone," said Stone, returning the bow. "I am told you have come to help us in our quest."

Gilgin, it transpired, was one of only a handful of English-speaking dwarfs from their city, his job being to deal with humans whenever it was necessary to trade with them. Learning the language was otherwise forbidden, as was any interaction with humans aside from guarding occasional prisoners, which was done by an elite squad of rather unpleasant troops. Clearly, Gilgin was taking a great personal risk by being there without permission, but such was his gratitude to them for saving Feenat that he felt obliged to assist them as best he could. Feenat, he explained, was his fiancée; they were due to marry in three weeks' time, and he'd been worried sick since she disappeared. He had no idea what he was there to help with, but he was willing to do whatever he could, his tone making it clear that he had no love for either his job or for those he was serving.

He listened intently as Stone explained their situation, although Vincent noticed that Stone played down their numbers and made no mention of any reinforcements, just in case Gilgin was not what he seemed to be. It was wise to keep some element of surprise, however small that might be.

When Stone was done, Gilgin conversed for a moment with Feenat in their own language. They appeared to be in agreement.

"One hundred men will not get into the city," Gilgin addressed Stone bluntly. "Even one thousand men is too few. One man, however, may get past the guards unnoticed, especially," he added, turning to Vincent, "if that man were invisible."

CHAPTER FIFTY

Once again Vincent found himself poking his head out from behind a bunch of rocks. It was getting to be a habit. The wind had died down so at least he wasn't treated to another blinding face full of grit, and the sun had risen some hours ago, already too hot for comfort, but for the life of him he couldn't see any entrance to the dwarf city, just a craggy cliff face with a few spiky shrubs clinging stubbornly to its surface. Admittedly, they were planning to sneak into the city the back way, through a disused and perhaps long forgotten tunnel, but as close as they now were to the cliff face he'd expected to see some sign of it, maybe a hole or a metal grill or something. Certainly there was no door.

They ducked back down behind the rocks. Feenat and Gilgin both looked at him expectantly, clearly waiting for the all-powerful wizard to do his disappearing act. Between them and the supposed entrance lay a hundred yards or so of open ground.

"Um," said Vincent.

The trouble was that he wasn't actually scared; tired, yes, oh so desperately tired, his legs like wobbly jellies after yet another long trek across this godforsaken desert, but not afraid. And unless he could manage to summon some fear they'd be looking at him all day. He hadn't had the heart to tell them that he wasn't really a wizard.

Ironically, it would have helped if the place was heavily guarded, but dwarfs, as Gilgin had explained, were forbidden from leaving the city without the correct papers, so they could hardly go strolling in through the main gates. As an emissary for the dwarfs, Gilgin was permitted to leave in order to conduct business on their behalf, but Feenat would have some serious explaining to do, not least because she had only just returned after being listed MIA for several days. Thankfully, she wasn't the first dwarf to have got lost out there, separated from the rest of her company when a sandstorm blew up in the middle of the night, but it wouldn't be good if she was caught outside the city again, especially not so soon. Instead they would have to use this secret way in, which was left unguarded for the simple reason that it was, well, a secret.

Vincent tried to imagine what was on the other side, tried to imagine it being a trap, but it was no use. If Feenat and Gilgin wanted to set him up then there were far easier ways of doing so than this, like, for instance, not telling him about the secret entrance, and just handing him over to the guards at the front gates. Invisible or not, there was no escape if he was surrounded. Besides which, the two dwarfs seemed a lot more scared than he was, so it was pretty obvious that they weren't setting him up; they were too worried about getting caught themselves. If they were apprehended then they could always claim that he was a prisoner, but that wouldn't explain what they were doing outside the city in the first place.

Vincent took one last look at where the entrance was supposed to be, still unable to spot anything that resembled a door. And then, for want of a better idea, he legged it.

In fact, the door, when they reached it, turned out to be not only extremely well hidden, but extremely well made. This probably shouldn't have come as a surprise to Vincent since dwarfs were known, among other things, for their excellent masonry skills, but still he couldn't help being impressed when Gilgin pushed the appropriate rock and the stone door swung open like it was on rollers. It must have weighed over a ton, and yet he'd never even have known it was there, much less that it could be opened so easily.

Another thing that probably shouldn't have surprised him was how low the ceiling was on the other side of the door, no more than five and a half feet high, which meant he'd have to walk with a stoop so he didn't crack his head. It was dark inside the tunnel, too, the bright sunlight penetrating no more than about ten feet, and offering no clues as to where the tunnel went or how long it was, although he guessed that it went deep into the mountain, a gentle declivity suggesting that it went down as much as in.

There was an oil lamp mounted on the wall, which Gilgin lit before closing the door behind them, and Vincent was thankful for the fresh batteries
in the torch that Chaos had loaned him, but still it took a while for his eyes
to adjust to the darkness. At last he felt a glimmer of fear, but not enough yet
to make him disappear. It was an irony not missed on him. When he'd first
started prospecting for Aberrant MC he used to vanish all the time, afraid of
his own shadow, but the braver he became, the less his invisibility ring was of
any use to him. It had yet to fail him when he truly needed it, but just in case
he dug into his jacket pocket for the tranquillizer darts he'd been armed with,
a gift from one of the Aborigines, made from plant extracts, and powerful
enough to render most people unconscious in seconds. They were supposed to
be reserved for the escape plan, a way out of here after he'd found Derain, but
it didn't hurt to keep a couple of them handy.

They walked in single file, Vincent following behind, and perhaps a mile
into the tunnel went down a short flight of stone steps, at the end of which was
a dead end. Gilgin extinguished the oil lamp, instructing Vincent to turn off
his torch, and for a moment they stood in pitch darkness.

"There is a door," whispered Gilgin. "Now would be a good time to be
invisible."

The door, another well-disguised stone construction, opened into darkness, and Gilgin relit his oil lamp to reveal what was once a storeroom of some
kind, perhaps a wine cellar, although there was no sign of any wine, just row
upon row of empty shelves. Thankfully, the room was empty, too, which was
just a well, since Vincent had still failed to become invisible. It was getting
rather embarrassing.

"I'm, er, saving it for when I need it," he told Gilgin, who was clearly
beginning to have his doubts about the so-called wizard.

The storeroom had a heavy wooden door at the far end, with a thick metal
grill at about eye level – or at least eye level for a dwarf. Gilgin peeked outside into the dark corridor beyond, and, satisfied that the coast was clear, he
stepped outside, beckoning for Feenat and Vincent to follow.

They walked in silence, Vincent stooped as ever to avoid head injuries,
and at last his nerves began to get the better of him. Somewhere off in the
distance, deep inside the mountain, there was a dulled thudding noise, like
a giant pounding on the walls. Thump! Thump! Thump! Heavy machinery,
presumably mining equipment, but it certainly added a layer of tension, and

Vincent let his imagination run wild, deliberately fearing the worst. Fear was good. Fear might save his life.

Presently they reached the end of the tunnel, and it branched off in two directions, one leading to the right, the other leading left and down. They turned left, and then, no more than a hundred yards farther, did another left where the tunnel offered three possible routes. They went down a short flight of stone steps, took a right and then another left. Vincent tried to remember them all – right, left, left, right, left – already knowing he'd be hopelessly lost without a guide to get him out of here.

Another right. Past two wooden doors and two more tunnels leading off to the left. Down, down, always down. Thump! Thump! Thump! And then, at last, they came upon a long corridor that was lit by oil lamps mounted along the walls. They turned the corner and suddenly found themselves face to face with a couple of stern-faced guards, all but walking straight into them.

Vincent had no idea what was said next, but angry words were spoken, the two guards having apparently been caught napping on the job. They looked behind Gilgin and Feenat as if expecting to find someone else, and Vincent had to press himself against the wall to avoid being discovered. Given that the guards looked directly at him, he could be sure that his ring was working, but he suspected that it had only worked at the last minute and that they may have caught a glimpse of him before he disappeared. Certainly, they were deeply suspicious of something.

Finally satisfied that there was no one else to be found, they demanded papers from Gilgin and Feenat, presumably ID, and their manner became less hostile. It appeared that Gilgin outranked them, but Vincent got the impression that, even so, neither of them were supposed to be down here. Or up here, as the case may be. Eventually one of the guards laughed at something Gilgin had said. The rest was just idle banter, polite conversation, body language suggesting that the guards were rather pleased with themselves.

At last the guards stood aside to let them pass and they continued on their way down the long, long corridor, Vincent ever careful to match the others' footsteps. Instinctively he knew that the guards were watching them go. He prayed that they wouldn't notice the third shadow.

CHAPTER FIFTY-ONE

The third shadow was a worry. In all the times that Vincent had done his disappearing act, he'd never noticed before that he cast a shadow when he wasn't there. Well, obviously he *was* there, just invisible, but the fact remained that it made him a great deal easier to catch if he didn't keep his wits about him. Which, evidently, he hadn't been doing if he'd only just noticed it.

He thought back to previous incidents, trying to pinpoint a moment when it might have been more apparent, but nothing came to mind. Not once had he or anyone else noticed a shadow, and the more he thought about it, the more it became a concern. An ill-lit tunnel with no easy escape routes was not the best place to be making such discoveries.

By now they were perhaps a mile or more inside the mountain, perhaps even as far down. They passed more doors, most of them closed, but Vincent saw occasional signs of life here and there, living areas, and through one half-open door, a busy kitchen. All the while the distant thumping noise continued, but it seemed like it was farther away now, more like a heartbeat than someone trying to kick down a door. Maybe he'd just grown used to it.

Once in a while Vincent would have to sidestep a dwarf who was coming the other way, and at one point Gilgin stopped to chat with a friend, his manner suggesting that he was keeping the conversation brief, just being polite so as not to arouse suspicion. He and Feenat appeared more relaxed now though, apparently no longer in a part of the city that was forbidden to them. It was somewhat reassuring when they moved on and Gilgin whispered to Vincent to make sure he was still with them.

The three of them had walked another half a mile or so when they stopped at a small wooden door – there were no other kind of doors – which opened into what turned out to be Feenat's living quarters. The room, little more than a hole carved into the stone, was sparsely furnished, just one chair and a wooden bed, more a prison cell than a home, although even a prison cell might have a toilet. As is so often the case for those who have nothing, the place was spotlessly clean.

"We will wait here until the guards change their shift," said Gilgin. "Please, take a seat. We will not be disturbed."

And so they waited, the two dwarfs sitting on the bed, both visibly relieved when Vincent reappeared. They were by no means the first to find it somewhat disconcerting being in a room with someone they couldn't see. It generally made people uncomfortable, even angry sometimes, but they both recognised that it was necessary in the circumstances. It wasn't like Vincent could just stroll in there as their guest.

Time passed slowly. Gilgin apologised for not being able to offer any food, but meals were served at set times, and there were heavy penalties for stealing even a loaf of bread. Beer was more readily available, but Vincent declined because it wasn't a good idea to pass out or start singing, and the last thing he needed was Dutch courage. Instead they sat in nervous silence, glancing towards the door at every passing sound.

Perhaps two hours went by, and then Gilgin got to his feet. He spoke briefly to Feenat, and although Vincent didn't understand the language, he understood well enough what was being said. It was a personal moment of reassurance and love, and, if they were caught, a last farewell. Gilgin and Vincent would continue from here, but Feenat had no authority to go beyond this point, and must wait behind, hoping for the best. It was a stark reminder of what was at stake if things went wrong.

Moments later they were back in the maze of corridors, Vincent needing no reminders that he should disappear, and having no problem doing so. Even his shadow was gone.

Finally they reached a gate with two guards on the other side, and Gilgin handed one of them his papers through the metal bars. The guard gave them a cursory glance and opened the gate, Vincent slipping quickly through on Gilgin's heels. So far so good.

"Still with me?" whispered Gilgin.

"Yes."

At the next gate, however, the guards were rather more officious and a great deal less friendly. They scowled at Gilgin, examining his papers as if they might be forged, and barked questions at him, obviously treating him with great suspicion even though he must have been this way thousands of times. Worse still, Vincent's shadow was back, as clear as day, and he had to quickly reposition himself behind Gilgin in order to hide it. Given that it had been some time since he'd taken a shower, Vincent was also beginning to worry that the dwarfs would start to notice the smell, particularly in such close confines. He was, he had to admit, getting a bit whiffy.

Try as they might, the guards could find nothing wrong, and they grudgingly opened the gate, Vincent slipping through once more, and it wasn't long before they reached Gilgin's living quarters. They were rather more comfortable than Feenat's place, with running water for both the sink and the toilet, a more comfortable bed, and a wooden desk, presumably for work purposes, Gilgin's higher status affording him slightly more privilege. But it was still little more than a hole in the wall. When they were married he would have to give up even these small luxuries as his future wife had no clearance for this part of the city.

According to Gilgin, they had an hour to wait before the guards changed their shift at the next gate, and Vincent would have to take that opportunity to sneak past, as Gilgin had no clearance to go any farther. If he missed his chance then he'd have to wait another twelve hours. The first time they'd waited because Gilgin knew the guards personally, now they waited because Vincent would be going alone.

It was probably the shortest hour of Vincent's life, but that was something of a relief. There was no going back, and no sense in dragging it out. Best to just get on with it. He stepped out into the dimly lit corridor, just in time to follow the guards to their post, Gilgin heading back the way they had come, his part in the rescue over for now.

The final obstacle proved to be almost embarrassingly easy; the guards were mean looking, hard-bitten warriors, but since they obviously weren't expecting any problems, they were lackadaisical at best, standing around chatting with the gate open, and taking their time handing over the keys. All the same, there was no escaping the fact that once Vincent was on the other side he was locked in and would have to find his own way out.

He wondered, briefly, how long it would take, should he get caught, for a rescue party to show up and get him, but there was a distinct possibility that they wouldn't show up at all. Not that they wouldn't try, of course, but as Gilgin had already pointed out, they were too few in numbers to storm the place. And, now that Vincent had seen it for himself, he knew they'd never even get past the first gate without resorting to explosives that might bring the roof down on top of them. Dum Dum could probably bend the bars, but he could still be days away, and, more to the point, he'd never fit in these tunnels. And that was assuming they could even find a way into the place without charging the heavily defended main gate.

Either way, the club weren't expecting Vincent back yet, so he pushed the thought to the back of his mind, letting it linger amongst his many other fears as he pressed on into the semi-darkness. According to Gilgin, the lower levels of the city, way down underground, had electricity, but here the corridors were still lit by oil lamps, some of which needed refuelling, and had either gone out or were flickering their last.

It wasn't long before Vincent came to the first prison cell, and with it the stench of human waste. At first glance it appeared to be unoccupied, but as he peered through the metal bars he saw a movement beneath a pile of old rags, and a gaunt, white face peered back at him, so thin as to be not much more than skin stretched over a skull. The man struggled to pull himself upright, clearly close to death.

"Please," he said, his voice hoarse, barely more than a whisper.

"You can see me," said Vincent, somewhat redundantly. Obviously the man could see him.

"Please..." Again, just a whisper.

Vincent dug inside his jacket pocket and pulled out a bottle of water, recently refilled in Gilgin's room. He rolled it across the floor to the living skeleton.

"I'm looking for someone called Derain," he said. "Aborigine bloke, would've been brought here in the last few days."

The skeleton regarded Vincent through sunken eyes, then, slowly, he nodded, even that small movement taking all his remaining strength. "That way," he said, as if there were any other way. "I don't know if he was still alive."

Vincent stared at him through the metal bars. He had no words. What do you say to a dying man? Whatever the man had done, he surely didn't deserve to starve to death in this godforsaken place.

Finally the moment was gone. "I'll be back," said Vincent. "I'll get you out of here."

But the man was already dead.

CHAPTER FIFTY-TWO

Several hundred miles to the south, the Land Rover rattled along a dirt track, an impenetrable cloud of orange dust in its wake, and an equally impenetrable cloud of Bingo filling its interior. Above it, a mere dot in the sky, flew Puff the massive dragon, roughly equivalent in size to the jumbo jet that had brought them to Australia, but rather lacking in complimentary peanuts.

Snot liked to think that she knew a thing or two about aerodynamics, but even she was impressed by how effortlessly the dragon stayed airborne, and more so by the languid fashion with which it got off the ground. Admittedly, the gust of air created by those giant wings had almost tipped the Land Rover onto its side, but it had taken no more than a few lazy beats for the creature to get into the air, and once there it seemed able to ride the thermal winds like a hawk.

Faeries, by comparison, had to expend an enormous amount of energy in flight, flapping their wings like hummingbirds, at about fifty beats per second. In human form they could, if they so wished, retain their wings, but only for decorative purposes; they couldn't actually fly with them. They were basically little more than glorified ostriches. On the other hand, Snot could function reasonably well on the ground, the occasional stubbed toe notwithstanding, whereas Puff, when he was not in flight, was arguably among the clumsiest creatures she had ever seen, barely able to take more than two steps without tripping over his own feet.

The dragon had showed up just after dawn, swooping down from the cloudless sky like some vast, black hang-glider, and landing with all the grace of a sack of potatoes thrown from a tower block window. Backing up like a heavy goods vehicle it had turned to face the Land Rover and peered into the passenger side windows, its head being a little bigger than the Land Rover itself. George had stepped out to do the talking, and then they'd unloaded the gold, the dragon sniffing at it, presumably to make sure it was real, its ebony scales gleaming in the morning sun.

Snot had harboured doubts that they would ever see the creature again, but she kept them to herself, George having assured them several times that the dragon could be trusted. And, sure enough, it had caught up with them sometime after midday, a majestic flypast announcing its arrival, and almost blowing the Land Rover off the road.

"F-f-foolish show-off," muttered George, his smile betraying his admiration.

Despite the heat and the ever-present stench of Bingo, it was a pleasant journey, white sands stretching out to cobalt seas on one side, and verdant trees on the other, not a soul in sight. Snot half expected them to come across a cocktail bar or some sort of tourist trap selling toy koalas and boomerangs that were unlikely to come back – or sticks as they should more properly be known. Indeed, if not for the black dot high up in the sky, it would be possible to think they were just going to do a spot of sightseeing.

A few hours later, however, the dirt trail came to an abrupt end, its path blocked by trees, and George was forced to take the Land Rover onto the beach, which itself soon turned from sand to rocks. Progress became slow, and more than once they were forced to climb out of the vehicle and move large boulders by hand, even Dum Dum straining to lift the biggest ones. The only other alternative was to go back and take a route that was, according to the ravens – all of which had now returned – several hundred miles longer. As the crow, or indeed the raven, flies, this way was considerably shorter, but unfortunately Land Rovers don't fly.

Or at least that was what Snot had reasonably assumed, but apparently Puff had other ideas.

They'd been toiling for about an hour, the Land Rover crawling along at a snail's pace, when the dragon grew tired of circling above them like it was in a holding pattern over Heathrow, and landed nearby, its great wings kicking up all manner of sand and ocean spray. George went over to have a word, an odd expression on his face when he returned.

"Well, I've never heard of such a thing," he said, "but Puff said he'll give us a lift."

"We're going to ride a dragon?" asked Dum Dum, not a little excited.

"No." George shook his head. "I mean he's going to carry the Land Rover."

And so it was that twenty minutes later they were dangling several hundred feet off the ground, the Land Rover gripped firmly in the talons of a giant reptile that could, if it so chose, drop them onto the rocks at any moment. Being so ungainly on the ground the dragon had to swoop down on the vehicle, catching them like prey and giving them all an all too vivid idea of what it felt like to be a small rodent that was about to become breakfast to an owl. It was not a pleasant experience.

Needless to say, the takeoff had been terrifying, but perhaps more unnerving was the way the Land Rover creaked and groaned above the howling wind at every beat of the dragon's wings, and the way that the tips of Puff's great claws had pierced the sides of the vehicle upon takeoff, like some massive tin opener. Understandably, George was not at all happy about this and seemed just one horrid squeaking noise away from letting loose some most unsavoury language. Snot could only imagine what he'd be saying if there weren't 'ladies present'.

Still, there could be no doubt that they were making considerably faster progress, and once you got past the abject terror of the situation the view was quite incredible. They turned inland from the ocean, passing over many miles of rain forest, and then farther still, over wide mountain ranges with great, jagged peaks, where the forest seemed to determinedly cling on with trees growing from the cliff face at the most bizarre angles. Snot had lived most of her life in a forest, but never had she imagined anything so magnificent as this. She wondered for a moment if faeries lived here, too, but then she remembered all the spiders and snakes and horrible creepy-crawlies that were down there, and dismissed the notion as foolish, glad to be seeing the place from a distance.

Beyond the mountain range the land turned to desert, a sun-scorched, featureless earth that stretched as far as the eye could see. It was difficult to imagine being farther from home, and while Snot was pleased to have seen such a place, she was quietly relieved when at last the sun began to sink low over the horizon, a breathtaking sunset slowing giving way to darkness. Somehow the terrain was a little less scary if you couldn't see it.

She rested her head on Numb Tongue's arm, his shoulder being rather too high, and must at some point have drifted off to sleep, because she awoke with a start as she felt a sudden blast of cool night air. The driver's side window was wound down, and she watched as one of George's ravens flew out into the darkness, the other five birds still lined up like beady-eyed dashboard ornaments. Presumably it was being sent off with a message and would travel faster than a dragon that was hauling a fully laden Land Rover.

Numb Tongue noticed her move: "Hungry," he said, not a question but a demand, and she rummaged around in the back for food, wondering, not for the first time, why the club didn't do things for themselves sometimes, rather than waiting for a prospect to do it for them. Then again, she had asked for no special privileges when she signed up and would not have received them anyway; all prospects were treated the same. And although it was an odd balancing act, being both Numb Tongue's girlfriend and a prospect for the club, it was no less difficult for Vincent being Mad John's son.

She found bread and cheese in the cooler, and an assortment of truck stop snacks, which would have to do for now. There was tinned food, but nothing to cook it on. She made Numb Tongue a sandwich and grabbed him a beer, helping herself to a bottle of water and something that professed to be a fruit bar, but tasted like it was made of rubber. She chewed on it until her jaw began to hurt.

The raven returned no more than a couple of hours later, which suggested that they were close now to their destination. It flew alongside the Land Rover, keeping pace until George wound the window down to let it back in.

"All good?" George asked.

"Well, I found 'em, if that's what you mean," said the raven.

"And?"

"And I wouldn't want to be you when you try to land this fucking thing!"

"Language," scolded George. "Ladies present."

CHAPTER FIFTY-THREE

As a runway it was far from impressive, but then, as an aeroplane, neither was the Land Rover. On the ground a reasonably flat strip of desert had been cleared of rocks, and two rows of small fires were lit to act as landing lights. The dragon came in low.

"Hold onto your hats, fellas," said George. "Could be a bumpy fucking ride."

No ladies were present.

Against her wishes, if not necessarily her better judgement, Snot had been instructed to vacate the vehicle before they attempted to land, adopting faerie form and leaping from the open window into the chill night air. The ravens had followed without needing to be told. Everyone else strapped in as best they could.

And then, perhaps five feet from the ground, Puff let go.

The dragon had slowed as much as possible, but they were still doing thirty or forty miles an hour, and the Land Rover came down hard, bouncing as it hit the makeshift runway, and then careening to the right as George struggled to maintain control. For a moment it rattled along on two wheels, and if not for Dum Dum's weight acting as a counterbalance might have rolled and flipped end over end. Instead there were some terrible grinding noises, and much of the luggage that had been strapped to the roof decided that now was a good time to scatter itself across the desert, but the vehicle finally came to a halt on all four wheels.

Behind them the fires were hurriedly extinguished so as not to draw any further attention, although, with Puff still circling, anyone coming to investigate would be in for a nasty surprise. Doubtless the dragon was hungry after such a long journey, and a dwarf patrol would make for a tasty snack.

"Everyone alright?" asked George, as the dust settled. "Dum Dum, you're bleeding."

Dum Dum had cracked his head against the inside of the Land Rover and there was a trickle of blood running down his temple, but it was not a serious injury, and aside from a few scrapes and bruises everyone appeared to be unharmed. Even the Land Rover started first go and appeared to be relatively unscathed. They clambered out to a cold night and a warm welcome, exchanging hugs with fellow Aberrant members, all of whom were suitably impressed by the manner of their arrival. The club had a habit of making rather grand entrances, but even by their standards getting airdropped by a dragon was pretty cool.

"Your timing is perfect," Stone told them. "We just received news from Vincent."

"News?" Mad John looked concerned. "I thought he was with you?"

"Change of plan," said Stone. "Don't worry, he's fine. Come and get yourselves settled and I'll get you up to date."

Settled, it transpired, meant sitting on the ground behind a large rock, but it was not particularly uncomfortable, or at least not to Dum Dum, who much preferred being outdoors to being crammed inside the Land Rover. He welcomed the opportunity to stretch his legs, and was more than happy when someone handed him a slab of wild boar, his stomach having long complained that truck stop snacks weren't sufficient to keep it from grumbling.

Stone, meanwhile, got them up to speed with the latest news. Apparently, with the assistance of a couple of friendly dwarfs, Vincent had made his way to the dwarf city where Derain was being held captive, and, having successfully freed him, was now deep inside the mountain somewhere, awaiting further instructions. Understandably it was suggested that those further instructions might be something along the lines of 'get the hell out of there so we can all bugger off home', but unfortunately it wasn't quite as simple as that. It rarely was.

Vincent had walked the long corridors, peering into each dark cell, often gagging at the smell. At the end of each corridor was a sharp turn leading to yet more cells, beyond which was more of the same. He was appalled by what he saw; there were hundreds, if not thousands of prisoners down there, dwarfs and humans alike, many of them close to death, starving and badly beaten. It had taken some time to find Derain's cell, and if not for the iron cage, a cell within a cell, to prevent him from doing any magic, he might have continued past it.

"Er, is your name Derain?" Vincent asked.

The man nodded.

From what Stone had told him, he'd been expecting to find an old man – the oldest man in the world – but instead he found someone who didn't appear to be any more than middle-aged, perhaps fifty at most. Admittedly, black people seemed to age rather better than white people, and Vincent wasn't sure he'd ever seen anyone as black as Derain, more like an absence of light than a colour, but it was difficult not to notice that the man was also incredibly fit. Mostly because the man was incredibly naked, and, frankly, hung like a shire horse. So much for stereotypes.

Thanks to the skills he'd learned from Joker, it had taken Vincent no more than a few minutes to pick the lock on the cell door, employing a device that had been custom-made for such things. And although it took a little longer to crack the lock on the iron cage, it wasn't long before that, too, gave a satisfying click and fell open. As much as possible in such a small cell, Derain unfolded himself to his full height, about six foot three of solid muscle, liberally covered in welts from when the guards had bravely given him a good kicking after he'd be safely restrained.

"Thank you," he said, clearly a man of few words. His voice was deep, like how you'd imagine a digeridoo would sound if they could talk.

Once they were out of the cell, Derain paused, using his telepathic abilities to let Stone and the others know what was going on. Even though he was capable of conversing over great distances, the signal was weak because of all the iron. He didn't say as much, but Vincent could read it in his expression. Doubtless this was also what had rendered Vincent's invisibility ring so ineffective. Derain was probably giving everyone headaches, but clearly he was having trouble hearing their response.

At Vincent's suggestion they moved farther along the corridor to where there was less iron, just stone walls, Derain doing the mental equivalent of a phone commercial. "Can you hear me now?" He stopped for a moment, that odd, glazed expression on his face, like how Stone got when he was talking to someone who wasn't there. He smiled to himself.

Vincent, of course, was used to such behaviour from Flashback and Stone, although Stone tended to close his eyes when he was conversing telepathically, and Flashback's behaviour was generally so bizarre that drifting off mid-conversation was the least of his worries. Derain just stood there smiling, which Vincent took to be a good thing, even though it was a bit disconcerting that he was naked.

Presently, Derain's eyes snapped back into focus and he smiled at Vincent, rather than to himself.

"They have a dragon," he said.

"Um, that's good."

Vincent expected Derain to elaborate, perhaps tell him how exactly a dragon was of any use to them deep inside a mountain, where neither of them could stand up straight without banging their heads on the ceiling. Or perhaps whether it was the same dragon he'd seen back in the caves. Instead they just kind of stood there, Derain looking off down the long corridor towards the cells. For fuck's sake, you'd get more conversation out of Numb Tongue, and that was saying something, or not, as the case may be. And if Derain was trying to speak to him telepathically, then he was definitely wasting his time. Vincent had no telepathic abilities whatsoever.

Indeed, when they'd done a few tests a couple of months back, it had turned out that Vincent was, if anything, rather less talented in that department than someone with absolutely no talent at all; he may as well have been guessing. Stone had held up the standard cards, star, square, wavy lines, etcetera, and then tried to project the image to him, and Vincent had got it wrong every time. It was all rather disappointing, particularly since his father, Mad John, had once been quite an expert, which suggested that it might be hereditary. Then again, Mad John couldn't ever actually use it, and had effectively turned it off a long time ago so it didn't drive him insane. With an estimated two and a half billion Christians in the world, it tended to get a bit noisy if they were all sending him messages. It wasn't so much that Mad John didn't listen to people's prayers, it was that he couldn't because they were all shouting at once, most of them with no idea they were doing so.

"Um," said Vincent, feeling not a little uncomfortable, not to mention somewhat annoyed, given that he'd just rescued this taciturn twat, and now felt as if he'd lost control of the situation. "So, er, what's the plan?"

Derain looked at him, as if remembering that he was there. He smiled again, maybe not a twat after all but some sort of higher power, who had trouble communicating with mere mortals.

"We free them," he said.

CHAPTER FIFTY-FOUR

Footsteps. Someone was coming.

Shit.

Vincent looked about in panic, but there was nowhere to hide, just a long row of prison cells, at the end of which there was more of the same.

The footsteps drew closer, dwarf guards casually chatting. Any second now they would come around the corner. Fight or flight. The guards would be armed, but they wouldn't be expecting anyone. Derain was a big guy, together they could overpower them. Flight was out of the question: where would they fly to? Vincent steeled himself, digging in his jacket pocket for the tranquillizer darts, just in case. He glanced to Derain for confirmation.

Derain raised his finger to his lips: "Ssh!"

And then he did the most remarkable thing; he stepped backwards into the wall.

A few years ago, Vincent had read a book called The Men Who Stare At Goats in which a retired army major general had spent a considerable amount of time walking into walls, apparently with the firm conviction that it was possible, in the right circumstances, to walk through said walls. It was something to do with molecular physics, if Vincent remembered correctly. It was also, Vincent remembered, impossible, and the major general had spent much of his time flat on his arse. Convinced that he was right, he never gave up; convinced that he was wrong, people largely believed him to be an idiot, and laughed at him. Far from being an idiot, however, it appeared that the man just needed to practice for a couple of hundred years.

Thus, as the guards rounded the corner, they were completely oblivious to the fact that there was anyone lurking in the corridor, and they continued past Vincent and Derain without so much as a second glance. Evidently Vincent's ring was working again, and he was tempted to jab them with the tranquillizer darts as they passed, the thought having crossed his mind that they could then be locked in Derain's former cell while the pair of them set about releasing all the other prisoners.

There was just one problem.

When the guards were safely out of sight Derain stepped out of the wall, and Vincent explained the situation. Derain then explained to Stone, who further explained to everybody else.

"Two days!" Mad John exclaimed. "Are you sure?"

"I'm afraid so," affirmed Stone. "Give or take a few hours. And that's without a break. They estimate that there's about a thousand cells down there and it took Vincent about three minutes to pick the lock..."

"Good lad," Joker muttered approvingly.

"Quite," agreed Stone. "But at that rate, as I said, we're looking at about two days just to get all the cells open, and then we still have to figure out how to get them all out of the city. Vincent's pretty sure that the guards have keys, which would cut that time in half if he can get them, but that would assume that they didn't notice the keys were missing, which is unlikely at best. As you'd imagine, they're open to suggestions."

There were, in fact, numerous suggestions, but none of them were very helpful, most of them trailing off into "Oh no, wait, that won't work." The original plan had simply been for Vincent to go in and rescue Derain, and it had gone exceptionally well so far. Getting him out was always going to be a bit tricky, but not impossible. Vincent could tranquillize the guards, tie them up so they didn't raise the alarm when they came to, and with a little luck, sneak out the same way he'd got in before anyone was any the wiser. Getting up to a thousand prisoners out of there wasn't going to be quite so simple, particularly when some of them were in such a bad way, malnourished or sick.

After the dwarf guards had completed their patrol and gone back to the gate, Derain and Vincent were free to wander the corridors unchallenged, but aside from a few ventilation shafts in the corridor above them – just wide enough for someone to fit inside, but too steep to climb – there was only one way in or out of the place. There were shafts below them too, but they were smaller, more like drainpipes, and had metal grills over them. Once again, Derain reported back to Stone and the others. They were still fresh out of ideas.

"Well, they may as well get started on the locks," said Mad John. "In the meantime, I want everyone back here in an hour. Go and have a walk, whatever it is that helps you to think."

Dum Dum rummaged in his belongings for a pen and paper, then dug out his iPod and selected shuffle mode. He stuck his earphones in: *Jailbreak* by Thin Lizzy. Appropriate, but not especially helpful. *"Tonight there's gonna be a jailbreak, somewhere in this town..."* He wrote it down anyway, even though it seemed fairly obvious where the jailbreak would be, and then, for want of a better idea, began to write down anything else he could think of that might be useful.

Dragon, he wrote. Breethes fire. Flys. Cannot get inside mountain.

Vincent. Invisable. Cannot get out of mountain.

Land Rover?

Keys. Need more.

Aborij... Aborige... Native people. About 300. 300 more from north. Here soon.

He chewed on the end of his pen, the song still playing through his earphones.

"Tonight there's gonna be a jailbreak. Some of us won't survive..."

He didn't like the sound of that. Despite the so-called immortality of several members of Aberrant MC, Dum Dum had learned that it was possible for anyone to die. As proved by Andy One-Leg, if you lost a limb, it stayed lost, it didn't grow back. Likewise, if you lost your head then that, too, would stay lost. Immortal, as he understood it, just meant that you didn't really die from natural causes. If you got shot in the face, it still wouldn't do you any favours.

Besides, Dum Dum himself wasn't immortal, he just had a very long lifespan ahead of him, perhaps three or four hundred years, if the average bridge troll was anything to go by. Since his parents were mixed, no one really knew for sure. And there were others in the club whose lifespan was equally uncertain. Zig Zag, for instance, was part dwarf and part orc, and while orcs, on account of their violent nature, tended not to live past about thirty or forty years old, dwarfs had been known to reach six hundred years or so. Either way, the lyric was not encouraging. As much as he liked the song, Dum Dum would rather have heard *Give Peace A Chance*. The only real chance of that was if Mad John could speak to the dwarf leader, but evidentially that wasn't possible.

And so Dum Dum sat for the next twenty-five minutes listening to songs and writing down anything that might be useful, which, though he hated to admit it, wasn't a great deal, and involved quite a lot of misspelling and crossing out. He wrote down the names of each of the club members, and beside them any particular talents they possessed that might be helpful. A number of them were good at fighting, of course, which would undoubtedly come in handy, but only if the dwarfs could be persuaded to leave their city. Since they'd be unlikely to give up such an advantage, Aberrant would need to employ other skills to even the odds.

Unfortunately, Dum Dum couldn't really see how any of those other skills could be of much use. Mad John could walk on water and, indeed, turn water into wine, but since they were in the middle of a desert that wasn't exactly beneficial. He could also talk sense into people, talk them out of fighting in the first place, but only if they were willing to listen. A couple of the club could perform magic, not least Flashback, who was pretty much a sorcerer and could turn motorcycles into flesh and blood creatures, but, again, that wasn't a great deal of use in these circumstances. They already had a dragon at their disposal and no idea what to do with it.

Dum Dum chewed on his pen some more. Time was nearly up. He looked again at the list of songs that had been playing while he worked, but as far as he could tell they were all fairly random. *Jailbreak* made sense, obviously, but The Cult's *Here Comes The Rain* hardly seemed relevant in a place where it probably hadn't rained in years, and all the rest were mostly about politics. He looked again at the titles in case he'd missed something, but still nothing jumped out at him. Groop Dogdrill, *Low Sperm Count*... Great song, but, seriously, what the fuck did it have to do with anything? He clambered to his feet as the song came to a close with a wail of feedback and a looping refrain, the same four words repeated over and over. *"The king is dead, the king is dead..."*

Oh well, hopefully the others had come up with something that might be a bit more helpful.

CHAPTER FIFTY-FIVE

One thing that hadn't been fully anticipated was the language barrier: It was one thing to start unlocking cells, but quite another trying to explain to whoever was inside them that even though they were being rescued they would have to remain in their cell with the door closed until such time as they were told otherwise. Vincent had managed to pick dozens of locks so far, and was getting quicker with each one because they were all the same, but his task would have been considerably easier without all the confusion.

Derain, meanwhile, was deep in conversation, that faraway look in his eyes suggesting that he was involved in some sort of telepathic conference call. Possibly he was on hold and listening to dreadful music. Presently Vincent became aware that the conversation was over and that Derain was just standing there looking at him, as he poked and prodded at another lock. He was starting to get a little tired of the lack of communication. They'd come a long way to rescue this dickhead, after all.

"Well?" he said, somewhat irritably.

"They have a plan," said Derain.

"Oh good. And would you care to share that plan with the rest of the class?"

Derain looked bemused, clearly not one for sarcasm.

"Class?"

"Never mind. Would you care to tell me the plan? Please."

Derain told him the plan. It was the abridged version, of course, since he wasn't much of a talker, but it was certainly ambitious, and it was a lot better than flicking a dwarf on the nose and then running off with his beer. If nothing else it would put Vincent in the vicinity of a toilet, which would be most welcome. Not that the smell down here could get much worse, but the idea of adding to it by dropping a Trump in the corner of a prison cell was far from appealing. It would also give him a chance to refresh his memory concerning how to get back to Gilgin's place; not that it was a particularly complicated route from here, but it would be best to know exactly where he was going if he was supposed to be leading everyone out of there. He didn't want to be hesitating or doubling back. And, of course, it was necessary to warn Gilgin in advance that there would be more than just him and Derain breaking out, since that was what the dwarf would be expecting.

Vincent poked his head around the corner to see the two dwarf guards standing vaguely to attention by the gate, both of them looking rather bored. Moments later they were unconscious and Derain was helping him drag them down the corridor, where they were relieved of their keys, stripped of their uniforms, and locked in a cell. They'd barely had time to react before the tranquillizer darts knocked them out, and it would be a good six or seven hours before they woke up.

With any luck Derain would be able to explain to a couple of the prisoners that they should put on the uniforms and stand guard in their place, but it wasn't as if anyone came down this way to check on them, and if Gilgin was right, the next shift wasn't due for several hours. Assuming that nothing went wrong, Vincent would be back long before then.

With the gate locked behind him, he made his way along the dimly lit corridor towards Gilgin's room. So far, Gilgin had been a man – or dwarf – of his word, and during their walk to the city he'd made his feelings about his bosses abundantly clear, but Vincent had a tranquillizer dart ready just in case. It would be a shame to have to jab him, but it wouldn't do for him to be raising the alarm.

Having found it with ease, Vincent knocked on the door. There was a flicker of confusion on Gilgin's face when he answered, not least because Vincent was invisible, but also because he wasn't expecting him to be alone.

"Come in, come in." He ushered Vincent inside. "Your friend, you did not find him?"

"Yes, I found him. He's back at the cells. We have a small change of plan. Do you mind if I use your toilet?"

"Is it part of the plan?"

Twenty minutes later Vincent was on his way back to the cells, relieved in every sense of the word, a load taken off more than just his mind. Not only was Gilgin still conscious but he'd be working with them when the time came to try and get everybody out. As they'd hoped, he had a few friends who he trusted enough to pass on word of what was going on, and if all went according to plan... Well, it had to go according to plan. One weak link would break them all.

Vincent found the theme tune for The Great Escape stuck in his head, and it was all he could to stop himself from whistling it, but he was promptly reminded against such carelessness when a couple of dwarfs came out of one of the side doors, almost walking straight into him. He stepped neatly aside to let them pass.

Arriving back at the gate, Vincent's heart sank for a second at the sight of two guards on the other side, but he quickly realised that they were just a couple of prisoners in uniform. Both of them were startled when he demanded to be let in, and even more so when he suddenly became visible, but after a bit of confusion one of them went off to get the keys from Derain, who was still busy unlocking cells. It seemed that he'd found a dwarf who could speak a little English, which was helping everyone to understand what the hell was going on, but even with a key it was taking a while to get all the cells open. Vincent got to work with his lock pick, the English-speaking dwarf translating for him as he went along.

When they got to the next cell the dwarf stopped him. "Not this one," he said. "We leave here."

"Why, what's he done?"

"My words English not good," the dwarf replied. "This not good dwarf. Stay prisoner. Bad dwarf."

Vincent shrugged and moved on to the next cell. From what Gilgin had told him, most of the prisoners down here were locked up for petty theft, usually for stealing food, and most of the rest were political prisoners of some sort. It hadn't really occurred to him that they might be freeing a bunch of murderers and rapists.

"Er, can I ask what *you* were in here for?" he ventured, as he started on the next lock.

"I learn speak English."

"Yes, I understand that, but what were you locked up for?"

"I learn speak English," the dwarf repeated. "I read book."

"Oh, I see," said Vincent. "What was it called? What was title of book?"

The dwarf thought for a moment, not familiar with saying the words aloud. "One, nine, and eight four," he said. "I get rest of life in prison."

"Fuck!"

"Yes," agreed the dwarf. "Bad fuck."

The dwarf, it transpired, was called Buttock, which was slightly unfortunate, and had so far served seven or eight years of his – or indeed, quite possibly her – life sentence; it was difficult to mark the passage of time down here with any more than a notch on the wall. Like most of the inmates he – yes, yes, or she – was painfully malnourished and had expected to die here. Suicide was not uncommon.

For the first two years there had been a human in Buttock's neighbouring cell, which rather defeated the purpose of sending him – or her – to prison for learning English, except that that neighbour had been French, so Buttock had learned that instead. Most of the humans, perhaps a few dozen or so, had made the mistake of doing business with the dwarfs, but among them were a couple of spelunkers, cave enthusiasts who'd got lost, never to be seen again, their only crime being that they'd chosen to explore the wrong mountain. The rest, apparently, were electricians and engineers who'd helped to get the power working in the lower levels of the city. Evidently the dwarfs didn't want anyone to know where they lived.

"The king is, how do you say, gourmand...greedy," said Buttock. "He think only of l'or."

"Or what?"

"L'or," Buttock repeated. "Sorry, my English. En Français l'or is...gold. He think only of gold."

"No need to apologise," said Vincent, as another lock gave a satisfying click. "I can't speak Dwarfish or French. Your English is very good."

Buttock admitted to struggling with 1984, understanding the context but not really grasping a lot of the words. He – or Goddammit, possibly she – had also been under the impression that it was a historical document rather than a work of fiction or, indeed, a terrible prophecy. Vincent had no idea where to even begin with an explanation, especially since he hadn't actually read the book, just seen the movie, but thankfully he was saved from making such an embarrassing admission when a small rock struck him on the top of his head.

CHAPTER FIFTY-SIX

Dangling from one of the air vents above Vincent were a pair of motorcycle boots, apparently scrabbling for purchase on something that wasn't there. White Alpinestars with a most unpleasant splash of yellow. Only one person could possibly think they looked cool. He would, in the vernacular of the genuine Cockney, refer to them as 'daisy roots'.

"Apples?"

"Vincent?"

"What are you doing?"

"What's it fuckin' look like I'm doing? Stop fuckin' about and help me down."

With a hand from Vincent, Apples deposited himself into the corridor, followed moments later by a couple of backpacks, a parachute, and then, with slightly less swearing, by Chaos. They seemed to think that Vincent would be expecting them. This was news to Vincent.

"Where's Snot?" snapped Chaos.

"Snot?"

"Is there an echo in here?"

"Um," said Vincent, correctly surmising that 'up my nose' wasn't the right answer. "No, I just don't know what you're talking about."

"Snot," repeated Chaos, as if this would help. "Female. Prospect. Faerie..."

"You mean Snow? I haven't seen her since Berlin."

"Oh, right," said Chaos. "Forgot about that. Long story, but she's changed her name."

"Well, she's not down here, mate."

In fact, Snot was not far away, but was not, all things considered, having the best start to her day. Naked and afraid, she inched her way farther down the inside of the stone-walled ventilation shaft, her fingers clinging on for dear life as her bare feet tentatively prodded for any footholds, all the while praying that she didn't step on something furry and venomous.

Under the last cover of darkness they had set off towards the mountain, Apples and Chaos riding the dragon's back, while Snot, in faerie form, hung on to one of the backpacks. According to George, they were probably the first people ever to ride a dragon in such a way, and certainly the first to attempt such a thing with Puff, who, much to George's amazement and everyone else's relief, seemed to be enjoying himself.

They flew high, an ice-cold wind cutting the three passengers to the bone, the dragon gaining altitude with each beat of those mighty wings. The ground was no longer visible, a sea of black beneath them. Any higher and it felt as if they'd reach the stars. And then the great dragon began to circle.

"You ready?" said Chaos.

Apples nodded. "Let's fuckin' 'ave it!"

It was too late for second thoughts. Apples and Chaos jumped, a tandem skydive into nothingness. Moments later Snot followed, performing her second jump of the night without a parachute. If everything went well she would rendezvous with them on the mountain, where she would retrieve her clothes, and from there climb down an air vent to assist Vincent and Derain with the escape.

Everything did not go well.

Blown off course and finding herself alone on the wrong side of the mountain, Snot then discovered that there were dozens of vents leading down into the underground city, and she had no idea which was the right one to get to the prison cells. Apparently there were stars that were visible from below, and since Chaos could navigate by the stars it was up to him to lead them to the right shaft. Without him it was anyone's guess. So she guessed.

It should have been no more troublesome than simply flying down and having a quick look, then flying back up and trying a different shaft if she'd got the wrong one. Apples and Chaos would have to climb down, so with any luck she'd find them fairly quickly. Unfortunately, what she found instead was huge cobwebs.

Panicking, Snot had transformed to human size in an instant, and almost plummeted to the bottom of the shaft before she got a grip of herself and the walls. Her heart thumped now, as she continued her descent. Getting caught in the web in faerie form would not have been inescapable, but still, a bite from one of the many venomous spiders that lived in Australia could have nasty consequences even when she was human-sized and would certainly have been fatal to a faerie. The book she'd been reading may have insisted that bees were more of a danger than spiders, but it also cheerfully pointed out that there were over forty species of funnel-web spiders in Australia, and that their venom attacked the nervous system. This made her extremely nervous. Whoever came up with the old adage 'they're more scared of you than you are of them' was clearly an imbecile.

Snot stopped climbing. She wasn't much for swearing, but she swore. "Bollocks." Of all the stupid... She started climbing up instead of down.

One of the things that Apples and Chaos had with them when they jumped, aside from a few medical supplies, a small bag of tranquillizer darts, and Snot's clothes, was a length of rope. If they'd climbed down one of the vents ahead of her then it would still be tied to something at the top. All she had to do was find it.

Morning was breaking and Snot allowed herself a few moments to take in the breathtaking vista that stretched out beneath her from the top of the mountain, sunrise slowly lighting the desert in glorious shades of umber and orange. There really was no end to the beauty of this country, and it felt, from here, as if she could see pretty much all of it. Thankfully she couldn't see any sign of the Aberrant camp, some fifteen or twenty miles away, which was obviously a good thing, but there was very little cover out there for anyone who might be thinking of sneaking up on the place. In every direction but one there was just wide open desert, and to the south lay a dried up riverbed carved into rock that seemed to disappear into the mountain. No doubt it was guarded, but luckily their plan did not rely on the element of surprise. Unless, of course, you counted the surprise that the dwarfs were going to get when they found out all their prisoners had gone.

By the warm light of the morning Snot found the rope in a matter of minutes, still firmly knotted to a crampon that had been hammered into the rock. She could also see now that there was smoke coming out of some of the other vents, so it was probably just as well that she hadn't hastily flown down the wrong one. Her arms were tired from the previous climb though, so safely assuming that Apples and Chaos would have dealt with any spiders, she adopted faerie form once more and dived in.

She arrived at the bottom and heard familiar voices, Apples explaining to Vincent why they couldn't just sneak everyone out through the vents rather than making their way out through the corridors; namely that it would take days and that food was already running short on the outside. By the time they'd rescued everyone, half of the rescuers might have starved. Also, that sneaking everybody out that way would leave a lot of innocent dwarfs "up to their Gregory Pecks in tom tit." Given that he was explaining this in his usual Cockney gibberish, she only understood about half of it.

"Psst. Apples."

"'Ello?"

"Up here."

"Alright, Snot," Apples grinned. "Been doin' a bit of sightseeing?"

"I went down the wrong hole."

"I 'ave that problem a lot meself."

"I don't doubt it. Can you pass my clothes up, please?"

Fully clothed, having for modesty's sake dressed herself with some great difficulty whilst hanging onto the rope, Snot busied herself with picking locks. It was not a talent she'd picked up readily, if at all, and it was a good twenty minutes before she got the first one open, only to discover that the dwarf-shaped pile of rags in the darkened corner was in fact just a pile of rags.

"Best to get a response first," advised Vincent. "I've opened two so far that were empty and another one with a corpse inside. At least the locks are all the same, but it would be helpful if we had more than one key between us."

"It would be even more helpful if they had some decent light down here."

"Yeah, but I'm not sure you really wanna see what's in some of these cells. That smell isn't making itself."

And so the hours went on. Buttock had found another English-speaking dwarf and the two of them helped with translation, once in a while insisting that a cell remain locked. A former torturer for the king's inquisition could be left to rot, as could the informant who'd taken such great delight in getting most of them sent to the former. Upon realising that he wasn't going to be released the informant had started yelling blue murder, so Vincent jabbed him with a tranquillizer. The dwarf in the next cell had served three of seven years for stealing a loaf of bread from the kitchen, and now found that his sentence came with an early full stop.

On the subject of food, Vincent discovered that the prisoners were fed every other day, a bowl of slop and leftovers that may or may not contain cockroaches. You were generally considered lucky if you got cockroaches since they were a source of protein that was otherwise missing from said slop. Sometimes they ran out of slop before they reached the farthest cells, other times they just couldn't be bothered to walk that far. Today was not a food day, so they would not be disturbed by the slop-slinging process. No one else came down here other than the guards. Visitors were not allowed.

When the next shift arrived some hours later, Vincent was already waiting for them on the other side of the gate. He was, perhaps, feeling a little overconfident, and there was an unfortunate moment when they both stopped and stared at him. They raised their weapons and barked something at him in Dwarfish.

"Oh shit!"

The dwarfs looked at each other, completely baffled. Where the hell did he go?

Seconds later they were both unconscious.

CHAPTER FIFTY-SEVEN

Seventeen rifles and three shotguns. It didn't sound like much. It *wasn't* much. A couple of the rifles didn't even have ammunition and were, if it came to actually using them, essentially just clubs. Aside from that, all they had were sticks and stones, and while, admittedly, some of the Aborigines seemed incredibly adept at using them, it was still a far from impressive arsenal.

The lyric kept running around Dum Dum's head, like it was on a loop: "*Some of us won't survive.*" He wished it wouldn't. He'd spent a couple of hours, before it got too hot to think, trying to learn how to use a boomerang, but it had basically been time spent throwing a piece of wood away. The one time it had come back it had hit Joker on the ear.

But still there was hope. There was *always* hope, always a chance. Billy Toothless was busying himself making 'bat poo bombs', having apparently carried said bat poo in his backpack from some caves, which explained why he was unusually fragrant even by his own standards. And while their army may have been small they did have a dragon on their side, even if it was currently MIA having flown off to find food. With any luck it would find some dwarfs and thin their numbers down a bit so there'd be less of the little buggers to fight. If it came to that.

Maybe they wouldn't take the bait. Maybe they'd stay inside their nice cool mountain and just wait until there was nothing outside but a couple of hundred puddles of grease.

Fuck, it was hot.

Dum Dum preferred cooler weather at the best of times, but this was just ridiculous, sapping all strength, slowing thought to a crawl. So much for *Here Comes The Rain*; there wasn't a cloud in the sky, and the sun glared down at them like a... like a... big fucking hot thing. Furnace, that's the one. And poor old Mental was a ginger! No wonder he was hiding under the Land Rover; poor sod could get sunburnt by candlelight!

"Some of us won't survive..."

Dum Dum wiped the sweat from his brow with his T-shirt. He was starting to get a headache. He daydreamed about cold beer for a while, trying to take his mind off who might not survive. At this rate none of them would survive, although it had to be said that the Aboriginal blokes didn't seem too bothered by the heat.

Another thought crossed his mind.

"Why'd you wanna throw bat shit at dwarfs, Billy?"

"Flam'ble, unnit."

Given his affinity to strange odours, it probably shouldn't have come as a surprise that Billy was something of an expert on the subject of bat guano. Indeed, those who could understand what he was saying – and were able to tolerate the smell long enough to engage him in conversation – were often surprised by the depth of Billy's knowledge in general. Apparently bat guano was not only flammable but explosive due to its high nitrogen content. It was also a valuable plant fertilizer, and, according to Billy, could be used as a laundry detergent, although this may have explained why people tended not to stand too close to him.

Dum Dum always enjoyed a good chat with Billy, so long as the wind was blowing in the right direction, and he'd always come away knowing a little bit more than he knew before. Waterloo Teeth, that was a good one. Given that Billy was known as Toothless, even though his teeth, though a curious shade of brown, were all present and vaguely correct, Dum Dum had asked him about his nickname during one of their little chats. Evidently it was common practice, as far back as the sixth century BC, to make dentures out of real human teeth, and the battle of Waterloo in 1815, which left 50,000 dead, created such a surplus of teeth that they became known as Waterloo Teeth. Which is where Billy's somewhat stained chompers came from.

Admittedly it was useless information, but it was interesting nonetheless, and there were times when such trivia was good for taking your mind off other things. Like whether there might be another surplus of teeth after they'd faced off against an army of dwarfs. Perhaps it wouldn't come to that, but there seemed little doubt that there would be a battle. Until then, there wasn't much else to do but wait. And make 'bat poo bombs'.

The weight of responsibility sat heavily on Dum Dum's shoulders as he worked. What if he'd got it all wrong? What if they were just random songs? What if they *weren't* just random songs and they'd been misinterpreted? What if? What if?

Mad John seemed to think otherwise, but even he made mistakes sometimes. After they'd reconvened and discussed whatever ideas they'd come up with – most of which weren't particularly helpful, apart from sending a couple of people in through the vents to help with the lockpicking – he'd gone off on his own for a while to mull things over. When he returned he'd headed straight for Dum Dum.

"I've been doing some thinking about your list of songs," he said, sitting himself down.

"Oh yes?" said Dum Dum, who'd been doing much the same and not really coming up with much.

"Could I take another look at it?"

"Knock yourself out." Dum Dum handed over the crumpled paper to which he'd added a few notes, but nothing that appeared especially useful. It had surprised him to learn that Mad John was rather a good DJ when he put his mind to it, and although his repertoire was somewhat limited once you'd heard it a couple of times, it wasn't unexpected for him to be familiar with most of these songs. Some of them had been top 40 hits in their time, and most of the rest weren't exactly obscure: *Here Comes The Rain, Talkin' 'Bout A Revolution, Jailbreak, Children Of The Revolution,* Twisted Sister's *We're Not Gonna Take It...* The only one he questioned was *Low Sperm Count.*

"Beats me," shrugged Dum Dum. "It's a brilliant song, but I'm fucked if I know what it's got to do with dwarfs. I thought it might be because they're short or something, y'know, low, but I'm just guessing. I've got a few more notes I wrote down if you wanna have a look."

"Please, yes."

Mad John spent a while pouring over the notes, occasionally asking Dum Dum to decipher some of the handwriting.

"Did you know," he said at last, "that Joker's granddaughter owns the hearse that took Marc Bolan to his grave?"

"Yeah, he told me," said Dum Dum. "I thought he was making it up."

"Oh no. It used to belong to his wife before she gave up driving, and she gave it to their granddaughter. They've kept it in pristine condition."

"Um," said Dum Dum, "does that have anything to do with dwarfs?"

"I shouldn't think so," Mad John shook his head. "I just thought you'd be interested. This, on the other hand," Mad John pointed to the notes, "could be extremely important."

"It could?"

"Indeed it could, Dum Dum."

"Oh," said Dum Dum. "That's good. Would you mind explaining how?"

So Mad John explained.

"Gentlemen, if I might have your attention," he said, climbing to his feet.

Though Dum Dum had grown accustomed to it, it never ceased to amaze him how the world seemed to go quiet when Mad John spoke. It didn't seem to matter where they were, they could be in a crowded bar or standing next to roadworks, he never needed to raise his voice; the world just turned it down a notch. Contrary to what Monty Python might have thought, there was unlikely to be anyone standing at the back going "Speak up!" or "What's so special about the cheese makers?" Admittedly someone was going to have to translate what he was saying for the benefit of those Aboriginal guys who didn't speak English, but there was no doubt that he could be heard. Moreover, there could be no doubt what he meant. He was used to giving speeches in deserts.

"Today," he said, "we will not just free our friend from captivity. We will not just free the prisoners from captivity. Today we will free an entire city from captivity! Today...we will begin a revolution!"

And then he explained how they were going to do it. Mostly they would be singing.

CHAPTER FIFTY-EIGHT

The song began in hushed tones, a sonnet of serenity whispered through the ages, as old as time itself. Slowly, so slowly, it rose into the air, a gentle crescendo lifting higher and higher until it seemed to reach the darkening sky.

They sang louder, and louder still, three hundred or more voices carrying far across the plains, their silhouettes dancing by the light of numerous camp-fires. And from the north, another three hundred voices from the Aborigines on the other side of the mountain, who had arrived as the sun began to set.

Again it started as no more than the lightest of showers, a delicate pitter-patter that barely moistened the hard-baked desert earth.

A little over a quarter of a mile away were the vast iron gates of the city. They were far bigger than was necessary for dwarfs, perhaps fifty feet high, as much a statement – a warning – as an entrance, and above them, carved into the rock, were a couple of lookout posts, each of them manned – or dwarfed, as the case may be – with the same archers who had taken potshots at George's raven. Already they had loosed a few arrows at the small army, but they fell short of their targets, who remained safely out of range.

"Well," said Stone, rolling himself the obligatory joint, "I think we've got their attention. Let's see what they're going to do about it."

"Don't they, like, send people out to have word and find out what we want?" asked Dum Dum. "Emissaries or something?"

"What do you think this is, fucking Braveheart?" scoffed Joker. "Course they won't!"

Moments later, however, the great gates opened and out came half a dozen dwarf soldiers, fire torches in hand, striding purposefully towards them across the plains.

"Told ya," grinned Dum Dum.

Together with one of the Aborigine nomads, a man named Kalti, Mad John, Stone, and George walked out to meet them halfway. As they drew closer Stone realised that one of them, the one wearing a different uniform from the rest to indicate a higher rank, looked rather familiar.

"That's Gilgin," he told Mad John. "He's our man on the inside."

"Dwarf," corrected George.

"You know what I mean. Let me do the talking."

Both parties stopped about five feet from each other, Gilgin speaking first. His voice was loud and authoritative, as if demanding to know why they were here.

"Pretend not to know me!" he barked. "The others do not speak English."

"Excellent," replied Stone. "What news do you bring from the inside?"

"The king is preparing to send out his armies. He is angered by your presence, but he sees you as no threat. He will not yet send his best troops."

"How many?"

"A thousand. They are poorly trained. He does not care about casualties. If you kill them, if there are many casualties, it will make him stronger because people will be in fear. He does not know that they will not fight for him. They will join your side."

"How many will join our side?"

"All of them! Only then will the king send out his elite guard."

The elite guard, Gilgin told them, numbered some ten thousand, well paid, well fed, well trained, well-armed, and loyal troops. They would show no mercy and take no prisoners. Below ground were another five thousand troops, the dwarf equivalent of the Royal Marines or the SAS, who would guard the king with their lives. In the unlikely event that ten thousand troops weren't enough to defend the city, they would lock themselves in with ample supplies to last at least two years.

"We'll see about that," said Stone. "But first things first. Vincent has told you our plan?"

"Yes."

"Good. In that case, get back to the city and prepare as best you can. Make sure your people are ready with the gates."

"I am instructed to report to the king," said Gilgin. "What message do you have for him?"

"Personally, I'd tell him to go fuck himself," Stone grinned. "But I don't want to get you locked up, so tell him whatever you like."

"It will be my pleasure to pass on your words," Gilgin replied sternly, trying his best not to laugh. "I wish you good luck. May we meet again when our people are free."

"May fortune be with you. And sing loud."

Gilgin gave Stone a questioning look.

"Trust me," said Stone. "It will help."

With those words the two parties went their separate ways, Gilgin and his men back to the city, Stone and company back to their campfires. There was a rumble of distant thunder as they turned, an omen. But for which side?

"Can we trust him?" George asked as they walked back.

"I certainly hope so," said Stone. "But there's only one way to find out."

"Fuckin' hell of a way to find out if we can't."

"Either way, we can't trust the king," said Stone. "He's just sent some of his men out the back way by the riverbed. Obviously thought they could launch a sneaky attack on our reinforcements while we were all out here talking. It didn't quite work out how they expected."

"How do you...?" began George, before remembering Stone's telepathic abilities, something he usually associated with his Aborigine friends. "Are they okay?" he said instead.

"Oh yes," Stone smiled. "They took seven prisoners and sent the rest packing."

"Good lads."

The Aborigines on the other side of the mountain had, it transpired, anticipated some sort of attack, and they were well prepared. The riverbed exit was not big enough to send out a substantial amount of troops, just a small hit squad whose job was to sneak out and bash a few heads. Unfortunately for them, the heads that they bashed, as they crept up on them from behind in the darkness, were decoys made of clay and contained a large number of very short-tempered and extremely aggressive wasps.

Word of this small victory spread around the camp as they readied themselves for battle, but still there was no doubt that they'd need more than a few wasps' nests to defeat the vast army of dwarfs that would be heading their way. There weren't even enough weapons to go around, and many of those who *were* armed didn't really know what they were doing. Then again, word had also got around that the first wave of troops – a thousand in all – would be joining them rather than fighting them, and if you looked at the top of the mountain and knew what you were looking for, you'd see the great black shadow that was otherwise known as Puff. All was far from lost.

And still they sang.

Again there was a rumble of thunder, closer now, a timpani of war, electricity in the air, and at last a flash of forked lightning in the distance.

Dum Dum started counting: "One – one thousand, two – one thousand..."

"What are you doing?" asked Joker.

"I'm counting to see how far away the storm is. You count between the thunder and lightning, and it's how many miles away it is."

"Yeah, but you're doing it wrong. You're supposed to count from the lightning not the thunder, cos the speed of light is faster than the speed of sound."

"Is that so?" smiled Dum Dum. Yeah, right, he thought. He rarely believed what Joker told him, especially since he'd once asked Joker what the difference between wizards and warlocks was. "Warlocks are hairier," Joker had told him, straight-faced, "and they tend to hang a bit lower."

Beside them was Flashback, who was definitely one or the other, possibly both. Although it had to be said that he looked more like some sort of witchdoctor at the moment, with a crocodile's head for a hat, and his face smeared in ash from the fire, like warpaint. A jug of dwarf beer dangled from his left hand, while his right hand grasped his magical wand, a fifteen-hundred-year-old fulgurite that he'd fashioned to resemble a walking cane, complete with a silver skull tip. He seemed to be talking to himself, but that was perfectly normal. Well, perfectly normal for Flashback, anyway. It was usually best not to ask.

Another drum roll of thunder, and the rain began to fall harder, proper rain that hissed in the campfires. Ian Astbury would be proud. Here comes the rain, indeed. More lightning. One – one thousand, two – one thousand... The storm was getting closer.

And then, across the plains, the great doors to the dwarf city swung open once more...

CHAPTER FIFTY-NINE

Deep inside the city the heavy industrial thumping noise had stopped, its absence only noticeable when it was gone, like when you turned air conditioning off. It was replaced by a different sound that seemed to come from everywhere as it drifted through the air vents and along the ill-lit corridors. The dwarfs inside the city had joined in with the rain song. It was an altogether more pleasing sound than the stomp of mining machines, but also rather unnerving because it meant that when the song was over there was no going back.

Not that there was ever any going back, it being difficult – not to mention pointless – locking all these prisoners back in their cells, but perhaps more worrying was that it meant going forwards. Those who were too sick or too weak would stay behind and await their fate, the rest would arm themselves as best they could and head out into these long, cramped tunnels, either to join the ranks of the dwarf resistance or to walk straight into a trap. The latter seemed unlikely – why go to so much trouble? – but the former was no less daunting.

Furnished with directions from Buttock, Vincent had already been out to find the armoury and made a couple of journeys bringing back whatever he could steal, but with the place on a high state of alert it had been busy with soldiers and he hadn't been able to get more than a few axes. They were heavy and difficult to carry, which made the prospect of running into the wrong end of one of them all the more terrifying. The dwarfs seemed to throw them around with ease, while Vincent could barely lift them, and not for the first time he wished that he didn't have arms like spaghetti. Still, at least all the activity amongst the dwarfs meant that he didn't have to wait at any gates for long, what with all the coming and going.

They stood now, Vincent, Chaos, Smiler, and the rest, Snot, Buttock, Derain, and a multitude of former prisoners, all jammed into the corridor like sardines, rainwater dripping on their heads from the vents above, waiting, waiting, waiting for the song to end and the war to begin, tension and stench filling the air.

"How many fucking verses are in this song?" moaned Apples. "It's like Bohemian fucking Rhapsody!"

"Quit complaining," warned Chaos. "It'll be over soon enough."

"Mama, just killed a cunt. Put a gun against his 'ead, pulled the trigger, he's brown bread."

"Shut up, Apples."

The rain fell harder, predictably finding the back of Vincent's neck, just to add an extra layer of discomfort. The vents had been constructed to circulate air – some of them fitted with pumps for the purpose – and weren't designed to deal with rain. It hadn't rained here for years. Already the floor was getting wet, which meant, invisible or not, he would leave footprints, another thing to worry about when invisibility is your only advantage. Not for the first time, he wished he was pretty much anywhere else, anywhere but this damp, stinking corridor. But the trouble with wishes like that was that they tended to come true, and more often than not he'd end up somewhere worse. Don't want to be in a cave full of bat shit? How about a freezing cold desert? Or hey, how about a tunnel that stinks of death and shit? Unlike Apples, Vincent wasn't sure that he ever wanted the song to end.

But end it did, an eerie silence falling over the place, just the white noise of the rain far above, the song having worked its magic tenfold. Vincent had expected to hear the sounds of battle, perhaps yelling and screaming, or the clash of axes and shields, but instead there was just this creepy quietness, broken only by running water and the sound of their own breathing, clothes rustling, someone coughing... But certainly no battle.

"You reckon we've missed it?" Apples suggested hopefully.

Chaos shook his head.

"Didn't think so. Go 'an 'ave a butchers up the top, Snot, see what you can see."

"Butchers?"

"A look."

"That is not necessary," said Derain.

"Oh yeah. I forgot you've got a built-in dog."

"Dog?"

"Dog 'n' bone. Phone. Never mind. Just see what you can find out."

And so, still completely naked, Derain dialled Stone's number on his mental telephone. Apparently it rang for some time because Stone was a little preoccupied with an army of dwarfs that was heading his way, and their conversation, understandably, was rather abrupt, the psychic equivalent of "can't talk now, I'll call you back."

Across the plains, the dwarfs drew closer, illuminated, because nature has a flair for the dramatic, by a flash of lightning. Ill-trained or not they looked a formidable bunch, stern-faced, and ready to kick some ass. Or at least kick some knee, depending on their height. The darkness was helping to disguise Aberrant's lack of numbers, but it made the approaching dwarfs seem all the more sinister, a wall of shadows, an unstoppable tide. But stop they did, no more than twenty feet away. No one dared to breathe.

The moment lasted less than a minute, probably much less, but it seemed as if time itself was holding its breath along with them. It was Mad John who broke the spell, stepping forwards, his arms outstretched, palms facing upwards, in what Soundgarden might have called the Jesus Christ Pose. Bone dry in the pissing rain. If the water was deeper he'd be walking on it. In full-on messiah mode, he was quite an impressive sight to behold. No words were spoken. No words were necessary. The dwarfs simply walked past him, a nod of respect as they passed, to join the other side.

"It's like them Irish fellas in Braveheart," grinned Dum Dum, rather wishing that Joker was within earshot.

Of course, it hadn't escaped his notice that Mel Gibson died a horrible death at the end, so it was probably for the best that no one was paying attention to him. All eyes were upon the city gates, barely visible now in the rain and dark. It wouldn't take long for word to get back to the dwarf king about his soldiers changing sides, and it was a safe bet that he wouldn't be at all happy about it.

It was half an hour or so before the gates opened, the longest half hour in history, during which time Stone received some potentially unpleasant news from Derain, namely that the families of those dwarfs who had defected were being rounded up and taken to the prison cells. Fortunately the guards had been rather noisy, obviously not expecting a welcoming committee, so the families were safe and the guards themselves were now locked up, having been relieved of their weapons. But it was proof, if it were needed, that the dwarf king was a ruthless bastard, who would stop at nothing when it came to dealing with his enemies. There were two dozen families down there so far, and more coming all the time.

When the gates finally opened it was Gilgin who came out, flanked, again, by half a dozen soldiers, a grim expression on his face, until Stone explained the situation to him. It was another small victory, and so far they were winning without anyone getting hurt, some nasty wasp stings notwithstanding. It would be foolish to think that it was all going to be so easy, but every little helped to even the odds and brought them closer to a nice warm bath and a change of clothes. The look of terror on some of their faces suggested that a change of underwear might be in order. Gilgin had been right about that, at least; these were not well-trained troops who had defected, just conscripts, cannon fodder. It was decided not to tell them about their families getting dragged off in case they panicked, and for the more practical reason that Gilgin couldn't tell them the truth in front of his own guards without them knowing that he was colluding with the king's enemies.

"I'm guessing you were sent out here to tell them," said Stone.

"Yes," Gilgin nodded, "but these guards don't know that. I will tell them that you would not let me speak with them."

"Fair enough. Just don't get yourself in trouble."

"I fear it may be too late for that," Gilgin allowed a small smile to cross his face. "Are we not already in trouble?"

They stood for a moment in the rain, a moment of strange tranquillity, as if it were just the two of them there, but it lasted no more than a few seconds.

"Until we meet again..." said Gilgin, and turned back towards the city.

"Some sunny day," Stone said to himself, unheard beneath a low rumble of thunder. He watched the dwarf walk back across the plains towards the city gates, soaked to the skin, tired and frightened, but oh so brave.

The next time the gates opened it would be, in the words of another Australian, to unleash hell.

CHAPTER SIXTY

If the first wave of dwarf troops had appeared like an unstoppable tide, then the second wave was a tsunami, row upon row of them pouring from the city, forming ranks, beating axe handles against their shields, their helmets and chain-mail suits glistening in the rain. The shield-beating was an old tactic employed to instil fear in the enemy, but Dum Dum rather liked it because it reminded him of Sepultura. He'd been tempted to put his earphones in and crank up some Slayer or something to get fired up, but this would serve just as well.

Still, there was no denying that they were an intimidating foe, and even Dum Dum would confess to feeling some nerves. Around him there were some who were all but ready to turn and run for their lives, but instead they were helping to distribute strips of hotel bedsheets for the defecting dwarfs to tie around their arms, so they'd know which side they were on in the heat of battle.

"So many," gasped Tike. "We don't stand a chance."

The poor kid was terrified, understandably so; he was just a kid. And some of the rest, Dum Dum had learned, were no better qualified to be facing such odds. Which was all the more reason for him to be proud to stand alongside them.

"Stick with me, kid," he winked at Tike. "You'll be fine."

Across the plains, the dwarf commander was giving the traditional pep talk, marching up and down the lines, wasting his breath. It wasn't like any of them could hear him over the racket they were making, but clearly he thought it was important to be seen doing his job. It was also making him a rather obvious target for Andy One-Leg who, lying flat on his stomach, was taking aim with one of the rifles. Luckily for the dwarf, he was out of range, and while it might have been a little morale booster for Aberrant's side if he got his head blown off mid-speech, it was a waste of ammo if Andy missed. Every bullet needed to count.

"Hold your ground," Mad John reminded. "Let them come to us. Good luck everyone!"

The thing about torrential rain, in a place where it hasn't rained in decades, is that the ground can very quickly turn to mud. Adding ten thousand dwarfs to the mix, as the king's army found when they charged, rapidly turns it into a quagmire. And because dwarfs are not, as a rule, known for their height, many of them became stuck. The result was horrific, a Hieronymus Bosch painting made flesh and bone, as the first in line were trampled by the hordes still coming from behind, like too many people trying to get out of a fire exit.

And then came the real fire, Puff swooping down from the mountain top, belching flames, death from above, while Billy lobbed his bat shit bombs, and those with rifles and shotguns blasted away, the dwarf commander being among the first to fall. Panic spread throughout the ranks, some of those at the rear trying to get back into the city and finding that the gates had been closed behind them, locking them out. On slightly higher ground, rock and not dirt, Aberrant were safe from the mud, and their small army threw everything they had, before, eventually, it came to hand-to-hand combat. Or boot to face, knee to groin, and in Zig Zag's case, teeth to nose.

Dum Dum grabbed the first dwarf to come at him, swinging him by the ankles and using him as a club. A few yards away, Flashback was zapping them with his wand, electric blue light shooting from the skull tip, like some supercharged stun gun, knocking them off their feet where they lay twitching in the mud and the blood. So much blood...

Below ground the fighting was no less intense. The king's guards had rounded up about two hundred families before it all kicked off, and there were groups of them spread throughout the corridors, many of them rapidly finding themselves on the wrong end of a beating when word got out that most of their number were locked outside. Others were not so easily persuaded to give up, and they fought like cornered rats.

Derain and Snot stayed near the prison cells to tend the wounded, both of them better suited to the task than to fighting. Not that they couldn't fight, but both had medical knowledge, and Derain was too tall to be much use in such a confined space, while Snot's martial arts had yet to be tested against weapons. They'd also come a long way to rescue Derain, so it would be a cruel irony if he was killed now, and although she was supposed to receive no special treatment, quite frankly no one wanted to be responsible for telling Numb Tongue if Snot got injured.

Vincent, Chaos, Apples, Buttock, and a bunch of the freed prisoners, meanwhile, had gone out into the dimly lit tunnels, and quickly became involved in vicious pitched battles, the stone floors awash with rainwater and blood. Luckily, by this point no one was really looking out for extra footprints, so Vincent was able to inflict damage on his opponents without being seen, but this also meant that those on his own side couldn't see him, and twice he came close to being hacked down by so-called friendly fire. Which was the only thing that was remotely friendly about the situation.

Around each corner there was fresh fighting, fresh blood, but with each skirmish came more reinforcements from the dwarf rebels who had won their own battles, each of them with a white band tied around their right arm to indicate which side they were on. After an hour or so there were no more guards.

But there was no respite. No sooner had they secured the tunnels than they had to hurriedly make their way to the main gates, charging outside to join the battle that was still raging in the rain and mud. They were met by a scene of utter carnage – charred and burning bodies filling the centre of the battlefield and piled against the gates, where the dwarf troops had tried to get back in – and beyond them the grotesque savagery and terror of war. Vincent probably didn't make it look any more attractive by throwing up on the spot, although, to be fair, he didn't make it look any worse. Given that he was still invisible, the sudden appearance of his vomit might have been a surprise if anyone was paying attention, but there were rather more pressing matters at hand. On the other side of this sickening bloodbath, Aberrant and their allies were close to being overwhelmed.

And so they fought on until they could fight no more. Vincent would remember seeing Zig Zag tear out a throat with his teeth; he would remember seeing Smiler hack off a head; he would remember someone driving a Land Rover at the dwarfs, mowing them down like some modern-day terrorist nutjob, a severed arm caught in the grill; he would remember seeing Andy One-Leg fall, his wooden leg stuck in the mud... But most of all he would try to forget.

When it was over, he sat and cried, his head in his hands as he sobbed into the bloodstained dirt. Around him were the moans of the wounded, but he could no more help them than he could help himself. Presently he felt an arm around his shoulder, and through the tears he saw Tike by his side. "You made it," he managed, the words sounding strange, like his friend had arrived unexpectedly at a party.

In the end, victory had come, as it should in times of revolution, at the hands of the people. When all had seemed lost, they came from the city, thousands of them, the poor, the oppressed, young and old, armed with hammers, kitchen knives, anything they could lay their hands on, each one with a white band around their arm. They were not trained to fight, but had everything to fight for. Everything to die for, and so much to live for.

Tike and Vincent sat for some time, clinging together in the rain, unseen and unnoticed. It was perhaps not the most opportune time for Tike's cell phone to ring, the annoying generic ringtone startling them both, but maybe it would give them something to laugh about one day. How on earth it had a signal out here in the middle of nowhere was anyone's guess.

"It's me mum," said Tike, who had all but forgotten he even had a phone. "I'll call her back later."

They sat in silence a while longer until, eventually, Dum Dum trudged over and lifted them gently to their feet.

"C'mon," he said kindly. "Let's get you two somewhere warm and dry."

"Andy?" said Vincent, remembering his fallen friend.

"He's alright," Dum Dum nodded. "Lost his leg somewhere, but luckily it was the wooden one. It was about time he got a new one."

They walked back to the city, boots squelching in the mud and gore, and Dum Dum ushered them into the hands of friendly dwarfs, blankets, baths, some sort of warm liquid that claimed to be tea.

"Gonna go an' see what I can do," said Dum Dum, turning back to the battlefield. "I don't fit in them tunnels anyway, and the rest of the bad guys have locked 'emselves in down the bottom somewhere. We'll deal with them tomorrow, it's not like they're going anywhere. You two go an' get some sleep."

The pair were led to a room somewhere, vaguely aware of the hustle and bustle around them, the wounded being rushed past them on makeshift stretchers, vaguely aware that they were getting special treatment, but too exhausted to take it in. The bed was uncomfortable and lumpy, and the room spartan, but after so long without rest Vincent was asleep before his head hit the pillow.

CHAPTER SIXTY-ONE

No one really knew what to do with the pig. When dawn broke the next day, the storm of the night making way for the usual scorching desert heat, it revealed many strange and hideous sights sticking out of the sludge – severed limbs, bodies twisted, contorted and burned beyond recognition, like some vile and terrible soup – but perhaps nothing was quite so disturbing as the pig. Happy as the proverbial swine in shit, it was currently munching its way through something that might once have been an arm.

Smiler had suggested eating it, the pig that is, not the arm, but that really didn't seem right, not right at all. It was the eyes that freaked Dum Dum out, looking as they did rather less porcine and rather more, well, dwarfish. Thankfully, Flashback had promised to change it back, as soon as he'd had a bit of a lie-down and got his powers back. Which might be a couple of days from now, since he was currently replenishing those powers in a dwarf bar.

It wasn't the first time Dum Dum had witnessed lightning being employed in magic, nature's jump leads, but it was still an impressive sight, and terrifying if you were on the wrong end of it. In the midst of battle, Flashback suddenly lit up like Blackpool Illuminations, a blinding burst, and just as suddenly there were three very startled-looking pigs in front of him, each clad in chainmail, and a whole lot of dwarfs trying to run in the opposite direction. No one had asked what happened to the other two pigs. It was probably best not to know.

Dum Dum was helping to dig the Land Rover out of the slowly drying mud when he heard the news that the dwarf king was dead. He crossed *Low Sperm Count* off his list. Sometimes the songs only made sense after the fact, but they all seemed to fit into place eventually, those last four words repeating in his head: "*The king is dead, the king is dead.*" The rumour was that he'd drowned when the lower parts of the city became flooded, his body found amongst those that had washed out of the now running river on the other side of the mountain. Either way, the body had been identified and few would mourn his passing, not least those who had been sent to fight a senseless battle and now found themselves prisoners. Easily able to withstand a siege, all the king had needed to do was lock the gates and wait, but such was his arrogance that he hadn't even waited for daybreak before he sent them to die.

And so many were dead.

Aberrant had been lucky, a broken bone here, a flesh wound there, nothing that wouldn't heal, but hundreds, thousands of others were not so fortunate. No one knew yet how many. Families wandered amongst the carnage looking for loved ones, missing presumed dead, their task made all the more ghastly by the intense heat of the day. The stench was unbearable, and all too often so was what they found. It would be days before the true cost of the battle was known, and years before that price was paid.

When Vincent awoke, he found Tike by his side, and the news was broken to him that Gilgin was dead, his body discovered among those that had washed up on the banks of the river. By now there was talk that the king and his men had been electrocuted, not drowned, when the city was flooded – a fitting irony given that they were the only ones who had electricity. Gilgin had been executed, presumably for treason. Some truths would never be known, others were best unknown, but Gilgin would be buried a hero with the highest honours. Or burned, to be precise, since the dwarfs, out of tradition and necessity, opted for funeral pyres rather than graves. With so many dead, the fires burned day and night.

Given that dwarf funerals involved an excessive amount of drinking, those days were something of a blur. Vincent was awarded a medal for his bravery, but his recollections of the ceremony were vague at best. Feenat had presented the medal, Vincent kneeling so she could pin it to his cut. He remembered that she'd cried a lot, and that he'd had trouble standing up after the presentation. No one seemed to mind. Among the other honours handed out, Andy One-Leg was presented with a new leg.

A couple of days earlier there had been another ceremony, a coronation in which Buttock was crowned as the new king...or possibly queen. Vincent didn't remember much about that either, but the dwarfs appeared to be happy enough about it, the new king – or queen – being rather less of a tyrant than the old one. Certainly, they drank a lot of beer and sang a great many songs, and even though there was only one book in the new library – a very worn copy of 1984 – it was a vast improvement on no library at all. Mad John had promised to send them more books. Possibly starting with some books on learning English.

And so the days turned into weeks, and some semblance of normality returned to the city. Led by the nomads, the Aborigines began their long walk home, although a handful, since they had little to go back to, decided to stay in the city and start new lives. The mining machines began thumping again, this time with the workers receiving a fair wage, decent meals, and the promise of working toilets. Obviously there was rather more to it than that, the freedom to leave the city, the freedom of education, but some changes couldn't happen overnight. The important thing was that there *was* change.

George was the next to leave, hitching a ride from Puff, since the battered Land Rover was low on petrol and in no state to survive such a long drive across the desert. Mortified to discover that he couldn't tell the difference between dwarf ladies and dwarf men, and had frequently used foul language when there were "ladies present", he'd been reduced to a stuttering imbecile, and was keen to get home. It didn't seem to matter that the dwarf ladies couldn't understand what he was saying. The dragon had been paid another large amount of gold, and would return to begin ferrying Aberrant back to somewhere in the vicinity of their long-abandoned coach.

Having recharged his powers, mostly, it seemed, by drinking copiously, Flashback offered to change the pig back to a dwarf, but on reflection it was decided that it was best if he didn't. Before it was running around on four legs and oinking a lot, the pig had been – as identified by its uniform – one of the former king's guards, a particularly unpleasant fellow by all accounts, and was now facing a long stretch in prison. Besides, they'd all grown rather fond of the pig, and if nothing else it was a poignant – or porknant – reminder that the new monarch needed to be a bit nicer to everyone. Dum Dum had christened it Strutter after the pig in Time Bandits, and no one had the heart to tell him that he'd got it wrong.

Derain, meanwhile, had been demonstrating some of the magic that made his life worth taking so many risks for, not least with his ability to heal broken bones by simply waving his hands over them. Admittedly, he'd given up with Smiler's nose – some damage being beyond even his capabilities – and he was still less chatty than Numb Tongue, but it was easy to see why he was held in such high regard. The oldest man in the world, steeped in knowledge from the dawn of time. Proper earth magic.

When it was time to leave he simply vanished into the desert, no more than a mirage and memories. A group of friends gathered to say their good-byes, Stone, Flashback, Vincent, some of the Aborigine nomads, and as they watched Derain walk away, still naked and without possessions, a small dust devil appeared out of nowhere. It was there for no more than a few seconds, and when it was gone, so was Derain.

CHAPTER SIXTY-TWO

Soon enough it was time for Aberrant to leave. As promised, Puff returned to give them a ride, but he would take no more than four of them at a time in case someone fell off, so it took a few more days before they were all gone from the city. Passengers aboard what had been dubbed Dragon Airlines travelled at their own risk, but it was a lot better than walking. And riding a dragon wasn't something that many people got to cross off their bucket list, even if it hadn't been on there to start with. Vincent was rather less disappointed, now, that he hadn't seen a kangaroo. Besides, with thirty-five million of them hopping around Australia, it still wasn't too late.

It felt a little strange being back in civilisation after what seemed like such a long time away, surreal almost. Not that the dwarf city wasn't civilised, especially after they'd got rid of the former king, but with the exception of Zig Zag they'd all grown accustomed to walking with a stoop so they didn't keep banging their heads on the ceiling, Numb Tongue and Dum Dum choosing to sleep outside. Warm, comfortable hotel beds had become a luxury they'd almost forgotten. As had air conditioning, cigarettes, coffee shops, cold, smooth beer – dwarf beer being warm and lumpy – and all manner of small things like toothpaste that didn't taste like chalk.

Perhaps most of all, however, Aberrant Motorcycle Club had missed motorcycles, and the day they dropped the coach off at a depot in Perth, Mad John surprised them all by taking them to a barn on the outskirts of town in which was a vast collection of bikes, the owner having agreed to loan some of them out for a week or so. Well, Dum Dum wasn't entirely surprised, since he'd been listening to his iPod a lot now that it was fully charged and had been treated to at least a dozen classics like Montrose's *Bad Motor Scooter*, Motörhead's *Iron Horse/Born To Lose*, Zeke's *God Of GSXR*, and even Arlo Guthrie's *Motorcycle Song*. He'd pretended to be surprised though, because it was the right thing to do and he wasn't a dick.

Life was good. The club blasted around doing some sightseeing and bar-hopping, soaking up the sunshine and enjoying the ride. Tike tagged along on the back of Vincent's bike, grinning from ear to ear. There was talk of him maybe prospecting for Aberrant one day, although he'd have to wait a few years before he was old enough. For now he was their guest and, given that he'd had to call his mother and explain where he was, their responsibility. He was also a stark reminder of the cultural disparity in Australia, an Aboriginal face on a motorcycle often turning as many heads as the bikes themselves.

It was a lazy Saturday afternoon when, at Dum Dum's request, they all headed to Fremantle Cemetery to check out Bon Scott's grave. Another beautiful sunny day. It took them a while to find the site because the large cemetery was divided by denominations and they figured that the man who wrote *Highway To Hell* was unlikely to be in the Jehovah's Witness section, but it wasn't as if they were in a hurry. It was Mental who noticed the cop car on the other side of the wide street, the occupants clearly watching them.

"Fuck's sake, seriously?" muttered Smiler. "We're just trying to pay our respects here."

"Yeah, really," nodded Chaos. "Cunts have been watching too much Sons Of Anarchy."

"All the same," said Mad John. "I think we should be moving on. We don't need any trouble today."

Numb Tongue shrugged: "Wouldn't be any trouble."

"I don't doubt that, but we don't want to risk the bikes getting impounded."

They followed Mad John up Carrington Street away from the cemetery, obeying the traffic laws, sticking to the speed limit. The cops followed. Right on McGregor Road, left on Adrian Street, just to be sure. The cops were definitely following.

Right again on Solomon Street.

Now the cops had backup, another squad car.

Fuck.

Stop and search was one thing, but Australian authorities had some serious beef with bikers. Aberrant may have had protective spells cast into their colours, but the spells had their limits, enough to confuse the average traffic cop. As far as the law was concerned they weren't even allowed to wear those colours. Somehow the club had kind of forgotten about that until now, and it was far too late for disguises.

They pulled up at some traffic lights, engines thundering. It was a nice residential neighbourhood, so the cops were unlikely to hassle them here in case they were armed, but the farther they went, the more time the cops had to get reinforcements. No doubt an armed response unit would be showing up. After all they'd been through, it looked like they were going to get busted for nothing. Well, probably not for nothing, since Numb Tongue had replenished his coke supply, and Stone, as ever, was a walking pharmacy, but they hadn't really done anything wrong as such. They certainly weren't planning on selling the drugs. It was strictly for personal use.

"Now what?" Smiler yelled above the engine noise. "Split up and lose them?"

"Fight them?" Numb Tongue offered hopefully.

Mad John shook his head: "If George was correct there's a pub around here, over by the old Round House Prison."

"Prison?" said Smiler. "Well, I suppose that will save them some bother."

"Pub?" said Numb Tongue.

"Trust me," said Mad John.

The club doubled back, cops still on their tail. Vincent moved up to the head of the pack, while Tike looked up directions to the old prison on his phone. It had been a long time since any of them had employed such technology, but sometimes Google maps came in handy.

Built between 1830 and 1831, The Round House is the oldest standing building in Western Australia, and, in its time as a prison, had just eight cells. One of its most famous occupants was an Aboriginal folklore hero named Yagan, from the Noongar people, who fought against British colonialism before he was beheaded in July 1833, his head then sent to England where it was displayed as an 'anthropological curiosity'. Today the Round House is a tourist attraction, Yagan's head having been rightfully returned to his people and given a proper burial. Close to the old prison, however, is a place that is neither a tourist attraction nor mentioned in any folklore. Probably because it looks like a bit of a dump. A wooden sign hangs outside, so weather-worn and faded that it's barely possible to read the name: The Roo Inn.

Aberrant Motorcycle Club pulled into the empty car park around the back, beyond which was a small beach, and the sparkling blue waters of Bathers Bay. The pub looked closed, its windows either boarded shut or filthy, but Mad John knocked on the door just so – tap-tap-tap, tap-tap, tap-tap-tap – and the door was opened by a tall, surly-looking man with a mutton chop beard. He didn't seem particularly pleased to see them, but he warmed slightly when Mad John explained who had sent them.

"George, eh?" The man gave a scowl that was attempting to be a smile. "Well, I s'pose you'd better come in."

The pub was as grubby inside as it was outside, a thick layer of dust on every surface. Judging by the décor it had been built around the same time as the old prison, and hadn't been cleaned since. Not surprisingly, there were no other customers. The man introduced himself as Buckley, shook Mad John's hand with a vice-like grip, but didn't seem to be interested in who the others were.

"What is your business here?" he asked bluntly.

"We've got some unwanted company," Mad John nodded towards the front windows. "I was hoping there would be a back way out of here."

Buckley walked over to the front window, taking his time. He wiped away a layer of dirt and peered outside. At least four squad cars, several meatwagons, a lot of bulletproof vests and assorted weaponry. Outlaw biker clubs were considered terrorists and the cops weren't fucking about. Buckley spat on the floor. Ptah! He ambled back to the bar and poured himself a shot of rum.

"If they break my door you lot can pay for the damages."

"Of course," said Mad John.

"In advance. No cheques."

"As you wish."

Buckley poured himself another shot. "Got no time for the law," he growled.

"So you'll help us?"

Buckley considered this for a small aeon, no time for the law, but plenty of time to stand around thinking about it. Outside, one of the senior officers was barking into a megaphone, apparently quite keen to meet Aberrant MC in person, preferably with their hands on their heads. By rights, they needed a search warrant, but they'd no doubt argue probable cause before they gate-crashed the party.

"You know you came in the back way?" said Buckley, finally. "S'pose you'll be wanting the other back way?"

It was a rhetorical question, a fucking stupid question. Buckley poured himself a third shot of rum, still yet to offer the rest of them a drink. A familiar expression on Numb Tongue's face suggested that any moment now Buckley would be horizontal with a couple of missing teeth. Either Buckley hadn't noticed or he didn't care.

"Damages paid up front," he reiterated.

Mad John handed him a bag containing what was probably enough gold to buy the pub, a parting gift from Buttock.

"Out that way," Buckley nodded. "I'll let you know when they're gone."

There was a popping sensation in the ears when they opened the door, like a change in altitude on a plane, or indeed a magical change in location. It was the same door they'd come in by, but the car park was gone, and in its place, beside the clear blue waters of a totally different beach, was a cocktail bar, complete with deck chairs and parasols. The bar was untended, but there was music playing, a local band called AC/DC, and a song called *Have A Drink On Me*.

For once, Dum Dum didn't have to figure out what it meant.